L'AGENT DOUBLE: A NOVEL

SPIES AND MARTYRS IN THE GREAT WAR

KIT SERGEANT

THOMPSON BELLE PRESS

CONTENTS

OTHER BOOKS BY KIT SERGEANT

355: The Women of Washington's Spy Ring

Underground: Traitors and Spies in Lincoln's War

The Spark of Resistance: Women Spies in WWII

Be sure to join Kit's mailing list at www.kitsergeant.com to be the first to know
when my newest Women Spies book is available!

Contemporary Women's Fiction:

THROWN FOR A CURVE

WHAT IT IS

This book is dedicated to all of the women who lived during the First World War and whose talents and sacrifices are known or unknown, but especially to the real-life women upon whom these characters are based

GLOSSARY OF TERMS

Aerodrome: a small airport

Boches: derogatory term for Germans

Croix de Guerre: a French military honor

Deuxiéme Bureau: France's military intelligence agency; translated as the "Second Bureau of the Second Staff"

Franc-tireur: a civilian sniper

Feldwebel: a German military rank, approximately equivalent to a sergeant

Gefreiter: a German military rank, approximately equivalent to a corporal

Gendarme: an armed police officer

Grand Place: the town square

Hauptman: a German military rank, approximately equivalent to a captain

Huns: another derogatory term for Germans

Kermis: a Dutch summer fair

Lorry: a motor vehicle used to transport goods or passengers

Meneer: Dutch for "Mr."

Mevrouw: Dutch for "Mrs."

Oberarzt: a senior physician

Ordnance train: a train carrying military supplies

Unteroffizier: a German military rank, approximately equivalent to a sergeant

Zouave: a soldier usually linked to the French North African territories; they are known for their distinct uniforms

PROLOGUE

OCTOBER 1917

The nun on duty woke her just before dawn. She blinked the sleep out of her eyes to see a crowd of men, including her accusers and her lawyer, standing just outside the iron bars of her cell. The only one who spoke was the chief of the Military Police, to inform her the time of her execution had come. The men then turned and walked away, leaving only the nun and the prison doctor, who kept his eyes on the dirty, straw-strewn floor as she dressed.

She chose the best outfit she had left, a bulky dove-gray skirt and jacket and scuffed ankle boots. She wound her unwashed hair in a bun and then tied the worn silk ribbons of her hat under her chin before asking the doctor, "Do I have time to write good-byes to my loved ones?"

He nodded and she hastily penned three farewell letters. She handed them to the doctor with shaking hands before lifting a dust-covered velvet cloak from a nail on the wall. "I am ready."

Seemingly out of nowhere, her lawyer reappeared. "This way," he told her as he grasped her arm.

Prison rats scurried out their way as he led her down the hall. She breathed in a heavy breath when they were outside. It had been months since she'd seen the light of day, however faint it was now.

Four black cars were waiting in the prison courtyard. A few men scattered about the lawn lifted their freezing hands to bring their cameras to life, the bulbs brightening the dim morning as her lawyer bundled her into the first car.

They drove in silence. It was unseasonably cold and the chill sent icy fingers down her spine. She stopped herself from shivering, wishing that she could experience one more warm summer day. But there would be no more warmth, no more appeals, nothing left after these last few hours.

She knew that her fate awaited her at Caponniére, the old fort just outside of Vincennes where the cavalry trained. Upon arrival, her lawyer helped her out of the car, his gnarled hands digging into her arm.

It's harder for him than it is for me. She brushed the thought away, wanting to focus on nothing but the fresh air and the way the autumn leaves of the trees next to the parade ground changed color as the sun rose. Her lawyer removed his arm from her shoulders as two Zouave escorts appeared on either side of her. Her self-imposed blinders finally dropped as she took in the twelve soldiers with guns and, several meters away, the wooden stake placed in front of a brick wall. *So that the mis-aimed bullets don't hit anything else.*

A priest approached and offered her a blindfold.

"No thank you." Her voice, which had not been used on a daily basis for months, was barely a whisper.

The priest glanced over at her lawyer, who nodded. The blindfold disappeared under his robes.

She spoke the same words to one of the escorts as he held up a rope, this time also shaking her head. She refused to be bound to the stake. He acquiesced, and walked away.

She stood as straight as she could, free of any ties, while the military chief read the following words aloud:

By decree of the Third Council of War, the woman who appears before us now has been condemned to death for espionage.

He then gave an order, and the soldiers came to attention. At the command, *"En joue!"* they hoisted their guns to rest on their shoulders. The chief raised his sword.

She took a deep breath and then lifted her chin, willing herself to die just like that: head held high, showing no fear. She watched as the chief lowered his sword and shouted *"Feu!"*

And then everything went black.

A Zouave private approached the body. He'd only been enlisted for a few weeks and had been invited to the firing squad by his commander, who told him that men of all ranks should know the pleasure of shooting a German spy.

"By blue, that lady knew how to die," another Zouave commented.

"Who was she?" the private asked. He'd been taught that everything in war was black and white: the Germans were evil, the Allies pure. But he was surprised at how gray everything was that morning: from the misty fog, to the woman's cloak and dress, and even the ashen shade of her lifeless face.

The other Zouave shrugged. "All I know is what they told me. They say she acted as a double agent and provided Germany with intelligence about our troops." He drew his revolver and bent down to place the muzzle against the woman's left temple.

"But is it necessary to kill her—a helpless woman?" the private asked.

The Zouave cocked his gun for the *coup de grâce*. "If women act as men would in war and commit heinous crimes, they should be prepared to be punished as men." And he pulled the trigger, sending a final bullet into the woman's brain.

CHAPTER 1

M'GREET

JULY 1914

"*H*ave you heard the latest?" M'greet's maid, Anna, asked as she secured a custom-made headpiece to her mistress's temple.

"What now?" M'greet readjusted the gold headdress to better reflect her olive skin tone.

"They are saying that your mysterious Mr. K from the newspaper article is none other than the Crown Prince himself."

M'greet smiled at herself in the mirror. "Is that so? I rather think they're referring to Lieutenant Kiepert. Just the other day he and I ran into the editor of the *Berliner Tageblatt* during our walk in the Tiergarten." Her smile faded. "But let them wonder." For the last few weeks, the papers had been filled with speculation about why the famed Mata Hari had returned to Germany, sometimes bordering on derision about her running out of money.

She leaned forward and ran her fingers over the dark circles under her eyes. "Astruc says that he might be able to negotiate a longer engagement in the fall if tonight's performance goes well."

"It will," Anna assured her as she fastened the heavy gold necklace around M'greet's neck.

The metal felt cold against her sweaty skin. She hadn't performed in months, and guessed the perspiration derived from her nervousness. Tonight was to be the largest performance she'd booked in years: Berlin's Metropol could seat 1108 people, and the tickets had sold out days ago. The building was less than a decade old, and even the dressing room's geometric wallpaper and curved furniture reflected the Art Nouveau style the theater was famous for.

"I had to have this costume refitted." M'greet pulled at the sheer yellow fabric covering her midsection. When she first began dancing, she had worn jeweled bralettes and long, sheer skirts that sat low on the hips. But her body had become much more matronly in middle age and even M'greet knew that she could no longer get away with the scandalous outfits of her youth. She added a cumbersome earring to each ear and an arm band before someone knocked on the door.

A man's voice called urgently in German, "Fräulein Mata Hari, are you ready?"

Anna shot her mistress an encouraging smile. "Your devoted admirers are waiting."

M'greet stretched out her arms and rotated her wrists, glancing with appreciation in the mirror. She still had it. She grabbed a handful of translucent scarves and draped them over her arms and head before opening the door. "All set," she said to the awaiting attendant.

M'greet waited behind a filmy curtain while the music began: low, mournful drumming accompanied by a woman's shrill tone singing in a foreign language. As the curtain rose, she hoisted her arms above her head and stuck her hips out in the manner she had seen the women do when she lived in Java.

She had no formal dance training, but it didn't matter. People came to see Mata Hari for the spectacle, not because she was an exceptionally wonderful dancer. M'greet pulled the scarf off her head and undulated her hips in time with the music. She pinched her fingers together and moved her arms as if she were a graceful bird about to take flight. The drums heightened in intensity and her gyrations became even more exaggerated. As the music came to a dramatic stop, she released the scarves covering her body to reveal her yellow dress in full.

She was accustomed to hearing astonished murmurs from the audience following her final act—she'd once proclaimed that her success rose with every veil she threw off. Tonight, however, the Berlin audience seemed to be buzzing with protest.

As the curtain fell and M'greet began to pick up the pieces of her discarded costume, she assured herself that the Berliners' vocalizations were in response to being disappointed at seeing her more covered. Or maybe she was just being paranoid and had imagined all the ruckus.

"Fabulous!" her agent, Gabriel Astruc, exclaimed when he burst into her dressing room a few minutes later.

M'greet held a powder puff to her cheek. "Did you finalize a contract for the fall?"

"I did," Astruc sat in the only other chair, which appeared too tiny to support his large frame. "They are giving us 48,000 marks."

She nodded approvingly.

"That should tide you over for a while, no?" he asked.

She placed the puff in the gold-lined powder case. "For now. But the creditors are relentless. Thankfully Lieutenant Kieper has gifted me a few hundred francs."

"As a loan?" Astruc winked. "It is said you have become mistress to the *Kronprinz*."

She rolled her eyes. "You of all people must know to never mind such rumors. I may be well familiar with men in high positions, but have not yet made the acquaintance of the Kaiser's son."

Astruc rose. "Someday you two will meet, and even the heir of the German Empire will be unable to resist the charms of the exotic Mata Hari."

M'greet unsnapped the cap of her lipstick. "We shall see, won't we?"

Now that the fall performances had been secured, M'greet decided to upgrade her lodgings to the lavish Hotel Adlon. As she entered the lobby, with its sparkling chandeliers dangling from intricately carved ceilings and exotic potted palms scattered among velvet-cushioned chairs, she nodded to herself. *This was the type of hotel a world-renowned dancer should be found in.* She booked an apartment complete with electric Tiffany lamps and a private bathroom featuring running water.

The Adlon was known not only for its famous patrons, but for the privacy it provided them. M'greet was therefore startled the next morning when someone banged on the door to her suite.

"Yes?" Anna asked as she opened it.

"Are you Mata Hari?" a gruff voice inquired.

M'greet threw on a silky robe over her nightgown before she went to the door. "You must be looking for me."

The man in the doorway appeared to be about forty, with a receding hairline and a bushy mustache that curled upward from both sides of his mouth. "I am Herr Griebel of the Berlin police."

M'greet ignored Anna's stricken expression as she motioned for her to move aside. "Please come in." She gestured toward a chair at the little serving table. "Shall I order up some tea?"

"That won't be necessary," Griebel replied as he sat. "I am here to inform you that a spectator of your performance last night has lodged a complaint."

"A complaint? Against me?" M'greet repeated as she took a seat in the chair across from him. She mouthed, "tea," at Anna, who was still standing near the door. Anna nodded and then left the room.

"Indeed," Griebel touched his mustache. "A complaint of indecency."

"I see." She leaned forward. "You are part of the *Sittenpolizei*, then." They were a department charged with enforcing the Kaiser's so-called laws of morality. M'greet had been visited a few times in the past by such men, but nothing had ever come of it. She flashed Griebel a seductive smile. "Surely your department has no issue with sacred dances?"

"Ah," Griebel fidgeted with the collar of his uniform, clearly uncomfortable.

Mirroring his movements, M'greet fingered the neckline of her low-cut gown. "After all, there are more important issues going on in the world than my little dance."

"Such as?" Griebel asked.

The door opened and Anna discreetly placed a tea set on the crisp white tablecloth. She gave her mistress a worried look but M'greet waved her off before pouring Griebel a cup of tea. "Well, I'm sure you heard about that poor man that was shot in the Balkans in June."

"Of course—it's been in all of the papers. The 'poor man,' as you call him, was Archduke Franz Ferdinand. Austria should not stand down when the heir to their throne was shot by militant Serbs."

M'greet took a sip of tea. "Are you saying they should go to war?"

"They should. And Germany, as Austria's ally, ought to accompany them."

"Over one man? You cannot be serious."

"Those Serbs need to be taught a lesson, once and for all." Upon seeing the pout on M'greet's face, Griebel waved his hand. "But you shouldn't worry your pretty little head over talk of politics."

She pursed her lips. "You're right. It's not something that a woman like me should be discussing."

"No." He set down his tea cup and pulled something out of his pocket. "As I was saying when I first came in, about the complaint—"

"As *I* was saying…" she faked a yawn, stretching her arms out while sticking out her bosom. The stocky, balding Griebel was not nearly as handsome as some of the men she'd met over the years, but M'greet knew that she needed to become better acquainted with him in order to get the charges dropped. Besides, she'd always had a weakness for men in uniform. "My routine is adopted from Hindu religious dances and should not be misconstrued as immoral." She placed a hand over Griebel's thick fingers, causing the paper to fall to the floor. "I think, if the two of us put our heads together, we can definitely find a mutual agreement."

He pulled his hand away to wipe his forehead with a handkerchief. "I don't know if that's possible."

M'greet got up from her chair to spread herself on the bed, displaying her body to its advantage as a chef would his best dish.

"Perhaps we could work out an arrangement that would benefit us both," Griebel agreed as he walked over to her.

Griebel's mustache tickled her face, but she forced herself to think about other things as he kissed her. Her thoughts at such moments often traveled to her daughter, Non, but today she focused on the other night's performance. M'greet always did what it took to survive, and right now she needed the money that her contract with the Berlin Metropol would provide, and nothing could get in the way of that.

M'greet was glad to count Herr Griebel as her new lover as the tensions between the advocates of the Kaiser—who wanted to "finish with the Serbs quickly"—and the pacifists determined to keep Germany out of war heightened throughout Berlin at the end of July. Although Griebel was on the side of the war-mongers, M'greet felt secure traveling on his arm every night on their way to Berlin's most popular venues.

It was in the back room at one such establishment, the Borchardt, that she met some of Griebel's cronies. They had gathered to talk about the recent developments—Austria-Hungary had officially declared war on Serbia. M'greet knew her place was to look pretty and say nothing, but at the same time she couldn't help but listen to what they were discussing.

"I've heard that Russia has mobilized her troops," a heavyset, balding man stated. M'greet recalled that his name was Müller.

"Ah," Griebel sat back in the plush leather booth. "That's the rub, now isn't it?"

Herr Vogel, Griebel's closest compatriot, shook his head. "I'd hoped Russia would stay out of it." He flicked ash from his cigar into a nearby tray. "After all, the Kaiser and the Tsar are cousins."

"No," Müller replied. "Those Serbs went crying to Mother Russia, and she responded." He nodded to himself. "Now it's only a matter of time before we jump in to protect Austria."

As if on cue, the sound of breaking glass was heard.

M'greet ended her silence. "What was that?"

Griebel put a protective hand on her arm. "I'm not sure." He used his other arm to flag down a passing waiter. "What is going on?"

The young man looked panic-stricken. "There is a demonstration on the streets. Someone threw a brick through the front window and our owner is asking all of the patrons to leave."

"Has war broken out?" M'greet inquired of Griebel as she pulled her arm away. His grip had left white marks.

"I'm not sure." He picked up her fur shawl and headed to the main room of the restaurant. Pandemonium reigned as Berlin's elite rushed toward the doors. Discarded feathers from fashionable ladies' hats and boas floated through the air and littered the ground before stamping feet stirred them up again. M'greet wished she hadn't shaken off Griebel's arm as now she was being shoved this way and that. Someone trampled over her dress and she heard the sound of ripping lace.

She nearly tripped before a strong hand landed on her elbow. "This way," the young waiter told her. He led her through the kitchen and out the back door, where Griebel's Benz was waiting. Griebel appeared a few minutes later and the driver told him there was a massive protest outside the Kaiser's palace.

"Let's go there," Griebel instructed.

"No." M'greet wrapped the fur shawl around her shoulders. "Take me home first."

"Don't you want to find out what's happening?" Griebel demanded, waving his hand as a crowd of people thronged the streets. "This could be the beginning of a war the likes of which no one has ever seen."

"No," she repeated. It seemed to her that the Great Powers of Europe: Germany, Russia, France, and possibly England, were entering into a scrap they had no business getting involved with. "I don't care about any war and I've had enough tonight. I want to go home."

Griebel gave her a strange look but motioned for the driver to do as she said.

They were forced to drive slowly, as the streets had become jammed with motor cars, horse carts, and people rushing about on foot. M'greet caught what they were chanting as the crowd marched past. She repeated the words aloud: "*Deutschland über alles.*"

"Germany over all," Griebel supplied.

The war came quickly. Germany first officially declared war on Russia to the east and two days later did the same to France in the west. In Berlin, so-called bank riots occurred as people rushed to their financial institutions and emptied their savings accounts, trading paper money for gold and silver coins. Prices for food and other necessities soared as people stocked up on goods while they could still afford them.

Worried about her own fate, M'greet placed several calls to her agent, Astruc, wanting to know if the war meant her fall performances would be cancelled. After leaving many messages, she eventually got word that Astruc had fled town, presumably with the money the Metropol had paid her in advance.

She decided to brave the confusion at the bank in order to withdraw what little funds she had left.

"I'm sorry," the teller informed M'greet when she finally made it to the counter. "It looks as though your account has been blocked."

"How can you say that?" she demanded. "There should be plenty of money in my account." The plenty part might not have been strictly true, but there was no way it was empty.

"The address you gave when you opened the account was in Paris. We cannot give funds to any foreigner at this time."

M'greet put both fists on the counter. "I wish to speak with your manager."

The teller gestured behind her. M'greet glanced back to see a long line of people, their exhausted, bewildered faces beginning to glower. "I'm sorry, fräulein, I can do nothing more."

She opened her mouth to let him have the worst of her fury, but a man in a police uniform appeared beside her. "A foreigner you say?" He pulled M'greet out of the bank line, and roughly turned her to face him. "What are you, a Russian?"

M'greet knew her dark hair and coloring was not typical of someone with Dutch heritage, but this was a new accusation. "I am no such thing."

"Russian, for sure," a man standing in line agreed.

"Her address was in France," the teller called before accepting a bank card from the next person.

"Well, Miss Russian Francophile, you are coming with me." For the second time in a week, a strange man put his hand on M'greet's elbow and led her away.

. . .

M'greet fumed all the way to the police station. She'd had enough of Berlin: due to this infernal war, she was now void of funds and it looked as though her engagements were to be cancelled. She figured her best course of action would be to return to Paris and use her connections to try to get some work there.

When they arrived at the police station, M'greet immediately asked for Herr Griebel. He appeared a few minutes later, a wry smile on his face. "You've been arrested under suspicion of being a troublesome alien."

M'greet waved off that comment with a brush of her hand. "We both know that's ridiculous. Can you secure my release as soon as possible? I must get back to Paris before my possessions there are seized."

Griebel's amused smile faded as his lip curled into a sneer. "You cannot travel to an enemy country in the middle of a war."

"Why not?"

The sneer deepened. "Because…" His narrowed eyes suddenly softened. "Come with me. There is someone I want you to meet." He led her to an office that occupied the end of a narrow hallway and knocked on the closed door labeled, *Traugott von Jagow, Berliner Polizei*.

"Come in," a voice growled.

Griebel entered and then saluted.

The man behind the desk had a thin face and heavy mustache which drooped downward. "What is it, Herr Griebel? You must know I am extremely busy." He dipped a pen in ink and began writing.

Griebel lowered his arm. "Indeed, sir, but I wanted you to meet the acclaimed Mata Hari."

Von Jagow paused his scribbling and looked up. His eyes traveled down from the feather atop M'greet's hat and stopped at her chest. "Wasn't there a morality complaint filed against you?"

M'greet stepped forward, but before she could protest, Griebel cleared his throat. "We are here because she wants to return to Paris."

Von Jagow gave a loud "harrumph," and then continued his writing. "You are not the first person to ask such a question, but we can't let anyone cross the border into enemy territory at this time. People would think you were a spy." He abruptly stopped writing and set his pen down. "A courtesan with a flair for seducing powerful men…" He shot a meaningful look at Griebel, who stared at the floor. "And a long-term resident of Paris with admittedly low morals." He finally met M'greet's eyes. "We could use a woman like you. I'm forming a network of agents who can provide us information about the goings-on in France."

M'greet tried to keep the horror from showing on her face. Was this man asking her to be a spy for Germany? "No thank you," she replied. "As I told Herr Griebel, I have no interest in the war. I just want to get back to Paris."

Von Jagow crossed his arms and sat back. "And I can help you with that, provided that you agree to work for me."

She shook her head and spoke in a soft voice. "Thank you, sir, but it seems I'll have to find a way back on my own."

"Very well, then." Von Jagow picked up his pen again. "Good luck." His voice implied that he wished her just the opposite.

CHAPTER 2

MARTHE

*M*arthe Cnockaert didn't think anything could spoil this year's Kermis. People had been arriving in Westrozebeke for days from all over Belgium. She herself had just returned home from her medical studies at Ghent University on holiday and had nearly been overcome by the tediousness of living in her small village again. She gazed around the garland-bedecked Grand Place lined with colorful vendor booths in satisfaction. The rest of Europe may have plunged into war, but Belgium had vowed to remain neutral, and the mayor declared that the annual Kermis would be celebrated just as it had been since the middle ages.

The smell of pie wafted from a booth as Marthe passed by and the bright notes of a hurdy-gurdy were audible over the noise of the crowd. She had just entered the queue for the carousel when she heard someone call, "Marthe!"

She turned at the sound of her name to see Valerie, a girl she had known since primary school. "Marthe, how are you? How is Max?" As usual, Valerie was breathless, as though she had recently run a marathon, but it appeared she'd only just gotten off the carousel.

15

Marthe refrained from rolling her eyes. "Max is still in Ghent, finishing up his studies." Valerie had never hidden the fact she'd always had a crush on Marthe's older brother, even after she'd become betrothed to Nicholas Hoot.

Valerie sighed as she looked around. "There's nobody here but women, children, and old men. All the boys our age have gone off to war and now there's no one left to flirt with."

"Where is Nicholas?"

"He was called to Liége. I suppose you've heard that Germany is demanding safe passage through Belgium in order to get to Paris."

"No."

Valerie shrugged. "They are saying we might have to join the war if Germany decides to invade. But the good news is some treaty states that England would have to enter on our side if that happened."

"Join the war?" Marthe was shocked at both the information and the fact that Valerie seemed so nonchalant about it. There were a few beats of silence, broken only by the endless tune from the carousel's music box, as Marthe pondered this.

"Ah, Marthe, I see you have returned from university." Meneer Hoot, an old friend of her father's, and Valerie's future father-in-law, was nearly shouting, both because he was hard of hearing and because the carousel had started spinning.

"Yes, indeed. I am home for a few weeks before I finish my last year of nursing school," Marthe answered loudly. "Glad to see you are doing well. How is your wife?"

"Oh, you know. Terrified at the prospect of a German invasion, but aren't we all?"

Marthe gave him and Valerie a tentative smile as the church bell rang the hour. "I must be getting home to help Mother with dinner."

Marthe knew something was wrong as soon as she entered the kitchen. "What is it?" she asked, glancing at her father's somber face.

"It's the Germans. They have invaded Belgium."

Marthe fell into her chair. Mother stood in the corner of the room, ironing a cap.

"Belgium has ordered our troops to Liége." Father sank his head into his hands. "But we could never defend ourselves against those bloody Boches."

Mother set her iron down and then took a seat at the kitchen table. "What about Max? Will he come home from Ghent?"

Father took his hands away from his face. "I don't know. I don't know anything now."

"I suppose we should send for him," Marthe said.

Mother cast a worried glance at Father before nodding at her daughter.

For the first time Marthe could remember, Kermis ended before the typical eight days. That didn't stop the endless train of people coming into Westrozebeke, however. The newcomers were refugees from villages near Liége and were headed to Ypres, 15 kilometers southwest, where they had been told they could find food and shelter.

Max sent word that he would be traveling in the opposite direction. He was going to Liége, a town on the Belgian/German border that was protected by a series of concrete fortifications. The Germans were supposedly en route there as well. Both Father and Mother were saddened by Max's decision to enlist in the army, but Marthe understood the circumstances: Belgium must be defended at all costs. She wrote her brother a letter stating the same and urged him to be careful.

As Westrozebeke became a temporary camp, Marthe's family's house and barn, like many of the other houses in the village, were quickly packed with the unfortunate evacuees. Soon the news that Liége had fallen came, and not long after, the first of the soldiers who had been cut off from the main Belgian army arrived.

Marthe stood on the porch and watched a few of them straggle through town. Their frayed uniforms were covered in dark splotches, some of it dirt, some of it blood. Their faces were unshaven, their skin filthy, but the worst part was that none of them were Max.

Upon spotting Nicholas Hoot's downtrodden form, Marthe rushed into the street. "Have you heard from Max?" she asked.

Nicholas met her eyes. His were wide and terrified, holding a record of past horrors, as though he had seen the devil himself. "No."

"C'mon," Marthe put his heavy arm over her shoulders. "Let's get you home."

Mevrouw Hoot greeted them at the door. "Nicholas, my son." She hugged his gaunt body before leading him inside.

After his second cup of tea, Nicholas could croak out a few sentences. After a third cup and some biscuits, he was able to relay the horrific conditions the Belgian soldiers had experienced at Liége, especially the burning inferno of Fort de Loncin, which had been hit by a shell from one of the German's enormous guns, known as Big Bertha. De Loncin had been the last of the twelve forts around Liége to yield to the Boches.

"Do you know what happened to Max?" Marthe asked.

Nicholas shook his head. "I never saw him. But it was a very confusing time." His cracked lips formed into something that resembled his old smile. "The Germans are terrified of *francs-tireurs* and think every Belgian civilian is a secret sniper out to get them." The smile quickly faded. "The Fritzes dragged old men and teenagers into the square, accusing them of shooting at their troops. It was mostly their own men mistakenly firing upon each other, but no matter. They killed the innocent villagers anyway." He set his tea cup down. "The Huns are blood-thirsty and vicious, and they are headed this way. We should flee further west as soon as possible."

Mevrouw Hoot met Marthe's eyes. "I'll tell Father," Marthe stated before taking her leave.

Mother was ready to depart, but Father was reluctant, stating that if Max did come home, he would find his family gone. Marthe agreed and disagreed with both sides. On the one hand, she wanted to wait for her brother, and judge for herself if the Germans were as terrible as Nicholas had said. On the other hand, if he was indeed correct, they should go as far west as possible.

The argument became moot when Marthe was awakened the next

morning by an unearthly piercing noise overhead. The shrieks grew louder until the entire house shook with the crescendo, and then there was an even more disturbing silence.

Marthe tossed on her robe and then rushed downstairs. No one was in the kitchen, so she pulled Max's old boots over her bare feet and ran the few blocks to the Grand Place. She could see the mushroom cloud of black smoke was just beginning to clear.

She nearly tripped in her oversized boots when she saw someone lying in the roadway. It was Mevrouw Visser, one of her elderly neighbors. She bent over the bloodied body, but the woman had already passed.

The sound of horse hooves caused Marthe to look up. She froze as she saw the men atop were soldiers in unfamiliar khaki uniforms.

"Hallo," called a man with a thin mustache and a flat red cap. He stopped his horse short of Mevrouw Visser. "Met her maker, has she?" The way he ended the sentence with a question that didn't expect an answer made Marthe realize the British had arrived. The men paused at similarly lying bodies, giving food and water to those who still clung to life, but after an hour or so, they rode off.

Marthe went home, her robe now tattered and soiled, her feet sweaty in her boots. "What now?" she asked her father, who was seated at the kitchen table, also covered in perspiration, dirt, and blood.

"Now we wait for Max."

A knock sounded on the front door and Marthe went to answer it, fearing that she would greet a Hun in a spiked helmet. But the soldier outside was in a blue uniform. "The bloody Boches are on their way," he stated in a French accent. "You must flee the village, mademoiselle."

She glanced at Father, who was still sitting at the kitchen table. "I cannot."

The French soldier took a few steps backward to peer at the second floor before returning his gaze back to her. "Our guns will arrive soon, but we are only a small portion of our squadron, and cannot possibly hope to hold them for long. We are asking the villagers to allow us access to their homes in order to take aim."

She nodded and opened the door. He marched into the kitchen and spoke to her father.

Marthe went outside, and looked up and down the street, which was now dotted with soldiers in the blue uniforms of the French. The sound of hammering permeated the air. The soldier she had spoken to went upstairs to pound small viewing holes into the wood of the rooms facing the street. She helped Father barricade the windows and front door with furniture.

Marthe and her parents sequestered themselves in her bedroom, which faced the back of the house. Although half of her was frightened, the other was intensely curious as to what would happen. She used her father's telescope to peer through a loophole in the wood-barricaded window.

"I see them!" she shouted as a gray mass came into view.

"Marthe, get down!" her father returned.

She reluctantly retired the telescope, but not before she peered outside again. The masses had become individual men topped by repulsive-looking spiked helmets. There were hundreds of them and they were headed straight for the Grand Place.

The windows rattled as the hooves of an army of horses came closer. Marthe knew that many of those carts were filled with the Boches' giant guns.

The French machine guns, known as *mitrailleuse*, began an incessant rattling. *Rat-a-tat-tat:* ad infinitum. Marthe couldn't help herself and peeped through the hole again, watching as the gray mob started running, men falling from the fire of the *mitrailleuse*.

Mother's face was stricken as a bullet tore through the wood inches above her daughter's head. Wordlessly Father grabbed both of their hands to bring them downstairs. At the foot of the stairs was a French soldier rocking back and forth, clutching his stomach. Father tried to pull Marthe toward the cellar, but she paused when she saw the blood spurting from the soldier's stomach. All of her university training thus far had not prepared her for this horrific sight, his entrails beginning to spill out of the wound, but she reached out with trembling fingers to prop him against the wall. "You must keep still."

His distraught eyes met hers as he managed to croak out one word. "Water."

Marthe knew that water would only add to his suffering. The sound of gunfire grew closer, and Father yanked her away.

They had just reached the cellar when a shell sounded and a piece of plaster from the wall landed near Father. He struck a match and lit his pipe. "Courage," he said. "The French will beat them back," but the defeated tone of his voice told Marthe that he did not believe it to be so. Nothing could stay that rushing deluge of gray regiments she had spotted from the window.

When the *mitrailleuse* finally ceased its firing, Marthe crept upstairs to retrieve water. The man at the stairs had succumbed to death, and there seemed no sign of any live blue-clad soldiers anywhere in the house. The hallway glistened with blood and there were a few spots where bullets had broken through the exterior wall. An occasional shot could still be heard outside, but it sounded much more distant now. Marthe glanced at her watch. It was only two o'clock in the afternoon.

The front door burst open and she turned to see a bedraggled young man standing in the doorway with his eyes narrowed. Something in the distance caught the sunlight and she glimpsed many men on the lawn, their bayonets gleaming. Marthe marveled that the sun had the audacity to shine on such a day.

The soldier before her holstered his revolver and spoke in broken French. "*Qui d'autre est dans cette maison avec vous?*" He marched into the room, a band of his comrades behind him. Marthe assumed he was the captain, or *hauptmann*. The men outside sat down and lit cigarettes.

She felt no fear at the arrival of the disheveled German and his troops, only an unfamiliar numbness. She replied in German that her parents were downstairs.

"There are loopholes in the walls of this house," the captain stated. "Your father is a *franc-tireur*."

Marthe recalled what Nicholas had said about the Hun's irrational fear of civilian sharpshooters. "My father is an old man and has never fired a shot at anyone, and especially not today. The French soldiers who were here were the ones shooting but they have gone."

"I have heard that story many times before. Yours is not the first village we have entered."

You mean demolished, Marthe corrected him silently.

"Fourteen of my men were shot, and the gunfire from this house was responsible. If those men who were with him have run, then your father alone will suffer."

"No, please, Hauptmann." But the captain was already on his way to the cellar. Two other burly men stalked after him. Marthe was about to pursue them when the first man appeared on the steps, dragging her mother. The other soldier, a sergeant judging by the gold braid on his uniform, followed with her father, who held his still smoldering pipe.

The soldiers shoved her parents against the wall of the hallway. Marthe bit her lip to keep herself from crying out in indignation, knowing that it couldn't possibly help the situation they were in. She cursed herself for her earlier curiosity and then cursed fate for the circumstances of having these enemy men standing in her kitchen, wishing to do harm to her family. If only they had left when Nicholas gave her that warning!

"Take that damned pipe out of your mouth," the sergeant commanded Father.

The soldier who had manhandled Mother grabbed it from him, knocking the ash out on Father's boot before he pocketed the pipe with a chuckle.

"Old man, you are a *franc-tireur*," the captain declared.

Father shook his head while Mother sobbed quietly.

"Be merciful," Marthe begged the captain. "You have no proof."

"You dare to argue with me, fräulein? This place has been a hornet's nest of sharpshooters." He turned to one of the men. "Feldwebel, see that this house is burned down immediately."

The sergeant left out the door, motioning to some of the smoking men to follow him to the storage shelter in the back of the house, where the household oil was kept.

"Hauptmann—" Father began, but the captain silenced him by holding up his hand. "As for you, old man, you can bake in your own oven!" He dropped his arm. "Gefreiter, lock him in the cellar."

The corporal seized Father and kicked him down the steps, sending a load of spit after him.

"Filthy *franc-tireur*, he will get what he deserves," the corporal stated as he slammed the door to the cellar.

Mother collapsed and Marthe rushed to her. "You infernal butchers," she hissed at the men.

"Quiet, fräulein," the captain responded, taking out a packet of cigarettes. "Our job is to end this war quickly, and rid the countryside of any threats to our army, especially from civilians who take it upon themselves to shoot our soldiers."

The feldwebel and two other men entered the house carrying drums of oil. Mother gave a strangled cry as they marched into the living room and began to pour oil over the fine furniture.

The captain nodded approvingly before casting his eyes back to Marthe and her mother. "You women are free to go. I will grant you five minutes to collect any personal belongings, but you are not permitted to enter the cellar. Do not leave the village or there will be trouble." He lit his cigarette before dropping the match on the dry kitchen floor. It went out, but Marthe knew it was only a matter of time before he did the same in the living room where the oil had been spilled.

Marthe ran upstairs, casting her eyes helplessly around when she reached the landing. *What should she take?* She threw together a bundle of clothes for her and Mother, and, at the last second, took her father's best suit off the hanger. She shouldered the bundle and then went back downstairs, grabbing Mother's hand. They went outside to the street to gaze dazedly at their home where Father lay prisoner in the cellar.

The German soldiers walked quickly out of the house, carrying some of the Cnockaert's food. Gray smoke started coming from the living room. Soon reddish-orange flames rose up, the tongues easily destroying the barricaded windows. Marthe put her hands on the collar of her jacket and began to shed it.

"What are you doing?" Mother asked, her voice unnaturally shrill.

"Father's in there. I have to try to save him."

Mother tugged Marthe's jacket back over her shoulders. "No," was all she said. Marthe lowered her shoulders in defeat. As she stared at the conflagration, trying not to picture her poor father's body burning alive, she made a vow to herself that she wouldn't let the Germans get the best of her, no matter what other horrors they tried to commit.

Eventually Mother led Marthe away from the sight of their burning home and down the street to the Grand Place. The café adjacent to the square was filled with gray-uniformed men who sang obscene songs in coarse voices. A hiccupping private staggered in the direction of Marthe and Mother as the men in the café jeered at him. Marthe pulled her mother into the square to avoid the drunken soldier.

The abandoned Kermis booths had now become makeshift hospital beds for wounded Germans. The paving stones were soaked in blood and perspiring doctors rushed around, pausing to bend over men writhing in pain. In the corner was a crowd of soldiers in bloodied French uniforms. Marthe headed over, noticing another, smaller group of women and children she recognized as fellow villagers. She had just put her hand on a girl's forehead when a German barked at her to move on.

"Where should we go?" Mother asked in a small voice.

Marthe shook her head helplessly, catching her eye on Meneer Hoot's large home on the other side of the square. They walked quickly toward it, noting the absence of smoke in the vicinity. Marthe reached her fist out to knock when the door was swung open.

Marthe's heart rose at seeing the man behind the door. "Father!"

"Shh," he said, ushering them into the house.

"How on earth—" Marthe began when they were safely ensconced in the entryway of the Hoot home.

"I took apart the bricks from the air vent. Luckily the hauptmann and his men were watching the inferno on the other side of the house."

Mother hugged him tightly, looking for all the world like she would never let him go. Father brought them into the kitchen, where Meneer and Mevrouw Hoot greeted them. Several other neighbors, including Valerie, were also gathered in the kitchen, and they waited in a bewildered silence until darkness fell.

Meneer Hoot finally rose out of his chair. Taking the pipe from his mouth, he stated, "We have had no food this morning, and I'm sure it is the same for you all. Unfortunately," he swung his arms around, "the bloody Boches ransacked our house and there is nothing to eat here." He put the pipe in his mouth and gave it a puff before continuing, "I am going to get food somehow."

Mevrouw Hoot clutched his arm. "No, David, you cannot go out there."

Father also rose. "I will join you."

Meneer Hoot shook his head. "No, it is safer for me to go alone."

Mother gave a sigh of relief while Mevrouw Hoot appeared as though she would burst into tears. Meneer Hoot slipped a dark overcoat on and left through the back door.

An eternity seemed to pass as they sat in the dark kitchen, illuminated only by the sliver of moon that had replaced the sun. The silence was occasionally broken by Mevrouw Hoot's sobbing.

Marthe was nodding off when she heard the back door slam. Someone lit a candle, and Marthe saw the normally composed Meneer Hoot hold up a bulky object wrapped in blood-stained newspaper. His rumpled trousers were covered in burrs and his eyes were wild-eyed. He tossed the bulk and it landed on the kitchen table with a thud.

Mevrouw Hoot unwrapped the package to reveal a grayish sort of meat from an unfamiliar animal.

"I cut it from one of the Boches' dead horses," Meneer Hoot told them in a triumphant whisper. He lit a fire and put the horsemeat on a spit. Marthe wasn't sure if she could eat a dead horse but soon changed her mind as the room filled with the smell of cooking meat. Her stomach grumbled in anticipation.

Just then the kitchen window shattered. Marthe looked up to see a rifle butt nudging the curtain aside. The spikes of German helmets shone in the moonlight beyond the window. The Hoots' entire backyard teemed with them.

"We must get downstairs, now!" Meneer Hoot shouted. He grabbed his wife and rushed her into the hallway. Father did the same with Mother, and Marthe followed, stumbling down the steps to the Hoots' cellar.

To Marthe's amazement, she saw the large room was already nearly filled with other refugees—men, women, and children of all ages—with dirty, tear-stained faces.

The sound of many boots thundered overhead and it wasn't long before the Germans once again stood among them. One of them pointed his rifle at the opposite wall and shot off a clip, the bullets ricocheting around the room, followed by wild screaming. Somebody had been hit, a child Marthe guessed sorrowfully by the tone of its wail.

She wanted to go aid the poor creature, but she felt the sharp point of a bayonet at her chest. "Get upstairs," the bayonet wielder sneered.

The soldiers lined up the cellar's occupants outside, and separated out the men. Without allowing a word of parting, the Germans led the men of the village down the hill, and Marthe watched Father's lank form until she could no longer see him. The remaining soldiers shepherded the women and children back down into the Hoot's now blood-covered cellar.

CHAPTER 3

ALOUETTE

AUGUST 1914

The smell of gasoline and the wind in Alouette's hair was as intoxicating as ever. She eased back on the stick of her Caudron, enjoying the adrenaline rush that always ensued when the plane rose higher. The French countryside below appeared just like the maps in her husband's office: the rivers, railroads, even the villages seemingly unchanged from her vantage point. The world beneath her might soon be engaged in combat, but, a few thousand meters above the ground, she was alone in the sky, the universe at her beck and call. She flew along the Somme Bay at the edge of the English Channel, marveling at the beautiful beaches and marshes that must be thronging with wildlife.

After half an hour, she began heading back to the Le Crotoy aerodrome to land, using the coastline as a navigation guide. She held the tail of the Caudron low and glided downward.

Alouette found the aerodrome in a state of commotion, with men running all about on the ground. As she turned the engine off, Gaston

Caudron, the inventor of the plane, climbed up the ladder to stare into the cockpit.

"What's going on?" Alouette shouted over the noise. It sounded as though every plane in the aerodrome was running.

"We're taking the planes to the war zone."

"Okay." Alouette refastened her seatbelt and tilted her head, indicating she was ready for Caudron to spin the prop to start the plane up again.

His eyes, already jaundiced, bugged out even more. "You can't possibly think you can go to war."

"This is my plane."

He held up a hand to his mouth and coughed. "As I recall, I designed it for your husband."

"You know that Henri lets me fly it any time I want to." She tapped the ignition switch with impatience.

"Still, civilians can't fly planes during wartime." His voice softened. "You wouldn't want to hurt the war effort, would you Madame Richer?"

Alouette's hand dropped to her side. "No. No I would not."

Caudron stepped as close as he could to the edge of the ladder as she climbed out of the plane. "I guess I'll see about my motor-car in the garage at Rue," she said, navigating down the ladder as Caudron arranged himself in the cockpit.

"You'll find it a challenge to get back to Paris—all the petrol supplies have been requisitioned for the army."

"I'll be able to get as far as Amiens," she said, jumping down to the ground. "After that I shall find a way to manage, somehow."

"Good luck," Caudron replied ominously as he started the engine.

She saluted as he pulled her plane out of the aerodrome.

Alouette estimated that her car had enough petrol to carry her 30 miles, figuring she could stop at the aerodrome in Amiens, or at least a garage somewhere along the route to Paris. But near Picquigny, the car began to sputter and soon stopped completely. Alouette walked a few miles and was relieved to find a garage, albeit looking abandoned. She knocked on the closed shutters of the attached house.

A woman's hand opened the window a sliver. "Yes?"

"Can you please tell me, madame, where the mechanic is?"

The woman opened the window enough to eye Alouette up and down, from the lace neckline of her fashionable dress to the flower-trimmed hat she had donned after changing out of her flight gear. "He's gone to war," the woman finally replied.

Alouette got a similar response from the next garage she tried. One elderly woman seated on her porch did not appear as hostile and Alouette called out to her. "Do you have any vehicle I could use to take me to Amiens? My car has stalled and I need to find a mechanic."

The woman appeared likely to flee back into the house, so Alouette pulled her wallet out of her purse. "I can pay you."

Alouette soon found herself in the back of a hay cart pulled by reluctant horses, and being jolted from side to side at every rut in the road. They had to pull into the ditch almost every mile, at least it seemed to Alouette, as regiment after regiment of soldiers passed them, heading north. They drove by several villages in turmoil, the residents packing every belonging they owned onto motor-cars, rickety carts similar to the one Alouette found herself in, or even on the backs of donkeys.

"Why are you leaving?" Alouette called to one man as he balanced his rocking chair on a small wagon.

"The Germans are advancing toward the Marne," the man replied, the terror obvious in his voice.

Alouette tipped her flowered hat and focused her eyes on the road ahead of them. She had to get back to Paris as soon as possible.

The farm woman pulled back on the reins when they reached the aerodrome, about half a mile outside of Amiens. "You sure this is where you want to be?" she asked, eyeing the aerodrome. The doors had been left open, revealing its nearly empty chambers inside.

"Yes, madame." Alouette placed a few extra bills into the farm woman's hand. "If you could just wait a minute."

The farm woman gave a deep sigh before nodding her acquiescence.

When Alouette entered the practically deserted cavern, she heard someone call, "Madame Richer! Whatever are you doing here?"

As she turned, she caught sight of the well-built Captain Jeanneros. "Oh, Captain, is it possible for you to send a mechanic to help me with my car? It has stalled on the road."

The captain threw his head back and laughed. "Only such things could happen to you, Madame Richer. The Germans are pushing toward here and I only have a few litres of petrol left. Of course, you can have some if you need it. But as for the mechanic, I cannot spare one. I'm very sorry, but I'm the last of the squadron now. All the others have gone."

Alouette sighed. "I'm not sure the petrol will do me much good if I cannot get my motor-car fixed."

Captain Jeanneros scratched his head. "I can give you one tip, madame. Do not stay long in this district, or soon you may find it impossible to leave at all."

They had passed the first houses in Picquigny on the return journey when Alouette heard the farm woman suck in her breath. Alouette sat straighter in the cart, catching sight of a crowd assembled in the spot where she'd left the car. To her horror, she noted two armed gendarmes approaching.

"Now you've really done it," the farm woman muttered.

The gendarmes paused near the back of the cart. "Hand over your papers," the shorter one commanded.

Alouette did as she was bid, her heart racing. She garnered that her presence in the back of the farm cart, combined with her Parisian attire, not to mention her presence in the war zone, must have looked suspicious to the rural population of Picquigny.

The short gendarme folded Alouette's papers and tucked them into the pocket of his uniform.

"Sir," the farm woman spoke up. She hesitated for a brief second before resignedly pointing a gnarled finger to the cans of fuel in the rear of the cart.

Alouette's heart sank at her escort's sudden betrayal.

"Where did you get that petrol?" the other officer demanded. "Why are you harboring fuel when the Allies are in desperate need of it?"

"Monsieur—" Alouette attempted an explanation, but the short gendarme cut her off. "You must come with us." He gave a sharp whistle and the farm woman set the horse in motion, both officers keeping pace on either side of the cart.

"Death to the spy!" an old man shouted as the crowd of villagers also started moving forward.

Alouette felt terror rise in her chest. The mob swirled around the cart like an ocean tide. The villagers had already deemed her a traitor and any attempt she made to contradict them would be futile.

She was under arrest.

The mob of villagers followed the gendarme-escorted farm cart to the police station.

One of the gendarmes pulled Alouette out of the cart. "Lynch the spy!" someone shouted as a spray of gravel landed at her feet. She looked up to meet the angry glare of a white-haired man. The tears that gathered in her eyes did not soften him—if anything, they seemed to be an admission of guilt—and he drew back his arm to launch the next cluster of rocks. "Die, double-crosser!" This time a sharp stone connected with Alouette's jaw and the tears coursed their way down her face.

Although the villagers were not permitted into the police station, the window in the room where Alouette was taken for questioning stood open and the crowd gathered outside of it.

The evidence of Alouette's supposed damnation was spread out on the table. Her revolver was placed prominently in the center, surrounded by the cans of petrol and the documentation she had presented to the gendarme.

An older officer sat himself at the table across from the still-standing Alouette. "Name?" he demanded.

"Alouette Richer," she replied, a hint of pride in her voice. She briefly crossed her fingers behind her back, hoping he would recognize her name from the newspapers.

The village gendarme gave no sign of appreciation as he copied it down. "Sit."

She fell into a chair with a sigh. She had recently flown from Crotoy to Zürich, to great fanfare, and the Parisian papers followed her triumphs, publishing several articles and photographs of her in aviator gear standing beside her plane. But now that war had come, a curtain had dropped over everything that had occurred before its outbreak.

"You have no right to a revolver," the officer commented, a growl in his voice. "How did you come by it?"

"My husband, Henri Richer, gave it to me. He knew I'd be traveling alone and wanted to ensure my safety."

Once again, the gendarme showed no recognition of the name. "Let me see your handbag."

Reluctantly, she passed it across the table.

He dug out her wallet and pulled out a wad of bills. "Who gave you all this money?"

Alouette bit back another sigh. She supposed the 300 francs in her wallet was a small fortune to the country inspector, who probably earned less than half that in a month.

"I am not a spy," she insisted. "My husband is a wealthy man…"

"I know, I know," the gendarme held up his hand. "He must have given you all that money to ensure your safety." He rose heavily to his feet. "What he didn't understand was how incriminating carrying that amount of cash would be in a warzone. I have no choice but to detain you."

"But monsieur—"

"Pending further inquiries, of course," the inspector remarked as he shut the door behind him.

Alouette was left in the room for over half an hour. She used that time to compose herself. The last thing she wanted was to show fear to the men at the station. Indeed, when a younger officer at last unlocked the door, she kept the expression on her face neutral. He escorted her to an empty cell.

Alouette patted the pillow and then spread her skirts prettily before she sat on the bed.

The young gendarme watched, an amused expression on his face. "This is not the first time you've spent the night in jail," he stated.

"Oh, it is monsieur," Alouette said, taking her hat off and running a hand through her golden hair. "But it's better than sleeping in my broken-down motor-car by the side of the road."

"Indeed, it probably is." He returned shortly with a packet of biscuits and stale coffee. Alouette could sense that she'd at least made a friend of one of the aloof gendarmes.

That same young man came in early the next morning to announce that Alouette had been released. He waved a telegram with the word PARIS stamped on the front. "It seems you have friends in high places."

Alouette picked her hat off of the chipped nightstand and tucked her hair beneath it. "It would seem so, wouldn't it?"

"Where will you go now?"

She pursed her lips. "My petrol?"

He shook his head. "Seized for the army."

"Then I shall walk to Amiens."

The young man's face spread into a smile. "Good luck, Madame Richer."

"And to you, monsieur."

Alouette passed many villagers going the opposite way as she. They were obviously refugees, judging from their weary, and in some cases, panic-stricken expressions. The pronounced silence was only broken by the occasional droning of an airplane. As soon as one became audible, the bewildered townspeople would duck their heads, as if heeding an unheard call, the call of terror that an enemy warcraft was about to drop a bomb upon them.

Alouette found Amiens in utter chaos. Every door stood open as the townspeople rushed to and from their houses, packing up all of their belongings. Children, dogs, and a few roosters ran wildly through the streets. All roads that led to the town seemed to be filled with refugees repeating the same desperate phrases: "The Germans are coming. What shall we do?"

She headed through the hordes of anxious people gathered outside the railway station. She found a man in a conductor's uniform to ask about the next train to Paris.

"Trains?" he asked in an incredulous voice. "My lady, this station is closed, and the rest of the staff has been cleared out. Gone to war," he continued proudly, but Alouette was only half-listening.

For a moment, she thought she would give in to the same useless panic that had overcome the people surrounding her. She allowed herself a few seconds of despair before returning to reality. She needed to find some other way to get to Paris if she desired to not be in a region that was about to be infested with the enemy.

She spotted an open garage across the street and walked over to it. A young woman in a tattered dress sat on the steps leading toward the door. She glanced up as Alouette approached. "They say that the Germans murder any children they see." She sniffed. "And I have two little boys." She buried her head in her handkerchief.

Alouette climbed up the steps and put a tentative hand on the woman's shoulder. "Nobody can be so cruel as to hurt young innocents," she stated. "Not even the Germans."

She handed the woman a soiled but dry handkerchief. The woman blew into it noisily before stating, "If you are looking for a vehicle, I have nothing left."

"Not even a cart?" Alouette asked, the hopelessness threatening to surface again.

The young woman looked doubtfully at Alouette's dress. "I do have a man's bicycle. Do you know how to ride?"

Alouette took a deep breath. Her brother had had one when they were growing up, but she was never allowed to ride since it couldn't be ridden sidesaddle. "Not exactly, but if I can fly planes, surely I can ride a bicycle." She dug into her purse to find the gendarme had left her a few francs, which she extended to the young woman. The woman pulled herself up, using the banister to steady herself, and led Alouette into the garage.

Alouette walked the bicycle along the road until she was well out of the way of the crowds. The threat of falling on her face paled in comparison to the possibility of being taken as a German prisoner if she stayed here. Mounting the bicycle proved a difficult feat given her dress and handbag. As she pushed down on a pedal, the bicycle wobbled sideways instead of going forward and she hopped off, the bicycle plunging into the dust of the roadway.

She heard a low noise and turned her head with her eyes closed, hoping that it was not the stomping of German boots. A young soldier in a blue coat and bright red trousers was sitting on a nearby bench, laughing.

Alouette put her hands on her hips. "Well, don't just sit there. Give me a lesson, would you?"

He pointed at the bandage covering one of his eyes. "Even I can see that is a man's bicycle."

"Oh, do you have a woman's available?"

The soldier shook his head.

"Then do you know of another reason why I should not ride this bike straight to Paris?"

"Yes," he said, recovering from his earlier mirth. "The road to Paris has been captured by the Germans."

Alouette wiped her sweaty palms on her skirts and gazed at the dust blowing across the road. A German invasion in the carefree French capital seemed as far-flung a threat as someone predicting a thunderstorm on a sunny day. "My husband is in Paris."

"Oh?" The soldier's voice dropped an octave. Alouette smiled to herself. There was something so naively amusing about young men thinking that every woman was ready to fawn over them.

"At least I think so," Alouette replied. "He enlisted as an ambulance driver, but hasn't gotten orders yet. I had to detour to Crotoy to check on our plane."

The young man raised his eyebrows.

"Confiscated," Alouette said in answer to his unasked question.

"Yes, the military will do that. When I was at Charleroi—"

"You were in the Battle of the Sambre?"

"Yes, why?"

Alouette looked down. "No reason." They said that war had a way of turning boys into men, but the young man's affable manner hadn't struck her as though he'd seen many hard battles. Even despite that bandaged eye.

"Anyway, both sides are using airplanes for reconnaissance now." He shrugged his shoulders. "What war innovations will they think of next?"

Alouette was lost for a second, dreaming of being in the sky, finding the enemy among the trees. When she returned to reality, all she could focus on were the man's bright red pants. "Those uniforms... are they new?"

"They are, but the style dates back to Napoleon."

"Perhaps General Joffre might want to reconsider the color of your trousers. A line of soldiers all wearing those would be quite easy to spot from the air."

"Perhaps," he agreed with a smile. "I think that trains are still running to Paris from Abbeville."

Alouette picked up the bicycle. "Well, what are you waiting for, then?"

The soldier taught her how to keep her balance. In only half an hour's time, Alouette was able to ride steadily, although she was only able to mount the bicycle from the curb and could not stop except by jumping off. "I think I'll be able to manage myself, now. Thank you for your kindness."

The young soldier tipped his hat toward her, revealing a bruised and bloody forehead. "Good luck, mademoiselle."

Alouette had no idea riding a bicycle could be such taxing work. She passed numerous refugees on her way to Abbeville. So preoccupied were they in their own misery that they did not pay much heed to the girl wobbling along, trying both to balance and keep her dress out of the bicycle's chain at the same time. She kept her berth wide, lest she fell again, and called out to a man pushing a wheelbarrow, who heeded her by moving closer toward the side of the road. As Alouette overtook them, she realized the wheelbarrow was not filled with food or worldly possessions, but an invalid woman.

Alouette saw she was approaching a hill and leapt off the bicycle. She tossed her hat into a ditch before picking the two-wheeler back up and walking up the summit. She could feel her stamina fading fast, but would not allow herself to rest, fearful that if she sat down, she might not be able to get back up again.

Catching a train proved just as difficult in Abbeville as Amiens. The watchman there told Alouette that there was no way to know when the next train to Paris would leave.

Alouette was about to turn around in anguish when the man told her there was a branch line in Sergueux. Knowing that was her last chance, Alouette managed to get her aching limbs mounted once again on the bicycle and pedaled off.

She was relieved to see a train sitting in the station, although it seemed to consist mostly of open cattle wagons. "Will that be leaving shortly?" Alouette inquired of an official standing near a car.

The man shrugged. "We are waiting for information on the movement of the troops."

Still, Alouette bought a ticket and boarded a cattle wagon.

CHAPTER 4

M'GREET

AUGUST 1914

M'greet was able to catch a train bound for Switzerland, but it was stopped by frontier police. All occupants were ordered to disembark for questioning.

"Papers?" a portly man asked her.

She handed him her ticket.

He looked at it in consternation. "What nationality are you?"

M'greet sighed. "Dutch."

"Really?" He glanced up from the ticket to peer at her.

"Yes, meneer." She softened her brown eyes as she met his gaze.

"Let me see your passport."

"I don't have it with me. I haven't been asked for my passport in years, despite the fact I am a world traveler."

"Well, fräulein, now that Europe is at war, we need to see passports from everyone. If you don't have one, you will have to come with me."

A whooshing noise sounded from the train. "No, meneer, I cannot." She gestured toward the steam rising from the engine. "My belongings are on that train."

"I am sorry." The portly man nodded at a uniformed soldier, who stepped forward.

M'greet ducked out of his grasp as the train began to pull away. She ran after it, banging on the side of a car. "My suitcase. My jewelry. My furs!" The last word came out as a shrill shriek as she stopped, panting. The train had picked up speed.

The soldier appeared beside her. "Now, fräulein, if you would come with me."

She turned to the guard, her eyes blazing. "You've just cost me 80,000 francs."

M'greet was deported to the last place she wanted to be: Berlin. She checked into a hotel, one of a much lower quality than the Adlon, near the train station. She called her former lover Griebel three times that afternoon, but he did not answer any of her messages. She was truly on her own, and without even a change of clothes.

As evening fell, she made her way down to the bar and, casting her eyes around the room, found a likely evening companion, a blond man with wire spectacles. He introduced himself as Meneer Jansen and stated that he was in Berlin on business, but would be leaving for Holland the next day.

M'greet frowned. "Holland. Oh, how I miss my home country."

He choked back on his drink. "You are Dutch? I did not perceive that."

"No one usually does. They think I am of a more exotic descent. But I assure you I am as Dutch as you."

"Where did you grow up?" He took a sip of beer, his wedding ring flashing in the electric light of the hotel bar.

"Leeuwarden, but I have a home in Amsterdam now." This was not technically true.

"You are without your husband?"

"I'm a widow." This, also, was a lie. Her ex-husband was very much alive, and the flat in Amsterdam had been sold in 1902, not long after that terrible day when M'greet returned from running errands to find their small apartment bare of both Rudy and her daughter's belongings.

"And now I have no money and no clothes." She filled him in on the previous day's tribulations. "I'm not sure what to do," she said in a helpless tone. "I am a lonely woman with no one to aid me."

Jansen's expression softened in sympathy and M'greet knew she had hit her mark.

"I cannot help you with your passport, but," he reached into his coat and pulled out his wallet. "I can buy you a ticket to Amsterdam." He took out more bills. "If you go to the consulate in Frankfurt, they can assist you in crossing the border."

In a few days' time, M'greet was back in Amsterdam. The consulate had indeed issued her new papers with relatively little complications. After a clerk handed over the new passport, M'greet had discreetly changed her age from the correctly reported 38 to 30.

She found herself in Amsterdam once again, as poor as she had been when she left the city for Paris more than a decade before. She looked up Jansen in the phone book and then traveled to his sizable house in the fashionable Herengracht neighborhood. She sighed to herself as she walked past the stately houses along the canal, alike in their tall, narrow structures and square windows, but differing in their vibrant exterior paint colors and the shape of their gabled roofs. This would be the perfect place to stay while she figured out her next step.

She paused on the porch of a red brick building and consulted the slip of paper in her hand before knocking on the heavy door.

A woman answered. Her eyes traveled up from M'greet's dark blue skirt, which ended just above the ankle to better show off her Parisian boots, to her matching tailored jacket, and landed on the navy and cream lace hat pinned jauntily to the side of her head. "Yes?"

"Is Meneer Jansen home?"

"No. He is at work." Her tone implied that, while it was obvious Meneer Jansen did honest work, it was equally obvious M'greet did not.

"Oh, I do not mean to intrude. I merely wished to thank him. I was stranded in Berlin, and he lent me some assistance."

"Yes." The woman's voice was still cool. "He told me he did so."

M'greet could tell she was unwanted. "Well, thank you and please give my regards to your husband. I will be going on my way." She began walking down the steps.

"Wait.'"

M'greet turned.

The woman glanced over her shoulder before shutting the door and stepping onto the portico in her stockinged feet. "Aren't you Mata Hari, the dancer?"

"Yes, madame."

"Can I ask..." the woman looked up and down the quiet, tree-lined street. "Did you seduce my husband while you were in Berlin?" Her voice was barely above a whisper.

"No," M'greet answered truthfully.

The woman's voice rose. "Can I ask why not? He's handsome enough, isn't he?"

"Indeed. But I would never do so without a clean chemise or a bath and at the time I had neither."

"Oh," the woman's voice filled with relief. Her comfort seemed to stem more from the fact her husband had not done anything to repulse the famed Mata Hari rather than that he hadn't accepted her non-existent advances. M'greet did not recall ever feeling the same about her own philandering husband, who would often do cruel things to women, but was never in want of mistresses. She adjusted her hat. "G'day, madame."

"G'day. And good luck."

M'greet still had no money and no luggage, but her foray into the fancy canal neighborhood inspired her to book a room at the opulent Victoria Hotel. As was custom, she made sure that her room had a private bathroom.

The next day she went to call on Anna, who had been able to return to Amsterdam much earlier than her mistress. As M'greet headed down Prins Hendrikkade, she heard footsteps behind her and peeked backward to see a man in a striped suit. He must have seen her exit the Victoria and assumed she was a courtesan.

M'greet had dealt with such situations before. She decided to detour into the Church of St. Nicholas. Standing in the vestibule, she pushed the heavy door open to get a better look at the man, who was now searching up and down the street. She could see that the cut of his suit and his leather shoes hinted at money. She decided he did not pose a threat and exited the church to deliberately walk in front of him.

"Bonjour, mademoiselle." He removed his hat to reveal a head of thick hair.

"Bonjour, monsieur," M'greet returned.

"I was wondering, if you weren't busy, if you would like to have brunch with me."

She laughed. "I don't even know your name."

The man looked taken aback. "I am Lucas van der Schalk. And you are?"

"Margaretha Zelle-MacLeod." She held out her hand for him to kiss it. It had been a while since anyone had been interested in getting to know the real her, and not just Mata Hari. "I am terribly sorry, but I have other plans this morning."

Van der Schalk appeared to be disappointed.

"But you can call on me at the Victoria Hotel," M'greet shot over her shoulder as she continued on her way.

"I will do so… this afternoon!" Van der Schalk called as she crossed the street. She smiled to herself instead of glancing back at him.

"Where's Non?" M'greet asked Anna when she answered the door of her mother's tiny apartment in De Wallen.

"Madame!" Anna shouted as she hugged her mistress. When she ended her embrace, Anna said that M'greet was as elegant as ever.

"And Non? Where's my daughter?"

Anna waved her toward a table before pouring tea from a cracked pot. "She is in The Hague with Monsieur MacLeod."

"Have you seen her?"

Anna nodded. "I took the train to The Hague and walked past their house. I passed her on the street, but she didn't recognize me. She looks just like you, madame. Dark hair, dark eyes. She has your skin coloring as well… and she carries her lunch in a box with a picture of Mata Hari dancing on it."

M'greet's eyes filled with tears. "Oh, my Non, my beautiful

daughter." She wiped her face with a napkin. "I curse that bastard every day for taking her away from me. A girl should be with her mother."

Anna bit her lip as she nodded.

"Oh, Anna, I know what you are thinking—that my lifestyle is not conducive for raising a child." M'greet tossed the napkin. "But I would never have become a dancer if I had my daughter with me. And after Normie died…" The tears were threatening again, but she refused to give into them. She stood up and glanced disdainfully around at the dilapidated furniture and crumbling plaster walls. "I've taken rooms at the Victoria. You are welcome to join me."

"Yes, madame." Anna began clearing the tea.

"I must get going now. I believe I have a dinner date tonight and my nails are much due for a manicure, not to mention I have to buy a dress."

True to his word, her newest beau called her that afternoon and M'greet met him for dinner at De Silveren Spiegel. She had purchased a Paul Poiret-style dress at a boutique after leaving Anna's, and paid extra for the seamstress to fit it right then.

"Have you ever been here?" Van der Schalk asked after he'd kissed her hand.

"No," M'greet admitted as she gazed around at the old-fashioned candelabras and Dutch portraits on the walls. Unaccompanied women were not to be found in fancy restaurants, and her ex-husband would never have been able to afford such a meal.

"It dates back to the Dutch Golden Ages," van der Schalk commented as he sat down.

M'greet gathered her silk skirts before sinking onto the flimsy chair. "Are you a historian?"

"Am I? No," he replied, the amusement obvious in his voice. "I am a banker."

She leaned forward and put her hand under her chin. "How interesting."

A waiter came by with a decanter. His eyes dropped to stare openly at M'greet's décolletage as he poured her wine.

Van der Schalk took a long drink before setting his glass down. "Tell me more about yourself, madame. You are Russian, no?"

M'greet sat straighter and put her hands in her lap. "You really don't recognize me?"

He gave her a searching look. "Should I?"

She was about to reveal herself as the famed Mata Hari, but then thought of an even more glamorous role than the one she'd been playing for over ten years. She did her best to affect a Russian accent. "I'm a ballet dancer. I've danced with Sergei Diaghilev's Russian ballet company for some time." This was almost legitimate: in 1910, her manager had nearly convinced the ballet impresario to hire her, but Diaghilev insisted that Mata Hari audition, which she, of course, would not deign to do.

"Ahh," van der Schalk said delightedly as the meal was served. "I thought you had a dancer's physique."

She dipped her chin, pretending to be bashful at the compliment.

"Are you married?" he asked. "I don't see a wedding ring."

"Widowed," M'greet replied without hesitation. "You?"

"Never been married." Van der Schalk took a bite of meat. "You know," he stated when he finished, "Peter the Great once visited Holland in order to learn the art of shipbuilding. The little house he stayed in is still there, in Zaandam. I could take you there if you'd like."

"Of course. I'd love to see where the great Tsar resided." M'greet had no such desire, but wouldn't mind touring the town with the handsome van der Schalk. "But then again…" she frowned.

"What is it?"

"I have nothing to wear." She explained what happened in Berlin, emphasizing the banker's accusations of Russian ancestry for good measure. "So you see, I have no clothes and no money."

His eyes traveled over her beaded dress. "Perhaps I could take you shopping beforehand."

M'greet beamed. "That would be lovely."

The next day, van der Schalk took M'greet all over Amsterdam's shopping district, buying her shoes, jewelry, and the latest styles of dresses to replace all that had been left behind in Germany.

Despite the pleasure she obtained from having a full closet once again, M'greet was almost overcome with melancholy when she returned to the hotel. She realized as she walked up the wide staircase to her room that it was due to being back in Holland after so many years abroad. Save for Normie's death, which occurred in Java, some of the worst things M'greet had to endure had transpired in her native country: it was where her father abandoned her all those years ago, and also where her marriage had officially fallen apart.

"I need to see Non," she told Anna when she entered the suite.

Anna's normally pinched face relaxed into a sorrowful look. "Perhaps you should contact Monsieur MacLeod."

M'greet grimaced. "I don't want to have any contact with that brute. I should write to Non herself."

Anna sat across from M'greet at the little table. "I suppose Non is old enough now that she's heard stories about you."

"I'm sure her father has filled her head with lies."

"If you did write to Non, you could tell her about your life. Explain what happened from your perspective."

M'greet tucked a manicured hand under her chin. "Yes, that is a good idea. She should know that I never willingly abandoned her."

She pulled a piece of clean paper from a drawer in the writing desk and dipped a pen in ink. *I did love your father when I first met him,* she wrote before pausing and replacing the pen in the inkwell. How could she describe to her teenage daughter the passion they had experienced when they first met? M'greet was only 18 when she answered the ad John Rudolph MacLeod had placed in the local newspaper. It read *Captain in the Army of the Indies, on leave in Holland, seeks a wife with a character to his taste, preferably with means.*

M'greet certainly did not have means, as much as her father used to pretend it to be so. Her father was a hat-maker, but like his daughter, preferred to live beyond said means, and his fellow Leeuwardeners nicknamed him the Baron. He had invested in oil shares at a time when coal ruled the world, and had completely wiped out his wife's meager inheritance before M'greet was thirteen. The words she had written to Non blurred as M'greet became lost in thoughts of the past.

After her father declared bankruptcy, he moved to Amsterdam to live with his mistress, taking M'greet's two younger brothers with him.

She was left to take care of her heart-broken mother, who died eight months later.

M'greet had bounced from family member to family member and had just gotten kicked out of college, where she had been training to become a kindergarten teacher, when she spotted Rudy MacLeod's ad. Even then she had favored men in uniforms.

Their infatuation with each other quickly grew stale, but M'greet married him anyway, seeing no other viable opportunities. They sailed for the West Indies soon after she gave birth to her son, Norman John. Rudy spent most of his off-time drinking, gambling, and consorting with the local women, and M'greet and her baby son were frequently left alone. Rudy was given a new posting in Malang in 1897, and things looked up: they had more money and Rudy started sharing M'greet's bed more. A year later they had a daughter, Jeanne Louise, nicknamed 'Non,' a shortening of *Nonah*, which meant "Little Miss" in the local language. After Non was born, Rudy returned to his old ways, and the marriage had already fallen apart when Normie died at just a little over two years old.

But M'greet couldn't explain any of this to her daughter. Back in the present, she shook off the haunting memories and wrote some nonsense about how she still loved Non's father, but circumstances had forced them apart. She depicted what living in Paris had been like, the excitement of being on stage, but made no reference to why she never again demanded to see her daughter after Rudy left that day.

She ended the letter stating she looked forward to seeing her pretty face once again and sealed it with a kiss. Anna immediately left to post it.

CHAPTER 5

MARTHE

SEPTEMBER 1914

The women and children of Westrozebeke were forced to spend two weeks in the Hoot's cellar. The atmosphere down there grew foul and damp. They were not allowed to light fires and, as August dragged into September, the nights grew chilly. Their water supply became dangerously low and Marthe worried the Germans might have forgotten about their cellar hostages.

Finally a hauptmann, different from the one who had terrorized Marthe's family, appeared. "You can come out now." He spoke so quietly that a near-starved Marthe wasn't sure she had heard him right.

"What is he saying?" Mevrouw Hoot inquired.

"We are free to go?" Marthe asked him in German.

"You may leave the cellar. We will escort you to the town of Roulers, as it is not safe here for civilians anymore."

Marthe nodded her thanks to the hauptmann before leading her mother upstairs. Mevrouw Hoot followed closely behind.

They emerged in the Hoot's kitchen to see five more German soldiers gathered around the kitchen table, smoking cigarettes.

Mevrouw Hoot coughed and waved her arms, but the smoke refused to dissipate. "*Dit is mijn huis.*"

"Not anymore, fräulein," a man with a pock-marked face replied in German. "This house has been confiscated. Move along."

Mevrouw Hoot, too emotional to process the soldier's words, cast a helpless glance at Marthe, who motioned to follow her outside. She didn't need the German soldiers to overhear her explain to Mevrouw Hoot that the house, which had belonged to the Hoot family for nearly a century, was no longer hers.

As the former prisoners walked out into the sunshine, their eyes traveled over the blackened remains of their village. The houses that hadn't been completely burned down had shattered windows and doors —from the Germans searching for hidden villagers, Marthe assumed. Most of the trees that had once lined the broad main avenue had been felled and the street was littered with debris from the carnage: wooden shoes, broken saddle buckles, beer bottles, and other various discarded materials.

Marthe couldn't bear to look at what remained of her beautiful village any longer. As she passed an abandoned spiked helmet, rage took over her mourning and she had to refrain from kicking it.

The soldiers accompanying them to Roulers allowed any woman whose house was still standing to collect a few belongings and pile them onto the dilapidated cart that would accompany them to Roulers. Most of Mevrouw Hoot's clothing had been tossed out along with her family's personal items, and she stood watch as the rest of the women gathered what was left of their lives.

As the women were escorted along a muddy highway, they frequently looked back to gaze at the ruins of their native village, wondering if they would ever see it again. It must have rained every day that Marthe was in the Hoot's cellar as the mud, a constant presence in the low country of Belgium, was even more ubiquitous now that the masses of soldiers, horses, and guns had destroyed the roads. The Germans had tried to abate the flowing muck by strewing flax and looted curtains and carpets along the roadside, but still the sticky red sludge oozed, coating the refuges' boots and skirts during the six miles to Roulers.

· · ·

48

The larger town of Roulers was still unharmed, and Marthe stared wonderingly at the unscathed houses, their gabled roofs rising triumphantly over the intact cobblestone streets. When they reached the Grand Place, Marthe saw a market was taking place, with Belgian civilians readily mingling with German soldiers. No one paid much notice to the now homeless women and Marthe wondered what to do.

A kindly, gray-haired woman finally approached Mother. "You are refugees?"

Mother nodded.

The woman sized Mother up before stating, "I can take you as a lodger in my house, and I think I can find places for the rest of you."

"And my daughter?" Mother asked, hugging Marthe to her.

"Yes, I suppose I can take her too," the woman acquiesced.

A relieved Marthe began pulling their scant belongings from the cart.

That evening Marthe and her mother found themselves sharing a comfortable bed in a warm, spacious house. The gray-haired lady was the wife of a prominent grocer and she served them the first decent meal they'd had in weeks. After Marthe and Mother had explained their ordeal, the grocer's wife promised to make inquiries as to the whereabouts of Father. They still hadn't heard any news of Marthe's brother, Max, and she wished that all of her family could once again be united under one roof.

Wanting to make herself useful in the best way she could, Marthe set out for the Roulers hospital the next morning. She'd washed her face in an effort to look presentable, a task not easily accomplished in her ripped, muddy clothes.

The hospital was established in Roselare College on Menin Road and recognizable by the Red Cross flag that flew from a spire on the main building. An orderly standing propped against a pillar near the main entrance directed Marthe to the office of the senior physician, or *Oberarzt*.

The Oberarzt was a kindly-looking man with a well-trimmed

beard. He nodded his gray head as Marthe explained her nursing background. "I am thankful for your presence," he stated when she finished. "We are in dire need for a nurse as we have none."

"None?" Marthe repeated. "That seems unusual for such a large hospital."

"We have some Belgian women here who cook and wash, but none of them have any medical training." The Oberarzt stood up. "Come, I will show you around."

He led her into the first ward, where rows of cots in uneven lines filled the room. A doctor with drooping eyelids moved slowly among the men while two burly German orderlies assisted. The Oberarzt went to the aid of one man in the corner who was writhing in pain. Marthe could smell the gangrenous wound even before she looked down on the bandages covering his leg. The Oberarzt met the eyes of another doctor and mouthed the words, "amputate." The other doctor signaled for the orderlies, who picked up the man's stretcher and carried him away.

"It has been calm lately, relatively speaking," the Oberarzt commented as he led Marthe into the civilian clinic, which was nearly empty except for an elderly man with a bandaged arm and a woman with a toddler on her lap. It seemed the Germans in Roulers were not nearly as barbaric as those who conquered Westrozebeke, or else they had paused their burning of homes and shooting of townspeople. Marthe bent down in front of the toddler to inquire what was wrong.

"It's his stomach," his mother told her.

"Right here," the little boy added, pointing.

"It looks like you are ready to begin working here, then, fräulein," the Oberarzt said, the approval clear in his voice. "I will see you tomorrow, then?"

"Yes, Herr Oberarzt," Marthe replied, placing a stethoscope on the little boy's chest.

Marthe soon fell into a routine where she would wake up early to arrive at the hospital by seven, and then leave by the same time in the evening.

A few mornings later, she was greeted by a new sight hanging on the door of the hospital: a piece of paper with a declaration from the new Town-Kommandant typed in large print:

My task is to preserve the public order in Belgium. Every act of the population against the German forces, every attempt to interfere with our communications with Germany, or to trouble the railway, will be met with severe punishment. Any resistance against the German government will be suppressed without pity.

The declaration, the type that would henceforth be known as an *affiche*, went on to establish a regular curfew from 7 pm until 5 am, stating that no unlicensed civilian should be out on the streets at that time. The Town-Kommandant ended his message by adding that, if he became displeased, he could move the curfew earlier and perhaps fine the town as well.

Marthe walked into the hospital with a scowl on her face. Roulers might have been visually in a better state than her hometown, but German occupation was equivalent to German tyranny. The Belgian government had left Brussels and was now in exile somewhere in France while King Albert was at the Yser Front with his troops, leaving the people of Belgium to be ruled by the iron fist of the Kaiser.

The Oberarzt greeted her with the same amicable tone as yesterday. "Ah, Fräulein Cnockaert, I am grateful to see you have returned."

She forced a cordial smile. "Yes, Herr Oberarzt, I am reporting for duty."

He nodded toward a smaller room off the main one. "We've had some Belgian soldiers arrive overnight. You can start with them."

Marthe entered to find two men covered in bloodied bandages. She approached the first one, whose chest was wrapped in a dressing, the blood darkest on the lower part.

"He was shot in the stomach during the retreat to Namur," his companion stated.

There was something familiar about his gravelly voice. Marthe turned to see her old schoolmate, or, what remained of him anyway. "Nicholas Hoot," she remarked, surprised. Bandages covered his left shoulder, but she could see that some of the flesh of his upper arm was gone, and his left leg had been amputated below the knee. His face and body had been cut severely and the skin that wasn't lacerated was peppered with bruises.

She poured him a glass of water and held it to his lips. "What happened?"

He took a small sip, but most of the water trickled down his chin. "The Boches. After that night they invaded Westroosebeke, I went out to look for Valerie."

Marthe wiped at his mouth with a cloth. "She wasn't with us in the cellar at your parents' house."

"I know." He stared at the wall instead of meeting her eyes. "She tried to run from them…"

"Was she… did they…" Marthe couldn't find the right words. She crumpled the washcloth in her hands instead.

"Kill her? Yes, but not before they'd each had their turn with her."

"Oh Nicholas." Marthe's eyes filled with tears. "I'm so sorry."

"I tried to get revenge as soon as I'd heard. I became a true *franc-tireur* and shot at them from the church tower." The right side of his face turned upward in a strange half-smile. "I managed to wound a few of them before they found me. They shot me, beat me, and then left me lying on the road as a warning. The good nuns of Westroze-beke took me in and nursed me till the Boches accused them of being Allied informants. They ordered the nuns to strip down right in front of me. I swear, had I any strength left, I would have pummeled them until the Huns were bloodier than me if they so much laid a hand on them."

"Did they?" Marthe was horrified at the thought of anyone, including the Huns, would even think of raping a woman of God.

"No. They just kicked them out of town and then evacuated the hospital. And here I am, a German prisoner. And a crippled one at that."

"Nicholas, I…," but once again Marthe had no words.

"Do you know anything of my parents?"

Thankful for some good news, she explained how Mevrouw Hoot had been taken in by Roulers townspeople. "I will get a pass for her to see you as soon as I can."

"And Father?"

Marthe shook her head. "I don't know what happened to him, or my father either."

Nicholas shifted his body painfully.

"You should try to sleep now," she told him. "I'll come back as soon as I can."

He didn't reply as Marthe attended to the other, still sleeping, soldier, filling his water glass and then checking his bandages.

She could barely look at Nicholas's pitiful form as she left the room.

Marthe checked on Nicholas one more time before she left the hospital that night. She had to hurry home, as it was nearly seven in the evening and the last thing she needed was a run-in with the military gendarmes who trolled the streets at night and harassed anyone about who was not a soldier.

She had just returned to the grocer's house when she heard a rustling in the shrubbery outside the back door.

"Hello?" she called loudly.

"Shh," a woman's voice commanded.

Marthe blinked a couple of times as someone backed out of the bushes. "Aunt Lucelle!" she whispered in an excited tone.

Her aunt held a finger to her lips and, once again, shh'ed her.

Marthe opened the back door as Lucelle darted inside. Once in the kitchen, her aunt glanced furtively around. "Do they have a cellar here?"

Marthe pointed to the basement.

"Get your mother," her aunt commanded before going downstairs. Marthe did as she was bid.

As expected, Mother was pleased to see her older sister. Aunt Lucelle seemed much more comfortable in the basement and stopped her shh'ing. "It's the Berlin Vampires," she explained, clearly referring to the German curfew enforcers. "They could be anywhere, and have the authorization to walk into houses unannounced."

"Are you a criminal?" Mother asked.

Lucelle shrugged. She found a bottle of brandy and poured some into the cap before gulping it down. "I've come from the front. I have seen Max."

"Max?" Marthe asked at the same time Mother said, "You've seen my son?"

Lucelle held up the cap of brandy. "He is fine and with the Army at the Yser. My own sons are also safe, thank God. But that is not why I'm here."

"You are a spy." As far as Marthe could tell, Lucelle had said nothing of the sort, but there was no question in Mother's voice.

Lucelle nodded. "I am part of the British Secret Intelligence Commission."

Marthe put a shocked hand over her chest. She'd heard of many Belgians accused of espionage, but had never actually met anyone who truly was a spy. The spy-paranoia of the Roulers Town Kommandant could have almost been laughable had the punishments not been so deplorable. When he accused the Staden town priest of spying, he ordered soldiers to drag the aged man out of the church to dig his own grave and then shot him into it. Marthe found it hard to reconcile the ill-famed notion of a spy with the gray-haired elderly aunt standing before her.

Marthe noted wonderingly that her aunt had lost her front teeth as she spoke again. "I have to do something to help our people fight off the Boches."

"We all do what we can for the war," Mother replied in a quiet tone. "Marthe here is a nurse at Roselare."

Lucelle looked at her niece with renewed interest. "You are in contact with enemy soldiers?"

Marthe nodded.

"Do they ever talk of military formations or troop movements?"

"I just started there," Marthe responded. "But I did overhear some talk yesterday, though all the places sounded foreign."

"You must pay attention!" Lucelle hissed. Her eyes gleamed in the dim light. "How would you like to do more for your country?"

"You mean like espionage?" Mother demanded. "No. It's too dangerous. They hang people on mere suspicion now."

"It's no more dangerous than Max being at the front," Lucelle challenged. "And may be even more necessary if we are to win this war."

Mother opened her mouth again, but no words came out. She was probably thinking what Marthe was—of Max, of Father, of all the townspeople that had been harmed by the Germans.

Marthe drew in a breath, her thoughts traveling to all she had seen that day—the oppressive *affiche* and poor Nicholas's broken body at the hospital. She would sacrifice anything to help her fellow Belgians. "What would you have me do?"

Lucelle tapped her lip in thought. "I must communicate with my intelligence handlers, for it is through them that I get my orders. But I will be back around Roulers in a few weeks' time and will send for you. However I can get my message to you, Marthe, you must show no surprise." She set the nearly empty brandy bottle on the shelf and wiped her mouth. "I must leave—I've been here too long as it is."

Marthe and Mother followed her up the stairs, where Lucelle slipped out as quietly as she had come in. They watched as she headed toward the fields and then was eclipsed by the darkness.

Mother's eyes were wide as she looked upon her daughter, but she did not speak of what had transpired in the cellar.

CHAPTER 6

ALOUETTE

SEPTEMBER 1914

*W*hen Alouette finally returned to her Paris home, she burst in, the heavy door no match for her excitement at seeing her husband again. "Henri!" she shouted, setting her valise on the tiled floor of the entrance hall. "Henri, I'm home."

The maid, Hortense, appeared in her usual spotless uniform. "Madame Richer you've finally returned."

"Where's Henri?"

A flicker of disapproval flashed across Hortense's face as she glanced at Alouette's torn dress. "Monsieur Richer has left for the front."

"No. He couldn't have gone yet." Alouette's eyes filled with tears. "I was trying to get back, but the trains weren't running from Crotoy."

The maid handed her an envelope. "Monsieur Richer left this for you." She gave the slimmest curtsy before she walked away.

Alouette frowned. Hortense had been Henri's housekeeper for years and she'd clearly never cared for his young wife. Alouette wasn't sure if it was the vast age difference between Henri and his new bride, her refusal to adhere to the strict rules that governed upper-crust

Parisian society, or something else entirely that provoked Hortense's distaste. Not that it mattered all that much. Alouette always did what she wanted, regardless of who found it unacceptable.

She walked into the parlor and sat down in a plush velvet chair before tearing the envelope open.

My dearest wife,

I was hoping to set my eyes upon your beautiful face one last time before I had to leave for the front, but alas I was called up. I heard that Amiens was now in German control, but I'm not worried. You have gotten yourself out of worse scrapes before and I am confident you will be able to take care of yourself. I know you wish that you could fight this war and while I believe that someday women will be looked at as men's equals, this is not your time. Please look after the house. I will return soon.

Your affectionate husband

Alouette refolded the letter and put it in a nearby drawer. Henri had volunteered to be an ambulance driver, and she supposed she should be grateful that he wouldn't be at the front line. And the monotony of military life would probably suit him very well.

As for her on the other hand… what should she do now? Ever since she'd married Henri, her life had been one carefree adventure after another, all financed by her husband's considerable fortune, including her plane, which was now probably being flown by a French aviator. She stood, casting her eyes around the Victorian-styled parlor. *Take care of the house,* Henri had written.

Suddenly Alouette felt overwhelmed: the velvet drapes, the Persian rug, the gilded mirrors, even the various knick-knacks spread over the piano from their travels seemed to weigh on her. Hortense had kept everything impeccably neat and free of dust, but it appeared incongruous and foreign to the lifestyle Alouette had once led.

Still in her blood-stained dress, the sudden urge to flee came over her. She walked purposefully out of the house and back into the Parisian sunshine. As her stomach protested against her quick movements, she realized she hadn't eaten anything for hours and, a bit slower now, headed down the street to her favorite café.

Instead of the familiar, chubby face of the shopkeeper, a hard-faced woman was behind the counter. "Husband's gone to the front," the woman replied to Alouette's inquiry after the owner.

"I'll have a croissant and a coffee, please," Alouette requested.

The woman arched her eyebrow. "Croissants waste precious flour and butter, and we've been ordered not to produce them anymore. We just have plain bread." It made a distasteful ringing sound as she dropped it onto a plate. "The Germans are approaching the Marne River. A battle will be on soon, if it hasn't started already." She handed Alouette the coffee. "But we will not know for weeks: the Parisian papers have stopped running since all the men have gone to war."

"Will your husband be in the battle?"

She shrugged. "If he fights, he will fight hard, like every other Frenchman. And yours?"

Alouette gave her a small smile and nodded, embarrassed to explain that Henri was too old to be a soldier.

"You can't make an omelet without breaking a few eggs!" the woman called as Alouette walked away from the counter.

She drank her coffee and ate the stale bread on a little table outside of the café, pondering the woman's casual remark. It seemed that everyone, and everything, had gone a bit numb since the war started. Talk of the destruction of whole towns and the murder of innocent people had become almost commonplace now, and it was both spoken about and heard with a degree of indifference. *But,* Alouette supposed, *maybe that's to keep from surrendering to the ever-present misery that is war-time.*

She dusted the crumbs off her dress, and, still avoiding returning to her empty house, decided to stroll down the street. She had gone a few blocks when she heard a plane overhead.

"Is it French?" a female passerby asked in a shrill voice.

"No," Alouette said, gazing at the fan-tailed plane, which was flying just over the tops of the buildings. "It's a German *Taube.*" Indeed the *Taube*—German for dove—resembled its namesake in both form and flight, yet she was sure its graceful maneuvering belied the plane's menacing intentions. Alouette and the passerby stared warily at the black crosses on the plane's wings as it made several passes, coming closer and closer.

Suddenly, Alouette caught sight of something small being hurled from the cockpit. "It's a bomb!" she shouted. "Get down!" She flung herself to the sidewalk in time to feel a small tremor in the ground.

When it stopped, she got unsteadily back to her feet. The buzzing of the plane was fainter now. Smoke filled the air and Alouette coughed.

When it began to dissipate, she ran toward the source of the smoke. Her heart sank as she saw that the café she had visited just half an hour before had been obliterated. She covered her mouth against the black smoke rising into the air, cloaking the bright sunlight and making the afternoon seem dark as dusk.

A crowd had gathered in front of the ruins. Alouette tried to move some of the debris in search of survivors, but she burned her hand on a still-hot piece of metal.

"It's no use," the woman Alouette had passed earlier on the street said as she came up beside her. "Anyone buried under there is now the latest victim of the Huns."

"Look at this," a young man said, waving a banner in German colors he had pulled out of the wreck.

Alouette reached for it. There was a message printed in German and she translated it aloud. "The German Army stands before the gates of Paris. You have no choice but to surrender."

"Surrender?" the young man repeated, the indignation obvious in his voice. "To the Boches? Never."

The skin on Alouette's arm grew cold and, despite the warm day, she shivered as she took stock of the felled café, imagining the charred body of the owner's wife among the smoking embers. *Looks like a few eggs have already been broken.* She glanced again to the sky, just being able to make out the dark form of the *Taube* over the eastern part of the city. She would have given anything to be in her own plane at that moment, armed with a machine gun, the German plane centered in the crosshairs. And suddenly she had an idea.

She rushed home, once again throwing her bag on the floor, before entering Henri's office. She wrote a hasty letter to the Ministry of War, offering her aviation experience to France and the Allies. "It does not matter where I would be stationed, of course, but I request to be put to use. I have risked my life for sport as an aviatrix, and therefore the sacrifice I now propose to make is of no consequence."

A week passed without word from either Henri or the Ministry of War. The *Taube* had become a frequent fixture in the skies over Paris, occasionally dropping its bombs, which were always accompanied by a note full of threats. There was nothing else to do but make light of the macabre matter. The clerk at the postal office had told Alouette that the German plane's flight pattern was so regular he'd begun to set his watch by it.

Alouette's restlessness turned to worry over Henri's fate. Every day she awoke faced with two choices: carry on her day as she'd done before the war and pretend that everything was normal, or wallow in self-pity that her husband was at the front, possibly getting killed at that moment. Most days she went with the former choice, but one morning it was the latter, and she stayed under the covers until well past noon.

Hortense burst into the room with a tray of bread and tea. "Madame, will you not go out today?" She set the tray on the bed before raising the blinds.

Alouette blinked in the sudden sunlight before burying her head under a pillow. There was nowhere to go, anyway. Most of the population believed the Germans were indeed at the city gates and had fled for the countryside, turning the once-bustling Paris into a ghost town. The theaters and museums had all been closed, and the gas lamps that had given the city its nickname, "The City of Lights" remained dark.

"Madame." Hortense's voice was hesitant, but closer this time.

"Yes?" Alouette reluctantly pulled the pillow away.

"It is your husband you worry about, no?"

Alouette met her maid's eyes without reply. For once Hortense's gaze held no animosity, only sympathy.

She stepped toward the bed to set a gnarled hand on top of Alouette's. "My son-in-law is also at the front. I pray for his safety each day. I will add Monsieur Richer's name to my prayers as well."

Alouette was uncomfortable with this unexpected show of affection from the normally aloof maid, but she nodded in agreement. "We must pray for all the Allies at the front."

Hortense dropped her head in acquiescence. "Perhaps it's just that Monsieur Richer's letters have been held up in a German blockade."

Alouette's indignation rose. Wasn't it enough that the Germans were bombing their city and killing their men? Did they have to steal their mail as well? She turned away, and Hortense, taking the hint, left the room as silently as she had come in.

The next day Alouette was pleased when Hortense handed her an official-looking letter, with the *Aéronautique Militaire,* the aviation department of the French War Office, as the return address. Her half-smile soon drooped as she read the opening lines. The letter was written in a characteristically French style: polite but standoffish, telling her with regrets that only males could be employed in the French air force.

"Madame?" Hortense inquired, a helpless look on her face.

Alouette folded the letter into a mock airplane and sent it flying across the room. It landed, as intended, in the fireplace. "It's nothing."

A few days later another official-looking letter arrived. This one summoned her to the office of a man named Georges Ladoux, from the Deuxiéme Bureau of the Ministry of War.

Alouette hurriedly dressed and rushed over to the address given in the summons, thinking at last the men of the *Aéronautique Militaire* had changed their mind.

The building at 282 boulevard, Saint-Germain had been built recently; the ornate doors led into a rotunda with high plastered ceilings and a mosaic tiled floor. None of it seemed like a suitable office building for the War Department.

Alouette was shown to an upstairs room and squinted at the hastily-scrawled lettering on the door indicating that this was the office of French Counterespionage Services. *That's odd,* she thought as she pushed the door open. *What do they want with me?*

As Georges Ladoux stood in greeting, it was clear he was much shorter than Alouette. He was stocky, with black hair gleaming with brilliantine product and a well-trimmed toothbrush mustache. He nodded as Alouette sat down across from him. "I presume you know why I have sent for you, madame." It was not a question. Ladoux's eyebrows arched and he leaned forward expectantly.

"I do not," Alouette replied as coolly as she could. Inside her heart was racing, but she relied on her experiences as a pilot to force herself to remain outwardly calm.

"I have proof that you have visited Germans in Paris."

Alouette covered her confusion by pulling a lipstick out of her purse and uncapping it.

"German spies," Ladoux continued.

She flipped open a compact mirror, hoping her shaking hands were not noticeable. The bewilderment in her voice was not fake, however. "And who would these German spies be?"

"Does it matter?" Ladoux sat back in his desk chair.

"I should think that it does. Such words could get me hanged, if they were true."

"Then you are saying it is not true?"

She snapped the lid back on her lipstick. "Of course it is not true."

He pulled a piece of paper from a file folder and unfolded it. "Alouette Richer was born in Lorraine, April 15, 1889. Her father was an adjutant in the Hussars. As a young girl, she took to sports with ardor. Before becoming an aviatrix, she had much experience with horseback riding and driving an automobile. She won second place at an international target practice competition in Lille, a sport which few women attempt."

Alouette's hands tightened, but he thankfully put the report down before he read any more. "Now, Madame Richer, if you could explain your recent visit to Crotoy."

She met Ladoux's eyes squarely. "I had to check on my plane. I am trying to join the air force."

He gave her an oily smile. "A woman pilot in the *Armée de l'Air?*"

His condescending tone was beginning to grate on Alouette's nerves. "Surely, if you researched me that much, you would know that I recently offered my services to them."

He shuffled some papers on the desk, and Alouette caught her name written at the top of a file folder. "I can tell that you are a woman of some character, Madame Richer. If you would just tell us about these Germans—"

Alouette, sensing there was no point in continuing the conversation, grabbed her bag and stood. "I'm sorry you have been so misinformed, Captain. I have repeatedly offered my services to the government, to no avail. If I knew of any German spies, I would be the first person to report them. But alas, I do not." She started for the door.

"Will you join my department?"

Alouette nearly dropped her purse.

"We need women like you—patriotic, sporty, not fearful of anything."

She stood frozen, thinking that only two of those descriptions were true. "If you are so convinced I'm a German spy, why are you inviting me to join your staff?"

He indicated her unoccupied chair in lieu of answering.

As much as she longed to leave this odious man's office, here he was offering her the chance she'd been longing for. She sat. "What would you want me to do?"

"I want you to, in fact, find the German spies I have been referencing." The hairs on his mustache fluttered with his breath.

Alouette replaced her purse on the floor and folded her hands in her lap as he continued, "When Germany closed its borders, we had not a single French agent within her lines, whereas they had managed to infiltrate France and many other Allied and neutral countries with *liaisons* ready to act at a moment's notice."

"And do what?" Alouette asked.

He stretched his hands out. "Spy. Spread German propaganda. Steal supplies. Defy the blockade."

"And we are at a loss as to the identities of these *liaisons*."

"Indeed." He pulled out a cigarette before offering her one. She declined. He lit it before continuing, "France's ability to detect these Trojan horses, if you will, was almost nil. That's when General Joffre recognized the necessity of a Department of Counterespionage. I am the man whom he appointed to begin this new type of combat, what I am dubbing the Secret War."

"What role would I play?"

"I'm told you speak German."

She gestured toward her file. "As you know, I grew up in Alsace. I had no choice but to learn the language."

He flicked ash into a nearby tray. "Our frontiers are like sieves: full of holes. Everybody and everything can pass through our borders at their will. I will give you 25,000 francs for every spy you expose."

The growl in his voice contained hints of intimidation and Alouette had the notion that his offer was as much of a disguised threat as the German *liaisons* that, according to him, lurked on every corner. Once again, Alouette stood. "You must know, of course, that I do not need the money. And also that I would need to consult with my husband before I can accept your offer."

He rose from his chair and bowed. "Of course. Take what time you need. Contact me when you are ready."

Alouette's demurral of Ladoux's offer was not merely an excuse. As typical of most marriages, she consulted Henri on all of her decisions, but he often did the same. They'd shared the same interests and had a trusting, if passionless, marriage. Still, they had never spent so much time apart, not since Henri had rescued Alouette from poverty when she had, misguidedly, left her hometown for good at sixteen to follow a lover to Paris.

She wondered what Henri, with his old-world sense of chivalry, would think of the pompous little Ladoux. She would never know if his letters couldn't get past the blockade.

The next afternoon, when Alouette finally got the motivation to get out of bed, she decided to demand news of Henri at the town hall. While she was getting dressed, Hortense entered without knocking and set an envelope on the bed. "Madame, this came for you by courier this morning."

Alouette could feel her maid's eyes boring into her back as she lifted the bulky letter with an equally heavy heart. Ironically it had come from the Sixteenth Arrondissement, the same destination she had been gearing up to set out for later that morning.

She tried her best to rip open the envelope in spite of her shaking hands.

Dear Madame Richer,

We regret to inform you that the soldier, Richer, Henri, aged 42, was engaged in bringing up transports while exposed to military artillery fire.

She looked up, her mind racing with indignation. *I know that already.* What do they think, husbands don't communicate with their wives?

She forced herself to read on:

After being wounded by a highly explosive shell, he showed an extraordinary coolness in bringing his lorry into a position of safety.

"Thank God," she exclaimed out loud, expecting the rest of the letter to contain news of Henri receiving the *Croix de Guerre.*

But the letter ended simply with the words, *A few minutes later he died.*

"No!" The letter landed on the bed as Alouette's hands flew to her mouth. She tasted blood and forced herself to look at her fingers. She must have sliced the tip of her finger opening the envelope, but sensed no pain. She felt nothing, in fact, but a numbness that penetrated her body.

"It's Henri," she told Hortense helplessly. Her eyes dropped to the terrible letter sitting on the bed. "He's dead."

"Oh madame!" Hortense glanced at the cream-colored letter, as if the French government, in opposition to their callous explanation, had included some sort of blueprint for what to do next. "Madame?"

Alouette glanced at Hortense, who was standing with her hefty arms opened wide. Wordlessly Alouette stepped forward until those arms were around her back and she was standing in Hortense's embrace. She clung to her maid, feeling as though the floor was sinking beneath them.

CHAPTER 7

M'GREET

OCTOBER 1914

M'greet's letter to her daughter was returned unopened, accompanied by a note from her ex-husband. He stated that if she wished to see Non, she should ask permission from him first. M'greet responded with a letter written, perhaps a bit pretentiously, in French, knowing that Rudy did not readily speak the language.

My dear friend,

If you so wish, I will ask you personally: be kind and let me see my daughter. There is much hate between us, but Non should not be deprived of a mother because of our bickering. I thank you in advance for allowing me what I've been craving all these years.

Sincerely, Marguerite

Finally, Rudy agreed to a meeting, though he was reluctant to meet in Amsterdam, where he lived, or even in the Hague. Instead he suggested lunch in Rotterdam.

The last time she'd seen Non was nearly ten years ago, at the railroad station in Arnhem. It had been shortly after M'greet had started to make it big as Mata Hari. She'd traveled from Paris in the first-class car, and was helped down by the liveried footman who'd been assigned to personally look after her luggage.

Non's eyes grew wide as she gazed at her mother's finery. She reached out to touch the fur lining on M'greet's coat, but Rudy brushed her arm away.

"You're looking... well." He had spat out the last word, as if it pained him to say it.

She glanced at him disdainfully, telling him she felt just the opposite about him with her eyes. She turned to her daughter and swept her into her arms. "Oh, Non, my baby girl. How would you like to visit Mammie in Paris?"

"That's not possible," Rudy replied.

"Oh, but she would love it."

Non's enthusiastic nod showed she agreed.

"What she would love is to have school supplies." He put his hand on M'greet's arm to pull her to the side and tell her in a gruff voice, "We are in a little bit of a financial problem."

"Of course." She shrugged off his arm; his grip and rough manner reminded her all too well of their terrible marriage. She then pulled out a wad of bills and counted them aloud before handing them to Rudy. Catching sight of her daughter's dirty face, she wet her thumb and swiped at Non's cheek. Non smiled up at her and M'greet pulled the rest of the money out of her purse. "Make sure you buy her a new dress," she told Rudy.

He had nodded and led Non away.

Throughout the years that had passed since, M'greet had often become melancholy when she thought of Non. How could she grow up a proper lady without a mother? But Rudy had always refused her visitation, though he never returned any of the money M'greet sent.

Now M'greet agreed enthusiastically to a visit, writing to Rudy, this time in Dutch, that she'd like to discuss the possibility of contributing to Non's secondary education. She wondered what her daughter looked like, if what Anna had said was true and her hair had darkened since she saw her last.

Rudy answered that if M'greet wanted to help with money, she should send five thousand florins for Non to take voice and piano lessons. He ended the letter stating that he had not received his pension that month and would not be able to meet in Rotterdam after all.

"Is something wrong, madame?" Anna asked, entering the room with a basket full of M'greet's stockings.

"It's Rudy." She wiped at a tear that was threatening to fall. "It's always the same with him. He tells people that he doesn't want any of my 'dirty cash' but at the same time insists I contribute something to Non." She clenched her fists. "But he won't let me see her. How can he deny me that, me, her loving mother?" M'greet finally broke down and wept openly.

Anna, unaccustomed to such a display of weakness from her mistress, seemed unsure what to do. She set down the basket and sat beside M'greet. "Madame, how is it that he can make such demands of you?"

M'greet focused her red eyes at a spot on the wall and shook her head. She'd spent most of her adult life spinning fantasies—it helped her escape from the fact that she was a penniless divorcé forbidden to see her daughter. Now she cried for the reality that was her existence, soaking her servant's blouse with makeup stained tears.

M'greet cleaned up in time to accompany van der Schalk to a dinner party hosted by Lady Hendriks, one of Amsterdam's most distinguished women. The guest of honor that night was the Baron Willem van der Capellen.

"Ah, the beautiful Margaretha MacLeod," the Baron said, kissing her ring. His lips lingered a bit too long on M'greet's hand as evidenced by the tsk-tsking emulating from his wife, a stick-figured woman with a pinched face and graying hair. The Baron himself was about fifteen years older than M'greet, and for a moment she was drawn back to those horrifying days after she'd returned on an errand to find that Rudy had left, absconding with everything in their little apartment, including Non.

She had met the Baron on the street one day soon after that. He approached her at a flower stall, and she asked him back to the small apartment she'd rented. She'd slept with him that first afternoon, and many afternoons after that. In return, the Baron paid her rent and bought her some clothes to replace the ones that Rudy had stolen.

Over dinner that night at Lady Hendrik's, the Baron mentioned he'd seen M'greet dance once. "I couldn't believe the little Margaretha MacLeod that I knew had become the famous Mata Hari." His wife's face seemed to become even tighter, her lips forming a hard line.

"Mata Hari?" van der Schalk coughed down the food he'd been chewing before turning to M'greet. "I thought you were Russian."

The Baron laughed heartily before hitting his heavy fist on the tablecloth. "Russian. That's rich. That's really rich." He gave M'greet a glance of appreciation before wiping his eyes with his napkin. "Russian," he repeated.

Lady Hendriks, evidently believing such conversation was not to be had at the dinner table, changed the subject to talk of the front. M'greet tuned out as she always did when the war was brought up.

After the second course, M'greet excused herself to go to the balcony for a smoke. She'd just lit her cigarette when she heard the door slide open.

"Mind if I join you?" the Baron asked.

"Are you not still married?"

He threw his head back and let out that same belly laugh from before. "Are you not still a courtesan?"

"Hush," M'greet said, looking around the empty balcony. While paid women were perfectly acceptable in Paris, it was still looked down upon in sanctimonious Holland. "I don't need to do that anymore. As you said, I am the famous Mata Hari."

"Then what are you doing with van der Schalk? And why did you tell him you were Russian?"

M'greet tipped ash from her cigarette onto the lawn before glancing inside at her latest lover, who was still seated at the table. He met her eyes, and she could tell by the barely concealed hatred on his face that their tryst was over.

It was no matter, M'greet decided. The Baron would keep her just as well. She took a step closer to him. "Are you staying in Amsterdam for long?"

"No. Holland has mobilized her forces against the possibility of a German attack. I must report to the border."

She angled herself so that no one inside could see her put her hand over his. "How will I see you?"

The Baron, pleased as pie to have her attention again, beamed. "I'll think of something."

The Baron's solution was to buy her a house in The Hague, at 16 Nieuwe Uitleg, facing a canal. The house was a charming three-story brick building, decorated with a quaint, old-fashioned air, which M'greet immediately decided would never do. She was able to find a Dutch contractor with Parisian taste, and, using the Baron's money, commissioned an entire redo of the house's décor, including putting in a bathroom with running water.

In the meantime, M'greet took a room at the Paulez Hotel. At the Baron's urging, she called Paris and requested to speak to her lawyer, Edouard Clunet.

"Margaretha?" Clunet asked when he got on the line. "What's your ex-husband done now?"

She filled him in on Rudy's latest antics. When she'd finished, he told her, "We've been through this before."

"I want to see her."

"Monsieur MacLeod has maintained—"

"Lies. They are nothing but lies."

Clunet knew they weren't. "I'm sorry, Margaretha."

Her voice rose as tears threatened to fall again. "Are you saying I have no recourse? That I can't see my daughter because he says so?"

Clunet was silent for a moment and M'greet imagined him biting his fingernails the way he always did when he was thinking. "I didn't want to tell you this, but..." she heard a drawer open, "she's in The Hague."

M'greet grabbed a piece of paper and wrote down the address he dictated. "She's attending school to become a teacher."

She set the pen down with shaking hands. "I went to school to become a teacher once."

Clunet's voice softened. "I didn't know that."

"I got kicked out for attempting to seduce the headmaster."

He cleared his throat.

She supposed he wasn't used to hearing women talk of such things, even after all those months they'd spent time together when Rudy had filed for divorce, claiming—falsely—that M'greet had committed adultery. Back then she'd been on her best behavior, trying to pretend she was more than the nearly naked woman in the picture Rudy had sent to Clunet. The lawyer had told her that any Dutch judge would have agreed with Rudy that his ex-wife was a depraved woman.

"Anyway, thank you for telling me." She pressed the address to her heart.

"You're welcome."

Without thinking, M'greet stepped outside to hail a cab, giving the driver the address on the paper. She had no idea what she would do when she got to the school. She feared that her daughter, who'd been forced to grow up without a mother, would be taken advantage of the way M'greet had.

M'greet was just an innocent teenager when Wybrandus Haanstra, the headmaster at her teacher-training school, had asked her to stay after class one day. He'd forced himself upon her, his bristly mustache chafing her face, his drool running down her school uniform. M'greet had tried to push him off, but he was far too heavy. He'd forced her to touch him and kiss him *down there*. Although he never entered her—even Rudy, who had invented many falsehoods against her, had never accused her of not being a virgin when they married—it was enough to get her expelled.

She'd seen Headmaster Haanstra as a sort of substitute father figure, and, like her real father, he had betrayed her. No one ever accused Haanstra of having corrupt morals: he kept his job at the school and was probably doing the same thing to some other girl. M'greet never wanted Non to experience such heartbreak. It was enough that she'd barely survived the mysterious illness that killed her brother.

"Slow down," she commanded the driver as they approached the school. Classes must have just let out as there were dozens of girls in maroon uniforms milling about the grounds. "That's her," M'greet said aloud as she spied a tall girl with long black hair. "That's my daughter."

M'greet pulled down the brim of her hat when Non laughed at something her companion said. She did resemble her mother, more so than even M'greet would have predicted, but there was a light-heartedness about her spirit. Non had something that she herself had lost a long time ago, or perhaps, with her tumultuous upbringing, she'd never had. *Innocence.* M'greet would never willingly take that away from her, no matter how much she longed to envelop her in a never-ending embrace. And, despite whatever lies Rudy had told her, that innocence would be shattered as soon as Mata Hari stepped out from the car and approached her daughter.

"That's enough," she told the driver. "Let's go."

She had the driver drop her off at the hotel in time to meet with her house decorator, Jan Dekker.

"Ah, madame, you will be so pleased with these newest plans," Dekker stated. He unrolled a long piece of paper that had been colored in with pencil.

"Is that lavender?" M'greet asked, her lip curling upward.

"Yes, as we had discussed, the main room will be a light purple."

M'greet sat back and crossed her arms. "I thought we agreed on pink. I want everything in shades of pink."

"But madame," Dekker had a confused look on his face. "You said…"

"You heard me wrong." M'greet tapped her finger on the plans and repeated very slowly, "Pink. Everything pink."

"Yes, madame," Dekker said, rolling up the plans again.

CHAPTER 8

MARTHE

OCTOBER 1914

*A*fter the meeting with Lucelle, several weeks passed and Marthe nearly forgot about her aunt's promise to make contact. She was just leaving the house on her way to the hospital one morning when she saw Canteen Ma, her wild gray hair dancing in the wind, humming to herself as she pushed her loaded cart up the street. The old lady was a favorite of the German soldiers because she had fresh fruit and vegetables for sale a few days a week.

"Good day, mademoiselle," she called to Marthe in a raspy voice. "What a beautiful morning to be out so early." She approached with a basket. "How about some nice beans, mademoiselle? For you, I give a special price."

She came up onto the porch and was so close that Marthe could see her cheekbones through her translucent skin.

Marthe was about to refuse when Canteen Ma shoved something into her hand. "Only look at that when you are alone," the old lady said in an uncharacteristically lucid tone before she resumed humming. As soon as Canteen Ma moved on to another house, Marthe ran upstairs to her room and unfolded the note.

Come to the second farm on the right-hand side of the road to Zwevezeele at nine tonight. Ask for Marie.

Marthe sat on the bed, her heart sinking. There was no way she'd be able to be on the streets at nine—the Berlin Vampires would be out in force and there would be nothing to explain a woman's presence outside so late at night.

"Marthe, aren't you going to be late for work?" Mother called from downstairs.

With that, Marthe had an idea.

When she got to the hospital, the first thing she did was find the Oberarzt. "Herr Oberarzt, now that I have been working here for some time, do you not think it necessary for me to be available for emergencies?"

The Oberarzt mulled this over. "Yes, I suppose I can write you a pass to come to the hospital if we need you at night."

"Thank you, mein herr."

She headed into the little room to check on Nicholas Hoot, only to find it empty. She ran into the hall and accosted the first orderly she came upon. "What happened to the two men who had been in that room?"

He scratched at his scraggly beard. "Weren't they Allies? They probably got moved to a prison hospital."

"But they were injured. You can't mean they just up and transferred them in the middle of the night."

He shrugged. "Then maybe they were shot."

Marthe frowned but didn't want to make a scene. She was still the lone Belgian woman amongst a sea of German men. She took one last look at Nicholas's empty bed, determined to learn of his fate for Meneer and Mevrouw Hoot's sake.

The day passed slowly, as did most in the hospital. There had not been much fighting nearby in the past week; the patients were therefore really only suffering from minor pains, such as earaches and blisters on their feet.

. . .

Marthe left the house at eight that night, giving her a full hour to get to her destination. She made her way through the same fields Lucelle must have used, the Oberarzt's hastily scrawled pass clutched in her sweaty palm. The ground was hard with early fall frost so her feet thankfully did not sink into the mud. Her heart was in her throat at the thought of the Berlin Vampires coming upon her. She intended to state that she was on her way to visit a sick patient should she encounter the gendarmes.

Marthe found the road and counted the farms with her finger, deciding that the red-roofed home must have been the farm referred to in the note. If it were possible, her heartbeat sped up even more as she knocked on the door. Perhaps it was a trap.

The door creaked and a gruff voice demanded, "What do you want?"

"I have come to see Marie," Marthe replied, wiping her hands on her skirts.

The voice gave a grunt and the door opened wider. She stepped inside to the dark hallway. A cool hand took her hot one and led her up the stairs to the back of the house before pushing her into a room illuminated only by a small fireplace.

"Thank you, Pierre," Marthe heard her aunt say. "Give me a warning if you hear anything suspicious." Lucelle sat in a high-backed chair facing the fire, but turned as Pierre shut the door. "I rejoice to see you, my child." She motioned for Marthe to come closer. "The British Intelligence Service has accepted my proposal. They have given you the code name 'Laura.'"

Marthe's tone was awed. "Thank you, Aunt."

Lucelle shook her head. "I'm not sure you should be grateful to me, but hopefully someday the Allies will feel the same way toward you. Spying is dangerous work and your mission at all times will be to avoid detection. You will therefore send all your messages in code. Your first task will be to memorize the key for this code so thoroughly you will never make a mistake. As soon as you have committed it to memory, you will destroy the formula." She handed Marthe a small piece of paper. "As I'm sure you well know, the sooner you burn this, the better."

Marthe began to stuff the message into the top of her stocking while Lucelle chuckled to herself.

"That is not a very clever place to hide such a damning piece of evidence—it's the first place anyone searching you would look."

Marthe cast a helpless look at her aunt, who tapped her bun. Marthe followed by tucking the paper in her hair under a pin while Lucelle continued. "You will receive your instructions through the old woman known as Canteen Ma. When you have a message to send, you will code it and then go down the Rue de la Place to reach the Grand Place. On the right you will see an alleyway. Stop at the fifth window on the left-hand side and tap three times, pause, and then two more times. Agent 63 will then take your message to be transmitted to the British Intelligence Service."

Marthe's head was spinning and she spoke slowly. "Fifth window, Grand Place, knock three times, pause, then two more. Agent 63."

Lucelle nodded approvingly. "It will be your duty to report any military information you overhear, no matter how insignificant it may seem to you. Whenever you have something to transmit, you must take it to Agent 63 immediately. Do not try to conceal it in the house until a more auspicious time. That puts everyone in danger."

"Yes, Aunt, I understand."

"In a few days' time, a man will call at the house and ask for you. He will show you two safety pins on his lapel. These 'safety-pin men' are an active branch of an anti-German espionage system and you must persuade your hostess to give the man lodging."

"There are German soldiers billeting with us now," Marthe informed her.

"It is no matter. He is on a special mission and will only be in Roulers a short while. During this time, you must code any messages he wishes to transmit and then deliver them to Agent 63."

Marthe nodded.

"And now, my dear child, I must leave as soon as you have gone. I have reason to believe the Vampires know that I am in the district." She rose and looked at Marthe. "A spy needs to keep her wits about her at all times, whether asleep or awake. Intelligence is an important tool of a good spy: if you are caught, in all probability it will be your own fault."

Her words struck a chord in Marthe and she decided to change the subject. "Where will you go?"

She waved her hand. "The less you know of my whereabouts, the better. And that goes for all other people in our network: the less you know about your fellow spies, the less the Vampires are likely to wring it out of you if they catch you."

Marthe shot her aunt a tentative smile, doing her best not to show how nervous she was. "God be with you, Aunt Lucelle."

"You too, my child."

The hallway seemed deserted as Marthe let herself out of the little room, but once again a hand grabbed her wrist, leading her through the dark house and to the same door she had entered.

As she made her way back to the grocer's house, she wondered exactly what her aunt had gotten her into. Marthe had always been an intelligent girl, but would she be able to outsmart the Germans enough to sabotage them… and stay alive?

Her stomach suddenly heaved and she had to pause her rapid pace to bend over and retch. After she was done, she stood up and glanced about the streets, which were mercifully still empty. She wiped her mouth and then started walking again, albeit at a much slower pace.

CHAPTER 9

ALOUETTE

OCTOBER 1914

*A*louette climbed the steps to the Deuxiéme Bureau with a much heavier heart than last time, her movements made difficult by the heavy mourning veil that covered her face.

If Ladoux was surprised to see her dressed all in black, he made no comment.

This time Alouette did not bother sitting. "I accept your offer."

"Your husband—"

"Has been killed." Her voice was devoid of emotion.

Ladoux's hand massaged his beard. "I'm not sure this would be the right time."

"If you please, Captain. As I have stated before, I am willing to do anything to help my country, and the timing is perfect: I need a distraction to keep me from brooding over the loss of my husband. Not to mention I'd like the opportunity to avenge his death."

"Come again to see me in two days. That will give you time to change your mind if need be."

"My mind will not be changed, Captain."

A wan smile appeared before he covered it with his hand. "The Secret War is more ruthless than what goes on at the front, madame."

Alouette, her face steely, did not reply.

"Very well, then. Go to 26 rue Jacob tomorrow. You will ask for Monsieur Delorme."

26 rue Jacob was an apartment on the ground floor of an opulent building with a courtyard in front. When a butler answered the door, Alouette requested Monsieur Delorme. He led her into a spacious but dark room with Persian carpets and brocade wallpaper.

The man sitting on the satin couch was none other than Captain Ladoux himself, dressed in civilian clothes. "I see you did not change your mind, madame."

"No." She looked around the parlor. "Why did you want to meet me here?"

"In case you were followed, it looks less suspicious than if you once again walked into the offices of the Ministry of War." He peered into her veil to catch her expression, but Alouette kept her face neutral. She would not show him that she was intimidated at the thought of being tailed.

"Very well, then," he continued finally. "You will travel to Geneva, Switzerland next Saturday." He seemed disinclined to provide any more details.

The possibility that the Deuxiéme Bureau was setting her up flashed through her mind. She sat in a nearby armchair. "Pardon me, Captain—Monsieur Delorme—" she quickly corrected. "But isn't looking for a German spy quite like searching through a haystack for one needle?"

"Indeed."

Even from across the dark room, Alouette thought she saw his eyes glitter.

"But that needle has a thread through it that extends beyond the haystack and leads to the center of the enemy espionage network. You must find a way to infiltrate the German Intelligence Department."

Alouette thought of exposing this so-called enemy network once and for all, the dream of glory trumping the gloom she'd found herself in since being informed of Henri's death. She forced herself back to reality. "Surely it cannot be that simple to secure employment as a German spy."

"No." He struck a match and the embers of a cigarette began to gleam. "But you have both beauty and brains, two traits that will entice our enemies. You will be engaged in an intelligence conflict, one for which I believe you are well suited. You wanted to play a part in the war so that must mean you do not value your life greatly. I would bet this role is even more dangerous than that which your fellow pilots have undertaken."

Alouette drew in a deep breath, picturing all of the closed doors and rejection letters she had received from the men in charge. This man, this Ladoux, was intimidating—she still got the feeling that he did not trust her—but he was giving her a chance. "Danger and I are familiar comrades, monsieur. I am aware of the perils that lie ahead, but I accept the mission."

He exhaled, the ring of smoke encircling his head. "We are not a wealthy department. Our funds are quite limited."

Alouette was taken aback by this admission, considering his initial hefty offer. She glanced around the room with all of its luxurious décor. "Is that so?"

"Indeed."

The smoke from the cigarette burned her eyes. "I have enough francs to assist me now, and my lawyer will allocate more money once my husband's will is settled."

"Good. However, I encourage you to demand money from the Germans after they employ you, in order to help deplete the enemy's war funds sooner and expedite an Allied victory. Wars are won with weighty pocketbooks and lost by lack thereof."

"Very well, monsieur."

He rose and, as he approached her, Alouette had a vision of a snake slithering toward its prey. He dropped something in her lap. She used the last of the light from the setting sun to see that it was a passport with her maiden name on it. *That was fast.* But then again, she supposed that the Ministry of War had the ability to get passports quickly. Or else Ladoux knew she'd be coming back the first time he met her.

"It is best for you not to travel as a widow or a married woman."

She nodded.

"If you need to contact me, write to Monsieur Delorme at this address." He held out his hand. "And, Alouette, be careful."

Alouette's smooth hand met his rough one. As she shook it, she realized that was the first time he'd called her by her given name.

CHAPTER 10

MARTHE

NOVEMBER 1914

The man Aunt Lucelle had mentioned arrived a few days later. He was dressed in the clothes of a laborer. He must have been at least fifteen years older than Marthe, and was tall, with thick glossy hair and a neat mustache.

"Good day, mademoiselle. is there any chance of finding lodging here? I've lost pretty much everything in the invasion, and I heard they still pay for work in this town." He shot a quick glance around and, after seeing they were alone, lifted his lapel for an instant, showing Marthe the two metal safety-pins underneath.

"Step inside for a moment," Marthe invited. "I will ask the owner of the house what she can do for you."

The grocer's wife had a reluctant look on her face when Marthe brought her to the door, as if she was going to refuse him. Upon catching sight of the handsome, friendly-appearing stranger, she must have changed her mind. "We only have a small attic room available. Is that acceptable?"

He gave her a grateful smile. "Perfectly so. Thank you."

The man carried himself with dignity and spoke fluent French and German and fair Flemish. At dinner that night, he beguiled the entire household, including the two German soldiers, with tales of his travels. He'd traveled to the Argentine as a sailor, and became somewhat of an engineer for a year while he was there.

"Say, Herr..." one of the Germans said through a bite of dinner. He swallowed before continuing. "I realize I don't know your last name."

"Jacobs," the man supplied.

"Herr Jacobs, I don't suppose you would want to join us for an after-dinner cigar?" the soldier inquired.

"I wouldn't mind it at all." Marthe couldn't be sure, but it looked as though Herr Jacobs winked at her.

A week passed and Herr Jacobs said nothing more to Marthe than good day and good night. She was beginning to wonder if he was indeed the man Lucelle had predicted would come until she returned home from the hospital one evening to find him standing alone in the kitchen.

"Good evening, mademoiselle," he said, taking a cigar out of his mouth. "It's a cold night outside, no?" He had the same furtive look on his face that Marthe saw the first day. He gave a searching glance about the kitchen before opening his cigar case and withdrawing a small cylinder. "I think, perhaps, you will know what to do with this," he murmured, placing it squarely in Marthe's palm.

She wrapped her hand around it. "It will go tonight." She tried to meet his eyes, but Herr Jacobs was staring into the fire. "What are you doing here?" she ventured.

"Secret service." He spoke so quietly it almost sounded like a sigh.

"Are there others like you?" She gestured toward his lapel.

"Yes, though as a rule, we safety-pin men prefer to work alone." He glanced at her sharply. "If you are approached by one of those others, make sure you note how the pins are placed. If they run straight, not diagonal, pretend to be puzzled... that means he is a Vampire masquerading as anti-German." He grimaced. "These so-called 'false safety pin men' are one of the reasons I am here." His voice had become a growl. "When I find one of these imposters, trust me when I say he will not get off lightly." His frown faded as quickly as it appeared as the German officers' voices could be heard in the hall.

Marthe loosened the fingers clutching the cylinder as best as she could as she passed by them on her way to her room. Inside the cylinder was a small piece of paper written in an unfamiliar code. She tucked the paper under a hairpin the way Aunt Lucelle had taught her before donning her nurse's cap.

No one was awake when Marthe left the house that night. The church bells rang the ten o'clock hour as she set out on her first mission. She was curious to find out whether Agent 63 was male or female, old or young like herself.

She carried the Oberarzt's pass, but knew that it would offer no protection should a Vampire wish to search her and find the paper in her hair. The streets were dark and she passed a few soldiers returning to their billets. Thankfully they mostly ignored her. Near the corner of the alleyway on Grand Place, a German gefreiter was speaking to a Vampire. Marthe felt a bead of sweat trickle down her face and she pulled her nurse's cap down further. Her heart thudded as she caught movement from the men, but when she glanced up again, they had moved on, revealing the black mouth of the alley. She walked quickly through it, counting to herself.

At the fifth window, she knocked in the way she'd been instructed. The window, like the others in the alleyway, was covered with brown paper. She startled when she saw it begin to rise. A white hand came out. After a quick glance up and down the alleyway, Marthe tore the paper from her hair and placed it in the extended palm. The hand retreated, the window closed, and she found herself staring once again at the opaque paper, wondering if she'd just dreamt what had happened. A stray tendril of loosened hair grazed her face, proving that she had indeed extracted the message.

She straightened her nurse's cap and started back up the alleyway, pausing as she saw a soldier approaching. She threw herself against a house until he passed and then hurried into the wide street off the

Grand Place, breathing a sigh of relief. Now if she was stopped, she could say she was returning from the hospital. Still she kept to the shadows as much as possible. When she finally reached the grocer's house, she congratulated herself. She'd successfully delivered Herr Jacobs' message. She hoped that whatever it was would soon bring an end to the German occupation of Belgium… and the war.

CHAPTER 11

M'GREET

NOVEMBER 1914

Van der Capellen was called away for a few weeks in the beginning of November, but he left M'greet several hundred dollars, "in case of emergency." She decided to use the money to travel back to Paris.

She was unable to go through Belgium due to the German occupation, so she set off by ship for the British port of Folkstone.

When the ship arrived, she was sent to a small room without any of her things. "Where is my luggage?" she demanded as soon as someone entered.

The man, of slight height with a clean-shaven face, looked taken aback. "Your luggage?" he repeated.

"Yes. You better not take it away from me. I have very expensive items in there."

His eyes narrowed. "What's in your suitcase that you are so concerned about?"

"My furs." He didn't seem impressed, so she continued, "The Germans confiscated my beautiful muskrat shawl at the beginning of the war."

"The Germans? What were you doing in Germany?"

"I was dancing. Don't you recognize me?"

"Should I?"

"I'm Mata Hari."

Again, the officer seemed nonplussed. He opened a notebook and flipped to a clean page before sitting across from her. "Okay, Miss Hari... is Mata your first name?"

She heaved a sigh as she sat down. "My name, my proper name, is Margaretha Zelle-MacLeod."

"Ah." He glanced at her ring finger. "Are you married, then?"

"Wid—divorced," she corrected herself.

"I see." He scribbled something in the notebook. M'greet tried to see what, but his hand blocked it. "You are obviously well-traveled. What languages do you speak?"

"All of them."

He looked up, his hand still covering his notes. "All?"

"Obviously English and Dutch, but also French and German."

He noted this new information before asking, "What is your intention in Paris?"

M'greet bristled at his tone. "If you must know, I am traveling there to collect some items from my house in Neuilly, as well as sign some contracts for my dancing performances."

"Your house in Neuilly... how long have you had it?"

M'greet was growing bored and no longer felt it necessary to explain to this low-class police officer the intimate details of her life. "Are we quite through now?"

"Mrs.—" he glanced down at his paper. "MacLeod. This interrogation is well within the provisions of the Aliens Act of 1914. Now if you would just tell me about the house in Neuilly."

M'greet answered with her usual blend of half-truths, half-inventions until at last the man got up to leave.

"What about me?" M'greet demanded.

"Mrs. MacLeod, I'm going to need you to stay here."

"What?" She rose out of her chair, but he had already walked out the door. She tried the handle to no avail. He had locked it.

. . .

They kept M'greet waiting for almost two hours. Her stomach was rumbling and she grew warm in her racoon-trimmed traveling clothes. Finally another man in uniform entered the room.

"Mrs. Zelle-Macleod, I am Captain Dillon of MI5."

"The what?"

"Military Intelligence, Section 5."

"My goodness, what do you want with me?" She pulled an old brochure out of her purse and began fanning herself with it. "It's mighty hot in here, don't you think?"

"Not overly." He sat in the chair across from her. "This house in Neuilly..."

"Oh, for heaven's sake, that again. I am planning on selling that house. I'm moving in with my lover, Baron van der Capellen."

Dillon paused, his pen in mid-air. "Your lover, you say?"

"Yes. He is a colonel in the Dutch army. I am relocating to The Hague to make it more convenient for his visits."

The captain rubbed at his chin. "We've searched through your baggage—"

"Did you take anything?"

He dropped his hand. "Of course not. We've found nothing incriminating thus far."

"And you won't." She rose. "Am I free to go?"

"Just one minute." Now he scratched at his hair. "Why didn't you tell Constable Bickers that you were selling the house in Neuilly?"

"I didn't think he needed to know everything."

"You are an educated woman traveling alone, not to mention this talk of..." he coughed, "an affair with a Dutch baron. Can't you see how this looks suspicious?"

"No, I can't. Women should be able to come and go as they please, educated or not." She hoisted her purse onto her shoulder. "May I go now?"

He gave his chin a final rub before raising a hand, as if in defeat. "Yes, you may."

After the unpleasantness in Folkstone, M'greet managed to make it to

Paris without any further delays. Once there, she installed herself in Le Grand Hôtel Francais on the Boulevard Voltaire. She spent her days sauntering around the city, recalling when she was one of the most sought-after women in France.

The Paris of war-time was remarkably different from when she had been there last: darker, more depressing. The once-familiar monuments had been hidden by sandbags and the churches' beautiful stained-glass windows had been bisected by wooden beams to protect them in the case of a German attack. But it was still a world away from her monotonous life in The Hague.

One morning she took a carriage to the *Musée national des arts asiatiques*, where she had made her debut as Mata Hari. After perusing the large collection of Asian art, she inquired after the museum owner, Émile Guimet, but was told he was away.

She decided she could use some air and sat on a bench outside. The November day was cool but sunny and there were a few people who had emerged from their cocoons to enjoy the weather. Across the Rue Boissière, two men in business suits stood talking. One of them looked familiar and M'greet squinted her eyes against the sun. She could have sworn that the taller man was Harry de Marguérie, an old lover of hers.

M'greet had known Harry since those early days in Paris, right after Rudy had left with Non, when she was dirt poor. A perpetual bachelor, he had been a rising diplomat. He called her Marguérite, a combination of his last name and her own given name, and paid for anything she needed.

Back then she'd been working as a riding instructor and barely paying off her enormous bills when her boss, Ernest Molier, had suggested she take up performing the can-can. M'greet knew that some of Paris's dancing girls had been able to land rich men as either lovers or husbands. But she was too tall and thick, not to mention untrained, to perform at the ballet or even at the Folies Bergére.

If that were indeed Harry, the years had been kind to him. Even from across the street, M'greet could see traces of the man he'd been ten years ago, when he'd taken her out to dinner and introduced her to the retired singer, Madame Kireyevsky. M'greet had told the Parisian socialite that she'd been born in the Orient, the daughter of a Buddhist priest, skilled in the art of holy worship in the form of dance. Kireyevsky styled herself as a patron of the arts and invited M'greet to show off these sacred dances at her next party.

"Why did you concoct that crazy story about being Buddhist?" Harry had asked in the carriage back to his apartment.

M'greet shrugged. "Why not? Didn't you see that she fell for it?" She giggled. The wine she had drunk at dinner had obviously hit her hard.

"But you know nothing of these so-called sacred dances."

"I know enough." She'd seen many performances when she'd been a bored housewife in Java. "And what I don't know, I'll improvise. You mustn't forget all I have experienced, which is worlds more than you have."

He touched the feather on her hat. "I am older than you."

"Yes, but it has not been so hard for you. You have yet to realize that life is an illusion."

"What do you mean?"

"I mean that what you believe is true one minute becomes a false-hood the next. Loving fathers desert you when times get tough, hand-some young officers become heartless brutes the minute you marry them, and," she forced the sob out of her voice, "perfectly healthy, wonderful sons die without any warning. Then..." she took a deep breath, "said brutes could steal your last living child away from you."

They arrived at his building in silence. M'greet knew she had broken the cardinal rule for being a Parisian courtesan: remain flirta-tious at all times. Although Harry was, as yet, unmarried, he still expected her to act a certain way. Mistresses were supposed to be enter-taining, mysterious, and—unlike society wives—remain unburdened by tasks like raising children or running a household.

"So you see..." M'greet faked a light-hearted tone as she exited the carriage, her gloved hand in Harry's, "life is but an illusion. Why shouldn't I be?"

"Very good point." He kept her hand as they walked up the steps. "But next time try this one: your father, now deceased, was a British lord, your mother Indian—"

"Why Indian?" she asked as he opened the door to his apartment.

"Because of your dark coloring. Your seductive coloring," he added, his eyes traveling up her body. "Anyway, you were raised to be a sacred Hindu dancer in a temple on the Ganges."

M'greet nodded thoughtfully as she sat on his couch. "That's good. That's really good."

They'd consummated their relationship that night. Harry had been a gentle, thoughtful lover. When they had finished, he sat up and reached for a cigarette. "You enjoyed that, didn't you?"

M'greet took the cigarette from him and drew in a breath of smoke. "Don't get such a big head—it was no more spectacular than any of the other men I've been with."

"That's not what I mean."

He bent his head toward her and M'greet held the cigarette to his lips before taking another puff of her own. "Respectable women are not supposed to enjoy sex. Wives use it to make babies, and mistresses use it to hold power over their men."

He blew smoke out in a perfect ring. "But you do find the act itself pleasing, don't you?"

"Perhaps." She put the cigarette out. Her role as a courtesan should have been passive: she was supposed to wait for men to make overtures to her, and never have more than one lover at a time. But, save for those long years when she'd been married, M'greet was never a patient person, and she definitely did not abide by society's rules. She chose which men to invite to her bed. And while she did enjoy sex to a certain extent, she found the most pleasure in the material things these chosen men provided her after the act was over and in promise of more to come.

Harry and M'greet managed to see a great deal of each other before he left for some appointment in St. Petersburg the day before her big break at Madame Kireyevsky's. One of the guests that night had been Émile Guimet, who invited the then-styled Lady MacLeod to dance at his museum for an audience of a few hundred people, including the German ambassador. Guimet had also encouraged her to take on a more exotic stage name; hence 'Mata Hari' was born. After the performance at the *Musée national des arts asiatiques*, her star had risen quickly and Harry was soon forgotten.

But there he was now, standing on a street corner outside that same museum. He must have sensed M'greet's staring because he suddenly looked up.

CHAPTER 12

ALOUETTE

DECEMBER 1914

*A*louette did not necessarily make any mental preparations before she embarked on the journey toward her new career; instead, she decided to rely on her instincts as an aviatrix to keep her out of trouble. Although Switzerland had declared neutrality at the onset of the war, Ladoux seemed to think the German espionage system was active in Geneva. Hence, Alouette's destination was the country placed both geographically and politically between Germany and France.

Her heart raced uncontrollably on the train ride to Geneva. She tried to calm it by sitting back in her seat and focusing on the tranquil, snowy landscape passing beyond the windows.

She caught the eyes of the man across from her. Knowing Ladoux would want her to use her youth and beauty to its full advantage, she shot the man a sweet smile. He nodded and then returned his gaze to the newspaper in front of him.

In the early evening, there was a commotion at the front of the cabin. A shiver traveled down Alouette's spine as she saw that the men boarding the train wore the uniform of the Swiss Army.

"What is happening?" she asked.

"We are about to cross the border," the man with the newspaper replied.

"May I see your ticket?" an austere officer asked in French as he approached her.

Alouette handed hers over, a coldness spreading through her entire body. It felt as though it took months instead of mere seconds for the Swiss officer to examine her ticket, but to Alouette's relief, he appeared satisfied when he returned it.

The Swiss officers did much the same to the rest of the passengers, going about their work methodically, with no undue sense of urgency yet they wasted no time. When the train stopped at Bern, the man across from her folded his newspaper and stood. As he passed Alouette's seat, he bowed toward her. "I wish you a pleasant journey, Madame Richer."

Alouette watched him disembark, her mouth open. She had not told him her name, and even if she had, she would have used her maiden name, the one she was traveling under—Betenfeld. Her only conclusion was that the man must be employed by the Deuxiéme Bureau. Ladoux must still suspect her motives and intended for her to know that she would always be under his surveillance. *Trust no one*, she reminded herself.

As the train continued on to Switzerland, a handsome dark-haired man sat next to Alouette. "You are French, no?" He spoke with a Spanish accent.

"*Oui*," she replied.

"I am so very fond of the French," the man replied. "Are you traveling alone?"

She thought fast for an excuse that would double as a reason for being unattended as well as to keep her distance from the man. "I am meeting my fiancé in Geneva."

"Oh?" His voice contained a note of disappointment. "I pride myself in knowing quite a few members of Genevan society. What is the name of your intended?"

Alouette narrowed her eyes. She wanted to retort that it was none of his business, but making enemies of fellow passengers would not heed her mission. "Karl Mather," she replied finally. Karl was the boy that she had traveled to Paris for in her youth, before she'd met Henri. Last she'd heard, he had left for medical school in Switzerland.

"I am not familiar with the man," the Spaniard replied and Alouette gave an inward sigh of relief.

The train arrived in Geneva a few hours later. To Alouette's delight, the city contrasted greatly with gloomy, dark Paris. Christmas wreaths and bright paper angels decorated the chalet windows and red ribbons were tied around the street lanterns. The cheery city seemed to be unaware that the rest of Europe was engaged in war.

As Alouette left the train, she asked a passerby to recommend a hotel. Since Switzerland had no official language of its own, Alouette used German, which resulted in him directing her to the Hotel Blumenhaus, which he said was run by a German man.

Alouette had only been in Geneva for a few days when she was awakened by a loud pounding. Her heart raced as she threw on a robe and opened the door.

"*Polizei!*" a man shouted with a Swiss accent as he and another officer charged into Alouette's room.

"What is this about?" Alouette asked in German.

"Hand over your papers," he repeated, louder this time.

Alouette went to her suitcase and fetched her passport. The man scrutinized it and then turned to his companion, a stocky man whose uniform buttons were threatening to burst, and shrugged. The first man turned to Alouette's suitcase and began tossing its contents onto the floor. Alouette sank down on the bed, wondering what she had done as the stocky man fingered her fine linens and underwear and the other officer searched every square inch of her hotel room.

"What are you looking for?" Alouette asked when she finally found her voice.

Neither man replied but the stocky man picked up Alouette's passport from the dresser and headed toward the door. The other man commanded her to get dressed.

They were both waiting in the hall when she emerged a few minutes later.

They took her to the police headquarters. An elderly man in the same uniform as her inquisitors demanded to know what she was doing in Switzerland.

She told them how she had come to see her fiancé, Karl Mather, but had discovered on arrival that she could not find his address.

"Why did you leave France?" the elderly man demanded in German.

"The atmosphere there was affecting my health." She coughed delicately. "I have come here to rest."

The two officers stood on either side of Alouette. The elderly man asked the stocky man something that Alouette couldn't discern.

"*Nein,*" he replied, holding out his hands.

The elderly man handed Alouette her passport back. "Geneva is not a place for the French at present. We've caught several belligerents recently crossing the border. Although we've found nothing to compromise you thus far, I'm going to give you some advice: go back to your own country."

Unsettled, Alouette returned to the hotel. Clearly she had made a bad start.

After her close call, Alouette made up her mind to leave Switzerland. Ladoux had been wrong: this was not the country to gain an introduction into the world of espionage.

At dinner the night before she planned to embark, a woman in a well-cut suit sat beside her. "Gerda Nerbutt." She held out a manicured hand covered with rings, their jewels flashing brightly.

"Alouette Richer." As soon as the words were out of her mouth, she realized she should have used her maiden name.

"You're French," Gerda replied in a surprised tone. "What brings you to Switzerland?"

Alouette told her the Karl Mather story in her best woebegone voice. "But as I cannot locate him, I've decided it best to return to France."

"Oh no," Gerda replied. "You cannot give up so easily!" She broke open a roll and buttered it. "You know what you need?"

Alouette shook her head.

"A holiday! You must be so lonely here in Geneva, wandering about an unfamiliar city, searching in vain for your lover. Why don't you come on a trip with me? Some friends have invited me to Zurich for the New Year." She set the butter knife down and gave Alouette a searching look. "That is, if my company isn't boring you."

"Oh no," Alouette dutifully replied. She watched as the older woman took a bite of bread. Gerda was obviously intelligent, and German. Perhaps these friends of hers would have some information that would be useful to Ladoux. At the very least, an impromptu holiday sounded better than returning to France a failure.

Alouette smiled. "That sounds lovely. When do we leave?"

CHAPTER 13

MARTHE

DECEMBER 1914

*C*hristmas Day 1914 was bright but very cold. With the Oberarzt's permission, Marthe decorated the bare hospital walls with green paper trees and gold crosses. Mass was offered in the largest ward, and voices from a boys' choir echoed through the rooms filled with wounded men. The pleasantries of the carol singing were enhanced by the absence of cannon fire—Marthe overheard an orderly say that the soldiers in the trenches must have declared a temporary cease-fire.

The sound of artillery fire could be heard once again the morning after, however, dulled only by the whistle of a train as Marthe passed the station. She always took the same route to work, and, as her daily hours varied little, she noticed the same couldn't be said about the trains, which arrived and departed at very irregular intervals. One was arriving now, puffing large clouds of black smoke as it pulled in carrying weary soldiers in rumpled uniforms and carts of ammunition from the German line.

Marthe watched the men hustle to unload an enormous gun. The thought occurred to her that an ordnance train such as this one would make a great target for the Allies. One of the soldiers gave her a strange look and she realized she had been caught staring. She hurried along, daring herself to not think such thoughts.

But what if? Marthe thought as she sat down to lunch. What if she could pass on the schedule of an ordnance train to Agent 63? *Nonsense,* she replied to herself as she chewed on a piece of stale bread. The ordnance train always came at random days and times and she had no way of predicting the arrival of one.

"Fräulein Cnockaert?" the Oberarzt approached her. "Will you be done with lunch soon? We need to send some of our men to another hospital, and I was hoping you would escort them to the train station."

She couldn't help her mouth from falling open. It was as if he'd just read her mind. The Oberarzt averted his eyes and she realized she'd just displayed the half-chewed contents of her lunch. She coughed. "Of course, Herr Oberarzt. I was just finishing."

"Very well then," he replied with his usual impersonal politeness. "We are not too busy today, so take your time."

The day was sunny and unusually warm for December, and, after loading the men on the train, Marthe told the ambulance driver she'd prefer to walk back to the hospital. She thought perhaps she'd be able to pick up some information on the arrival of the next ordnance train.

He replied that he was going to the pub for a quick lunch. "Would you care to join me, fräulein?"

She shook her head, hoping he would blame her denial on her shyness.

He shrugged and headed off as Marthe turned back to the platform. There were no posted time tables anywhere at the depot, no signs, no coded numbers, nothing.

A short man came out of the small train station. From the way he paused to admire the shine of his new field boots in the sunlight, Marthe could only guess he hadn't held his post for long.

"Ah, fräulein," he said upon catching sight of her. "You are on nurse duty today?"

"Yes, mein herr." She had never noticed the little man before and was surprised he recognized her. "I was just enjoying the beautiful weather today."

"Me too," he replied. "I am usually very busy, but thought I could spare a few minutes to speak with a lovely lady." He peered up at her before digging a cigarette case out of his pocket. "Do you smoke?"

Marthe usually didn't, but she suddenly had an idea. Perhaps, if she could maneuver her way into the inner station offices, she could get a hold of a schedule. "Not in the open, mein herr."

"My name is Alfred Fischer." He paused in fiddling with the case. "You will come back to my office for tea and a smoke?"

Marthe nodded her consent.

"This way, this way," Fischer waved her on.

Marthe followed, determination outweighing any nervousness she might have about going to a strange man's office. There was something endearing about the little man, however resolved she was in using him for information to supply to his enemy.

He escorted her through a large front room filled with close-shaven men answering phones and banging away on typewriters before ushering her into the inner office. The clamor from outside ceased mercifully when he shut the door.

"I am happy to finally have company," he told her as he sat in his desk chair. "I've just recently lost my wife, and I'm lonely in Belgium."

"I'm sorry," Marthe told him, accepting the proffered cigarette.

"And you? I do not see a wedding ring."

"I am not married."

"Do you have a boyfriend? A soldier serving in the war?"

She shook her head. "No boyfriend. But my brother is a soldier. He was somewhere in Liege last I knew, but I have heard no more of him."

The man's pudgy hand closed around hers. "I am sorry. War is a terrible thing, but sometimes it is necessary."

She agreed with him on only one of those assertions, but smiled at him anyway.

Just then the door opened, bringing in a gust of air and the commotion from the outer office. A soldier stuck his head in. "You are wanted on the telephone, Herr Fischer. Headquarters."

"Will you wait here, fräulein?" Fischer's pleading eyes appeared ready to pop out of his head. Marthe nodded demurely as he rose.

As soon as the door closed behind him, she leaned forward and gazed about his desk. There were papers everywhere, and a few that resembled a train log, but Marthe did not want to be caught reading them and kept her hands tightly clasped, her cigarette still burning in the ashtray.

Fischer returned a few minutes later, and Marthe stabbed her cigarette out. "I must be getting back to the hospital." She stood up.

"I'd like to see you again. Would you mind?"

Marthe hesitated, thinking about how to once again demur, but then an idea popped into her head. "My job keeps me quite busy, as I'm sure yours does as well. It would be hard for us to find a time to get together."

"Oh," he said, reaching under a pile of papers to pull out a leather-bound book. "I'm sure we could find a day that could work for us both." He flipped through the book. "Today is Monday…hmmm." As he ran his pudgy finger down his datebook, Marthe had no trouble reading it upside down. An ordnance train was scheduled to arrive at 3 am this Wednesday.

Marthe looked away as the little man glanced up. "Would Friday afternoon work for you? I could get us a special pass to go to Ghent." His eagerness reminded Marthe of a puppy.

"Friday will work just fine," she assured him. "Goodbye, Herr Fischer, and thank you…" Her mind raced. She couldn't thank him for revealing the schedule. "For the cigarette," she quickly filled in.

"Any time, fräulein."

Marthe felt not a little sad as she made her way back to the hospital. If her plan actually worked, there would be no more Fridays, or any days past Wednesday, for the little man.

She paused her steps as a ghastly terror overtook her. Could she really go through with it? She thought back to her childhood: she'd always been quiet little Marthe Cnockaert, going out of her way to please everyone. Max was the one who did what he desired without worrying how it would affect others. Her brother was so personable that people barely noticed how he manipulated them into doing exactly what he wanted. And, on the rare occasions when his victim figured out they'd been duped, he would bestow his customary grin on them, and they had no choice but to forgive him.

If those Germans so much as dare lay a hand on Max. She had a vision of many short men in shiny boots rushing forward with guns to harm her brother and his fellow soldiers. A grey tidal wave of destruction, like what she had witnessed from the window of her family's home in Westrozebeke. At that, Marthe took a deep breath, knowing what she had to do.

Upon returning to the hospital, Marthe found a scrap of paper at the nurses' station. She took a pencil and then went into the bathroom and wrote out what she had seen in Fischer's diary before rolling up the paper and sliding it into her bun.

When she returned, the Oberarzt was rushing by. "Ah, Marthe, I'm glad you are finally back. We have an emergency surgery I will need you to assist with. An amputation."

Marthe patted her head to make sure the message was secure in its hiding place. "Trench foot?"

The Oberarzt nodded. "Turned gangrenous. Are you ready?"

She followed him into the operating room. He threw back the sheet of the patient, revealing the man's legs. The skin that was not red, raw, and covered with blisters had turned an unearthly black color. The Oberarzt began washing his hands as Marthe lined up the surgical instruments on a nearby tray.

She had witnessed several amputations in her short time at the hospital, but there was something about this one that made her sick to her stomach. Perhaps it was how young the soldier was, or the fact that his beardless face was handsome, or—most likely—the realization of what she was about to do regarding the train station was manifesting itself physically. Would she have to stand over surgeries of Fischer or anyone else if she succeeded in her mission to bomb the ordnance train? Would they die horrible, painful deaths because of her? How could she reconcile destroying lives as a spy with her duty to save lives as a nurse?

"Excuse me," she croaked before grabbing a bedpan and retching into it.

The Oberarzt paused and looked up from the leg, scalpel in hand. "Fräulein Cnockaert, are you well?" he asked through his surgeon's mask.

"I'm so sorry, mein herr. I don't know what got into me."

"It's alright," his muffled voice replied. "This is hard to handle even for a man. Can't imagine how a woman could stomach it." He resumed his cutting. "You go home and get some rest and we'll see you tomorrow."

"Thank you, Herr Oberarzt," Marthe said, leaving the room with the bedpan. She rinsed it thoroughly before she left.

It was already dark when Marthe set out for Agent 63's. The veiled streetlamps threw a muddled gray light onto the pavement, only to be disturbed by distant flashes of light in the West. *Véry shells*, she thought before quickening her pace.

Everything was quiet as Marthe entered the alleyway. She passed the windows without counting and then tapped on the fifth. As before, the pane slid open noiselessly. Marthe pulled the paper from her hair and placed it into the white palm. The hand disappeared and the window was dark again.

She headed home, relieved that the responsibility was literally out of her hands and into Agent 63's… and then hopefully the Allies.

As Marthe crept to the back door of the house, she was surprised to see the kitchen light on. Her heart dropped into her raw stomach as she saw a tall man in a German uniform standing under the dim porch light.

"Fräulein Cnockaert?" he asked.

As Marthe's mouth had gone numb, she could only nod.

He opened the porch door. "Please come inside. There are some officers with questions for you."

Two men in the uniforms of the military police were seated at the kitchen table. They rose as she entered.

"Please sit, fräulein," one of them said, extending his hand toward an unoccupied chair.

As if a dream, Marthe sat. It was only her first true coup, and she had already been discovered before she had a chance to be successful.

The other policeman, a red-haired, stocky man, leaned forward. "What can you tell us of Lucelle Deldonck? I hear that she is of relation to you and that she was recently seen in Roulers."

Marthe dug the nails of one hand into the sweaty palm of the other at the mention of her aunt's name. She hadn't seen her since the night at the farmhouse, but hopefully these men hadn't learned anything of Aunt Lucelle's business with the British Intelligence Service.

The red-haired man searched Marthe's face. "Lucelle Deldonck?" he prompted.

She blinked rapidly.

The man from the porch had come in as well, and Marthe could feel three pairs of eyes boring into her. *Speak. Say something!* she urged herself. But still nothing would come from her mouth.

"There is no reason to be afraid, fräulein," the other man said. "Just tell us what you know."

Marthe met his gaze. His eyes were brown and drooped at the corners like a basset hound. *And basset hounds really aren't that scary, after all.* She took a deep breath. "My aunt Lucelle disappeared when your soldiers raided Westrozebeke." She let her voice raise in anguish. "Most of them were drunk that night. I wouldn't be surprised if they shot her accidentally, or on purpose."

The red-haired man took a cigarette out and lit it in the kitchen fire. "We heard she was in Roulers a month ago."

"In fact," the other man laid his forearms on the table, "we've heard she was in this very kitchen."

"No," Marthe replied. "I have not seen her since we left Westrozebeke." She forced herself to look straight into the man's face.

His arms dropped back to his side. "Very well then." He nodded at the red-haired officer, who tossed his cigarette into the fire. "It is Lucelle Deldonck we want, not you. I have good information that places her here, but if you insist you have not seen her, I have no choice but to believe you. I hear you are doing excellent work at the hospital." He nodded at his comrade before starting for the door. "However, if you are lying, I would hate to have to report you to the Town-Kommandant."

"I assure you that I speak the truth, mein herr," Marthe stated as she crossed her arms in front of her.

Each man gave a small bow as they walked out. Marthe stared out the window, making sure they had really left, before she went upstairs to her room. She fervently hoped that her lies would help Aunt Lucelle avoid detection by the suspicious Germans.

The interrogation in the kitchen almost made Marthe forget about her previous mission that night. As she laid in bed, she wondered if the Allies would receive the message in time. If so, and they decided to bomb the ordnance train, the whole town might be destroyed. When she finally fell asleep, she dreamed of explosions and amputees.

CHAPTER 14

ALOUETTE

DECEMBER 1914

Gerda's friends turned out to be two German brothers, Otto and Charles. They were both handsome in the coolly-indifferent way that Alouette recognized as being inherently German. They greeted the women at the railway station, and when Alouette asked them to direct her to the nearest hotel, both men protested loudly.

"Any friend of Gerda's is more than welcome to stay at our house. We have plenty of room," Charles, the elder brother, stated. In contrast to his brother's light hair and blue eyes, Charles had dark hair, with matching, soulful brown eyes.

"Thank you for the lovely offer, but I do not wish to intrude," Alouette replied.

Gerda's slim hand gripped Alouette's. She gave the brothers a flirtatious smile before leading her aside. "Accept their invitation, my friend. They are sincere, and would be terribly hurt if you refused their offer of hospitality." She narrowed her eyes, her tone challenging. "Or are you afraid?"

Alouette gave a nervous laugh. "Why should I be afraid?"

Gerda's half-whispered reply almost sounded like a hiss. "Well, we are all German, and you are French."

Alouette stuck out her chin. "If I were as tainted by narrow-minded nationalism as some of my compatriots, I wouldn't have come here looking for my Swiss fiancé. I just don't want to cause anyone inconvenience."

"Nonsense, Alouette, you are not inconveniencing anyone." Gerda led her back to the gentlemen. "My friend has decided to accept your offer," she told them.

"Wonderful," Otto declared.

They all piled into an enormous motor car. Gerda sat up front with Charles while Alouette got comfortable in the backseat beside Otto.

"What brings you to Switzerland?" he asked.

Once again, Alouette related the lost fiancé fable.

"That is so heroic of you, facing the perils of the mountains and the frontier of a foreign land in the middle of a war to find your lost love."

Alouette realized that the Karl Mather storyline also provided her a convenient way to fend off any advances Otto might make, a likely possibility considering the way he was staring at her. "Yes, indeed." She gave a deep sigh. "This will hopefully be a nice break from worrying about him all the time."

Otto nodded as the car pulled up in front of a large, hammered-iron gate. A guard in uniform nodded at the car as he opened the gate. The long driveway eventually curved past an enormous snow-covered park to reveal a typical Swiss mansion with a grand turret peeking through a maze of tiled roofs and arched windows. The house was painted a friendly yellow, which was like a ray of sunshine over the white landscape and immediately appealed to Alouette.

As soon as she crossed over the threshold, however, the feeling that she had just entered a hot-bed of German spies washed over her. There was nothing tangible to indicate this, just a general notion that stemmed from the trio's watchful eyes. It struck her that Gerda Nerbutt was testing her and Alouette made up her mind right then that she would pass any challenges the brothers and Gerda put forth to convince them to recruit her in whatever game they were playing.

. . .

After a five-course dinner, the foursome sat in the drawing room and chit-chatted. Her companions stuck to banal information: where each of them had grown up, where they had gone to school, their most and least favorite subject matter at said schools. The heavy food had caused Alouette to become sleepy, but she forced herself to remain alert and not give away too much information. However cautious she was, it seemed that whenever she spoke, her hosts would exchange knowing smiles with one another.

"Did you know that Gerda graduated from the University of Freiburg?" Otto asked.

"No," Alouette replied. "I didn't know such a prestigious school allowed women."

"She was one of the few they let in," Charles added. "She earned a doctorate in political science."

"Congratulations," Alouette tried to fake a bright tone. "Your line of study must have been fascinating."

"Yes," Gerda agreed before taking a long drag on a cigarette.

Alouette looked down. In another life, she supposed she and Gerda might indeed have been at least allies, having the ability to prove themselves as women in spheres normally reserved for men—Gerda's at university and Alouette's in aviation. However, the German woman's dismissive tone, combined with their opposing allegiances, made it clear that the two would probably never truly be friends.

Alouette yawned. "I should be getting to bed. I've had a long day of traveling, and that wonderful food at dinner did me in."

At this, Gerda exchanged a furtive glance with Charles. "Do you need me to walk you to your room?" he asked.

"No thank you, I'll be quite all right."

At breakfast a few days later, Charles leaned in toward Alouette. "I have news of your fiancé."

Alouette, feeling both Charles and Gerda's eyes on her, refrained from dropping her fork. "Karl? You have heard of him?" With great effort, she managed not to stumble over her words.

"Yes. Guess where he is."

Her heart pounding, Alouette ventured, "Is he in Zurich?"

"No, he is at a hospital outside of Munich."

She looked down and sniffled, doing her best to conjure up tears.

Gerda shifted in her seat with a derisive sneer on her face, obviously not fooled by Alouette's crocodile tears.

"I must return to France immediately. It is clear that I have no business being here," Alouette added for good measure.

Otto put his hands on her shoulders. "I can help you," he whispered.

Alouette shook her body, giving the effect she was heaving with sobs. "What can you do? I cannot get to Germany to see him. I am French, remember?"

"Don't despair," Gerda's tone was sympathetic, but Alouette detected a sinister note underneath it. "Otto here has a plan."

"That's right," he said. "I'm just off to Munich myself. I will look up Karl and ask him to give me a letter for you."

Alouette glanced at Gerda. She had never noticed how cruel Gerda's eyes were. She had thought they were blue when they first met, but now they had become steely gray. "Why don't you go with Otto, Alouette darling?" Her voice dropped on the word darling. "I'll lend you my passport—Charles can substitute your photograph for mine. He's very clever at that sort of thing, aren't you Charles?"

"Oh yes," he answered, nodding enthusiastically. "It's quite easy."

Alouette felt like a butterfly on whom the net was closing in. "I couldn't possibly manage it—my French accent would surely give me away in Germany."

"Oh bother," Gerda dismissed Alouette's misgivings with a wave of her bejeweled hand. "Otto will do all the talking for you. You won't even have to open your mouth."

"I'm not sure I'm willing to risk paying so dearly to see Karl." Alouette tried to make light of the situation. "Imagine how awkward it would be for Otto if I were arrested and shot before a firing squad!"

Gerda narrowed her eyes as Otto burst into laughter. "Don't worry about me—they would never dream of suspecting me of being a spy."

Although they had not accused her of anything, Alouette was convinced they knew she was a spy for France and were trying to do exactly what she'd joked about—get her shot.

Gerda insisted Alouette was making a great mistake in throwing away the chance of accompanying Otto and seeing her fiancé.

Alouette was so preoccupied in her own thoughts that she only half heard her, but replied anyway. "Please don't insist. I shall not go."

"But why not, Alouette?" Gerda inquired, her eyebrows raised over those gray eyes. "There would be no danger involved whatsoever."

Alouette thought fast, and began, in a halting tone, "If you must know, it's because I do not have enough money for such a journey. I spent all of my savings just coming to Switzerland. If Karl had been in Geneva, he would have replenished my bank account, but as it is, I only have enough to return to France." If they did suspect she was a French spy, she'd just admitted that she was low on money, daring them to recruit her to spy for Germany.

Charles smiled as though he thought Alouette was cracking another joke and then changed the subject, begging his brother to bring back samples of his favorite chocolates from his visit to their home country.

Later that afternoon, Alouette decided to take the house dog, Mina, for a walk in the park. She wanted to be alone with her thoughts and it was the perfect excuse. Although the sun shone brightly, the weather was cool, and she quickened her stroll in an effort to keep warm.

She was still cursing herself for the Karl Mather story, never having figured he would have joined the German Army. What excuse did she have for staying in Switzerland now? And they had definitely not taken the bait she'd laid for them to recruit her as a German spy.

Alouette and Mina walked down through the thick trees at the back of the mansion. As they came to a clearing, she noticed a little wooden hut tucked underneath several pine trees. She started on the path toward it, but then Mina broke free and ran… straight to Charles who was just coming out of the hut.

"Oh, do you sleep here?" Alouette asked, rather stupidly she thought, since she knew perfectly well where Charles' bedroom was.

"No. Our workshops and offices are here."

"Workshops?" Her voice was tentative. She didn't want to let on how curious she was. She realized that the subject of how Charles and

Otto were able to afford such a lavish lifestyle had never come up. *Some spy you are*, Alouette chided herself.

"Come in," Charles said. "I'll show you around." Inside the hut were two large desks upon which sat fat typewriters, with paper strewn all over the desks and floor beneath them. The wall behind the desks was covered with a large map studded with colored flags.

Charles waved at the map. "The green flags represent the German armies. The black show the Belgian positions while the red and blue flags represent the French and English positions, respectively."

"What are these?" She pointed to a conglomeration of differently colored flags to the right side.

"Those are for Russia. Otto's favorite pastime is moving the flags to keep up with the latest news from both fronts."

He led Alouette closer, taking a green flag from the desk drawer and placing it in Germany, just a little east of Switzerland. "That's where your boy is."

Alouette ignored his comment. She started toward an open doorway in the back which led to a smaller room with no windows. "What is this?" she asked.

"Nothing," Charles replied tersely, hurrying ahead of her to shut the door, but not before she spied a bunch of chemicals and large trays.

"Are you a photographer?" she asked, trying to cover up her nervousness at Charles' abrupt change in manner.

"Yes." He glanced down at Mina, who seemed as anxious to leave the little hut as he was. "I think the dog needs to make it."

Alouette wanted to stay and find out what exactly Charles and Otto were up to, but she realized her curiosity had made her wear out her welcome. "C'mon Mina, let's leave Charles to his work."

At dinner that night, which was served earlier than usual, Gerda appeared as distracted as Alouette. Alouette was trying to come up with a plan to investigate what the little room in the hut was for while Charles and Otto were deep in conversation. She half-heartedly tried to follow, especially after she thought she heard the word for "develop," but they were speaking Italian and she was unfamiliar with the language.

"Well," Charles spoke at last in German. "It can only be done during the day. You must telephone the Schwartz Brothers that we expect them this evening. They can find me in the office."

Gerda gave him a strange look before setting her fork down and turning to Alouette. "What will you do when you get back to France?"

"Probably take up nursing." She wanted to add that she'd help the war effort however she could, but didn't think her German dinner companions would appreciate her enthusiasm to aid the French army.

As they left dinner, Gerda said she had some letters to write in her room. Charles and Otto were obviously going to be meeting with the Schwartz Brothers, whoever they were. Alouette declared she was tired and would retire early.

When she got to her room, she chose the darkest dress she had, a dingy shade of gray, and a matching overcoat to protect her from the cold. She walked as quietly as she could through the forest to the hut. Heart pounding, she crouched in the darkness of a large tree. It was only a matter of minutes before she saw Charles and Otto exiting, accompanied by two short, heavy-set men. They paused in front of Alouette's tree and she bent lower, trying to make herself nearly invisible despite the bare branches.

Otto's voice rang out clearly as he spoke in German, "You must hurry up because she is leaving soon."

She was sure they were talking about her.

Alouette had just changed into her nightdress when she heard a knock. With a heavy heart, she put on her dressing gown and then opened the door. She was not exactly surprised to see Otto standing in the hallway, but the look on his face plunged her into terror.

She forced the fear out of her voice. "What do you want with me?

Before he had time to reply, Gerda barged in. Behind her were the two heavy-set men from the hut. Alouette backed into the corner of the room.

"Do not be afraid," Otto stated. "We just want to ask you a few questions."

"Yes?" She sat down in the corner chair, acting as nonchalantly as she could.

Gerda looked at her. If it were possible, her eyes were even colder than they had been at breakfast the other day. "Alouette, you came to Switzerland to spy for France."

"We can prove it," Otto added.

Alouette laughed, a hollow laugh, but she hoped her interrogators wouldn't notice her lack of mirth. "I am very surprised to hear this. I have been living in this house for nearly a week. If I've overstayed my welcome, you could have simply said that. Although I intended on leaving tomorrow, I could go tonight."

"We want to know why you came to Switzerland," one of the unfamiliar men said.

"I'm getting tired of explaining my situation," Alouette replied.

"Your story is a lie," Otto said, his voice filled with an uncharacteristic rage. "Karl Mather is married and has two children. You couldn't possibly have been engaged to him."

Alouette could feel her face blush. "Gerda," she turned to the woman she once thought of as a friend. "Gerda, haven't I always stated that I haven't received news from Karl for years?" She took a breath. "I went looking for him because I was tired of the war and wanted to get away from it. But what I would like to ask you is why you are demanding all of these explanations. Why do you need to know my personal business?" She cursed herself for that last statement: clearly it was because they were suspicious of her.

Otto got into her face. "You are a spy for France and you cannot deny it."

"Fine, then I will leave." All five pairs of eyes fixed themselves on her suitcase in the corner. It was open, and obvious to Alouette that someone had ransacked it earlier.

"You know what your fate will be in a neutral country if you are found guilty of espionage, don't you?" Gerda asked. "You would be endangering Switzerland's declaration of neutrality, and they won't take kindly to that."

"Dear Gerda," She made her tone equally derisive. "If there are spies in Switzerland, you are on the wrong track if you suspect me." Gerda's expression did not change, so Alouette added, "At any rate, I presume they don't condemn people in Switzerland without having proof."

As calmly as possible, Gerda went to the suitcase and pulled out two envelopes that Alouette had never seen before.

"Can you explain these?" Gerda asked.

The two unfamiliar men, whom Alouette now assumed were policemen, followed Gerda's movements with keen interest.

"What a dirty trick!" Alouette shouted. "You must have put those in earlier, when I was…"

"Spying," Otto filled in.

Alouette grabbed the envelopes from Gerda. One had been addressed to the Hotel Blumenhaus in Geneva, postmarked from Germany. The other was purportedly from France and addressed to Alouette care of the mansion. She tore out this letter and gazed over it. The lines between the original words had been painted over with a glaze and showed a lightly stained code. She dropped the letter. "These are forgeries."

Gerda narrowed her eyes, but Otto's glance at the policemen revealed his concern they would believe Alouette. "You must go with these two gentlemen," he stated tersely.

"I presume there is a French consul in this town. I will go to them in the morning. Kindly clear out of my room. Now," Alouette emphasized.

One of the stock officers stepped forward. "Madame, he's right. You must come with us."

Alouette gave a deep sigh. "Do you mind if I change first?"

The man looked uncertainly at his companion, who conceded. The first man bowed, and then left, the other police officer following suit. Gerda planted her feet and crossed her arms, as if to say, you can't make me leave, but Otto told her, "She's in the hands of the police now. She can't do any more harm."

"How do we know she won't escape through that window?" Gerda asked, nodding at it.

"She won't. Come on." He grabbed her by the elbow and practically pulled her out of the room.

Overcome by an inexplicably childish impulse, Alouette stuck out her tongue at the closed door. She dressed slowly, mulling over Gerda's suggestion as she tied a scarf around her neck.

She walked to the window and pulled back the curtain to reveal a peaceful view of the countryside, the light of the moon outlining the roadway beyond the mansion. Her room was on the second floor, and she therefore risked breaking a leg, or both legs, if she jumped to the ground. Not to mention escaping would be a full admission of guilt. But then again, she was accused of spying in a neutral country, and even the flimsiest proof would land her in prison, not to be liberated until the war was over.

She sighed, deciding it would be better to face the charges brought against her rather than run from them. She emerged from her room to find the policemen waiting in the hall.

"Gentleman, I am ready," Alouette told them.

It must have been around 9 pm, Alouette guessed as the police led her to a carriage in the driveway. They rode into town and parked in front of the police station. There was not a gleam of light in any of the shop windows facing the deserted streets. Only the footfalls of the three of them broke the silence of the night. Everything in the town appeared strange to her; if the Swiss police decided to throw her into prison, Alouette knew no one would ask any questions. She was absolutely alone.

One of the men opened the door to the station and gestured for her to enter first. As she stepped into the dimly lit room, another man who had been dozing in a corner woke up with a start. He sleepily led Alouette to yet another badly lit room, this one windowless with only a sorry-looking bed in the corner for furniture. She heaved her bag onto it with a sigh. Swiss jails were apparently no better than French ones.

The new policeman told her that the commissary had gone home for the night and she would need to spend the night in the lock-up.

Somehow Alouette managed to fall into a fitful sleep. She was determined not to despair, no matter how grim the situation seemed from a Swiss jail cell.

Based on the dim light in the hall outside, dawn had broken when the policeman from the previous night reappeared. "The chief wants to see you."

CHAPTER 15

MARTHE

DECEMBER 1914

*M*arthe did not sleep any better in the days leading up to the bombing. She was especially restless Tuesday evening and, around 3 am, when the ordnance train was due to arrive, rose and went to the window.

She gasped as she saw a low light coming into town. The buzzing of an airplane followed, and she was filled with elation when she realized that the Allies were indeed going to bomb the ordnance train. The message had gotten through! A low, thunderous noise started, and her heart sank as she realized it was the sound of a German anti-aircraft gun.

She hurried to her mother's bed and shook her awake. "The cellar, Mother. You must get underground!" Her mother rose sleepily and, without asking questions, allowed Marthe to lead her and the grocer's family to the cellar.

Once she was sure her mother was secure, Marthe ran back upstairs and threw a cloak over her nightdress. Seized with a sudden need to make sure the train station was destroyed, she went outside through the back door and crouched underneath some shrubbery.

She tilted her head upward and, using the German searchlights combing the sky, tried to track the Allied planes. Marthe could only discern one single-engine plane.

One plane? It seemed ill-advised to send a solitary aircraft to face the onslaught of German guns. But the plane was holding its own among the clouds of shrapnel.

Then came a ghastly shriek, growing louder and louder until the earth shook. A yellow light flashed above the rooftops of her neighbors. The airplane was bombing the town. She closed her eyes and pictured the ordnance train—loaded with weapons of destruction meant to destroy the Allies—obliterated.

Thud after thud shook the ground beneath Marthe's feet, but still she could see the long shadow of the train waiting at the station. The bombs missed their mark! Soon the spraying of machine guns started, the projectiles creating red and yellow stars against the gray smoke.

Marthe's legs crumpled and she hit the mud hard as another explosion sounded. Covered in soot and evergreen needles, she rose unsteadily. The shingles from the house next door floated in the air as if they were dust being blown by unseen lips. The view toward the train depot was obscured by smoke, but she knew that last bomb had hit its target and once the smoke cleared, nothing more would be seen of the ordnance train.

Still, the rat-a-tat-tat of German machine guns filled the air, aiming for the Allied plane above. She heard screams and sobs from her neighbors, the sound of broken glass shattering as people ran from burning houses. Was this harrowing situation her fault? Would innocent bystanders, acquaintances or even friends, die because of the intelligence she passed on to the Allies? *But it's war,* she reminded herself, clenching her hands. And the Germans have done far worse to many Belgian villages. That thought didn't stop her from shivering uncontrollably, however.

Marthe considered going to the Grand Place to see if anyone needed help, but her feet seemed cemented to the ground. She raised her head again, only just able to catch a glimpse of the plane as it climbed higher, trying to reach the clouds and the safety they provided from the German guns. But then its tail caught fire, as if it were a dragon breathing from the wrong end.

The terrible burning grew brighter and brighter against the black sky. Marthe barely had time to register that the plane was falling before it crashed into the ground. The roar it made on impact reverberated through her entire body. She pictured the British aviators lying mutilated in a field, their khaki uniforms engulfed in flames, suffering a slow, agonizing death. In the morning, nothing would be left of the heroes but unrecognizable, charred remains. Once again, bile rose in her throat, and she leaned over to vomit in the nearest bush.

As she straightened, she saw that both the station and the ordnance train had indeed been demolished. The mission had succeeded, but at what cost? The machine guns were still rattling and smoke permeated the night air—there was nothing she could do until morning. She wiped off the bile residue with her sleeve and headed back into the house.

After escorting her mother back upstairs, Marthe sat in her bed wide awake, knowing as busy as the hospital would be tomorrow, she'd never be able to sleep. When she closed her eyes, all she could see were houses in flames, crashing airplanes, and mangled bodies. What new horrors would daylight bring? And what had become of poor little Fischer, the train station manager with the shiny boots?

She finally broke down in tears, crying for all that the world had lost since the war began.

CHAPTER 16

ALOUETTE

JANUARY 1915

It took some convincing for the Swiss police to let Alouette go, but eventually she managed to prove the letters were fakes by pointing out that she'd only been at the mansion for a week, not nearly long enough to receive a piece of mail from France. Luckily the police commissary had an affinity for all things French and decided to allow her to return to her native land. Obviously Otto and Gerda had overestimated Swiss sympathy for Germany when they attempted to arrange to have her sentenced without a trial.

The first place Alouette went when she reached Paris was to visit with "Monsieur Delorme."

She barged into the parlor at 26 rue Jacob, intending to tell Ladoux just what she thought of his spying methods when he turned around, the same shrewd look on his face as before. "Madame Richer, I've arranged for you to travel to Spain."

Alouette was too flabbergasted to form a coherent reply. "But Captain—"

"Immediately," he continued.

She finally found her voice. "No. I don't need a repeat of my failed mission in Switzerland. Clearly I'm not cut out for espionage."

Ladoux shrugged his shoulders, as if he'd expected her to say as much.

Alouette's curiosity got the best of her. "What did you have in mind?"

"What you ought to have succeeded in doing in Switzerland." He sat down behind the desk and gestured to the chair in front of him.

Alouette crossed her arms, refusing the seat. "Spy on the Germans? But we both know that neutral Spain is cut off from the arena of war."

"On the contrary," he spoke quietly and Alouette had to lean in to hear him. "There is a great deal to be done in Spain. Many German officers have been stationed there, and your job will be to find out why."

"If you'll pardon me, Captain, I have been…"

He held up his hand. "Never mind all of that. You can make up for the missteps you took in Switzerland."

Alouette pondered this sudden change in the Captain's attitude. His manner had always been somewhat suspicious toward her, but now he seemed open, if not downright friendly.

She finally sat down to relate what had happened in Switzerland. As she began to describe Gerda, he interrupted her. "Ah, yes, I've heard of such a character. The blonde woman, your Gerda, is otherwise known as Elsa Shragmüller, a German spy. I suspect that 'Otto' and 'Charles' go by other names as well. It is also my suspicion that your friends were involved with illegal transmissions to and from Germany via Swiss wires. So you see, madame, your, as you called it, 'failed mission' was not such a failure after all."

Alouette shook her head. "I do not speak any Spanish."

"Well, if that's how you feel," Ladoux stood up. "I will have to find someone else."

"Wait," Alouette didn't mean for the word to come out, but she couldn't stop herself. "I can do it."

He frowned as his eyes dragged down from her rumpled hat and travel-weary clothes to her dust-covered boots. The suspicion was back.

Distrust must permeate every corner of the Secret Service, Alouette thought as Ladoux resumed his seat.

"It is my duty to warn you, Madame Richer," his voice had taken on a harsh tone, "that if you happen to carry off any coup successfully for us, it will be impossible for you to give up working for us afterwards. If you deviate from your duty and allow them to bribe you with their gold, don't forget the terrible fate that awaits you."

Alouette laughed at the thought of accepting German gold. "I could only guess that fate would be a firing squad."

He took no notice of Alouette's flippant reply and fixed her with a grim look. "You are taking your life in your hands."

Alouette's smile faded. "Yes, Captain."

"Have you any money?"

"No," Alouette answered. She hadn't been lying to the Germans about that point. "I shall write to my lawyer."

Ladoux extracted his wallet and tossed eight hundred francs across the desk. "That's all I have. Get the Germans to pay you. Our department is hard up for funds."

CHAPTER 17

M'GREET

JANUARY 1915

*A*fter approaching her old lover, Harry de Marguérie, on the Rue Boissière, M'greet convinced him to help her gather her things from Neuilly. Together they packed crate after crate of silverware, drapes, and furniture.

"I can't believe this stuff is still here," Harry stated as he tucked a fringed lampshade into one of the crates.

"Why wouldn't it be?" M'greet asked.

He straightened and put his hand on his back. "We're at war, remember? People are becoming desperate from starvation."

"Starvation?"

"Maybe not in Neuilly or that pretty house you are building in the Hague, but in many other places. And a lot of them are freezing to death, not just the soldiers in the trenches. France's coal supplies lie behind the German lines."

M'greet picked up a fur stole. She hesitated for a second as Harry frowned at her, but then she resumed wrapping the fur in tissue paper before placing it in a crate. She knew him well enough to know he was thinking she should donate the stole to some poor cretin off the street.

"Those Boches confiscated my full-length furs. I need something to keep me warm in the winter," she said by way of explanation.

He unceremoniously dumped the last of M'greet's things on top of the stole. "Are we quite done here?"

When M'greet nodded, Harry slid the lid over the crate and pounded it shut with a little more force than necessary.

"Care for a drink?" she asked when he stood up.

They walked down the block in silence. Harry seemed to be seething over something, but for the life of her, M'greet couldn't figure out what. Once they reached a main intersection, Harry hailed a motor-car and instructed the driver to take them to La Mère Catherine.

"This is a Renault," Harry remarked as the car pulled from the curb.

"Oh?" M'greet took out a compact from her purse and rearranged a few stray curls that had been ruffled by the January wind. At least Harry was speaking to her again.

"The kind of taxi that carried our boys off to fight the Germans?"

She snapped the compact shut. "Must we talk war?"

Harry, clearly lost in thought, ignored her and continued, "It was quite a sight to see all those soldiers in blue uniforms waiting for the bright red taxis. The army didn't have enough transports to take them all to the front, so the taxi drivers volunteered. What remained of Paris had come out to see them off. When the line of cars circled the Arc de Triomphe the crowd was so loud in their shouting '*Vive la France!*,' it was as if half the city hadn't fled in terror the week before."

"How very Parisian," she murmured. He fell silent and M'greet stared out the window. Maybe Harry was right, she mused as they drove by a long line of people outside a bakery, trying to buy bread. They looked cold and haggard in their threadbare frocks. M'greet pulled her own expensive raccoon-trimmed coat tightly around her body. *I hope that never happens to me.*

Harry took M'greet's arm as they arrived at the brasserie. He had quite a few people to greet before they took a seat at the bar.

"That's my Harry, always knowing everyone." M'greet commented as the bartender delivered their menus.

He shrugged. "I'm the second secretary to the Ministry of Foreign Affairs. It's part of my job." He closed his menu and laid a hand on hers. "But I'm all yours now."

M'greet beamed.

He ordered her a sherry and himself a bourbon. "Did you hear about the Christmas truce at the front?" he asked as the bartender moved down the bar to fill their order. "Apparently the Boches were the ones to start it: they approached our trenches unarmed, wishing our men a *Fröhliche Weihnachten.*"

"I don't want to speak of the war anymore." M'greet crossed her legs with a whisper of silk stockings. "I'll speak of anything but war."

Harry laughed. "All anyone ever talks about is war nowadays."

"Not me. I'd rather hear about your travels since we last met."

He took a long swig of bourbon. "Tokyo, Vienna, Burma, Lisbon. But nothing compares to Paris. Even during," he coughed, "the war."

"Oh, I agree that Paris is the most beautiful city in the world." M'greet twirled her sherry glass. "I wish I could stay, but I'm only on a traveling visa. I'm supposed to return to the Hague next week." She put a gloved hand on Harry's arm. "I was hoping to go shopping on the rue de la Paix before I go back."

She could feel his muscles stiffen. She was skilled enough in reading men's emotions to retract her hand.

He took another drink before setting his glass down with a clang. "Is that all you can think about—shopping? Is that what you want from me, to pay for you again?"

M'greet could feel her face grow hot as the other patrons fell silent. "How dare you?" she hissed under her breath. "You were perfectly all right with the situation as it stood ten years ago."

Harry's face softened and his voice was lower as he replied, "You know, when I was in Java, the supposed place of your birth... I learned of something called karma. I take it you've heard of it?"

M'greet nodded, but Harry continued anyway. "It's the principle that the actions you take in this life will determine your fate—whether you will be rewarded or punished—in your next life. I would have thought both of us would have changed in the past ten years, or at least once the war started. I came back to the Quai d'Orsay to volunteer my services." He finished off the last dregs of bourbon. "Did you hear me, Marguérite? I'm not getting paid." He swiveled his chair to meet her eyes. "If I can't afford to keep you, will you stay?"

M'greet snatched her coat off the stool beside her. "If that's who you think I am, then no, Harry, I won't stay." She marched to the door, expecting him to follow her, but when she glanced back, he was still seated at the bar.

CHAPTER 18

MARTHE

JANUARY 1915

*T*he days after the bombing were complete torture. Marthe's nerves, shocked by all the chaos she had witnessed, made her jump at every little noise. The Oberarzt offered to give her a few days' leave to recover, but to lie in bed alone, thinking about all the destruction she had caused was the last thing Marthe needed. In her nightmares, she walked along the ruined train station, the corpses of German soldiers and the British aviators staring up at her with glassy eyes. If she didn't wake herself up in time, the dream would continue on with Fischer, the short man from the train station, grabbing at Marthe's ankle, an endless stream of Why? coming from his blackened lips.

On the fourth day after the air raid, Marthe overheard the Oberarzt speaking to someone in his office. "How can we spare a doctor?" His normally calm voice held an uncharacteristic note of desperation. "Aufrecht and Nagle went to No. 8 hospital this morning, and Sudermann has come down with pneumonia. There is no one else."

"Do you not have anyone else who could perform emergency procedures?" an unfamiliar voice asked.

Marthe stepped into the room under the guise of retrieving some medical supplies. This could be her chance to redeem herself.

"Marthe," began the Oberarzt, but then he paused and waved his hand dismissively. "Never mind."

"Herr Oberarzt, did you need something?" Marthe's voice was innocent, as if she hadn't been listening in the doorway.

"We are in dire need of someone to work on the field at an advanced dressing station," he replied.

Marthe knew that advanced dressing stations were located very close to the line so soldiers injured in the trenches could be evacuated to receive prompt treatment.

"You can't mean..." the soldier who had been conversing with the Oberarzt stammered. "She's a woman!"

"A woman with a vast amount of medical training," Marthe put in. "I will go at once."

"Field work is no joke, fräulein," the soldier stated as he folded his arms across his chest. "You will be in constant danger."

"I am fully aware of that, hauptmann." She turned to the Oberarzt. "Give me a few minutes to gather some supplies and I will be ready to go."

The Oberarzt bowed. "Thank you, Marthe."

An hour later, Marthe found herself in a battered ambulance speeding down a gutted country road. The sound of gunshots grew closer, and she asked herself why she had volunteered to go any closer to the battlefield.

The ambulance shook as something thundered overhead "A welcome shell," the driver said, attempting a friendly smile. He was a tall, thin man in a German military overcoat. "Don't worry," he continued upon seeing her frightened expression. "The Allies seem to be taking it easy this afternoon. Let's hope for your sake they continue to do so, fräulein."

"Marthe," she corrected.

He took his eyes off the road again to glance at her. "Alphonse Martin."

"Are you German?" Though he wore the same uniform and had

the same close-cropped hair of many of the soldiers she had encountered, he somehow struck her as different. Maybe it was his amiable green eyes or the easy-going way he had mentioned the Allies.

"Sort of. Alsatian. My family has been in the same region for generations. They were French citizens until Germany took over Alsace during the Franco-Prussian war. I was conscripted by the Kaiser, but at least I was assigned to driving ambulances, not to die in the trenches like many of my brothers."

Marthe gave him a sympathetic smile, thinking of her own brother. Had he too died in the trenches?

The ambulance splashed to a stop a few minutes later. Looking out the cracked window, Marthe saw a muddied sign stating "Advanced Dressing Station No. 3."

"There is nothing here," she said, looking out across the soggy, desolate field. Only a few blackened trees marked that this area had once been forested.

"Been bombed to bits," Alphonse agreed. "The dressing station will offer some protection from the shelling. It's over there." Squinting her eyes at where he pointed, Marthe could see a circle of sandbags surrounding a hole in the ground near the side of the road.

She opened the door and stepped off the footboard into the mud.

"Good luck, Marthe." Alphonse's voice was muffled through the pounding rain. She watched as he yanked on the clutch and drove away.

She stifled the urge to run after him and headed toward the dugout.

A medical feldwebel was standing just inside the hole. "Fräulein?"

"I was sent by the hospital's Oberarzt," Marthe replied to his unasked question.

He frowned. "I suppose if the Herr Oberarzt recommends you, it must be because you do good work." He started down the slippery stairs, which were nothing more than thin wood planks stuck into the mud. "This is one hell of a place. We do the best we can. Sometimes we work all night and day, but there's been a lull up at the front lately."

As Marthe descended, she was greeted with a putrid stench of blood mixed with perspiration. She refrained from holding her nose as she gazed around the spacious underground dressing station. Directly in front of her was a small table, wet with something shiny. A gefreiter was laying out dressings on the cleanest part of the table. His blood-stained apron looked as though he worked at a slaughterhouse instead of a makeshift hospital. He touched his cap to her, but the orderlies smoking cigarettes to Marthe's right paid her no heed.

The feldwebel pulled a box out from under the table. "Have a seat, fräulein. All of that vibration from above means it's about to get busier down here." He offered her a tin of meat and called for an orderly to get her a cup of coffee.

Marthe glanced at the far corner of the room, where four corpses lay covered in coats. "I'm not all that hungry, but thank you."

"Ah, but you better eat now to keep up your strength. You might not have time when the cases begin to arrive."

The sound of voices and boots splashing in the mud above ground grew louder. The blood-stained gefreiter paused in his sorting and pulled at his long mustache. "Get moving lads," he instructed the smoking orderlies. "They are coming."

They threw their cigarettes on the ground and stamped on them before going to stand at the foot of the steps.

Two stretcher-bearers entered conveying a badly burned soldier. The feldwebel pointed to an empty bed and the stretcher-bearers deposited their burden before quickly heading back up.

Marthe rolled up her sleeves and went over to him. His face was black with a mixture of mud and blood and she dipped a cloth in water and began to wash his face. His lower arm had been shattered and the other was covered in burns. He reached out a hand that appeared as though it had been crisped in an oven to grab her arm. "Morphine, fräulein," he managed to gasp out.

She gave the feldwebel an inquiring look. He freed her of the burned soldier's grasp and pulled her aside. "We would have to have great tanks of morphine to supply the men who ask for it. But we have none." He took a syringe out of his coat pocket and then retrieved a small bottle, turning so that the soldier, had he been coherent, could read the label. *Morphium.* After filling the syringe, the feldwebel injected the burned soldier, who soon stopped moaning and fell asleep.

"What's in the bottle?" Marthe whispered.

"Water," the feldwebel replied just as quietly.

. . .

The time passed quickly. Marthe kept so busy that she didn't realize she'd been covered in mud and dust from the dugout. Wounded men trickled in all afternoon, battered men in tattered uniforms using their rifles as a makeshift crutch or clinging to their comrade's arms. Overworked stretcher bearers carried in the wretched men who could not walk.

The shrieking of shells was occasionally accompanied by a rumbling in the ground, but most of the workers ignored the disturbances. One shell hit so close that dirt and stones from the dugout roof fell into some of the men's open wounds. The feldwebel was quick to distribute his "morphine" after that incident.

At one point Marthe banged her head into the low ceiling and a splinter cut her forehead, but she was so intent on soothing the suffering of others she barely felt her own pain.

An ambulance arrived in the late afternoon to transport men to the main hospital. "Germans first," the feldwebel commanded. The orderlies sorted the men and helped a few to walk up the steps before coming back down with stretchers.

"'Ere, you haven't forgotten about me, have you?" Marthe turned to see a man with a bandage wrapped around his chest lying with his shoulders propped against the dugout walls. He was dressed in the khaki uniform of the British and winked at her before taking a cigarette from his pocket.

"Fräulein," another soldier called.

"Yes, mein herr," A German had appeared on the other side of the Englishman.

He held out his hand, which was misshapen and purple with bruises. "I've been waiting quite some time to have my hand wrapped."

"'E've all been waiting quite some time," the Englishman said quietly.

"Yes, but you are the enemy and I am not," the German replied. He took his gold cigarette case out of his pocket and flipped it open, only to find it empty.

The Englishman reached out to tap the German's well-kept boot, who looked down with a sneer. The German drew back his boot and Marthe thought for an awful second that he intended to kick the man.

"'Ere," the Englishman said, holding up his packet. "'Ave one of mine."

"You swine," the German replied. He raised his leg higher.

"Crikey," the Englishman withdrew his packet. "Yer a real gentleman, aren't you? Don't suppose you mind if I have a smoke, do you?"

The German's beady eyes narrowed even further. Marthe was about to offer to wrap his hand, if just to get him out of the way, when there was a commotion near the stairs.

A man stood at the entrance to the dugout shouting in pain. He appeared to be wearing a knee-length skirt, and Marthe first thought he'd lost his trousers, but then it occurred to her that it was her first sighting of a Highland soldier.

"Jesus Chrrist," he said with a long rolling R, as he took in the scene of the wounded men and the scurrying medical staff.

"Hullo Scotty," the Englishman called. "You ken take a seat over here. Ceiling's leaking above so it's made the ground nice and soft."

The Scotsman grunted and Marthe grabbed a swath of bandages before following him. Although she spoke some English, she could not understand a word of what the Scotsman had to say in his rough, Northern dialect. Whatever it was, his tale seemed to fill him with great indignation.

The Englishman offered him one of his endless supplies of cigarettes. He listened to the Scotsman's tirade, evidently understanding as he added an "Aye," here and there when the Scotsman paused to draw a breath.

Marthe had just finished wrapping his foot when the feldwebel called to her. "Time to go home, Fräulein Cnockaert. You can go with them to the hospital when the next ambulance arrives."

"Sir... mein herr," the Englishman corrected himself. "This man needs to go too." He nodded at the Scotsman, who had closed his eyes and was laying with his head against the dirt wall.

"Germans first," the feldwebel returned.

Marthe found space for the Scotsman next to her and the ambulance driver, Alphonse, the same man who had driven her to the dugout. It had only been less than twelve hours, but it seemed like a lifetime.

"We've got to get going," Alphonse said. "The Allies are putting stuff over tonight."

Marthe looked up as she heard the telltale shrieking sound. The shell burst into flame a few hundred feet away, stirring up a mountain of dirt that soon dissipated into the twilight. She knew she should probably be scared, but she was too tired and hungry to register much more than that.

Alphonse put the ambulance in gear and began to drive off, the Scotsman grunting at every bump in the road. Suddenly a flame arose immediately in front of the ambulance. Time slowed to a crawl as the windshield burst into tiny fragments that sparkled in the firelight. Marthe hair rose upward, defying gravity, and she had the peculiar thought that she was flying. And then she felt nothing.

CHAPTER 19

M'GREET

JANUARY 1915

*A*fter she'd fled from Harry at the bar, M'greet made her way back to the Grand Hotel. The night was frigid and she shivered uncontrollably as she exited the cab, either from the cold or latent anger at Henry. Or possibly both.

A tall man in an officer's uniform stood at the front desk. He tipped his cap at M'greet as she entered the lobby. "Evening, madame."

M'greet nodded back. Although his face was round and his hair graying, the body under the uniform appeared to be well-formed. She reached under her own coat and rubbed her arms, which at this point were covered in gooseflesh. She thought first of the women and children standing in the breadline, imagining many of them would either starve or freeze to death by the end of winter if something didn't change soon. Her mind then traveled to Harry and his accusations of her being a fortune hunter. *Forget Harry.* She saddled up to the officer. "Are you checking in?"

"Indeed." He waved a piece of paper in the air. "I'm filling out my foreign card, so they can make sure I'm not a spy."

M'greet laughed. "Of course not. Anyone can see you are an

officer of the…" she squinted as if to analyze his uniform, but in truth she never could discern between the different kits of the many countries at war.

He clicked his heels together. "Commandant of the Fourth Belgian Lancers, Division of the Cavalry of the Army of the Yser."

"That's quite a mouthful."

He shot her a grin, and M'greet was pleased to see his face looked much finer when he smiled. "Also known as the Marquis Frederic de Beaufort. But you can call me Freddy."

She met his smile with her own, carefully maneuvered to make her thin lips seem fuller, before she turned to the clerk. "I do believe the room next to my suite is empty, is it not?"

"Yes, madame."

"Perhaps you can give him that one, then. The Marquis must be starving. If you would please send a tray of charcuterie to my room."

The reasoning behind her suggestion was not lost on Freddy, who chuckled and then winked at the clerk. "Seems like my stay in Paris is going to be more delightful than I thought."

The clerk kept his face neutral as he handed over the key.

M'greet winked at Freddy, who was waiting for a porter, before she started up the staircase.

When she had entertained strange men in Paris previously, she usually had her escort rent a room in what was known as a *maison de rendezvous*, particularly the one run by Mademoiselle Denart at 3 Rue Galilee. M'greet knew that, like at many high-class establishments, the Grand's staff and fellow patrons would look down upon a strange man coming and going from a single woman's room, but at the same time, the ruse of adjoining suites would at least be tolerated.

She was not surprised to hear a knock on the inner door a few minutes later. She had lit an electric Tiffany lamp to bathe a soft glow over the small table on which she'd set the tray of cold meats and cheese.

"I mightily appreciate your hospitality, Madame…" Freddy said as he arranged a cloth napkin on his lap.

"Zelle-MacLeod. But you can call me Mata Hari."

Recognition flashed across his face. "I saw you dance once, here in Paris. With my," he coughed. "Wife."

M'greet sat down across from him and helped herself to a piece of cheese. "Did you enjoy it?"

"I did." Even in the dim light, M'greet could see his face redden. "Very much so."

They ate in silence for a few minutes until Freddy set his napkin back on the table. "Do you mind if I ask... are you always so kind to officers on leave?"

She shrugged. "It's how I contribute to the war effort."

He tugged at his collar. "Again, I appreciate it, but..."

"How would you like to have a private dance from the famed Mata Hari?" She stood with her back facing him. "Unzip."

Freddy began to pull down on the zipper. His fingers were unsteady at first, but became more certain as he finished the task. She let her dress fall to the floor and then turned around, knowing the shadows would hide her fuller belly and loose skin. She reached her arms above her head and began gyrating to a silent song only she could hear. Freddy's eyes widened in appreciation and he watched her move, his mouth slightly open.

CHAPTER 20

MARTHE

JANUARY 1915

*M*arthe awoke to something heavy on top of her, her nostrils stinging smoke, the words, "Jesus Chrrist," being muttered over and over again in her ear. The Scotsman moved off of her, heaving in pain, before extending his heavy hand to Marthe and helping her out of the car. The exploding shell had caused the ambulance to tumble into a ditch, and she had to grab onto plant roots to get back to the road.

She examined herself with the help of the moonlight. Except for a few scrapes and bruises, she was surprisingly unscathed. She looked around, taking stock. The moon cast an eerie glow on the gaping holes in the dirt road. Alphonse was sprawled on the ground next to the largest one, and Marthe started toward him when he rose and dusted off his pants, his eyes wide. He gave her an all-clear sign before he limped in the direction of the ambulance.

She returned to help the Scotsman out of the ditch and into a sitting position beside the road before she and Alphonse began evacuating the stretchers from the ambulance. They groped into the dark interior and followed the sounds of the men's moans before trying to extricate them from the ambulance as carefully as they could. Some passing soldiers were able to help her and Alphonse hoist the stretcher-bound men back up to the road. Miraculously, only one man was unresponsive.

Marthe was re-adjusting the bandages of a German whose fingers had been blown off in the trenches when Alphonse told her that she was bleeding. He picked up a clean rag and held it to her forearm. Both of the undersides of her arms were a maze of bright red scratches.

"You must have used them to shield your face from the windshield's glass," Alphonse said.

He was still picking glass out of her skin when another ambulance arrived. Marthe made sure that every patient had a spot before she climbed into the front seat. Alphonse waved them off, saying he'd walk back to the dugout and wait for another ambulance.

"Are you sure you're alright?" she asked from the open window.

"I'll be fine."

As the ambulance drove away, Marthe closed her eyes to the sight of shells streaking through the skies.

When she arrived at the hospital, she went to the civilian clinic to have her wounds properly looked after by the orderly on duty. She was so tired from her labors and emotion that she nearly fell asleep in the examining chair.

"You're lucky to have walked away from that," the orderly stated. "French shells are no joke."

She watched as the orderly extracted yet another piece of glass from her arm and heard it clink in the metal tray beside her. *I could have died.* The thought seemed too far away to grasp right then, like a cloud floating amongst the stars. *Or a French shell.*

"Thank you, mein herr," Marthe said, rising unsteadily to her feet.

"Get some rest tonight, fräulein," he replied.

She was about to head for home when two stretcher-bearers rushed in with yet another wounded man. "Found him in a ditch, fräulein," one of the helpers told her.

The words were a splash of frigid cold water onto her exhausted frame. "Oh no, was he one of ours?" She thought that she and

Alphonse had checked the area thoroughly, but it was dark and there was so much confusion.

"I don't think so. He was out on the street, and someone tried to cut his throat."

"Send for the night surgeon," she commanded as she approached the stretcher. The man was a ghostly white from loss of blood, and his clothes and sheets were stained dark red. Marthe moved back the collar of his uniform, trying to ascertain where the blood was stemming from. Something flashed in the dim light. Marthe exposed the underside of his lapel. Two safety-pins. But they ran straight, not diagonally.

She caught sight of a man standing in the corner. A military policeman, judging by his uniform. "Do you know who this man is?" she asked.

"That's Schneider. He's been on special assignment for several weeks now."

She nodded, recalling the warning Herr Jacobs, the safety-pin man boarder, had given her about Vampires disguising as his kind. The night surgeon rushed in, accompanied by a few orderlies. Marthe left the hospital and walked out into the coolness of the night.

When she reached the house, she found that Herr Jacobs was still up. Although Aunt Lucelle had said he was there to do "Secret Service," Marthe wasn't sure what his exact role was, besides befriending the Germans. Tonight he sat in the kitchen reading with his boots propped up next to the stove. If he was surprised to see Marthe in such a disheveled state, he made no comment.

"A man with safety pins facing the wrong way was brought into the hospital just now," she told him. "Someone tried to cut his throat."

He pulled off a muddied, blood-spattered boot before asking in an expressionless tone, "Did he die?"

CHAPTER 21

M'GREET

JANUARY 1915

M'greet had no notion that Freddy would become one of her habitual affairs, like Harry, van der Capellen, or the German Alfred Kiepert, but he was here, in Paris, and, unlike Harry, hadn't shunned her. Not to mention he was a marquis. He took her shopping on the rue de la Paix and they dined at fine restaurants, especially at the swank Pavillon d'Armenonville.

She could have stayed in Paris indefinitely, but knew she had to return to the Hague to supervise her house renovations. She planned her return trip for the same day that Freddy had to leave for the Front.

"Will you write to me?" he asked as they lay in bed the morning of their departure.

"Of course."

He sat up. "Good. All soldiers need a distraction from the monotony of the trenches, but my wife refuses to be in contact with me. She accused me of cheating long before I actually committed the act of being unfaithful."

"I'm sorry." M'greet lit a cigarette. "Wives should be more understanding when their husbands are away at war." She took a puff. "Or just in general."

Freddy laughed. "If only all wives could be more like you." His face fell. "Will you be all right in your travels? I would hate for the French police to treat you like the English did."

"And the Germans." She flicked ash into the bedside tray. "But don't worry about me. I can take care of myself."

She gave Freddy the goodbye he thought he deserved, even conjuring up some fake tears for good measure. When he finally left, she shut the door and leaned against it, thinking that faking affection for someone took more of a toll on her than actually feeling. The door vibrated under her back as someone knocked.

"Did you forget something?" she asked, flinging the door open. But the man who stood on the other side wasn't Freddy. It was Harry.

"I heard you were leaving," he said, stalking into the room.

"Oh? And who gave you such information?"

"The desk clerk. I asked him to let me know when you set a check-out date."

"Why?"

He gazed down at the floor. "I wanted to say goodbye. And apologize." He met her eyes. "Next time you return to Paris, be sure to contact me. No questions asked."

"You didn't ask any questions this time. You just made accusations."

"No accusations then." He sat down at the table, pushing Freddy's breakfast plate away. "I get it that you don't want to talk about the war. It's kind of nice, taking a break from the ever-present troop discussions, the analysis of how the Allies are doing compared to the Germans." He looked up, his eyes as sorrowful as his voice. "I'm sorry I ever tried to encourage you to be someone you're not."

M'greet wasn't expecting that response from Harry. She put a gloved hand on his shoulder. "Next time, I come to Paris, I promise I will call on you."

He eyed the myriad of trunks sprawled on the floor and the clothes and jewelry still covering almost every inch of the room. "Do you need help packing?"

Harry drove her to the train station to see her off. He gave her a long hug and then whispered, "Be safe," before he kissed her lips. As she mounted the steps, M'greet gave him one last wave, shedding a real tear this time.

Her ship was scheduled to leave from Vigo, Spain. While in town, she purchased a postcard of herself in her dancing days at a shop and addressed it to Harry de Marguérie, writing on the back, "The famed daughter of a British lord and an Indian princess wishes you well. Yours always, Marguérite."

CHAPTER 22

ALOUETTE

*S*an Sebastian, Spain was pleasantly balmy, especially after wintry Switzerland. If the Swiss were somewhat unknowledgeable of the war, the people of San Sebastian appeared downright oblivious to it.

But appearances could be deceiving, and after spending a few days wandering shops and beaches and overhearing a myriad of different languages, Alouette discerned that a host of foreigners had found solace from Central Europe's storm in the popular resort town.

She had booked a room at the Hotel Continental, yet she was unable to fully engage the fashionable crowd that flowed through its lobby. She didn't speak a word of Spanish, and her widow's dress and veil did her no favors. She thought appearing as a bored young widow desiring nothing but a good time away from the war zone would be a brilliant disguise, but all that black among the bird-of-paradise frocks the other women wore just caused people to shy away from her.

If only she had her airplane, or even her car! *The nouveau riche were alike everywhere*, she mused. They honed in on the gilt of the frame and paid no attention to the state of the picture beneath it.

Unused to being ignored, especially by the male population, she tried to compensate by buying new dresses, but nothing worked. Before long, Alouette's funds were running out and she was no closer to infiltrating any espionage rings. Ladoux had made it clear that his department was short on cash, and she would not be able to contact her lawyer to wire her money while on a secret mission in Spain.

She had just about given up and was considering crawling back to Ladoux when she passed by the casino off the lobby of her hotel and an idea occurred to her. The casino seemed the perfect locale for luring her fellow hotel patrons into conversation while at the same time, possibly winning some much-needed cash.

Alouette spent a considerable time getting ready that evening, dressing in one of her fanciest dresses, dark purple with a tight-fitting corset and silk skirt. But her reputation must have preceded her because the first man she passed as she entered the casino called out, "Look, it's the merry war-widow. She must be over her mourning."

She knew the man was a wealthy ne'er-do-well who had paid someone to take his place in the French Army. She choked down the impulse to box him in his deserter ears and joined a group of men in boiled shirts gathered around a roulette table.

An exceedingly tall man in a dinner jacket fixed a pair of gray eyes on her. There was something about the firm set of his lips and stern expression that hinted he was one of the German officers Ladoux had referred to. She looked down at the table and stated with more confidence than she felt, "500 pesetas on red."

The uniformed croupier spun the roulette wheel and Alouette watched the ball fall. "Red fourteen," the croupier declared.

"An excellent play," the man across from her said in German, confirming that her instincts had been correct.

Alouette shot him a distracted smile and put her winnings on red again. The German echoed her movements. After she'd won once again, she pocketed the money and excused herself for some fresh air.

As soon as she stepped onto the balcony, she heard footfalls on the tile. A man coughed and she glanced over her shoulder to see the German behind her.

"Fräulein, I..."

It was all Alouette could do to keep from stamping her feet as the big, timid German stammered something. She decided to not let on that she spoke German. "*Excusez-moi?*"

He switched to a halting French. "You were much in luck this evening."

"I always bet on red."

His grip around the balcony railing relaxed. "The color of passion."

The color of the blood shed by my French brothers from your black German machines. Alouette didn't know if his shyness was natural, or a cover for something more sinister. She blinked rapidly as she thought of a reply. If he was a spy, how could she hook him into recruiting her?

Although this time it was no fib, she decided to once again divulge her financial needs to a Hun. "It is a good thing I won tonight, since I can now almost pay my hotel bill."

His cheeks, illuminated from the streetlight below, flushed bright red. She supposed she crossed some unwritten rule that German men should not offer loans to French women. Nonetheless, she stuck out her hand. "Alouette Richer."

"Walter Halphan."

"You are German?" She placed a gloved hand over her chest as if she were surprised.

"Ja."

Perhaps it was the fact that they were on different sides of the war —or maybe because it was the first time since Switzerland that she felt she had the upper hand—something in her wanted to embarrass him. Using her native language, she stated, "And here you are in Spain, obviously a strapping young German, taking it easy while your fellow countrymen are shedding their blood to defend—"

"I would have preferred to go back to my country when the war started." Although he had interrupted her, his tone was not angry, but deferential, almost apologetic. "But I was too late and they interned me at Pamplona. That's where all Germans not in diplomatic service were sequestered."

Alouette, now feeling a touch of guilt for her outburst, gave a conceding nod.

Encouraged by her obvious change of heart, Walter asked if she would have breakfast with him tomorrow morning.

She nodded once again.

He reached for her hand with his mammoth one and laid his lips upon it. "Good night, fräulein."

The next morning, Walter took Alouette in his car to Saldivar, a little town on the road to Bilbao famous for its hot springs. Luckily the open-air car made conversation nearly impossible. When they arrived, he opened her door and helped her out. He attempted to keep her hand in his as they walked into the restaurant, but she squeezed it once before dropping it.

Once seated, they ordered coffee and then sat in silence for a few minutes. Walter's awkward chivalry caused Alouette to doubt he was involved in any sort of enemy espionage. Still, stranded in a strange town with nothing else to converse about, she decided to once again extend the bait. "I am leaving for Paris in a few days."

"Why are you leaving so soon?"

"I told you, I have no money."

"But you won quite a bit at the roulette table last night."

The waitress arrived with their coffee, toast, and a dish of creamy butter. *The best thing about Spain was the lack of rationing.* Alouette kept Walter waiting for her reply while she spread butter over the bread with gusto. "I didn't win too much," she said finally. "Just enough to cover my hotel bill and pay off some of the debts I've incurred here."

This statement was met by yet another uncomfortable silence. Alouette took a bite of toast, ruminating as she chewed that she made a faux pas by mentioning needing money to the German. The pensive look on Walter's face was probably a result of him trying to figure out how to change the subject.

She did him the favor. "Do you know many other Germans in San Sebastian?"

He took a sip of coffee. "A few."

"Have you met with any of them often?"

"Not really."

The rest of the breakfast continued in a similar way, with Alouette trying to pry into Walter's background without being overly obvious. His replies were vague, either out of caution or because he had no information of any pertinence whatsoever. Either way, she soon became bored.

As if desperate to fill the silence, Walter launched into a description of Madrid, where he had been conducting business when the war broke out. He maintained his idle prattle as they left the restaurant. Alouette had given up her attempts to get Walter to recruit her as an agent: it was obvious he was as honest as he looked.

As they made their way back to the car, he put his hand on her back and steered her off the sidewalk. She was about to protest when he muttered under his breath, "I don't want to greet this fellow walking toward us. He might prove a nuisance to you."

"Why?" she asked, her voice also low.

"He is a spy."

"Oh." She tried to keep her voice neutral while her innards jumped for joy.

Walter pretended to be engrossed in the store window in front of them, but Alouette made eye contact with the approaching man. He smiled at her before catching sight of Walter. "Herr Halphan! Fancy meeting you here."

Walter extended his hand with a slight hesitation. The tall, slim man shook it before his eyes traveled up and down Alouette's form. "Who is the lady?" he asked Walter in German.

Walter, ever the gentleman, answered in French. "She has come to Spain to win a fortune at the casino. From Paris," he added.

"Yes, and who failed to do so," Alouette said with a laugh. "And that's why I'm headed back to Paris quite soon."

The man cocked his eyebrow at Walter. He switched to French to ask, "Aren't you going to introduce us?"

Walter planted his feet and gestured to Alouette. "Madame Richer, this is Monsieur Stephan Kraut, a naval officer."

Kraut bowed. "What hotel are you staying in, madame?"

"The Continental."

His bushy eyebrow inched its way even more toward his hairline. "The Continental?"

She knew this time the bait had found a fish, and hooked a German naval officer at that. She glanced down at the ground, eyelashes fluttering. "I came to Spain hoping to find a rich husband. In France, there are none left." She glanced up. "But the men here are no good: half of them are deserters and the others desire only to have women as lovers." She emphasized the last word, her tongue caressing her teeth as she formed the *l*. "You aren't like that, are you Herr Kraut?"

Walter's face grew dark with anger. If looks could kill, Walter's visage would have been even more dangerous than his countrymen's Big Bertha howitzers.

"No," Kraut replied, taking Alouette's arm. "I am in the manufacturing business."

Walter coughed behind them.

"Oh, you must teach me your trade!" She made her voice sickeningly sweet. "I see everybody around me getting rich, while I fall further in debt." She fell into step with Kraut, who had begun strolling as though he hadn't a care in the world.

"They are profiteering off the war. Would you stoop so low to make money at the expense of others?" Kraut asked.

"Never," Walter commented from behind them.

Alouette, pretending to be deep in thought, stopped walking, "I would indeed. This war is a silly, needless display of power. It's as if Germany, and France, and all those other countries, are boys on a playground, fighting over possession of some ball."

Kraut nodded. "And by now, everyone has forgotten to whom that ball belonged in the first place."

She gave him a meaningful glance and dropped her tone. "If it's just a silly ball they're after, why not try to sell them a new one?"

"Exactly." He met her smile with an oily one of his own, and Alouette knew she had won the round.

Walter's voice broke their tête-à-tête. "Fräulein Richer, are you quite ready to go?"

"So soon?" Kraut's face fell. "I was hoping to have lunch, and perhaps fill this lovely woman in on a business proposition I have."

"Lunch? We just finished breakfast," Walter replied.

"You are her escort?" Kraut looked from him to Alouette. She suddenly understood that Kraut would not speak of anything confidential in the presence of his large countryman.

"Actually, I am her d——" Walter began, but Alouette interrupted him with a wave of her hand. "I don't need an escort. I plan on doing some shopping while I'm here, and then take the train back to San Sebastian. Alone," she emphasized.

Walter blinked several times before turning abruptly on his heel and heading back to his car.

"The train arrives at San Sebastian in late afternoon," Kraut said after Walter was out of earshot. "Perhaps I can interest you in an early dinner? I know of a great place near the Continental where we can discuss that," he cracked the knuckle of his forefinger with his thumb, "business arrangement I mentioned earlier."

She hoped her instincts had been correct and he was not referring to anything more nefarious than espionage. "Of course."

Perhaps it was only her imagination, but the staff seemed different when she returned to the hotel later that afternoon. The clerk, who had once been quite inattentive to her, came immediately out of the office, as if he had been just inside the door, waiting for Alouette to ring the desk bell. "Yes, señorita?"

"I'm meeting someone tonight at the El Torreón restaurant." She stumbled over the foreign words.

"Ah, yes." He pointed to a spot on the map behind the desk. "It is atop Monte Igueldo."

"On top of a mountain?" Kraut was definitely proposing to recruit her for something—hopefully as a spy and not a courtesan.

"Yes," the clerk ran his hand down a diagonal line on the map. "You will need to take the funicular railway to the top."

"How long will that take?"

"Less than an hour, but you should go soon if you don't want to be late."

Alouette nodded. She was already out of the hotel before it occurred to her that she never told the clerk what time she would be meeting Kraut.

. . .

She was still reflecting upon this fact as she boarded the Igueldo funicular, a train car that rode along a wooden track from the lower slope of the mountain to the summit. There was only one other passenger, an elderly man in a worn coat, who asked her something in Spanish.

Anxious to be left with her thoughts, Alouette shrugged her shoulders.

He tried again, this time in French. "Are you going to the fairgrounds?"

She shook her head, but he continued anyway, "They have a roller coaster. I hear you young people like such things. Personally, I don't trust these new innovations."

She gave him a tight smile and then fixed her gaze on the view outside. The green forests at the base of the mountain were giving way to the amazing panoramic view that was to be expected from one of the highest points in San Sebastian. La Concha Bay, and beyond it, the Cantabrian Sea, sparkled like vast sapphires. Tiny boats bobbed peacefully in the current, and Alouette wondered if anything as malevolent lurked underneath them. Kraut was a naval officer, but what was a naval officer doing in a neutral country during wartime?

"Tell me," she addressed the old man. "Have you ever seen any German submarines in these waters? I'm on holiday and am hoping to see one."

Something changed in the man's eyes as the train jerked to a stop. "Such talk could cause you to end up like that woman yesterday, fished out of the harbor with a dagger stuck in her back." He pulled open the door of the car. "Better to ask your officer friend," he said, nodding toward Kraut, who stood waiting a few feet away.

Kraut greeted her with an unexpected casualness. "Good evening, mein fräulein."

She was still reeling from the old man's words, but pasted a smile across her face. "Good evening, Herr Kraut."

He took her elbow. "I think you will quite enjoy this restaurant." He maintained his easy gait as they were shown to their table in the corner, a view of the bay on one side and the mountains on the other.

"You speak French quite well," Alouette commented as she arranged her napkin on her lap.

"I lived in Paris before the war." He took a sip of water, his eyes following their waitress as she retreated. He swallowed audibly before setting his glass down with a clunk. "I am to understand that you are in need of money, fräulein. Is that right?"

"Yes." She was taken aback at how quickly Kraut got to the point.

"And you know why I arranged for this dinner?"

"Yes," Alouette repeated, crossing her fingers underneath the table-cloth. "I have an idea of what you want me to do."

"And are you willing to undertake it?"

She picked up her fork and examined it, wondering how not to lose the upper-hand like in Switzerland. Kraut appeared to be a man she could handle, if only there didn't lurk a Gerda somewhere holding the puppet strings. She wanted to show him she'd be worthy of any offer the Germans made. "Am I to understand that you are the chief of your business?"

"No." He cleared his throat. "My superior is out of Madrid. But if I were to write to him, even with a telegram, you'd have to wait at least a day for a reply. I am authorized to make arrangements for new recruits."

She wiped a smudge from her fork with the napkin. She could hear Ladoux's voice, urging her to get the Germans to pay. "My case is not an ordinary one. The information which I am in a position to give you is exclusive. I am an airwoman and, as such, have access to all Air Force documents." This was, of course, not true, but Kraut didn't know that. "It is impossible for you to pay me sufficient money in return for those services."

"I knew you were an airwoman, even before I caught sight of your probing blue eyes. You are very astute, and the fact that you have no particular loyalties to any country makes your potential all the greater. If you come through for us, I would be able to put a fortune at your feet."

His voice was as slippery as the oil Alouette dipped her bread in, but at least her plan seemed to be working. "Are you so very rich?"

Kraut looked up as the waitress poured the wine. He waited until she had finished filling his glass and once again left before he replied,

"Personally, no. But Germany gives magnificent rewards to those who serve her."

"Serve her how? They won't allow women to fight in the trenches and my plane has been confiscated."

"Oh, come now." His tone became harsh. "You are too intelligent to misunderstand my meaning."

Alouette swirled her wine before sniffing it, the way her deceased husband had taught her. Stalling for time in order to steel her nerves, similar to how she once checked each instrument several times before starting her plane. She took a long sip and then set the glass back down. "And you are too much of a fool for me to continue this conversation."

He leaned forward as Alouette continued, "My dear Kraut, you are not much of a recruiting agent if you think a woman such as myself might have misunderstood what your business proposal was. There is no mistake about the goods you manufacture: you are supplying German submarines."

He gritted his teeth. "So we can indeed talk plainly. You know the end of the road I am proposing to you."

"The execution post at Vincennes."

"I am speaking about a stack of money larger than what is in the Bank of France's coffers."

"And I am speaking about being hanged for espionage." Alouette took another drink of the blood-red wine. Now she sounded like she was refusing his offer. She wiped her mouth with her napkin as she mentally switched gears. "But I do love money and want to earn it quickly. More than what you can offer me in your subordinate capacity."

"I only have one chief after the Emperor."

"If I am to risk my neck for said Emperor, and that of your employer, while they stay more than arm's distance away from the trenches, the risk is worth at least a discussion between the two parties concerned."

Kraut opened his mouth, but Alouette, in a rush of brazenness, continued, "And by that I mean myself and your chief, and nobody but your chief. Take it or leave it."

He heaved a deep sigh. "I would have liked to have been your handler myself. But you are right in your summary—your circumstances are indeed unique. I will write to my chief. I will leave a message at your hotel when I hear back."

As Alouette left the restaurant, twilight began to envelop the mountain, the remains of the sun turning the horizon crimson. Now the bay resembled a crown set with jewels.

The train was crowded with families leaving the fairground, but she didn't mind. All she could focus on was the words she would write to Ladoux, boasting of her success tonight in infiltrating a German spy ring.

A soothing evening breeze blew in from the sea as she left the funicular station and strolled back to her hotel.

Walter had been keeping sentinel outside. Upon seeing her, he moved forward. "Fräulein, will you—"

"I'm sorry, but something quite unexpected has come up."

Walter flushed. "Does this have anything to do with Herr Kraut?"

"Perhaps," Alouette called over her shoulder as she went into the lobby.

CHAPTER 23

MARTHE

FEBRUARY 1915

*T*he Englishman with the ready cigarettes and the nearly-unintelligible Highlander were installed in a small room at the hospital and assigned to Marthe's care. The Englishman, whose name was Jimmy, had two broken legs. He had been standing behind an ammunition wagon when a shell burst a few meters away and the horses in front of the wagon began galloping away. He'd caught hold of them, determined as he was to get away from the shells, but in the process both of his legs were shattered.

The Oberarzt set his legs a few days after he'd arrived, and Marthe was in the room when he awoke from the chloroform.

"I didn't cry like a baby, did I?" he asked her, genuine worry on his face.

She shook her head.

"Good."

He sat up suddenly, grabbed the chamber pot at the foot of his bed, and dry-heaved into it. "Oh, I'm sorry, miss." He wiped his mouth with the back of his hand, looking decidedly green. "I should be out there, at the front, working beside my boys, but 'ere I am, with these useless old things." He gestured toward his bandage-covered legs.

"What was it like being in the trenches?" Marthe asked as she dipped a cloth into a bowl and handed it to him.

Jimmy wiped his mouth as he thought. "Beastly, miss. Just plain beastly. Sometimes there are men whom you've gotten to know very well, and they are wounded, and you can't get to them for fear the Germans will send another shell over. And those boys whom you know —the ones you were not able to save—die of starvation right before your very eyes."

She hadn't expected such an honest answer. She glanced around to be sure there was no one else around before leaning forward. "And the war? Do you think the Allies are going to win?"

"'E're an obstinate lot—the British never know when they've been defeated."

"But…"

"Just you wait, miss. I'll bring you the Kaiser's head on a silver platter yet."

Both Jimmy and the Scotsman, whose name was Arthur, healed without much trouble, and the time came and went when they should have been evacuated. But still they lingered, and though both remained as cheerful as ever, Marthe could tell by their attitudes that they were growing troubled.

"Good morn', Miss Cnockaert," Jimmy greeted her one morning. "What have you brought me today for breakfast? Sausages, eggs, kippers, coffee?"

She set the tray down next to him and he eyed the goods: minced beef from a tin can and hardtack. "Only bully and a biscuit, eh? Well, never mind, never mind."

Arthur had been humming a tune under his breath, but paused to ask, "We're to be prisoners of war, aren't we, miss?"

Marthe, who was now able to understand most of what Arthur said, frowned. Nicholas Hoot had once been in that same bed, and then disappeared one evening. He was probably still a German hostage, if he hadn't been shot. "I don't know."

. . .

As she was leaving that evening, she caught sight of old Pierre shoveling snow in the courtyard. Before the war, Pierre had been a thief and a scoundrel, but now he was one of several civilian workers employed by the hospital. He paused in his shoveling to tip his cap at her. "Evening."

Marthe nodded at him, watching as he reached under his jacket. For a moment, she thought he might show her safety pins, but he pulled out a cigarette case instead, and she hurried home, away from the cold.

She had been living on edge ever since the murder of the false safety-pin man the night the ambulance had tipped over. She had a feeling that Herr Jacobs had something to do with the murder, but of course he never discussed it. It should have reassured her that people in the espionage network were looking out for traitors, but to her it was just a reminder of how easily such work could go foul.

She was therefore startled to hear knocking on the kitchen window after she'd heated a pot of soup on the stove. The man standing outside had a hat pulled down low over his gaunt face, but there was no disguising his identity.

"Father!" she exclaimed before hugging him tightly. When they broke their embrace, she ushered him inside. "Mother, come see!" she called upstairs. "Father's back!"

Marthe's mother rushed down the stairs. "Is it true?" She let out an excited cry as she caught sight of her husband sitting at the table. "Felix! Oh thank God you're alive."

Mother clutched him to her as if she never wanted to let him go, and Marthe encircled her arms around both of them, all three weeping with joy. When they'd finally had their fill, Mother sat down next to Father, grasping his hand while Marthe prepared tea and Father told them what happened to him. "I was taken in by a kind farmer in his house on the road to Ypres. He has a brother who lives in Roulers and was finally able to answer my inquiry as to your fates. I came as soon as I heard."

"And you weren't hurt?" Mother asked.

Father shook his head. "Germans are the same everywhere, but I kept my nose down and cooperated with them as best I could. They took all of the harvest for their army, leaving many of the townspeople starving."

"Not much different from here, then," Mother remarked.

"No." He took a sip of tea. "The brother of the farmer owns the Café Carillon in Roulers."

"I know it," Marthe said. "It's the little yellow brick building in front of the church by the Grand Place."

"Yes. It was recently struck by a bomb," Father replied. "Though it did minimal damage, the brother is taking his family further away from the front. He offered the café title to me." He bestowed a weary grin on his wife and daughter. "Don't you see, my lovelies? We can be together again under one roof, and this will provide us with a modest income."

"And Max? Have you heard anything?" Mother asked.

Father frowned before he shook his head.

After thanking the grocer and his wife profusely for their kindness in providing them shelter all those months, Marthe's family moved into the space above the café.

As their new business was adjacent to the Grand Place, it was usually not in want of customers, including German soldiers. Marthe had heard stories of the capture of "café girls," tortured by the Huns for trying to make men talk. But it seemed all too easy to overhear the soldiers' gossip, Marthe realized as she waited tables after a long day of nursing. She didn't want to appear overly friendly to the soldiers so as not to alienate the Belgian patrons. Not to mention it might attract the soldiers' suspicions.

She convinced Father to open the upstairs room, usually reserved for private parties, to double as a soldiers' lounge. One evening, when Marthe came home from the hospital, the smell of cigarette smoke and the chatter greeting her even before she walked into the café, Mother approached her, an anxious look on her face.

"There are some German officers in the lounge who have announced their intention to billet with us."

Marthe sighed. They'd just been reunited with Father, and now this? She walked upstairs with a heavy heart. Three officers were seated at the center table, their duffel bags scattered on the floor between them. A man in a disheveled tunic, his hauptmann's jacket draped over the chair, sat smoking a cigar. He had bright red hair, and, as he caught sight of Marthe, raised his glass. "Fräulein, will you do us the honor of toasting to our upcoming trip to Paris?"

Marthe paused, not wanting to offend the Germans but she would never deign to toast to the enemy. The other hauptmann, his uniform still intact, tightened his lips as he glanced at the third man, a younger man with golden hair. A dimple played in and out of his cheek as he winked at the red-haired hauptmann.

"I'm sorry, Herr Hauptmann," Marthe replied finally. "I have just come from duty at the hospital and am quite tired."

"The hospital on Menin Road?" the red-haired hauptmann demanded.

"Yes, Herr Hauptmann."

"Really, Red Carl," the blond man said in a gay voice. "You are not here to court-martial the young lady."

The other hauptmann, a cadaverous man with close-cropped hair, gazed at her through his thick glasses. "Perhaps the fräulein will show us to our sleeping quarters." There was nothing sinister in his words, but Marthe felt uneasy all the same. She guessed he was the senior of the three, and showed him to the single room, but he turned to her, his eyes glinting behind those large glasses. "Herr Hauptmann Carl and I have some work to do together. The Herr Lieutenant can take the single room instead."

"Excellent," the golden-haired lieutenant replied, clapping the other man on his shoulder. "Red Carl, if you snore tonight the way you did on the train in, you will not be long for this world if Hauptmann Reichman has anything to do with it!"

Red Carl waved his hand. "He would never kill me. I'm too valuable for that."

Marthe went to fetch some more linens. When she returned to the lounge, the blonde lieutenant was sitting at the table alone.

"I'm sorry if you found my companions rude, fräulein. They don't mean to be that way, they're just always wrapped up in their own ideas."

"What sort of officers are they? They weren't wearing the uniform of the Army of Würtemburg."

"No," the lieutenant agreed, finishing off his wine. "They are from a special unit, sent ahead to arrange our trip to Paris." He said the last phrase mockingly before letting out another laugh.

Marthe knew it would not be wise to make further inquiries of the lieutenant, but vowed to herself that she would send Agent 63 a message about the Paris warning later.

He took out a cigarette from an expensive-looking case and offered one to Marthe. She declined.

"Otto Von Prompft," he said, sticking out the hand that wasn't holding the cigarette.

"Marthe Cnockaert." As he grinned, she noticed his smile was not quite even, the one facial imperfection he exhibited. "You have a dueling scar."

He touched his left cheek. "I was a student at Stuttgart up until a few months before the war started."

"My brother Max was also at University."

"Did he duel?"

"No." It had been said that a man's courage could be judged by the number of scars on his cheek. But her brother looked down on the practice of dueling, cursing anything that society considered elite. "Max always said he preferred to have his courage judged in other ways."

"*Très intéressant*," Otto replied.

"You speak French?"

"*Oui.* I lived in Paris for a few years." There was something frank yet friendly in his voice and Marthe couldn't help but develop a fondness toward the young lieutenant as he continued, "I've recently come from Berlin, and I know that you Belgians bemoan the oppression you claim you are forced to live under, but the regulations in the German capital are quite similar." He flashed her that slightly uneven smile again. "It is war-time, you know."

Marthe wanted to protest against the deplorable pillaging his countrymen had done, but tightened her lips as he told her, "We Germans know how to endure, so it is no matter. We are bound to win in a few months' time."

She couldn't help her reaction. "Win the war? You might have been able to accomplish a few victories thus far, but you will not emerge from this war a victor."

"Marthe, as yet Germany has not even been tested. A crushing victory is forthcoming, and it is coming soon." His once friendly voice had taken on an ominous challenge.

A bell rang from downstairs and she rose.

"Thank you for the conversation, Marthe." His tone had once again become amiable and the twinkle in his eye reappeared, as if he had never made any threat.

Marthe went downstairs to find the café nearly empty, save for two men in plain clothes seated at a table.

"Alphonse?" Marthe asked, recognizing the ambulance driver who had been wounded with her. "Am I wanted at the hospital?"

"No, fräulein," Alphonse stated. "My friend Stephan here and I just wanted a drink."

The man named Stephan nodded. He was a stocky man with an incongruously thin, well-trimmed mustache.

Marthe's hands grew sweaty at the way they were eyeing her—so queerly, as if they knew something she didn't.

"Brandy?" she asked.

"Tea," Stephan replied.

She went into the kitchen, her heart pounding. How long had they been sitting there? Did they hear her conversing with Otto and suspect that she was working with the Germans?

Stephan was still seated at the table when she returned, but Alphonse had risen and was looking at the pictures on the walls.

"Your family?" he asked.

"No, the former owner's. My father has only recently taken over the lease."

"I see," Alphonse replied with a casual tone as he sat back down.

She began pouring the tea.

"How do you like your double-job, sister?" Stephan asked quietly.

Marthe, feeling the blood drain from her face, kept her head turned slightly away. She willed her sweaty hands not to drop the teapot.

"Alphonse," Stephan said, louder this time. "I see your button is coming loose. Perhaps you are in need of a safety-pin. I have two."

Marthe breathed an inward sigh of relief as she set the pot down. "I might need one as well. You say you have pins handy?"

Stephan lifted the lapel of his jacket to reveal them. They were pinned diagonally and Marthe could feel her heartbeat resuming a normal pace.

Alphonse copied Stephan. "So you see, sister, we both have pins."

Marthe nodded and glanced around the empty room. "How did you know about me?"

"The sergeant-major at the hospital told us."

"What? That German traitor—"

"He is not German. He grew up in France, and until yesterday, was our channel of communication. But alas, he was transferred." Alphonse replied. "Stephan here works at Brigade Headquarters, and, as you know, my frequent ambulance trips to the front put us in a position of being able," he too glanced about the room, "to provide certain information."

"We were told to pass this on to a girl named Laura," Stephan said.

"You can well imagine my surprise when I figured out who this Laura was," Alphonse filled in.

"Do you have information for me now?" Marthe asked.

"No." Stephan touched his mustache. "We come on another matter, concerning a man named Otto von Prompft."

"He is billeted here. I've only just met him," she stated. "He seemed nice enough, for a German officer."

"No." Stephan leaned in and Marthe did the same. "He is a spy-hunter."

"How do you know that?" Her voice had become a whisper. "Do the Germans suspect me?"

Alphonse's voice, though hushed, seemed to reverberate throughout the empty café. "They are no more distrustful of you than they are of all Belgians, unless they are imbeciles or on their deathbeds."

"And even then, they are still mildly suspicious," she murmured.

"Quite right." Alphonse looked over at Stephan expectantly.

"I sometimes open mail for the censor at HQ," Stephan began. "I recently came across a letter from this Otto to his mother stating that the 'special work' they had sent him to do in Roulers would be both 'easy' and 'interesting.' He is not employed by the army or the military police."

"I see." Marthe stood up straight, mentally stabbing Otto a hundred times for letting her like him. "I have another matter I'd like to discuss, though. There are two men in the hospital—"

"Is one of them the Scottish man from the night of the bombing?" Alphonse asked.

"Yes. Are they to become permanent prisoners of the Germans?"

Stephan and Alphonse exchanged uneasy glances before Stephan answered, "Most likely, yes."

"Isn't there something we can do for them?" Marthe begged.

Alphonse gave a resolute nod. "I will look into it."

CHAPTER 24

M'GREET

FEBRUARY 1915

Soon after M'greet returned to the Netherlands, she had an interview with the Dutch magazine, *Nouvelle Mode*, and they decided to feature her on the cover. Van der Capellen attended the photo shoot, and, on a break, asked her if she thought her outfit immodest.

M'greet glanced down at her low-cut bodice, a pearl necklace dangling in the space between her breasts. "Of course not."

He nodded, appearing for a moment uncertain, but then his face cleared as he replied, "Well, if you don't have a problem with it, then I don't either."

He took her out to dinner that night. The weather was unseasonably warm and they sat near an open window. The trickling of a water fountain outside could be heard whenever the string quartet performing that night was between songs.

"How's your house coming along?" Van der Capellen asked.

"Not well," M'greet replied. "I don't think it's any closer to getting done than when I left for Paris." She reached across the table to put her hand on top of his. "Perhaps you could speak to my decorator and urge him to hurry."

"M'greet," he replied with a sigh, "Dekker is the best in the Netherlands. He knows what he is doing."

"He is slow and stupid."

He shot her a mocking smile. "We all cannot be as smart as you. Have patience, he will get it done." He squeezed her hand before glancing toward the courtyard, a wistful expression on his face. "I have to return to the front tomorrow. If only it weren't for this infernal war, we could run off and get married."

A sharp breeze blew, causing M'greet's eyes to water. In the dim electric lights, the normally wide, friendly face of van der Capellen thinned, his mustache drooped, and his eyes appeared steely, making him look just like her ex-husband.

M'greet covered her gasp by dabbing at her wet eyes with a napkin. She could never marry van der Capellen; although the affable general with the ready laugh normally held no resemblance to Rudy, all she could think of was the brutality she suffered while married. And all of the philandering: on both of their parts. Although M'greet had affairs out of retaliation for Rudy's unfaithfulness, she wasn't sure she could ever remain faithful to one man again. She'd been on her own for more than a decade and relished her freedom too much to jump back into the role of dutiful partner. "But of course we can't. What of your wife?"

He shook himself out of the revelry. "You're right. We'll have to keep things just as they are." He took a bite of food and chewed thoughtfully before swallowing. "What does a beautiful woman like you want with an old soldier like me, anyway?"

M'greet giggled. "Oh, come now, you know you're not that old. You're just fishing for compliments."

He threw his head back and laughed that deep belly laugh. "You're right. Now, did you get everything that you needed in Paris?"

She gave a dainty shrug. "I got a few outfits and trinkets, but I couldn't bring too much over the border for fear it might get confiscated."

"You need to go shopping then." He slapped his heavy hand on the tablecloth, startling a passing waiter, causing him to spill water on the floor. "Of course you do." He dug out his wallet and gave her several hundred guilders. "Buy yourself some nice things tomorrow. I wish I could go with you, but my train leaves in the morning."

"Oh," she puckered her lips in disappointment. "That early?"

He took a long sip of whiskey. "If only the English troops could get it together. They missed their opportunity after that surprise attack in Artois."

M'greet suppressed a groan. How she hated to hear talk of war!

After one last night with van der Capellen, M'greet wandered some of her favorite stores in the morning and then made her way back to the house in Nieuwe Uitleg. She walked down the quiet street next to the canal, stopping to admire the new green shutters on the brick facade of her home before letting herself in, only to find the hallway strewn with scraps of wallpaper and fabric samples. Her immense trunks from Paris were stacked next to the stairwell, still unpacked. She kicked at a box before noting the two men in grungy overalls standing on the second-floor landing, staring with uncertainty at her beautiful new dresser of carved wood and copper pulls. One of them scratched at his greasy hair before he threw up his hands in defeat.

"What's going on?" she demanded.

The movers looked dumbly down at her as Dekker called, "Madame Mata Hari, you've returned."

"I have." She mounted the stairs. "What is all of this?"

He glanced at the movers, his frown deepening. "It seems we mismeasured—"

"*You* mismeasured."

He cleared his throat. "At any rate, it doesn't appear that this dresser will fit through the doorway of your bedroom."

"That's impossible." M'greet stomped over to the dresser. She approximated the width of the dresser and then pushed past the movers, walking to the doorway with her arms held tight. "It looks as if it will fit fine."

Dekker pulled the measuring tape out of his pocket and walked over, holding out the tape to demonstrate. "It's six centimeters too large."

"Well." For a moment, M'greet was at a loss for words. "Well," she said again. "I suppose all that money I paid for it is wasted, wouldn't you say?" She marched over to the landing to angle her body behind the dresser, pushing on it with all of her weight.

"Madame!" one of the movers called. But it was too late. M'greet heaved the dresser off the landing, watching with a sick satisfaction as it tumbled down the steps and then crashed into the newly plastered wall.

The movers exchanged looks of horror before simultaneously starting downstairs. They climbed over the splintered wood as best they could before wordlessly letting themselves out.

M'greet turned to Dekker, her arms crossed over her chest. "What do you think about that?"

He cleared his throat before replying in a quiet tone, "Madame, you do realize there is a war going on, don't you?"

"Yes, of course I do. Why would you ask such a stupid question?"

"Well, most people in Holland are cutting back on expenses, preparing for the slim possibility of a German invasion. But here you are, spending money like it is nothing." He picked up one of the photographs from the *Nouvelle Mode* shoot off a nearby table. "You chose to wear an outfit like that," he said, his finger stabbing at her likeness.

"That dress is a Paquin, from Paris," she replied, not understanding his point. "And that hat is made from endangered osprey."

"Yes, but look at these women." He pulled a newspaper out of his pocket and pointed to a picture of women feeding wounded soldiers. They were dressed in black dresses buttoned up to their necks. "This is what a woman your age and class should be wearing."

M'greet wrinkled her nose. "Never."

"And this." He flipped to a list of the latest casualties and waved it under her nose. "A war, madame. People are dying, and you are building an indoor bathroom."

"I know there is a war going on," Her voice rose in volume as she continued, "It's all anyone ever talks about. There are no parties, only fund-raisers for the army. There are no more glamorous ladies of the *haut monde* on the streets, only grieving widows and amputees. Is it such a crime that I want to be surrounded by color and style in my own house when the rest of the world is dreary and gray?" She narrowed her eyes at Dekker. "Not to mention that my decorating budget is keeping a roof over your head."

He walked down the stairs, muttering to himself how the Hague was not Paris as he investigated the hole in the wall.

CHAPTER 25

ALOUETTE

FEBRUARY 1915

A few days later, Kraut left a message for Alouette to join him that evening at the restaurant atop Monte Igueldo.

He was already seated when she arrived, and mournfully watched her walk across the restaurant. He glanced toward the ocean as she sat. "If it weren't for the war…" his voice trailed off.

"What would you do differently?"

"I would abduct you." He pointed beyond the bay, to the open sea. "We'd head off to somewhere exotic."

Alouette fiddled with her napkin, thinking if it weren't for the war, she wouldn't be a widow. "I did not come here tonight to flirt."

Kraut clasped his hands together, once again all business, the sentimentality of the previous moment forgotten. "My chief has agreed to meet with you."

A band started playing somewhere below them, haunting strains of a foreign song drifting in the breeze. Alouette felt a pang of misgivings as she recalled the mess with Gerda Nerbutt. "Your chief isn't a dreadful man, is he?"

A faint shadow covered Kraut's face. "He is a decent chap." He stood, throwing his spotless napkin on his plate. "Be at the foot of the funicular railway tomorrow morning at six. A man will pass close to you and say, 'Follow me.' Don't dress too smartly as to not attract attention." He met her eyes. "Good luck, fräulein."

Alouette rose at dawn the next morning and put on a simple walking dress. Her heart was beating double time as she checked her hair. What if Kraut had laid a trap for her?

Although it was nearly daylight when she left the hotel, Alouette did not see anyone up besides the desk clerk. The beach was equally deserted. She walked quickly to the train depot, her spirits rising in time with the sun emerging from the rose-tinted clouds in the east. Her favorite time to fly had always been in the morning, and she recalled the exhilarating feeling of being in the air, the wind in her hair, the view from above. She was ready for another adventure and this time she would get the information Ladoux wanted.

She arrived at the rendezvous point well before six. Two priests standing at the foot of the funicular railway looked at her, no doubt surprised to see an unaccompanied woman wandering the streets so early in the morning.

As Kraut had foretold, exactly at six a man appeared wearing a blue military suit and a yachtsman's cap. He passed so close to Alouette that she thought he might run into her. "Follow me."

Alouette noticed with a slight irritation that the priests were staring at her as the man strolled away. She impatiently glanced at her watch and then at the incline suspensions before shrugging to herself, as though she'd made the sudden decision to walk.

She walked down the platform of the funicular, noting that the man waited by a Mercedes. The man opened the door and climbed in the backseat and then reached a long arm across to open Alouette's door. She could feel his gaze on her as she entered, but kept her own eyes straight ahead as the chauffeur started the car.

The car sped up and Alouette began to feel uneasy as the rocky landscape passed by in a blur.

The German wore clunky black spectacles which partially hid his face but did not conceal the fact that he was scrutinizing Alouette in between crossing and uncrossing his long legs. His edginess got on her nerves. Where was this man taking her at such breakneck speed, and why hadn't he spoken to her yet?

Alouette's ears popped as the Mercedes ascended a hill. She was so preoccupied with staring at the winding road ahead that she almost didn't hear when the man finally spoke.

"Has Herr Kraut told you what we want you to do?" Although he addressed her in French, his low voice held the guttural resonance of a native German speaker.

"Not exactly."

He moved so close that his thin leg nearly touched Alouette's. "I'm told you are an airwoman."

"Yes." She gripped her hand on the door of the car and shrank away from the man. Although his actions—the long moments of silence and his overcrowding—would be considered quite rude, his next words were said in a surprisingly deferential tone. "Do you speak German?"

Once again, she thought it would be best to not admit she spoke the language fluently. "No, I do not. Is that a problem?"

"No." He removed his spectacles to clean them and she used the opportunity to do her own scrutinizing. His face was as gaunt as the rest of his body. The eye on Alouette's side stared forward instead of looking down at the task and she realized it was made of glass. "What do you want to know about France?" she asked, partially just to end the silence.

The man took his time replacing his glasses before digging into a valise at his feet. He retrieved an envelope and dumped it on her lap. "Open it."

She showed no surprise as she retracted 3000 pesetas and a sheet of paper. The paper contained typed questions followed by blank spaces, asking such things about the new anti-aircraft defenses around Paris, the places that had been bombed, and the morale of the army at the front.

Alouette refolded the questionnaire and was about to put it back in the envelope when the man took it from her.

"Leave nothing to chance," he said with a patronizing tone. He struck a match and held it up to the paper. The light from the burning questionnaire gave his features an ominous air, the fire reflecting off that strange glass eye. She refrained from shivering outwardly as he rolled down the window and threw the burning paper out.

He reached into his coat pocket and extracted a strange-looking pen. He touched the tip of it. "This bulb is to prevent the pen from scratching the paper when using invisible ink." He then produced a vial full of silvery powder and shook it. "Dilute this in two or three spoonsful of water. You need to use thick white paper on which you will write a gossipy letter to an imaginary friend. Between the lines you will trace the information which I want from you when you return to Paris. You will sign with the pseudonym S-32."

Alouette took the vial from him. "What is this powder? If I run out, I will have to secure more."

"Collargolium." He handed her another slip of paper. This one read *Madeline Stepino, Calle Algorta, Madrid.* "Always write to me at this address. Never call on me, no matter how important you think the information is."

"You make it sound dangerous."

"It is."

She closed her eyes, reminding herself what it felt like to be the only one in the cockpit, in complete control of her airplane. She must not lose the upper hand to this man. "Well, if that's the case, then I have to tell you I value my life more than 3000 pesetas."

"We want to see what your capability as a spy is. We can match your payments to your skill." He gazed at her searchingly before edging closer. She scooted as far away as she could until she was flattened against the door.

"And one more point, S-32. Now that you have pledged yourself to serving Germany, if you do not fulfill your undertakings, your life will be forfeit. If you play us foul, those 3000 pesetas will be the last payment you receive before your death in front of a firing squad."

Alouette refused to dwell on the consequences of becoming a double agent and flexed her hands, pretending she was easing up on an airplane lever. She shifted her eyes to meet his. "I have no desire to serve Germany. I only wish to serve myself."

His thin lips spread into a sinister smile. "When you are ready to return to Spain, you will place an advertisement in the *Echo de Paris* for a chambermaid. You will give your address and invite your imaginary applicants to call on you the day and hour that your train will be leaving."

The car pulled to a sudden stop. Alouette had been so distracted by the man's commands—and his movements—that she hadn't noticed the car had turned around. They were once again at the funicular station. "Thank you, mein herr," she said before she opened the door behind her and practically spilled out of the car. It wasn't until after they pulled away that Alouette realized she never caught her new spymaster's name.

CHAPTER 26

MARTHE

MARCH 1915

$\mathcal{A}$ few days after finding out that Alphonse and Stephan were safety-pin men, Marthe entered the hospital grounds as the old groundskeeper Pierre was trimming a bush. Once again he tipped his hat to her. "Morning, mademoiselle."

She nodded a greeting and then hurried along.

"Mademoiselle?" He followed her into the courtyard.

"Monsieur?" She met his eyes. One of them only half-opened, but the other one was fixed on her with a penetrating stare.

"Our acquaintance Alphonse wanted me to pass this on to you." He handed her a fat envelope.

She tucked the envelope into her coat pocket but hesitated before she went inside. She was expecting him to show her safety-pins, but he turned back to his work, whistling *Frère Jacques*.

No one was in the staff room when Marthe arrived, so she peeked into the envelope. A small slip of paper sat between several hundred francs. She pulled the paper out and hid the money in her skirt underneath her nurse's apron. The note contained instructions from Alphonse regarding helping the Allied patients escape. She memorized the contents before she ripped it into tiny pieces, swallowing them along with several swigs of chicory coffee.

She hurried into the room where Jimmy and Arthur were having a friendly argument. "You're a bleedin' liar!" Jimmy remarked.

"Jesus Chrrist, have ye no bin to schule?" Arthur replied.

Another patient was on the other side of Jimmy, so Marthe went to the Scotsman's bed. "Good morning, Arthur," she said in a bright voice.

"Mornin' miss," he returned.

On the pretext of tucking in his sheets, Marthe leaned in close and whispered, "There is an envelope full of francs under your mattress. This evening on your walk, you and Jimmy will look for a short man with a squinty eye near the civilian workers' cabin. He will be your guide to get you over the border."

Arthur's eyes widened as Marthe straightened. "Ye know, lassie, what I'm gonna do once this war is ohva?"

She shook her head.

"I'm gonna become a meenister."

It took her a second to translate his words in her head. *I'm going to become a minister.* She grinned at him, picturing the large Highlander who peppered his speech with Jesus Chrrist standing in front of a congregation. "You might get the chance sooner than you think."

She lingered as long as the busy morning would allot for, hoping that the men would be safe on their journey. For all she knew Pierre might be an agent of the Germans and had claimed knowing Alphonse to set her up. When an orderly barreled into the room, Marthe froze, thinking that she had indeed been double-crossed.

"Fräulein, there are two ambulances on their way from the front. We will need you to prepare for the arrival of more wounded soldiers."

"Yes, mein herr," Marthe replied. She gave the men a little wave before rushing off to change the empty beds in the German ward.

It was around seven o'clock that evening when there was a sudden ringing of bells outside the hospital. Marthe raced into Jimmy and

Arthur's room to find both of their beds empty. A feldwebel entered, his eyes jumping from one vacant bed to the other.

"What do you know of this, nurse?" he demanded. "Two patients from your ward walked off right under your nose! When did you last see them?"

"This morning, Herr Feldwebel. But they can't possibly get far without civilian clothes or money," she replied, knowing that, if things went as planned, they would have both.

He stomped away, shouting for orderlies to search the grounds as he did so.

As Marthe left that night, she passed by the civilian cabin. Alphonse was standing in the doorway. "Good evening, Marthe," he said, stepping toward her. His green eyes twinkled with merriment in the light from the torch in his hand. "A friend of yours wanted me to tell you he should be in Holland by midnight."

She smiled and nodded, her insides filling with gratitude. Perhaps Arthur would indeed become a minister someday, and as for Jimmy, well, she wouldn't mind him keeping the promise of delivering the Kaiser's head on a platter.

"Thank you, Alphonse." His thin figure seemed fuller underneath his heavy coat, and his once severely cropped hair had been allowed to grow. His gaze cut through the darkness of the night and Marthe hoped that he wouldn't be able to discern that her cheeks—judging by how hot they felt—must have grown crimson under his gaze.

CHAPTER 27

M'GREET

MARCH 1915

M'greet was bored. The Hague was no Paris, and van der Capellen, though generous, was not proving to be a very exciting beau. And she'd had enough of Dekker and the endless construction on her house. But Dekker refused to hurry and it was only after a letter from her attorney that he finally finished.

M'greet persuaded van der Capellen to pay for the immense bill from the Paulez hotel, where she had stayed during most of the heavy construction, as well as Anna's salary. She figured she'd wait a few more months before begging him for travel money so she could go back to Paris and get away from the dullness of The Hague.

She had not been in her new house for a month when Anna handed her a calling card. It was from Karl Kroemer, the German consul in Amsterdam.

"I wonder what he wants?" M'greet asked. "Perhaps the Germans have decided to return my funds and furs after all."

"I don't know, madame. He is coming tomorrow, so I'm sure you will find out."

. . .

The time of Kroemer's announced visit came and went, with no sign of the German consul.

Anna had gone to bed, and M'greet was writing a note to Harry de Marguérie when someone knocked at the front door. Deigning to answer it herself, she found a man of medium height standing on her doorstep. His dark hair was parted straight down the middle and he was wearing an impeccably neat suit.

"Herr Kroemer?" she ventured.

"Indeed, fräulein. You are as astute as they say. May I come in?"

M'greet moved aside. "Would you like some tea?"

"No, fräulein. What I have to say won't take long."

He sat in a pink armchair and she draped herself on the white velvet couch across from him.

Kroemer took his hat off and set it on a marble-topped end table "I have heard you have recently been to Paris."

"I have."

He leaned forward. "Tell me, what was the atmosphere like there?"

"Oh, the French are quite sick of the British. They are afraid the British will never leave and will decide to settle in. After all, both the weather and the fashion are much better on the Continent."

Kroemer coughed politely. "That is not exactly what I meant."

"No?" M'greet put a hand on her chest and let out a giggle.

"No." He sat back in the chair and steepled his hands together. "How would you like to return to Paris in order to gather some information?"

"What do you mean, 'gather some information?'"

"For our intelligence services. I've been authorized to offer you twenty thousand francs."

M'greet folded her hands across her chest. "That is not very much money."

He rubbed one of the sides of his mustache until the gap above his lip was no longer perfectly aligned with the part in his hair. "Well, there could be more, but you would have to prove your worth."

"I ask of you again, Herr Kroemer, what exactly would you have me do?"

"Just listen. Make some contacts in your usual way. I hear you have a knack for captivating officers. Get them to talk and then report what they say back to us."

Flattered, M'greet decided to play along. "How will I contact you?"

"You will send a letter to the Hôtel de l'Europe in Amsterdam. I have a suite there. You may address it to Kroemer—my surname is quite common so it should not arouse suspicion. You will sign it H-21."

"H-21?"

"Your code name."

M'greet's jaw dropped. Up till now she hadn't been taking Kroemer's offer very seriously, though she had to admit the money would have been nice.

Kroemer produced three small vials from his pocket, two of which were filled with a chalky-white liquid, and set them on the table. "You will write a letter full of meaningless gossip, but write your real messages regarding troop movements and the like in between the lines with this one." He moved a vial labeled with the number 2 on it forward. The liquid, in contrast to the others, was an emerald green, the color of absinthe. "You will use number one to dampen the paper, and the third to cause the messages to disappear."

She held up her hands. "I don't know. Invisible inks—disguises in general—are not my style."

Kroemer gave a cruel laugh. "Disguises not your style? Are you not in fact Margaretha Zelle-MacLeod, a Dutch citizen, giving the people," his voice dropped, "the false impression that you are Mata Hari, a Javanese princess?"

"But that—"

"Is exactly why we wish to hire you." He swept the vials toward her edge of the table. "Take them. Use them. Once again, we can increase your payment once you prove your worth as a spy." He stood and replaced his hat, dropping a pile of francs on the table. "That's ten thousand to start. You will get the other half when you get back from Antwerp."

"Antwerp? I intended to go to Paris."

"In time," Kroemer responded. "You will report to Antwerp for training." He gave her further instructions, including how to get to the Belgian city. "You will enjoy meeting Fräulein Doktor," he added. "Like you, she is a strong, worldly woman."

M'greet showed him to the door. He left with the impression that she would do as he asked, and she didn't want to contradict him.

After she'd shut the door behind him, she resumed her spot on the couch. Could she really be a spy? She'd never proclaimed loyalty to either side. Like Holland, she considered herself neutral. But of course, she'd always loved Paris. And there was the fact that the Germans had stolen her goods at the outbreak of this infernal war. She sat up and counted the money. While it was in no way a full reimbursement for all that Germany had taken from her, at least it was a good start.

CHAPTER 28

ALOUETTE

MARCH 1915

The startled expression on Captain Ladoux's face as she knocked on his open door amused Alouette.

"Back again so soon?" he asked.

She sauntered into the room and took a seat in front of his desk. "Yes, Captain, I've returned because, as the Yankees say, I've made good." She put the pen and the vial of the German's secret ink on his desk and then draped her arm across the chair.

Ladoux held the bottle under his electric lamp. "What is this?"

"They call it 'collargolium.'"

"Interesting. We will have to send some to our chemists to see if we can find a reagent. And if so, we might just be able to decipher intercepted German correspondence." He set the vial down. "Who was the man who gave you this ink?"

Alouette straightened. "I never caught his name."

The twinge of regret must have been obvious in her voice, for Ladoux reached into his desk and retrieved an envelope, which he dumped in front of her. "These are photographs of known German agents in Madrid."

She fanned out the photos. "This is him." She picked one of them up and handed it to Ladoux. The photograph must have been an older one for both of his eyes were intact, but the narrow shoulders and gaunt face were the same.

"Ah, you've met the Baron von Krohn, the German naval attaché, nephew of General Ludendorff." He slid the rest of the pictures back into the envelope. "Excellent."

Alouette glowed at his praise. Her failures at becoming an airwoman and the fiasco in Switzerland forgotten, she relayed how her flirtations with the big German, Walter, had led her to Kraut and then finally to von Krohn. "I must state, Captain, that the Baron's manners were very poor. I had to make it quite plain that his advances would not be accepted."

Ladoux frowned and Alouette was once again pleased at his reaction. "I never want to see that brute again," she added.

He got to his feet and walked the length of the room, mindlessly puffing on a cigarette. Brushing ashes off his waistcoat, he paused in front of her. "You entered into our service voluntarily. It is too late for you to withdraw."

Alouette opened her mouth, but Ladoux held up his hand and continued. "You are a woman and must be guided by your instincts on how to deal with people who have amorous intentions toward you." He stood motionless for a moment, his hand still in the air. "This wasn't something I wanted to mention, but I heard stories about you, in Paris, before you met your husband."

The exhilaration Alouette had experienced since she returned from Spain quickly vanished; in its place was a sense of debilitating helplessness. Although she hadn't experienced it for many years, the feeling was all too familiar. "That's all they were, Captain, just stories." She dropped her arm from the back of the chair and quashed the feeling back down to the depths of her consciousness. "As you know, I am anxious to serve my country, to even give my life, if necessary, for France. But no *patriote francais* would expect me to pander to such an unpleasant, one-eyed creature."

Ladoux, who had restarted his pacing during Alouette's protest, paused again, his hands gripping the back of an armchair. "Don't you dare walk in here and tell me you never again wish to see the very man I want you to exploit for all you are worth."

Alouette bit back her rage and tried to keep her voice as calm as possible. "There are certain things, Captain Ladoux, to which no woman of honor can submit to under any circumstances."

Ladoux's expression softened and she thought she might have gotten through to him. He stepped forward and stuck his hands in his pockets. "Alouette," he said in a soothing, fatherly tone. "Think of the sacrifices of our poor *poilus* in the trenches. Or the plight of our fair Paris, which may be overrun by the enemy at any time. You have the priceless opportunity to serve our dear country more than any other Frenchwoman. Or," he added quickly, "many other Frenchmen."

He put a hand on her shoulder and Alouette resisted the urge to shrug him off. "For the sake of the Cause, don't say you will never see the Baron again. He's probably just an old philanderer, with an archaic German sense of civility. Humor him as such. Laugh and flirt with him, keeping him at arm's length while at the same time manipulating him into giving you information." He finally released her shoulder. "There are many lives to be saved by doing so."

"It is a sacrifice more bitter than death to have to submit to the dalliances of an old brute like von Krohn." she stated bitterly.

Judging by his triumphant smile, Ladoux knew that he had won. "A mere flirtation is harmless," he countered as he retreated behind the desk. "You are a woman with sufficient prowess to protect yourself if I am not wrong, which I don't believe for a second that I am. Von Krohn is the mastermind for the naval movements of all German submarines on the Atlantic coast. If you can succeed in discovering his plans, just think of all the French mothers and young brides you will be assisting by helping their boys to come home safely."

Alouette heaved a deep sigh. "Very well, Captain Ladoux."

Ladoux pulled out the desk chair to dig into a drawer. "I have some other business matters to attend to, but you can respond to the Baron's queries with this information. It is accurate although out-of-date, the same we supply to all double agents."

He left the room as Alouette dipped a pen into the inkwell. She followed von Krohn's instructions and wrote a letter full of nonsensical gossip to Madeline Stepino in Madrid. Between the lines, she used the collargolium-filled pen to answer the Baron's inquiries on French maneuvers as supplied by Ladoux. She held the paper up and blew on it, watching as the secret ink disappeared without a trace.

Alouette spent the remainder of the week taking a course in Spanish through the Berlitz School. Captain Ladoux was relentless in his encouragement for her to return to Spain. "You must hit the iron whilst it is hot," he repeated.

A postcard arrived from Spain with a coded demand for intelligence in regard to von Krohn's questionnaire. Alouette dropped it in front of Ladoux.

"Your letter has apparently been delayed by the postal services," he said, clearly unconcerned. "I've booked you on a train to leave in the morning."

"How will I further communicate with you from Spain?"

"You will write an ordinary note just as you do for the Germans, but use antipyrine in between the lines. It's the best we have right now, until we analyze the ink that von Krohn gave you."

"Antipyrine? For headaches?"

"Yes," Ladoux said with a touch of impatience. "If you are caught with it, you simply swallow it. Otherwise, dissolve a packet in two table-spoonfuls of water." He passed her the collargolium inkwell. "And now to place your advertisement according to the Baron's instructions."

As Alouette began her letter, someone knocked on Ladoux's office door.

"Ah, Monsieur Davrichachvili, come on in," Ladoux called.

"Zozo?" Alouette set her pen down to gaze at the tall man in the kit of the *Armée de l'Air*. "What are you doing here?"

He pulled a chair right next to her. "You look shocked, Alouette. Don't you like me in uniform?"

Alouette had met the fellow pilot a few times through Henri. Zozo had played some part in the Russian uprising in 1905 and self-exiled to France, giving up politics to become an aviator. He claimed to be an anarchist and his self-righteous declarations had always gotten on Alouette's nerves.

Ladoux did not seem surprised that they knew each other. "Monsieur Davrichachvili was the one who first alerted me to you, Alouette."

She turned to the younger man. "You told him I knew German spies?"

Zozo crossed his leg over the other, his knee nearly touching Alouette's. "What does it matter? Besides," he shot her a grin, "it's true now, isn't it?"

Ladoux cleared his throat. "Monsieur Davrichachvili will be the one feeding you false information to pass on to Baron von Krohn."

She returned her gaze to Zozo. He had a dark complexion, his mustache and beard purposefully trimmed to appear unruly. He seemed uncomfortable under Alouette's gaze and ran a hand through his wavy hair.

"You do realize he is an anarchist?" she asked Ladoux.

He shrugged. "A true revolutionary is rarely a traitor."

"I am putting my own life in your hands, then," Alouette stated. This made her more nervous than she dared to let on. Zozo was the type of young aviator who assumed that death waited for him each time he took flight and consequently lived a life—both on the ground and in the air—of excess.

Zozo threw up his hands. "You can trust me."

Ladoux lit a cigarette. "Monsieur Davrichachvili was on the trail of the woman you knew as Gerda Nerbutt."

"The Germans call her Fräulein Doktor," Zozo added. "But I lost track of her when I left Switzerland."

The hair on Alouette's arms prickled as she thought about Gerda. She found herself inexplicably hoping that Zozo wasn't aware of her colossal failure on that mission. "I'm sure she'll turn up."

"I don't quite share your enthusiasm," Zozo replied. "The German secret service has a mass of funds and they are able to conceal their spies just as quickly as we find their trail."

Ladoux flicked ash from his cigarette. "Monsieur Davrichachvili will dispatch the letters using the password, 'Skylark,' and, should we need to contact any of our Spanish operatives, they will address you with the same code name."

Zozo moved his hand through his hair once again. "Be careful, Alouette. You are now embarking on the most dangerous career of them all, that of *l'agent double.*"

CHAPTER 29

MARTHE

APRIL 1915

When spring came, with its floods and bone-chilling rain, the long war seemed to just become a long wait. Men stood for months in the trenches, which, from Marthe's patients' descriptions, were little more than open graves. As her new patient with the burned arm put it, "Forget trying to shoot Tommies. All the boys had to see was a mud wall and had to focus most of their effort on just keeping their feet dry."

"Tommies?" Marthe asked.

"The British," the man replied.

"Oh," Marthe replied, a bit inadequately, but she wasn't sure what else to say.

The German peered at her and then his eyes grew wide as if he suddenly realized something. "You are German, fräulein?"

"No. Belgian."

He raised his charred hand. "Doesn't it bother you to be bandaging a Hun such as me?"

Marthe snipped at the gauze with a pair of silver scissors. "I'm a nurse. It's my job to help you, no matter what side of the war you are on." She nodded at the door of the ward. "Not to mention this town, and therefore this hospital, belongs to Germany now."

"As will all of France soon," he said with an oily smile. "*Nach Paris! Nach Calais!*"

Marthe collected the stray bits of gauze without saying anything. The man reached out with his good hand and grabbed her arm. "You will see, fräulein, we will win this mighty war... and soon."

She usually didn't pay much attention when her patients started in with their German swagger, but the way this man spoke hinted that he had intimate military knowledge. She pulled her arm away, ostensibly to pour him a cup of water. "Are you a soldier?" He was dressed in dark gray pants and a collared shirt, not necessarily a uniform, but there were so many different regimentals in the Hun army that she couldn't possibly recognize all of them.

"No. A scientist." He looked for some type of reaction from Marthe, but she kept her face neutral. He continued, "The type of man for whom generals of old wouldn't hold more esteem than a cobblestone under their feet." He raised his chin. "With this new type of warfare, men like me are going to play their part in winning the most colossal war the world has ever known, even more so than the generals."

She set the water glass down and asked as casually as she could, "Is that so?"

"You will see, fräulein."

Having made her rounds, Marthe went outside to get some air and think over what the man had told her. He could have just been talking cocksure military nonsense, like a lot of her other soldier patients. But there was something else behind his comments, something sinister. What on earth would a scientist know about military victories? Despite the warm April sun, Marthe shivered.

The scientist was sleeping when Marthe went to check on him before leaving. *He must have fallen asleep working,* Marthe decided, picking up the papers that were scattered all over the bed. Of course she glanced through them before putting them back into the folder by his bedside. They appeared to be weather logs, and some sort of wind graph.

She again mulled over the conversation with the scientist as she walked home. It was still light out, and, as she passed the Grand Place, she could see Canteen Ma surrounded by laughing soldiers as she spoke her nearly unintelligible German. She had a pint glass in her hand and, upon sighting Marthe, drank the rest of the beer. "Fräulein," she slurred, waving her glass. "Fräulein, please get me some more of your fine beer!"

Playing along, Marthe shook her head and put her hand up to her ear, which succeeded in drawing Canteen Ma closer. She stumbled along the sidewalk, but her voice was clear as she whispered, "Marthe, there is something in the air. The Boches talk of sweeping victories coming, but none of them are clear on the specifics."

Marthe curled her lip, as if disgusted by the old woman, as she replied quietly, "I heard something similar this afternoon. What do you think they are planning?"

"I don't know." One of Canteen Ma's hangers-on whistled at her. She held up one finger before shoving the beer glass into Marthe's hands. "But we need to find out… and soon."

Marthe set out that night to inform Agent 63 of the bizarre weather graphs just in case British Intelligence had a better idea of what was afoot than her or Canteen Ma. It was, after all, her job to report anything out of the ordinary, and this indeed seemed to fit that description.

Canteen Ma delivered the British Intelligence's return message a few days later: "Do not worry about weather reports. Troop movements, trains, etc. are of more value." Marthe crumpled the message and threw it into the fire, feeling a bit foolish, like a girl making ghosts out of laundry drying on a clothesline.

The next morning, Marthe reported to the hospital to find it in an uproar. Orderlies were everywhere, escorting those civilian patients that could walk outside or ripping sheets off beds.

"Are we expecting a rush of patients?" Marthe asked the Oberarzt as he hurried by.

"Yes," he shouted in an unusually curt manner.

She joined the orderlies in preparing the now vacant civilian ward, surmising the evacuation of the non-combatants must mean that the Germans were making an advance on Ypres.

Not more than an hour later, the ambulances began to arrive. The workers unloaded dozens of men in light blue uniforms choking for breath, their features twisted in the most awful of ways. Some of them were grabbing at their throats and eyes, leaving long, bloody scratches down their cheeks and chest. The men's faces, hands, and even the brass buttons on their uniform had turned an unearthly green and the sickly smell of bleach clung to their clothes and skin. "What horror is this?" Marthe asked when she had time to speak.

The Oberarzt seemed as perplexed as her. "I'm not sure."

"How shall we treat them?"

He scratched at his beard. "Once again, I have no idea. Never in my career have such cases presented themselves." His voice choked over and Marthe's grudging respect toward the head doctor grew deeper. The suffering men were all Allies, clad in the uniforms of the French, English, even some Canadian. But, just as for Marthe, the Oberarzt's number one obligation was to cure people, not to choose allegiances. He knelt over a man who'd clearly lost his struggle to survive and, almost as a reflex, placed his stethoscope over the lifeless chest.

More and more men arrived, and the hospital quickly ran out of room for them. They lined the dying men in the corridors, and when those were full, put them outside in the garden.

"What has happened?" Marthe inquired of a man in a khaki uniform, British she assumed. He looked at her with eyes so swollen they appeared ready to pop out of their sockets, struggling as he tried to form words in his useless throat. Instead of speaking, he coughed into a nearby bush, covering the green leaves with bright red blood.

Marthe felt her knees grow weak. She would have given anything to run away from the horrifying sight of these decrepit men, but she also knew that they needed her. Besides, they were Allies. She steeled herself and continued working until a deep voice commanded, "Marthe, you have to take a few minutes to sit down and eat."

She glanced up to see Alphonse holding an unappetizing-looking black cake. "Rouler's war-time best," he said with a wry smile. He gazed around the packed courtyard before leading her to the back of the hospital near the civilian cabin.

"What do you make of all this?" Marthe asked Alphonse after she'd swallowed a few bites of cake, which was more palatable than it appeared. Or else she was just too hungry to care what it tasted like.

"The men at the front were talking about the Germans releasing metal cylinders, and a greenish gas floating in the wind toward the Allied trenches. And then everyone just started gasping for breath."

Marthe's hand shook, dropping black crumbs on the ground. "That scientist. The wind graphs and weather reports. This is what they were planning. No wonder he talked about a sweeping victory."

Alphonse's face was grave as he stood, holding a hand out for her. "This isn't good, Marthe."

"No," she agreed as he helped her up. "But I don't have time right now to think about the implications—I have to get back to work."

When they arrived back at the courtyard, they found that a congregation of people had formed just beyond the line of bushes. The people of Roulers had come to see the Allied soldiers' plight for themselves. As Marthe carefully stepped between wounded men, she heard a voice shout, "*Vive La France! Vive les Allies!*" Someone else took up the cry and soon every Belgian man and woman in the crowd was screaming at the tops of their lungs. Even those soldiers that could talk sat up and chanted "*Vive L'Angleterre!*" Marthe's heart swelled and she could see by the strange expression on Alphonse's face that he was experiencing something similar. She couldn't exactly join the chorus, as the Oberarzt and some orderlies stood nearby, their arms folded across their chests, but she repeated the chants in her head as she poured water for a patient.

The clatter of hooves sounded and then several mounted gendarmes appeared, shouting "*Raus hier!* Go!" Their horses neighed, startling the crowd. One of the gendarmes reared his steed, once again commanding the villagers to disperse. Which they did, but not before showering the wounded soldiers with cigarettes and chocolate.

The walk home that night was especially long for the exhausted Marthe. Otto and his two companions had recently returned from their mysterious trip to Paris and she passed the young lieutenant on the stairs as she went up to her room.

"Care to join me for a drink, fräulein?" he asked.

"Not tonight, Herr Otto," she replied.

He shot her a grin. Where once she had thought the uneven smile charming, now that she knew he was a spy-hunter, it seemed to mock her. It was part of his job to lure unsuspecting Belgian girls into confiding in him, but she would never trust a German.

"Is something the matter, Marthe?"

"No, nothing." She gave him a tiny curtsy before brushing past him. "I'm just tired from a long day at the hospital."

CHAPTER 30

ALOUETTE

MAY 1915

*V*on Krohn met Alouette at the Spanish frontier station of Irun. This time he wore a monocle over his glass eye. He took his hat off when he saw her; his skin was so thin on his nearly bald head she could clearly see the outline of his skull. As he bowed stiffly, she was nearly overcome with trepidation for the role she had accepted.

"I have rented a flat for you," he stated as he helped her into his car.

Her first thought was to run as far as she could, back to France if possible, but instead she folded her arms across her chest. "Was that necessary?"

Von Krohn seemed taken aback by the vehemence in Alouette's tone. He shifted his legs as best he could in the narrow backseat of the Mercedes. "At present it would be impossible for me to see you elsewhere."

His voice was matter-of-fact and Alouette did her best to echo his manner. "San Sebastian is too close to the French border. If I were to go to Madrid, I shall be less likely to attract attention."

It was obvious from his wry smile that he had no desire for her to accompany him to Madrid. After a moment of tense silence, he complimented her on the outfit she was wearing.

As Alouette was dressed in a plain traveling dress, she dismissed his comment with a wave of her hand. He countered with a joke about her hat. "Those feathers complement your skin tone much more than they could have on the bird they were taken from."

Alouette did not reply, and the silence resumed.

Finally he sighed. "You would like to go to Madrid, then? Well, we can take it under consideration later on. I have to stay in San Sebastian for at least another few weeks. Don't you fancy the beach there?"

"Have you received the letter I sent with replies to your inquiries?" she asked, determined to keep the conversation on business matters.

"No." His eyes widened. "When did you post it?"

Alouette was as aghast as von Krohn. "The day after I arrived in Paris." She turned to face him. "Do you think it was seized by the authorities?"

"Don't be afraid," he replied. "Even if it was confiscated, your countrymen will never be able to reveal the collargolium. We have some crack chemists in Germany who had to spend a long time before they succeeded in the perfect formula."

His attitude exasperated Alouette. "We have crack chemists in France, too."

He sniffed. "I'm not so sure about that."

Alouette looked out the window. The Mercedes was speeding along the coast and it was almost impossible to tell where the cloudless sky ended and the sea began. Her mind raced with questions. *Was it possible that Ladoux never sent the letter? What would be his reason not to?*

The car stopped in a small suburb outside of San Sebastian, next to an ordinary-looking house. A sturdy woman with brown hair streaked with gray greeted Alouette while the chauffeur carried her trunk into the apartment.

The Baron followed Alouette inside. The sitting room was decorated with Victorian bric-à-brac and rich curtains with an intricate floral pattern.

"Does it suit you?" von Krohn demanded.

Not in the least. It was too similar to the décor of Henri's house in Paris—the type of heavy fabrics and moldings that seemed to close

Alouette in. She feigned indifference with a shrug. "It doesn't matter. I shall spend most of my waking hours on the beach or in the casino."

Satisfied with her answer, he asked her to excuse him. "I have an appointment now. You can get settled in and I will return later, Alouette."

His use of her first name irritated her even further. "No. I'm going to change my dress and then go for a stroll."

His face fell, and she sighed, remembering Ladoux's instructions to captivate and manipulate him. She couldn't do that if she pushed the Baron away completely. "But if you like, I will meet you tomorrow morning at nine on the beach." She gave a wan attempt at a smile. "We can have a swim together."

He nodded and tipped his hat before he left.

Alouette excused the housekeeper, wanting nothing more than to be alone. She was exhausted from her journey and perhaps something else. She flopped down on the ornate satin couch with a sigh, causing dust particles to dance in the air.

The apartment smelled of old lavender and mustiness. She closed her eyes, willing herself to sleep, but instead she saw Henri's face. What would he think if he could see her now, serving a man such as von Krohn? Henri had always been so supportive of her adventures. *It's for France,* she emphasized, maybe for her husband's ghost, or maybe for herself. She could feel a tear coursing its way down her cheek. She wiped it away and got up to wander over to the window. As she pulled back the curtains, she was surprised to find the heavy drapes hid a gorgeous view of the ocean, but even that couldn't shake her feelings of melancholy.

The promise she had made to Ladoux haunted her as much as Henri's ghost. There were not many people she could trust—she wasn't even entirely confident in the people who proclaimed to be on her side. She was starting to realize that being a double agent was a terribly lonely occupation and supposed the secret service door would always remain shut against friendship and love alike.

Needless to say, that night was a sleepless one. Alouette rose at dawn, collected her luggage, and returned to the Hotel Continental.

The Baron was waiting for her at the beach the next morning.

"My stay in San Sebastian has begun under unpleasant auspices," Alouette told him, biting back the wave of nausea that accompanied her at seeing von Krohn in his short-sleeved, form-fitting swim outfit. "I had to clear out this morning from that flat."

"Oh, why is that?"

She thought of an explanation that might just get him to keep his hands to himself. "I realized my fiancé wouldn't like me staying in a house arranged by another man."

"A fiancé?" Von Krohn's face darkened and Alouette knew his mind raced with questions. Luckily he was too polite to demand why she hadn't mentioned this before now. "What is his name?" he asked instead.

The first man that came to mind was the quarrelsome, dark-eyed Slav she'd last seen in her boss's office. "Joseph Davrichachvili. But I call him Zozo. He is also an aviator."

"Is he aware of the role you have taken on regarding German intelligence?"

Alouette shook her head. "But given his status as an anarchist, I don't think he'd mind."

"I see," von Krohn said, in a tone that meant the opposite. "Where will you stay now?"

"The Hotel Continental."

His eyes grew even colder. "What a pity that you did not consult me first. The Hotel Continental is run by French people."

Alouette did her best to conceal the thrill of delight at knowing that he could not call on her there. She tore off her cover-up to reveal her striped swimming costume and ran toward the waves.

CHAPTER 31

M'GREET

JUNE 1915

*C*M'greet arrived by train to Antwerp. She had been to the city before in her travels, and always thought it charming—although one of the biggest cities in Belgium, it stubbornly clung to its small-town atmosphere. Her favorite part had always been Old Town, which, with its maze of narrow cobblestone alleys, made her feel she was walking back through time. Europe once thought Antwerp, with its ringed outer fortresses, impregnable, but the Germans had proved them wrong in the fall of 1914 and now they occupied the city.

Grand Central station was newly built, and even M'greet marveled at the domed steel roof. The heavy, Gothic-style interior and dark tile floor might have seemed gloomy, save for all the light that gleamed through the hundreds of ornate glass windows.

She walked outside into the sunlight and hailed a cab. As they drove through the suburbs, M'greet was shocked by what she saw. The little houses and pubs ringing the city had been razed to the ground and the only thing remaining of the once beautiful trees were blackened stumps.

"What happened here?" she asked the driver, gazing out at the barb-wire scarred, desolate landscape. "Was it the zeppelins?"

"No, mevrouw. The Belgians did it themselves. They wanted to give their guns and cannons a better shot at the invading Boches. Fat lot it did them." He stopped to let a group of soldiers in spiked helmets cross the street. M'greet couldn't help but notice how similar the soldiers looked to each other: their uniforms impeccable, they were all about the same height and wore the same grim frown.

Half an hour later, the driver pulled up in front of a rundown castle. "What is your business here?" he asked, staring out at the ancient stone wall that snaked around the building.

"Just…" M'greet was at a loss for words. What was her business here? Kroemer had mentioned something about spy training. "It's a hospital," she replied finally.

It was clear from the look on the driver's face he didn't believe her.

"My trunks." M'greet snapped as she opened the cab door.

He threw them at her feet and drove off. She decided to leave her luggage inside the gate and walked toward the massive fortification. The iron knocker creaked in protest when she attempted to use it. She waited a few minutes, wondering if the sound could even penetrate the immense wood door. She reached up to knock again, but put her arm down as she heard the door start to open.

"*Ja?*" demanded a man's voice. The door and the shadows from the interior obscured his face.

Having forgotten her instructions, M'greet stated that she was there on the request of Karl Kroemer.

He opened the heavy door wider with little effort. "Kroemer?" The voice belonged to a stocky man in a German officer's uniform.

"Bring her in," a woman commanded. "We've been expecting the famous Mata Hari."

The crumbling appearance of the exterior belied the interior, M'greet discovered as she walked into a large anteroom full of modern military gear, uniforms, and maps. "I have some bags outside," she told the officer. He nodded and left.

The woman stepped forward. "H-21. Welcome." She was tall and thin, her face as taut as the chignon that held her blonde hair.

M'greet could feel the woman's steely eyes boring into her and she met them steadily.

"*Sich hinsetzen*," the woman commanded in a sharp voice.

M'greet sat. "How long will I be staying here?"

"You will be here until I am satisfied you can serve in the field," the woman replied, flexing her fingers, which were adorned with jeweled rings.

"Mademoiselle—" M'greet began.

"*Fräulein*," she corrected. "You may refer to me as Fräulein Doktor."

"Fräulein Doktor," M'greet thought hastily, trying not to insult the woman. Something told her that the Fräulein did not tolerate being asked the wrong question. "Are you in… charge here?"

She turned narrowed eyes on M'greet. "My duties include the instruction of new recruits, securing the lines of communication between our agents and headquarters, and debriefing any agents arriving back from the field. Does that answer your question?"

"Yes, quite. Thank you," M'greet added.

Fräulein Doktor frowned as the officer walked in, pulling a trunk with each hand, the leather straps of her handbags crossing at his chest, the bags adding girth to his fat hips.

She lit a cigarette. "Your first lesson, H-21, is that a spy should not draw undue attention to themselves. Traveling with so much baggage is inadvisable. You will learn to get by with fewer accoutrements." She took a long drag. "Spying is a science. It is not an adventure to be undertaken for tawdry pleasures or quick money."

M'greet opened her mouth to say something, but shut it as Fräulein Doktor continued, "You must rest now as tomorrow we will begin your intensive training." She nodded to the officer, who picked up M'greet's bags once again and began heading down the hall slowly.

M'greet, unsure what else to do, curtsied to the Fräulein before following the officer.

"Is the Fräulein a medical doctor?" M'greet asked the officer in a hiss. Even though they were out of earshot, something told M'greet that there were hidden microphones throughout the castle.

"No. She was one of the first women in Germany to earn a doctorate—in sociology."

"Oh," M'greet replied as the officer suddenly halted. His hands full, he kicked the door open.

M'greet, expecting to find a room worthy of a castle, let out a cry of disdain. "Are these my sleeping quarters?"

"Yes. Yours and Fräulein Benedix."

"I am to have a roommate?" M'greet could barely fit into the sparsely furnished room as it was, let alone with another person.

"Indeed." He rid himself of his burden, putting the handbags down on the rusted wire-framed bed.

"Who is this Benedix woman?" M'greet demanded.

He shrugged. "Another recruit."

Fräulein Benedix arrived later that same night, but M'greet had already fallen asleep on the hard bed, and didn't meet her roommate until morning. M'greet was awoken by the sound of her rummaging through her suitcase at what seemed like the crack of dawn.

Fräulein Benedix must have sensed M'greet stirring, as she turned with a friendly smile. M'greet noted that her coloring was similar to her own, but her bunkmate was much shorter.

"Clara," Fräulein Benedix said, extending her hand.

M'greet shook it and introduced herself.

"Oh," Clara's mouth formed a bow. "You're Mata Hari, aren't you?"

She nodded.

"I've heard so much about you. I too am a dancer."

"Is that so?" M'greet stretched her arms over her head. "I don't think I've ever heard of you. Where have you performed?"

Clara waved her hand. "Nowhere you've ever heard of, and nowhere near the famous halls you are familiar with."

M'greet glanced out the window. "The sun has not even risen yet."

"Yes, but we must be at breakfast in five minutes. The Fräulein's orders." She retrieved a comb from her bag and ran it through her hair.

M'greet heaved a deep sigh. "I'm not sure I could get ready in that short amount of time."

Clara stopped combing. "And risk the Fräulein's wrath? I'm not sure you want to do that."

M'greet pictured the monstrous frown that would surely appear on the blonde-haired woman's drawn face. "You're right." She threw back the covers on her bed. "Mind if I borrow your comb?"

After a meager breakfast, the recruits assembled in the anteroom. Besides Clara and M'greet, there were two males and two other women who appeared to be sisters. In contrast to the German soldiers M'greet saw on the street the other day, these men looked nothing alike: one was tall and thin, the other short and fat. The other two females were of medium height, both with dark hair and blue eyes and introduced themselves as Julia and Maria Manzanarés, proving that they were indeed sisters. The thought occurred to M'greet that none of them, herself included, looked like spies.

Fräulein Doktor entered carrying a riding whip with an ivory handle. She paused in front of them and smacked the whip on a table. "Silence!"

The other recruits stopped their chit-chat and looked up.

A diamond cigarette holder was pinched between the Fräulein's first two fingers and it, along with the myriad of jewels that covered her hand, caught the sunlight and threw sparkling reflections all over the stone walls of the anteroom. *So much for not attracting attention.*

The Fräulein ashed the cigarette holder with a graceful flick. "Today's lesson will be how to detect other spies, both those that work for our side and the enemy. This could quite possibly save your lives." She paced up and down the room as she spoke, occasionally shooting her new recruits looks that sent shivers up and down their spines.

"You must play up on the French spies. The English ones are respectable and undergo equally rigorous training, but the people employed by France are inexperienced and easy to turn into *Doppelagenten.*"

Double agents, M'greet translated. Unused to being intimidated— which she certainly was, by the surrounding stone walls of the immense castle, by the military paraphernalia scattered throughout, and especially by the Fräulein—half of M'greet wanted to run for the Belgian hills, but the other half was determined to make the Germans pay for the property they had stolen.

The Fräulein made them memorize a script to recite whenever they fell upon a suspected spy before calling upon M'greet and Clara to act it out.

"*Wie denkst du über das Vaterland?*" Clara asked in a loud, clear voice.

How do I feel about the Fatherland? Not very well, considering they took all of my furs at the beginning of the war. Which begs the question: what am I doing here? M'greet got so lost in her own thoughts that she forgot the next lines.

"*Ich bin mir nicht sicher,*" was M'greet's reply. I am not sure. She repeated the first line, asking in turn how Clara felt about the Fatherland.

"*Nein!*" Fräulein Doktor shouted, banging her whip on the nearest table. She waited for the sound to finish reverberating around the room before she said in her high, pinched voice: "Those are not the lines, H-21. You must stick to regulations, and never, ever improvise."

M'greet's rational brain told her to beg for forgiveness, but, as usual, her impetuousness won out. "I've been improvising all my life. I am an entertainer."

The Fräulein marched over and stood in front of her, her whip held between crossed arms. "Are you that stupid, woman, to contradict me?"

M'greet raised her chin and was about to argue, but logic won this time. "No, fräulein," she mumbled, avoiding those steely gray eyes.

"Again!" the Fräulein commanded, stomping a boot for lack of a nearby surface upon which to smack her whip.

This time M'greet managed to get it right.

CHAPTER 32

MARTHE

JUNE 1915

Summer had come to Roulers. Although the faint sounds of machine guns were ever-present, the equally ubiquitous bird songs somehow managed to mitigate some of the horrors of war. Stray shells still occasionally soared over the town, but they usually exploded in the air above or plunged into empty fields.

For once since the war started, Marthe felt surprisingly light-hearted. In May, the Germans had made the mistake of sinking the *Lusitania*. There were many U.S. citizens aboard, and all of Europe was holding their breath that America would soon join the Allies.

When Canteen Ma delivered a new message: "Take care: counter-espionage being strengthened throughout Belgium. Trust no one," Marthe crumpled the message in her hand before tossing it into the flames of the kitchen stove. The Germans were always tightening their counter-espionage measures and since she had come this far, there was no sense in worrying over something she had no control over.

That night was yet another busy one at the hospital, but, during a much-needed break, Marthe overheard two orderlies state that several hundred troops were to be billeted at an old brewery on the outskirts of town. This was an unusual development: most of the time soldiers were quartered in civilian homes in pairs or threesomes before going off to the front. Such a concentration in one place would make an excellent target for the "Seven Sisters"—a group of British planes that occasionally dropped bombs over Roulers. To many of the oppressed Belgian citizens, the Seven Sisters were a welcome sight, even though the Allied planes often flew low and positioned their machine-guns on anything within their targets.

It was nearly midnight when Marthe set out to deliver the news to Agent 63. She was just across from the window when she heard footsteps in the alleyway, so she crouched down in a doorway, doing her best to hide in the shadows.

Had she been followed? The slip of paper tucked into her bun, on which she had printed the brewery information, felt warm, as if it could spontaneously combust and set her hair on fire.

The footsteps grew closer and a vague figure paused in front of the fifth window. Marthe relaxed her stance, thinking it must be a fellow agent dropping off their own message. Indeed, she watched as the figure knocked on the window in the same sequence she used: three taps, a pause, then two more. She assumed it was safe to come out of her hiding place, but something inside prevented her from doing so.

The window slid open without a sound, just the same as it always did for her, and a white, outstretched hand appeared in the moonlight. But then the shadowed figure pulled something from its belt. A red flash and a booming sound interrupted the silent night. The sound echoed through the narrow alley walls before Marthe heard a strangled cry and an even more disturbing thud.

The figure located an abandoned crate and put it below the window before climbing into the apartment.

Marthe had no recourse but to sit there, crouched in the shadows. *Agent 63 had been discovered. Agent 63 had been murdered.*

She waited for at least half an hour, maybe more. She wasn't sure whether she wanted the dark figure to reappear, but it did not. Finally she rose, her knees stiff, and left the alleyway.

The walk home in the dead of night from Agent 63's window, while never pleasant, was the worst Marthe had ever experienced. She feared that a policeman lurked at every intersection with a rifle aimed straight at her heart. This was the penalty of espionage. This was what Canteen Ma had tried to warn her about.

When at last she was secure in her own bedroom and able to close her eyes against the terror of being caught, all she could see was Agent 63's white hand reaching out to the murderer. The last thing on her mind before she succumbed to a restless sleep was: now how she was going to pass on the information about the soldiers billeted at the brewery?

Mother remarked in the morning that Marthe must not have slept well.

"No," she admitted.

"What is it?" Mother asked. Marthe never told her mother the minute details of what she had been doing. Of course her mother knew that her daughter was a spy, but not the full extent. Now Marthe confided about Agent 63's death, expecting that Mother would persuade her to quit the espionage game altogether.

"What message were you trying to get to Agent 63?" she asked instead.

Marthe filled her in on the brewery.

"Perhaps I could run into Canteen Ma in the Grand Place this morning. The café is always in need of fresh fruit."

"You? You would take the message to Canteen Ma?" Marthe asked incredulously.

"With Agent 63 gone, you will need to find a new form of communication."

Marthe gave Mother the tiny piece of paper. "Just get as close as you can to her and slip this into her hand when no one is looking."

Mother nodded.

On the way to the hospital, Marthe mused over Agent 63's death, expecting every minute for the name Marthe Cnockaert to be called, a forcible hand to be placed on her shoulder, a man calling for her doom to appear.

As soon as Marthe walked in through the hospital doors, an orderly rushed up. "Fräulein Cnockaert, the Oberarzt wants to see you in his office."

Marthe's knees felt weak as she made her way down the hall. In her recollection, the Oberarzt had never once commanded her presence in his office. A buzzing began in the back of her forehead, which made its way to the front of her scalp when she saw the Town-Kommandant also waited for her. As this was probably the end of her spying career, and possibly her life, she hoped Mother would be able to pass on the brewery information.

The Oberarzt stood up from his desk and came over to greet her with an unexpected smile. "Congratulations, Fräulein Cnockaert."

Marthe, suddenly aware of her open mouth, closed it dumbly. *Was this a joke?*

The Town-Kommandant also stood. "His Royal Highness, the King of Württemberg, has graciously awarded you the reverent Iron Cross for all of your fine work and dedication to this hospital."

Marthe sank into a chair.

The Oberarzt coughed as the Town-Kommandant held out a black and white ribbon with a silver-trimmed black cross. Marthe rose and stood at attention as he hung it on her neck. "The Fatherland is proud of the work you've done."

She nodded, touching the black cross, which felt hot in her hand.

"Thank you, Herr Kommandant," she replied, longing to take the heavy necklace off as soon as possible.

Otto approached her that night. He glanced shiftily around the lounge before asking if she'd come with him to his room.

"That wouldn't be proper," Marthe replied.

"I need to speak to you about a serious matter." His gaze refused to meet hers, and Marthe could feel the blood drain from her face. Was this the moment she'd been waiting for since that shot rang out in the alleyway last night? Wordlessly she trailed him up the stairs.

Otto seemed somewhat more at ease with the door shut. He pulled a chair very close to the lone lamp before offering Marthe the chair and a cigarette. She politely refused the cigarette as she sat down, the lamp heating her cold face. Otto hunkered in the corner, his profile hidden in shadow.

She waited for the interrogation to begin, but Otto said, unexpectedly, "I've heard good reports of you, Marthe. Congratulations on earning the Iron Cross. How do you feel about the chance to earn an even greater distinction?"

News in the German espionage system travels fast. She knew that he could see every little nerve play out on her face, so Marthe proceeded with caution. "What is it you would have me do?"

"I have knowledge that there are at least three spies against Germany here in Roulers. One of them, a woman, was shot last night."

So Agent 63 was indeed a woman. She tried to meet his gaze, but his eyes were merely glints of steel in that dark corner he'd chosen.

What was Otto thinking? Could he have been the shadowy figure in the alleyway last night? She nearly startled visibly as the miserable thought struck that Otto had followed her home. She attempted to compose herself, fearing that he could hear her heartbeat from across the room. "Who are these people you suspect?" Even Marthe was surprised by how calm her voice sounded.

He tilted his head toward the light, looking like a boy who was proud of having a secret from his mother. "I shall have to reserve that to myself, Marthe."

"How can I assist you, then?"

"The Higher Command is aware that there is a rebel underground intelligence system operating here in Roulers. There are a few people whose confidence I would like you to gain."

"You want me to find proof that these people are spies."

He waved his hand. "Not necessarily proof. Just let me know if you see or hear of them doing anything suspicious."

"You are asking me to act as an agent of the German government."

"Not an agent. Just an aid. Marthe," he picked up his chair and moved it closer to her. "You are a very intelligent girl. Many people trust you." He reached a hand out to touch her hair. "Not to mention very pretty."

Marthe cringed inwardly. Her first thought was to flee the room, but she didn't want him to think it was because of his proposal. She faked a yawn instead, stretching out her arms and pulling her hair away from his fingers. "It's late," she said, standing. "I shall give what you said much thought and let you know my decision tomorrow."

"Good night and sweet dreams, *meine liebe fräulein.*" He opened the door for her.

As he closed it, Marthe clenched her hands into fists. She raised one of them, picturing it connecting with the fine bones of Otto's face. *What was he thinking?* Without knowing it, he had just proposed for her to become a double agent.

Marthe once again had a hard time sleeping. How could she possibly get out of the situation Otto had put her in? She decided her best recourse was to dig up some sort of information: something the Germans would look upon as valuable, but innocuous enough that it would not further endanger her allies. Finally she fell asleep, dreaming of being placed in front of a German firing squad.

Three nights later, Marthe was awakened just after midnight to the sound of incoming planes. She rushed to the window to see the "Seven Sisters" heading north. The German's anti-aircraft searchlights occasionally caught one of them in their lights. Soon the screeching of bombs was heard. Several explosions followed, then the screaming from the bombs turned into human screaming. Marthe got out of bed and hurriedly dressed and then headed to the hospital.

The hallways were filled with wounded soldiers, and blood appeared to seep from everywhere: the soldiers themselves, the mattresses, it even seemed to stem from the wall. Marthe threw herself into her work, trying to do anything to distract herself from thinking that she was the cause of all of this human wreckage.

It was nearly noon when she returned home in her ruined nursing uniform. Otto was sitting on the steps outside the café, smoking a cigarette.

"Marthe," he called upon seeing her. "That bombing of the brewery was the result of someone in this town reporting the billeted soldiers' location to the Allies. Such vermin deserve the same treatment as this cigarette," he added as he repeatedly stabbed it into the sidewalk before crushing it with his boot.

She didn't say anything as she stared at the black stain he'd left on the concrete.

"You will help me catch this spy, won't you, Marthe? I want you to report back to me in a week's time."

He walked inside the café, leaving her on the sidewalk, pondering what to do. After all, it was she, with the help of her mother and Canteen Ma, who had informed the Allies of the location of the soldiers. But maybe she could find a way to pin it on one of their secret detectives, a false safety-pin man, one of the men who made the lives of Roulers' civilian population so miserable.

A few days later, Otto grabbed her arm as she tried to pass him on the stairs. "Have you any news for me, Marthe?"

She shook her head. "Not yet. I need more time."

He peered into her face. "I should think you have had ample time to at least develop an inkling into who is helping these underground activities." He must have detected the fear in her expression for he grasped her hand and rubbed his thumb over her palm. "Do not be afraid, Marthe. Not a soul in Roulers will know of the work you are doing for us. You can trust us, especially me." He dropped her hand as though it were a hot plate. "I have always liked you, and I do not wish to make myself unpleasant to you." With that, he turned and hurried down the stairs.

Marthe continued to her room. Once there, she flung herself on the bed. She was no surer what to do now than she was when Otto had first hatched his terrible plan. Gradually she became aware of a bird's chirping and looked up to see a fat robin just outside her window. He kept up his trilling, as if he had not a care in the world. *I wish I could say the same.*

A gunshot rang out and the bird flew away. Marthe opened the window to see what the commotion was. A man in plain clothes was shooting at pigeons across the Grand Place. She narrowed her eyes in annoyance, but then smiled as an idea occurred to her.

She sat down at her little table and wrote a series of letters and numbers on a slip of paper, bigger than what she would normally have delivered to Agent 63.

Before Marthe left work the next day, she took the slip of paper and rubbed it across a piece of raw meat in the kitchen until the paper was good and bloody. She then delivered it to Otto. "I obtained this from a Belgian man who wishes to remain anonymous," she told him. "He found it on a pigeon lying dead on the road to Ypres. Neither he nor I could decode it, but I'm sure your men would have that ability."

He snatched the paper from her hands and Marthe watched as he scanned it. "Without a doubt," he finally replied, meeting her eyes. "You've done well, Marthe. This will go straight to the cipher department—they can crack any code within 24 hours."

Marthe sighed with relief as Otto left, the message tucked into his pocket, dried blood and all. She'd just earned at least a day's break from his pestering, but, like a patient leaving a grueling hour at the dentist's knowing they'd have to finish the procedure soon, she knew her respite wouldn't last forever. Once Otto realized he'd been duped and the message was nonsense, he'd be back.

A few days later, as Marthe passed by the Grand Place on her way to work, she saw Otto talking to a man she knew to be a German detective. Otto waved to her and she paused. He nodded at the detective before approaching her.

"I just can't figure it out, Marthe. That paper you gave me—the coding department can't make heads or tails of it." He took off his cap and scratched his head. "Do you think that the paper could have been a trick?"

Although she'd been expecting this, Marthe's breath still caught in her throat. "What do you mean?"

"I mean, we've had the best code breakers in Germany examining this, and even they can't solve it. No Tommy could be good enough at coding to outsmart our experts."

Marthe shook her head. "I'm not sure."

He replaced his cap. "At any rate, keep your eye out. We'll get to the bottom of this."

Both of them looked up as a robin landed nearby and picked at something on the ground. Otto tipped his cap to her, his smile holding no warmth as he bid her goodbye and returned to the detective, who had been observing them from a few meters away.

Marthe continued on to the hospital, her heart heavy. Even the sight of Alphonse exiting the courtyard did nothing to lift her spirits.

He held the courtyard gate open for her. "Is something wrong, Marthe?"

A denial of anything amiss was on her lips, but then she hesitated. Alphonse was clearly loyal to the Cause, and she desperately needed to confide in someone. She tilted her head toward a corner of the courtyard and he followed her. Once they were sure no one was in earshot, she told him about Otto's proposal for her to become a double agent. "If something doesn't happen soon to help me out of this dilemma, I think I might go mad," she added.

Alphonse tightened his hands into fists. "How dare that Boche put you in this predicament." He took a deep breath and relaxed his body. "Let me think on a solution, and I will get back to you."

She placed her hand on his arm, which immediately stiffened again. "Thank you, Alphonse."

"No, thank you, Marthe, for your service. And please don't worry, I will figure out a way to get you out of this."

She watched him stroll away, feeling much better about the Otto situation.

Two days later, as Marthe made her way down stairs to the kitchen, she heard a heavy thump on the landing. Red Carl stood in the threshold of Otto's door, a canvas kit bag at his feet.

"Is Otto going away?" Marthe asked.

"He's gone, fräulein."

"Gone? What do you mean?"

"He's dead," was his only response.

Marthe first assumed that Alphonse had something to do with Otto's death, but he had been at the front the night Otto was murdered by two bullets passing through his brain.

"It wasn't me," Alphonse insisted when they had found a moment alone, again in the courtyard. "I passed by Canteen Ma in the Grand Place the afternoon you told me about Otto. I informed her of the situation you'd been put in, and she replied, "'There are several safety-pin men that would be interested to hear of this.'"

"Thank you, Alphonse." Marthe reached her hand out, but he stepped backward.

"Have I ever told you what I'm going to do once the war is over?" he asked.

Numbed by his unexpected brush-off, she shook her head.

"I'm going to become a priest." With that, he left the courtyard.

Marthe watched his tall frame walk away, wondering if he told her that to convince her that it couldn't have been he who killed Otto. Or if it was for some other reason altogether.

CHAPTER 33

ALOUETTE

JUNE 1915

$\mathcal{T}$he days at San Sebastian passed relatively peacefully: the Baron was often away on business and Alouette spent a lot of time relaxing at the beach, trying to avoid the nagging feeling that she was not making much headway at spying.

Finally von Krohn stated that he was to return to Madrid and this time he had no objection to her joining him.

He installed her in Madrid's Palace Hotel, reserving the best room for her. The hotel was only a few years old, and, as her porter informed her, the only one in Spain to have both a bathroom and a telephone installed in each of its 800 rooms.

She arrived in her new lodgings to find a large bouquet of roses waiting for her on the table. When she saw the card was signed by von Krohn, she tossed it into the garbage pail without reading the message.

"Something wrong, señorita?" the porter asked.

Alouette shook her head and went to the window, which looked out onto the tree-lined Paseo del Prado boulevard.

The porter bowed. "Good evening, señorita."

Alouette decided to ease her irritation at von Krohn by going for a walk to explore Madrid and changed into a walking dress.

As she passed through the hotel's ornate double doors, she noticed a policeman walking a beat directly outside of the hotel. She crossed the Paseo del Prado into the park and paused by a fountain with a statue of Apollo. Giving a quick glance over her shoulder, she was surprised to see that the policeman had followed her.

Alouette decided to keep walking, and when she reached the intersection of the Calle de Acalá and the Paseo de Recolotos, she turned her head right and left, feigning that she was lost. The policeman was a few feet behind, watching.

She summoned up the little Spanish she knew and called, "*Perdóneme, señor.*"

He gazed around before realizing she must be addressing him. "*Qué?*"

She asked him to point her to the Plaza Hotel. "I'm supposed to be meeting the Baron von Krohn, the German military attaché, there soon."

He blinked twice at the name before pointing to the large building right behind her.

"Gracias," Alouette replied before walking off.

Alouette found herself completely alone in this new city. As her Spanish was not very good, she did not have anyone to speak to except von Krohn.

When she complained about her loneliness to him, he decided that he would introduce Alouette to his wife. "She is quite anxious to meet you and I know that you two will get along splendidly."

Alouette was not so sure, but the Baron persuaded her to join them for lunch. "She wishes for you to procure some toiletries for her the next time you are in Paris."

Von Krohn's wife, Ilse, was much younger than Alouette had expected; she looked to be only a few years older than herself, a brunette who held herself in a dignified manner. Ilse was an heiress and the von Krohns could afford a lifestyle unique to most of the other Germans in the area. They were the only ones in the diplomatic service with a chauffeur and motor car. Alouette wondered why on earth she had married the odious Baron, unless it was just that she desired to be styled as a Baroness.

"Do you speak German?" Ilse asked in French.

"No, madame," Alouette answered.

"It is no matter," Ilse said. "I am glad of the opportunity to practice my French." To her husband, she spoke in German, which Alouette easily translated. "Hans, are you quite certain she does not know German?"

"*Nein*," von Krohn returned.

"Well, if you want to know for sure, I know a way." She held out her hand to Alouette. "My husband and I are hosting a little dinner party tomorrow night. We would love it if you could come."

Dressed in a beaded navy-blue gown, Alouette arrived at von Krohn's house at the allotted time, but the guests were already seated. It seemed to her that their expressions were spiteful as they exchanged furtive glances with one another. Neither the Baron nor his wife introduced Alouette to anyone, and she took her seat at the end of the table with a sense of foreboding that they had been gossiping about her before she arrived.

There were thirteen guests at the table, Alouette noted, a mixture of German officers and some affluent-looking Spanish couples. As the soup was served, she tried to converse with the man on her right, a fat German with equally chubby hands sprinkled with dark hair.

"French people have a sort of holy terror of the number thirteen," she said in her native language.

"Oh, is that so?" His French accent was atrocious.

"Yes. If my mother were here, she would either make someone get up from the table or else invite the butler to dine with us."

"Are you afraid of death?"

Alouette, taken back by his abruptness, replied, "If that were so, I never would have been an airwoman."

The eyes of her companions focused on her. She expected to hear praise, or at least a few questions about her feats, but there was only silence which Alouette was desperate to fill. "This soup is quite tasty."

One of the officers turned to von Krohn and said in German, "God will punish England for entering this war." He spoke with the guttural accent typical of his countrymen. "When we have won, we shall make England a colony."

"Those French are utterly incomprehensible to me," the German with the hairy hands added. He glanced at Alouette, but she focused on her soup, once again pretending not to comprehend a word these brutes said. "They continue fighting for the English, knowing full well that they have not the faintest chance at success."

"What's more," added the original speaker, "the latest bulletins state that the French are surrendering, preferring to be prisoners of war than to fight. But we have no room for them in our camps, and head-quarters have ordered that they all be killed."

A man with a bulbous nose seated next to the Baroness spoke up. "The French are cowards. Their degenerate race is worn out by loath-some diseases, carried by their women, who are all harlots."

Alouette fought back the impulse to spit in their faces. Despite having no appetite, she forced herself to eat. Toward the second course, the German with the bulbous nose roared in German, "How long will it be before she shows the first symptoms?"

"Half an hour or so," von Krohn replied.

"She appears calm," the fat German said. "She would not be so calm if she was aware of the horrible death awaiting her."

Alouette willed her expression to not reveal her bewilderment. *It's only a loathsome trick they are playing to get me to admit I speak German.* She took a sip of water.

As the dessert and coffee were served, the young man on Alouette's other side seemed to take pity on her. "I too am an airman. What sort of plane did you fly?" he asked in French.

"A Caudron. I knew the inventor."

"Pity he died in that accident."

"Yes," Alouette agreed sadly. "A pity indeed."

She could feel the Baron's eyes on her and glanced up. His expression was stony as he said, "Madame Richer, you look quite tired."

"I am." She delicately wiped at her mouth before setting the napkin down.

"She can't be that tired. I'm sure there's some man waiting in her hotel bed," the bulbous-nosed German stated.

Von Krohn stood. "Gentlemen, should we retire into my office for a cigar?" He nodded at Alouette, giving his permission for her to leave the disastrous dinner party.

She had passed their hateful test.

The Baron met her the next day. "You are being followed by one of the German Embassy's military attachés. A man by the name of Major Arnold Kalle."

"What? Aren't you employed by the German secret service?"

"Yes," von Krohn stated with barely concealed impatience. "But Kalle is upset because I never give him information about my department."

"I had no idea that the Germans exercised such pettiness when it comes to espionage." The full meaning of his statement finally settled in. "What should I do? Can't you get this man recalled back to Germany?"

He sighed. "I don't have any solid proof. One day, one of my agents, a Frenchman, drowned under mysterious circumstances outside of San Sebastian. But I have nothing but my suspicions."

Alouette was silent as she contemplated this. She had no one to protect her, and it seemed that even von Krohn was unwilling to advise her. They walked to the Puerta del Sol Square, where the Baron took his leave of her, stating that he had errands to run. He looked deliberately at a motor car with a Spanish license plate as he did so.

Alouette headed back to the hotel, noting that the car followed slowly behind her, pulling off the street while she waited on a corner. Glancing behind her, she could see the shadowy figures of two men, but the bright sunlight prevented her from discerning much else.

It was tea time when Alouette returned. She sat in the corner of the hotel bistro by herself and flipped through a magazine to hide her agitation. Presently, a trio was seated at the table next to her. Alouette noticed the *Legion d' Honneur*, a medal recognizing the highest military honor, pinned to the suit of one man.

"You are French?" Alouette asked after the men were seated.

"*Oui*," replied the man wearing the *Legion d' Honneur*. "I am General Denvignes, military attaché to the French Embassy."

Alouette introduced herself.

"Will you be staying in Madrid long?" Denvignes asked.

She longed to confide in her fellow countryman about her true purpose in Spain, but Alouette steeled herself not to say anything compromising. "I'm not sure. Possibly till the end of the war." She smiled politely, but her grin faded as she caught sight of two men entering the room. She narrowed her eyes, surmising that they were the same men from the car that had followed her earlier. Were they French, German, Spanish, or another nationality all together?

She rose, bidding adieu to General Denvignes and his companions, before leaving the tea room. She headed back out onto the Paseo del Prado. As she predicted, the two men exited the hotel behind her. One of them, a tall young man dressed in an expensive suit, approached her. "Madame, will you be so good as to read this letter and give me an answer as soon as possible?" His accent was that of a posh Briton.

"Is there a return address on it?"

"Yes, madame."

Alouette felt uneasy as she accepted the letter. As soon as the men entered their car, she went back into the hotel.

The letter carried the address of the English Intelligence Department.

Alouette put it down on the desk with a sigh, thinking that a double agent must always be on the alert. A kindly invitation could be the first step toward a firing squad. She decided to pay a call on von Krohn.

The servant who answered the door delivered her straight into the Baron's office. The Baroness was also in there and had a look of feigned concern as Alouette displayed the letter to von Krohn. It seemed to Alouette that the Baroness's interest was not so false after all, and she wondered if she had indeed been set up.

Von Krohn sighed. "You must return to Paris straightaway," he told Alouette.

The baroness clapped her hands delightedly. "I will make you a list of things I would like you to bring back for me," she called before rushing out of the room.

Alouette sat in her seat. "Paris? Why?"

"I think it's best if you are away from here for a while."

"Am I in danger?"

"No, nothing of the sort. At least I don't think so. I just think you should leave Madrid for a few days, maybe a fortnight."

"Are you trying to get rid of me?"

"Of course not." Von Krohn gave a hollow laugh. "I'm just trying to protect you."

Alouette rose.

"I'll see you in a fortnight," von Krohn stated.

CHAPTER 34

MARTHE

Something unusual was happening in Roulers. There was a curious air of activity among the Germans, although not like that which preceded the poisonous gas attacks of the spring. It seemed as though all of the Germans had gone mad with cleanliness. The regular army's uniforms were new, their brass buttons catching the sunlight, their boots polished to perfection, and even their equipment lost its battered appearance. Non-combatant personnel were ordered to the hospital and spent their days polishing the floors until they shined like glass and using rags tied to long poles to expunge cobwebs and dust from the ceilings.

As Marthe passed the civilian cabin, she saw a familiar figure on the porch.

"Alphonse," she called, momentarily forgetting about the awkwardness of their last encounter.

He lifted a rag and waved at her.

"What are you doing?"

"Cleaning."

Marthe came onto the porch, where Alphonse was occupied in

rubbing an aluminum tub. "Why?"

"Don't know." He rubbed at a non-existent spot on the sparkling tub. "Do you think that's good enough?"

"It's like a mirror," she said as the aluminum caught the light from the dimming sun.

He sat back on his knees. "That's what I thought last night. I came in from a heavy day spent in the ambulance, under fire, mind you, and the hospital sergeant told me to scrub out this tub. When I presented it to him, he told me I'd done a terrible job, called me an idler, and then boxed me round the ears. So here I am, cleaning again."

"Why does everything need to be so immaculate all of a sudden?"

Alphonse threw his rag down. "I'm not sure, but something is definitely happening. The troops in Roulers are all being told similar things." He looked up at Marthe, his green eyes filled with worry. "I'm going to get to the bottom of this, just as soon as I finish up here."

She nodded, noting as she hurried home the hue of the verdant grass in the setting sun was not unlike the color of Alphonse's eyes.

A few days later, Marthe was grabbing bandages from the supply cart when a voice whispered in her ear, "The Kaiser will be in Brussels next week and then is due to pay a visit to Roulers after."

She nearly dropped her kit before turning to see Alphonse. "The Kaiser?" she repeated, a bit too loudly. She rubbed at the back of her neck, feeling the hairs standing up from Alphonse's proximity. Both gazed up and down the hallway, but luckily no one was in earshot.

"Yes," Alphonse answered. "Can you find out the date and time?"

She nodded.

Marthe went through the motions of nursing that day, her mind occupied by the information Alphonse had delivered. She might have guessed that these intense preparations could only be for the Kaiser himself. But how would she get reliable information about such a sensitive subject?

Suppose I could bring about his death. The thought occurred to her at lunch. If it were the Emperor of Germany that had brought this scourge upon them, would ending his life mean ending the war? And who in Roulers would be able to supply the vital information?

Canteen Ma called at the door early the next day. She handed Marthe the weekly vegetables before slipping a pincushion into her hand. Marthe headed to her room and ripped open the message hidden in the cushion:

"The Kaiser arrives in Roulers the latter half of next week for an inspection. Need the time and date etc. to inform Allied aircraft."

So British Intelligence knew no more than Marthe.

Soon polished officers with tight waistcoats flooded the streets of Roulers with their fancy cars. The General Staff arrived and began barking orders, making sure the heel-clicking of the marching soldiers was loud enough to be heard in Ypres. Their incessant commands to make sure everything was satisfactory for the mighty war-lord put everyone in a bad mood, including Marthe, who was no closer to finding out information on the Kaiser's visit.

A steely-eyed staff colonel visited the hospital, and the Oberarzt asked Marthe to show the officer around. When Marthe walked into the main office, the colonel rose, clicked his heels together and bowed.

"If you will excuse me, Colonel," the Oberarzt said, his manner as deferential as always, "a number of cases have been brought to the hospital and my presence is needed in the operating theater."

"It is no problem," the colonel replied, rubbing at his fair mustache. He nodded at Marthe. "After you, fräulein."

The colonel followed as she began the tour. "Everything is so spotless," he commented upon seeing the German ward. "You must spend every minute you are not with patients cleaning. I suppose if you run out of dinner trays, the patients wouldn't mind eating off these immaculate floors." He obviously found himself quite witty, and Marthe indulged him with a smile.

Their tour ended, as they approached the Oberarzt's office, the colonel asked if Marthe might have lunch with him tomorrow.

He had been very polite the entire tour—he was obviously well-bred, even if he was a German, and perhaps may be a source of more information regarding the Kaiser.

"Certainly, Herr Colonel."

. . .

Lunch was a pleasant, if uninformative affair. After his second schnapps, the colonel swallowed and stated, "Mein fräulein, life must be extremely tedious here in Roulers, especially for a girl of your character and education." He lit a cigarette. "Would you like to come to Antwerp with me, to experience society and eat decent food?"

Marthe felt her face growing hot. By the way he looked at her, he was not concerned about the food.

His hand reached out and found hers. "Do not be afraid, mein fräulein. I will make it my goal to have your stay be as pleasant as possible. You will not need to worry about getting a special pass."

The distaste must have lingered on her face for the colonel threw some money on the table. "I will let you think on it." He rose and pulled her chair out. "You should probably be getting back to the hospital. We wouldn't want to displease the Oberarzt."

As they neared the courtyard, the colonel caught Marthe's arm. "Have you decided mein fräulein?"

She had been thinking about it all the way back to the hospital. The little girl in her screamed *No!* but the spy, the one who desperately wanted to glean any information she could about the Kaiser's visit, demanded she explore every possible lead.

"Herr Colonel," she replied, tilting her head to meet his gaze. "I would indeed like to stay with you in Antwerp."

He kissed her hand. "*Wunderbar.*" He pulled on her arm, and Marthe thought he would kiss her had not a couple of soldiers marched past, saluting him as they did so. He dropped her hand. "Take the evening train Thursday. If I am working, an orderly will meet you and take you to my hotel, where a room will be waiting for you."

"I shall not be able to obtain more than three days' leave from the hospital," Marthe replied. As he was talking, she'd been calculating in her head the amount of time she might need to find out the necessary information and then transmitting it to British Intelligence in time for the Kaiser's visit.

"Mein fräulein, it will be three days of paradise. The pass will be ready for you Thursday morning." He once again clicked his heels together and bowed before swaggering up the dusty road, away from the hospital. Marthe watched him as if in a dream. Had she really just agreed to travel unaccompanied with this German officer? Why? Had she herself gone mad? The scent of heliotrope from the courtyard garden drifted past her nose reminding her this was no dream. *I did it for the sake of Belgium,* she told herself.

"Ahem."

Marthe turned to catch sight of Alphonse sitting on a bench in the courtyard.

"What did you hear?" she asked.

"Everything. You two weren't exactly discreet in your plans."

She plopped down on the bench next to him. She could feel his arms stiffen, but he was too polite to scoot away from her. "You wanted to know... things," she finished her sentence vaguely, in case anyone was listening to their conversation the way Alphonse had been.

"I didn't expect you to agree to... that. You do know what the colonel is after, don't you?"

"Of course I do. You sound more and more like my big brother, Max."

He shifted to look at her. "Is that what I am to you? Like a brother?" His gaze was that of a wounded puppy.

"Isn't that what you want me to see you as? A protector, nothing more?"

He put his hand over his face, obscuring his expression. "I thought that's what I—"

Marthe stood and crossed her arms over her chest. "I can take care of myself you know. And this is my chance to find out the information you, and others—" she was once again vague— "have been demanding of me."

Alphonse stared at the ground, waiting a beat before he replied, "I know you can take care of yourself. And I also know that the colonel might be a good source of information."

"So why are you so upset?"

"I don't know." He rose and plucked a handful of violets from the ground. "Here," he said, thrusting them at her. "Wear this as a corsage. I will find contacts for you in Brussels who will recognize you by these."

"Alphonse—" Marthe called. But his long legs had already carried him out of the courtyard.

CHAPTER 35

M'GREET

JULY 1915

M'greet was miserable. She was failing at spy school. The intricacies of learning all the minute details of espionage would not stay in her head, and Fräulein Doktor made it a point to never repeat orders. M'greet had no aptitude for codes or ciphers, and she disliked the secret inks on principle—for pretending to be something they were not. The only thing she was reasonably good at was recognizing the different uniforms of the Allied armies.

Normally when she was in trouble, she'd find the first man to help save her. But the male recruits were not in a position to help her and the Fräulein, of course, was immune to her charms. M'greet had managed to befriend the stocky officer who answered the door the first day, even convincing him to take her out to a party in Antwerp, but when he was called away on assignment, she was left with no one to help her.

One day M'greet arrived late to the anteroom to find only Clara and the two sisters.

"Where are Werner and Erich?" M'greet asked, getting in line with the other women.

"Gone," Clara replied. "They were asked to leave yesterday."

"Oh." M'greet wasn't aware that the recruits could be kicked out of training, but then she recalled how often the Fräulein's voice raised against their male counterparts. "I prefer women as spies, anyway," she'd once stated. "So much easier to make it through checkpoints, and, they—especially if they are beautiful—can flirt with the men to provide a distraction."

After a lengthy tutorial on lock-picking, the Fräulein dismissed the other women, and requested M'greet to stay after.

The Fräulein paced up and down the length of the room in her typical manner. She began by stating, "I think you are a demimondaine and more trouble than you are worth."

M'greet longed to shout at her to stay still. "Oh?" she asked, for lack of anything else to say.

"I wanted to terminate your training the way I did those others, but my superiors would not allow it. It seems you've made allies with some powerful men in the Supreme Command."

M'greet shot her best Mata Hari smile: seductive, with hints of buried secrets.

The Fräulein stopped abruptly, directly in front of M'greet. "But a spy works alone. That way, if you are indeed caught, you will have no one to blame but yourself." She raised her eyebrows.

M'greet did not change her expression. Fräulein Doktor sighed before sitting down behind her desk. She opened a drawer and took out a leather-purse. "There are 10,000 francs in here. I was instructed to give them to you."

M'greet took the purse, opening to check that there was indeed a pile of francs inside.

The Fräulein watched her with narrowed eyes. "Is this why you chose to spy for Germany?"

"I needed the money, and the German army pays the best."

"This isn't a game, H-21. If you think that, you will get yourself killed. And possibly others too."

M'greet put the purse over her shoulder. "I am well aware of the consequences."

"Well, if that's the case," the Fräulein clasped her jeweled hands together and set them on her desk. "You will be sent to Paris to await further orders."

Paris. M'greet could barely contain her excitement to be going back to her favorite city in the world. "Thank you, Fräulein Doktor."

"Don't thank me. Thank the Supreme Command."

M'greet nodded as she turned to go.

"And good luck, H-21."

Was it just M'greet's imagination, or did the Fräulein's tone sound even more ominous than usual?

CHAPTER 36

MARTHE

JULY 1915

*T*hursday evening a German soldier brought an official-looking envelope to the café.

"What is that, Marthe?" Mother asked.

Marthe opened it to find a special pass and a travel voucher. She avoided her mother's glance, not wanting to reveal too much in case something went wrong. "I have an errand to perform, which will take me several days. Don't worry," she continued as Mother frowned. "There is no cause for anxiety. And if I succeed," Marthe said, gazing around the café, "it will be a huge victory."

Mother nodded her acquiescence, but her eyes were still filled with worry.

The train ride was luckily uneventful. Marthe tried to sleep, but her mind was racing. She wasn't sure she could really go through with this, but she had to steel her mind against her doubts. Killing the Kaiser would mean a swift end to the war, and almost anything would be worth such an outcome, even losing her reputation, and her virginity.

A German military car was waiting outside the otherwise deserted train station at Antwerp. The driver set Marthe's suitcase beside her in the backseat and handed her a note from the colonel, excusing himself for his absence. *Thank goodness.* He ended the note by ensuring Marthe that he would not be so detained the rest of the trip.

After checking into the hotel, she fell gratefully into the soft bed. That night she slept better than she had in a long time.

Marthe awoke the next morning to find a maid letting up the blinds, flooding the unfamiliar bedroom with sunlight. The hotel was obviously one of Antwerp's finest, with thickly piled carpets, silk wallpaper and pillows of eiderdown. The maid set a coffee carafe on the bedside table before handing Marthe yet another note. It was from the colonel. Reality came crashing down as she opened the note with trembling hands. He requested that she meet him for breakfast in the dining room.

"Something wrong, fräulein?" the maid asked.

"No," Marthe said, refolding the card. She reminded herself that the Kaiser was somewhere in the area: the same man who commanded these German vandals to overrun fair Belgium. *I must keep a clear head, no matter what.*

The colonel sat in the huge dining room with an extensive breakfast spread in front of him. "Marthe, eat. You must be starving from your long trip."

She sat across from him, feeling overwhelmed. Because of rationing, she wasn't used to large meals, especially not at such an early hour. Not to mention the colonel's enthusiastic welcome grated at her nerves.

"What will you do today, Marthe?" he asked through a bite of eggs.

"Oh, are we not to spend the day together?" she replied, trying to keep the hope out of her voice.

"Sadly, I have some business to take care of, but I will be sure to have it completed by supper."

"In that case, I suppose I will explore Antwerp."

"Excellent." He dug his wallet out and held several bills toward her.

"No thank you, mein herr."

"Take it, Marthe. Deutsche marks are much more valuable here than Belgian francs."

She hesitated before picking up the money, feeling her face flush as the other patrons peered at her.

After breakfast, Marthe took a walk around the city. She'd never been to Antwerp before, but expected it had been much less shabby before the war. The roads were in dire need of repair and some of the buildings had the telltale burn scars and broken windows of a German invasion.

The shops, too, proved to be a disappointment. There were barely any goods for sale, and the prices they were asking for what little was left took Marthe's breath away.

She decided to head toward the Grand Place. A company of English prisoners led by a German officer paused in front of her as a tramcar clanged by. As the car passed, a shower of cigarettes and chocolates fell upon the ragged prisoners. "*Vive L' Angleterre!*" a man shouted as he threw more cigarettes toward the Englishmen.

The German feldwebel caught sight of the tramcar benefactor. Thankful for the distraction, Marthe watched the scene unfold.

"You there!" the feldwebel shouted. The tramcar happened to pause and he boarded, but not before the culprit vaulted out of the back. The feldwebel pulled out his rifle and ran the length of the car as the tramcar started moving forward. He jumped out to chase the tramcar benefactor down a side-street, past a group of civilians. Marthe saw one of them extend a foot, and soon the feldwebel lay sprawled on the sidewalk. She just caught a glimpse of the man to whom the foot belonged before he faded into the crowd. It was Herr Jacobs, the safety-pin man who had once boarded at the grocer's house.

The civilian voices grew louder as a balloon bearing Belgium's national colors rose above them and began to sail majestically in the July breeze. Marthe realized the date: July 21—Belgium's Independence Day. "*Vive La Belgique!*" someone shouted. "*Vive les Allies!*" came the return cry.

Another passing tramcar rung its bell loud and clear and a motor-car driver gave an answering toot on its horn. The sounds from the streets grew louder as the balloon soared higher, and then suddenly came the crack of a rifle and the balloon was destroyed. The crowd began to disperse, but proudly, defiantly, for Antwerp had managed to celebrate, in the most minute way, its Independence Day.

The colonel met Marthe that evening wearing a tuxedo, his chin fitting perfectly in the upturned collar of his crisp white shirt. He had heard of the demonstration and was furious. "How dare they permit such a stupid escapade to take place?"

Marthe remained silent as he led her to a motor-car. She disagreed with the assertion that the escapade had been stupid but knew the colonel would not appreciate her opinion.

As the car traveled through Antwerp, Marthe stared out the window, noting that all of the street-lamps had been covered with dark blue paint. The distant beat of anti-aircraft guns announced the presence of Allied airplanes, and soon beams of searchlights slashed through the night.

The car pulled up to an enormous private residence set back from the road. Several Mercedes were parked along the long driveway.

Strains of dance music floated in the light breeze as an attendant took Marthe's cloak. The colonel held her hand as they descended marble steps into a large room decked with flowers, their fragrance tickling Marthe's nose. Several small tables ringed a dance floor. Sprinkled in among the gray-coated officers were beautiful women of all nationalities. The orchestra broke into a lively dance tune as the colonel led her past a table occupied by a fat hauptmann and his companion, a dark-haired, exotic-looking woman.

"Colonel!" the hauptmann exclaimed, waving his champagne flute around, spilling most of it on the floor. "Can you believe we are in the presence of the famed Mata Hari?"

Marthe wasn't sure to whom he was referring, but the dark-haired woman, who appeared enormously tired, frowned before taking a long drink of champagne. In fact, despite their elegant costumes of beads, feathers, and pearls, most of the women seemed haggard, and Marthe realized that many of them were Belgian, probably driven into the arms of their oppressors by sheer starvation, unable to otherwise cope in a world gone mad.

The colonel was courteous at all times, and, had he not been an enemy officer, would have made a charming companion. He made no other move to be physical beyond holding Marthe's hand or occasionally caressing her arm.

"This is an exceedingly rare grape," he told her, admiring the almond-colored champagne in the light from the electric chandeliers. "Especially now that we've destroyed most of the grape-growing regions in that part of France."

Marthe took a sip of the rare wine in lieu of a reply.

As the hour became late, the German officers became more uproarious. When the fat hauptmann tried to get up from the table, his large belly swept the wine glasses off the table, which shattered on the wooden floor and stained his companion's dress. She struck his face so hard she left a red handprint. He raised his arm to her, calling her a "filthy Dutch sow," before the colonel pushed him away. He crashed into another table and passed out amongst the spilled food and drink.

A stern voice cut through the crowd. "Gentlemen, by orders of the High Command, all civilians not of German nationality must produce their identity cards for my inspection."

Voices of several females rose in panic as they grabbed their purses to seek their cards. Marthe watched as the dark-haired woman with the now-stained dress quietly slipped from the room.

The colonel took Marthe's arm. "Say nothing. I will arrange this with the major. Von Bissing has lost no time in determining Antwerp's punishment for the balloon incident from this morning."

When they reached the hotel, just before dawn, they learned that the town of Antwerp was to be fined 8,000,000 marks and the curfew was set at five o'clock until further notice. The Germans were determined to punish the Belgians for their behavior. Marthe fell onto her bed exhausted, glad that the colonel had once again made no mention of sharing a room with her.

Marthe awoke the next morning, blinking in the bright sunshine thinking optimistically that she just might be able to find out the information she needed without having to have an intimate relationship with the colonel.

Indeed, he wasn't at breakfast that morning, and Marthe was still in a grand mood when she returned to her room, only to find her door standing half-open. She walked in, expecting to see a maid cleaning the room, but instead a German soldier stood next to two black suitcases. Upon seeing her, he touched his cap and gave her a sly smile before walking out.

Marthe examined the suitcases, noting that each bore the colonel's initials in bold white letters. She flopped onto the bed in a huff, realizing the implications of the suitcases' presence in her room. There could be no mistaking the colonel's intentions now. Her thoughts traveled to that horrid scene in the garden, which then went to Alphonse's promise to secure an Antwerp contact. She hoped that he would be able to come through: she could have very much used a friend at that moment. Tears came to her eyes as she dug her fingers into the silk comforter, feeling alone in a world of German oppression.

After a few minutes of feeling sorry for herself, Marthe relaxed her hands, reminding herself she wasn't some silly girl. She was a secret service agent, a member of British Intelligence, and commanded herself to act as such. She took a deep breath before getting up from the bed to powder her nose and straighten her hair.

The colonel was waiting for her in the lounge that evening, a glass of vermouth next to him. He kept his well-bred face neutral and made no mention of the suitcases as he ordered Marthe a drink.

She longed to get drunk on brandy, thinking it would make whatever was in store for her that night easier, but at the same time she wanted to keep her wits about her. The colonel's breath smelled of alcohol, which was unusual for him. She looked away as he lit a cigarette and caught the eyes of a German lieutenant at the next table. The lieutenant smirked and then winked at her. Confused at his attention, she dropped her eyes to the tablecloth before peeking over at him again. He nodded at her before getting up from the table.

"Come on, Marthe, you must be tired," the colonel said, rising to his feet. "Let's go upstairs to our room."

There it was: our room. As Marthe followed him upstairs, she was as unsteady on her feet as the colonel, but for a different reason.

He opened the door with a key and then walked in. A maid had laid out Marthe's nightdress on the bed, and the colonel's lips turned up as he fingered it.

Marthe tilted her head and curved her lips into a passable smile, but she was unable to meet his gaze, afraid he would be able to see how much she hated him for what was about to happen.

"You seem nervous, Marthe." He dug a bottle of brandy out of his bag and poured some in a glass. "Drink some of this as you get dressed and I'll be back in a half an hour."

As he shut the door behind him, Marthe cast her eyes helplessly about the room, wondering what to do next. She went to the double doors that led to the balcony and stepped outside, gazing upon the unsympathetic rooftops of Antwerp, wondering if it would be safe to jump. But, even if she survived, her mission would have been a failure: she still hadn't gained any information regarding the Kaiser's visit.

She caught sight of a man on the balcony next to hers. It was the German lieutenant from earlier, although now he was dressed all in black. Wondering if this was Alphonse's promised contact, she took a wilted violet from the corsage pinned at her breast and dropped it over the banister.

The lieutenant watched the flower fall before he stepped onto the ledge. Wordlessly he scaled the distance between them and dropped onto her balcony. "Good evening, miss," he murmured in a low voice, lifting his lapel to reveal two safety-pins running diagonally. "I'm with the Antwerp Secret Service and have been detailed to shadow you." He pushed past her into the room.

Marthe followed him. "How did you manage to obtain a German uniform?"

"The War Office," he replied as he opened a case and shook out a cigarette. He put it to his mouth before replacing it. "I s'pose I oughtn't smoke for fear the old colonel will smell it when he gets back." He tucked the case back into his pocket. "Look here, have you succeeded in getting anything out of him?"

"Nothing so far," Marthe replied, the regret obvious in her voice. "Perhaps I might learn something more tonight." She shuddered.

He nodded, a compassionate expression on his face. "I wish I could somehow assist you."

"Me too," she said, her voice barely above a whisper.

His eyes fell onto the colonel's suitcases, which still sat exactly as the German soldier had placed them. "Are those your precious colonel's?"

"Yes."

"Have you searched them for papers?"

"Not yet." Marthe cursed herself for not having thought of that herself.

He got down on his knees. "Unsuspecting bugger left them unlocked," he said as he snapped them open. The counterfeit lieutenant ran his hands expertly through the suitcases' contents. "Nothing of value," he said as he got back to his feet. "But better to check all the same."

Just then, a knock sounded at the door. "The colonel!" Marthe gasped, her eyes widening as the doorknob began turning. She turned to warn the lieutenant, but he was nowhere to be seen. The doors to the balcony remained undisturbed and she reasoned he must have slipped under the bed.

The colonel's fingers gripped her arms. "Why have you not undressed yet, my pet?" He let her go, noting both the untouched drink on the nightstand and his open suitcases. "Oh, I see, you were engaged in unpacking my bags." He reached for her again, his lips pursed.

Marthe racked her brain for how to give the lieutenant a chance to leave the room. "I must leave after tonight," she told the colonel, stalling for time. "The Herr Oberarzt needs me. And what would I say to him if I were not there when the All-Highest arrives?"

"Do not worry your pretty head over such trifles," he replied. "The All-Highest will not arrive in Roulers until Saturday, around 11 o'clock to review the troops. He won't even spend the night, and I doubt if he will have time to visit the hospital. We still have several days to enjoy ourselves—I can put in papers to extend your leave if you want."

"But I promised the Oberarzt I would return in three days." Marthe was hardly aware of what she was saying; her mind was occupied by the information he'd just revealed. Hopefully the man under the bed would be able to pass on that information to British Intelligence. That is, if the colonel didn't discover him first. This time she didn't pull away as the colonel pressed his lips upon hers in a long, lingering kiss.

The ringing in her ears cleared just enough that she could discern a voice singing in the hallway. Who could possibly be singing while she was in such a ghastly situation?

The sound of breaking glass came from just outside the room, and, once again grateful for the distraction, Marthe broke the embrace to throw the door open. The drunk hauptmann from the other night stood outside, obviously up to his old tricks, while a waiter wordlessly picked up the broken glass.

"What happened here?" the colonel demanded, wiping saliva off of his face.

The hauptmann attempted a bow, which nearly caused him to tip over. "This pig-dog," he swept his hand toward the bent waiter, "and myself tried to pass each other, but as you can see, there was no room." Both Marthe and the colonel looked down the corridor, which was wide enough for at least four men the hefty hauptmann's size to walk shoulder-to-shoulder. The hauptmann clicked his heels together as several senior officers appeared. There was a flurry of salutes and more heel-clicking as the Germans greeted one another.

Marthe tried to slip back to the room unnoticed, but the colonel caught sight of her and called to her in a stern voice. "Mein fräulein?"

"Herr Colonel, why don't you join these men for a drink while I," she dropped her voice lower, "undress? I'll be waiting for you when you get back."

The colonel's lips spread into a wide grin. "*Au revoir,* my pet. I will see you quite soon."

Marthe refrained from running back to the room as the colonel headed to the lobby with the other officers. Now that she'd managed to gain the information she'd sought, she had no desire to repeat the kiss she'd shared with the colonel earlier. Or anything else, for that matter.

She hoped the fake lieutenant would be able to help her escape, but, after checking under the bed, she realized he'd disappeared. She'd have to figure out how to get out of this situation on her own.

There should be at least one train leaving for Roulers before dawn. Marthe crossed her fingers that the colonel would be so embarrassed by her sudden departure that he wouldn't tell anyone. She scribbled a note, telling him that she changed her mind and that she hoped he would eventually forgive her before grabbing her train pass. She locked the door from the outside, hoping to stall the drunk colonel for at least a few more minutes while she made her way to the train station.

An hour later, Marthe sat in the comfort of a train seat, breathless and disbelieving that she had managed to get out from under the colonel's grasp without causing a permanent stain upon herself.

A woman passenger on a train that late at night was unusual, but the military police passed her through without a hassle. It was nearing dawn when the train arrived at Roulers.

Everyone was asleep when Marthe arrived home and she was able to doze off for a few hours in her own bed.

In the morning, Mother did not question Marthe when she showed for breakfast. It was enough for her that her daughter had returned safely.

As she set out for the hospital that Saturday morning, Marthe saw that the Grand Place was adorned with brightly colored flags, in preparation for the coming of the Kaiser.

Alphonse's ambulance sat near the entrance of the hospital, and, upon circling it, Marthe caught sight of him tinkering with one of the wheels. His eyes traveled up and down her nurses' uniform. She straightened her spine and met his gaze squarely, trying to show him she was no different now than when she left.

"Have you heard the news?" he asked finally. "The Kaiser will not be paying us a visit after all. The Seven Sisters have been bombarding us regularly these last few days and the High Command has decided it would be too dangerous for him to come to Roulers."

Marthe didn't reply, for really, there was nothing to be said.

CHAPTER 37

ALOUETTE

JULY 1915

*V*on Krohn insisted that Alouette return to Paris. When she questioned his reasoning, he was deliberately vague, but mentioned that it would give her a break from Kalle's watchful eyes.

"I dare not go," she asserted, and then added for good measure, "I'd be arrested as soon as I crossed the border."

He thought for a moment. "I have a solution, Alouette. We have a way of getting to France by way of the Pyrenees. We use it to send our agents in with supplies."

Alouette's tongue felt numb. The Germans had a secret path through the Pyrenees, through which they could infiltrate France with their undocumented spies... and worse yet, weapons meant to harm her countrymen!

Two nights later, the Baron drove Alouette to Figueras. They arrived at a nearly desolate, treeless intersection between two long roads.

"I suppose you will be seeing your fiancé in Paris," von Krohn commented dryly as the chauffeur shut off the engine.

"Yes. I'm curious to see what Zozo has been up to these past months," she replied truthfully.

"You said he is a revolutionary. Is he willing to do anything you ask of him?"

"Of course." The lie came easily.

His good eye glowed with mirth as he took something out of his pocket. "Look here," he said, handing her a fountain pen. "This ordinary-looking pen doubles as an incendiary device. All you need to do is press this spring," he turned it over in her hand, "and then light a match. If you toss the pen into a warehouse's gas supply, you can blow up the whole building." His grin widened at the thought of a French factory crowded with men and women blasting sky high.

"German engineers are quite ingenious." Alouette carefully tucked the pen into her purse, thinking she'd get rid of it at the first possible opportunity.

"Indeed," von Krohn replied. "Ask your little Russian friend to throw it into Schneider's factory in Le Havre."

Ladoux's words came again into Alouette's mind: *Get the Germans to pay.* "Do you really think Zozo will risk his life if you don't make it worthwhile?"

"If he does the job, I will send him money," he stated as he opened the car door.

Alouette stepped out into the chilly night air, noting that a man with two mules was standing in the middle of the crossroads.

"Drop me a line when you are ready to return, Alouette," was von Krohn's parting statement.

Alouette assumed the man with the mules, a stocky, gloomy-looking fellow, was a smuggler, a fact she could not validate as the man spoke neither Spanish nor French. After she climbed aboard a proffered mule, they headed down one of the roads in silence. Ahead, she could see the jagged peaks of mountains. She shivered, not so much from the cold, but from an eerie sense of foreboding that enveloped her as much as the night fog. She felt sleepy, but forced herself to stay awake in order to note the landmarks they passed so she could mark the passage later on a map. She was determined that no more German assassins would pass into France.

When they reached the beginnings of a mountain path, the guide dismounted and then lay flat, his ear pressed to the earth. Alouette took the opportunity to get off her mule and stretch her sore legs.

At last the guide rose. He took a rug from the back of his mule and cut it into eight pieces with a long knife before tying the rug pieces to each of the mules' hooves.

The footfalls of the mules now muted, they headed up a very narrow, winding trail.

Dawn was breaking when at last the uphill trail became a downhill one. The guide straightened and pointed toward a white spot on the horizon, indicating a town. Without a word, he turned his mule around and began his journey back up the mountain.

Alouette headed toward the town until she came upon a white-capped stream. She dismounted and washed her hands and face. The cool water woke her completely. She then took the incendiary pen from her purse and flung it as far as she could into the rippling water.

The first thing Alouette did when she returned to Paris was to pay a visit to Monsieur Delorme at 282 boulevard, Saint-Germain.

"What now?" Ladoux asked, pushing a bunch of papers aside.

"What happened to my letter?" she demanded.

Ladoux put his hands in the air. "Alouette, I assure you I sent it." He lowered his arms and folded them across his chest. "Now, tell me, why have you returned?"

She filled him in on everything, from the dinner party where her claim to not understand a word of German was put to the test, to the secret path through the Pyrenees, to von Krohn's statement that a man named Kalle was following her all over Madrid.

"Ah yes, Arnold Kalle, the German Embassy attaché. We believe he is a fairly high-ranking officer with German Intelligence. I would suggest trying to meet him if the opportunity arises."

"Meet him? Should I demand an introduction from the lackeys he has following me?"

Ladoux was about to retort, but someone burst into the office. "Pardon me, Captain, but these just came in." Zozo set a manila folder on Ladoux's desk before catching sight of Alouette. "So you've returned once again."

She frowned, hiding the fact that she was unexpectedly pleased to see his tall frame. "What are those?" she asked, nodding her head toward the papers Ladoux took out of the folder.

"Radiograms from Spain to Germany," Zozo answered in his deep voice. "They have been intercepted by the Eiffel Tower."

Alouette leaned forward to get a peek at them.

"Don't get too excited," Ladoux slid them back into the folder. "We are unable to decipher their code. We have our best men working on it, but so far we haven't gotten anywhere. But hopefully we will soon and then we can stay abreast of their underhanded plans."

"Oh," Alouette put her hand to her mouth. "I almost forgot." She relayed the information about the incendiary device and von Krohn's request to have Zozo blow up the Havre factory.

"Do you have this pen?" Zozo asked eagerly.

She reluctantly shook her head, cursing herself for her impetuousness at getting rid of it. Ladoux could have given it to one of his so-called expert engineers to see if they could make heads or tails of it.

Sensing her disappointment, Zozo set a hand on her arm. "Don't worry, Alouette."

His fingers felt like hot coals. She pulled her arm away and then cursed herself again for letting Zozo get the best of her. She put a hand to her mouth and coughed delicately in it, as if that were the reason for her rash movements. "What will be my mission when I return to Spain?"

Zozo stretched his long legs in front of him. "We believe Germany is trying to stir up trouble in the French protectorate of Morocco."

Alouette nodded. "So that France will have to divert troops from the Western front to put down the rebellion in Morocco."

Zozo grinned at her. "Exactly."

Ladoux added, "See if your Baron has anything to do with

supplying Moroccan insurgents with supplies: rifles, munitions, that sort of thing."

"I will do my best." Alouette rose from her chair.

"Come back in a few days," Ladoux instructed. "We will get your papers and passport in order for you to get back to Spain."

When Alouette returned to 282 boulevard, Saint-Germain, Ladoux handed her a newspaper clipping. She read it silently, her hands shaking:

Unknown assassins, probably of German descent, instituted an incendiary device on a factory in Renault, inflicting very serious damage.

Alouette sank into a chair. "Were there many killed?"

Ladoux tilted his head back and let go a great belly laugh. "There has only been one copy of that newspaper made." Upon noting Alouette's blank expression, he continued, "It was printed for your von Krohn, so he can pay you the money he promised."

CHAPTER 38

M'GREET

SEPTEMBER 1915

M'greet was able to obtain a visa to travel to France with very little problem, but when she applied to the British Consulate to sail via England, she was refused. She then employed the Dutch Foreign Office to inquire as to what the holdup was. It never occurred to her to inform them of her interrogation session in Folkestone a year prior. She visited the Foreign Office every morning for a week before a clerk finally showed her the English ambassador's reply to her inquiry.

"What does this mean, they consider me 'undesirable?'" she demanded.

"It means," the clerk replied, snatching the telegram back from her, "that you are going to need to find an alternative route to France."

"Fine." M'greet turned in a huff and then marched straight to the Spanish Consulate.

She was finally given permission to board the SS *Zeelandia* in September, which sailed from Amsterdam to Vigo in Spain. From there she would travel by train to Madrid and then finally to Paris.

The ship stopped en route in Falmouth for inspection. M'greet waited in line as patiently as she could, noting that one of the ship's passengers, a stocky man with a bushy mustache that did nothing to lessen the bulk of his large, crooked nose, stood behind the British inspectors and occasionally whispered in their ears. After that, some of the passengers in the queue would be led away for further questioning.

M'greet nervously presented her passport when it was her turn, avoiding the eyes of both the police and the passenger.

The following evening, her dining companions included a merchant from Zaandam, Cleyndert, a short man with broken teeth and smallpox scars.

"Madame Zelle-MacLeod," he said, leaning forward, close enough that M'greet could see pieces of food caught in those broken teeth. "Do you know that man over there?" He nodded toward the same man with the large nose that had been behind the British inspectors.

"No."

"Well, he's telling everyone that he was in your cabin last night."

"What?" M'greet dropped her fork. "What do you mean, 'in my cabin last night'? There was no man in there. Are you saying he was in there without my knowledge?"

Cleyndert shrugged.

"What is his name?" M'greet demanded.

"Hoedemaker," Cleyndert stated. "A Jew," he added under his breath.

Lady Atline, another passenger, told M'greet a similar story the next afternoon as some of the passengers waited in the sun to take tea with the captain.

"Excuse me," M'greet stood and walked directly over to Hoedemaker. She tugged at his sleeve.

"Yes?" Hoedemaker replied, squinting at M'greet as though she was a fly he was about to swat.

"Are you telling people you were in my cabin two nights prior?"

"Me?" He cast a sly look around the small crowd that had gathered to listen. "I have said no such thing."

"That's not true," Cleyndert insisted, pushing his way forward. "You said something to me about it."

"And me," Lady Atline added.

Hoedemaker cast a helpless glance about the unfriendly crowd. Realizing he was caught, he replied, "I said I was in your room, but I didn't imply that you were also there."

"You're exactly right," M'greet said, her rage mounting. "I wouldn't dare be any closer to you than I am now." Her right hand reached out and connected with the side of Hoedemaker's face. One of her rings must have scratched him, as his face began bleeding. He pulled out a handkerchief and placed it over the red mark. Without a word, he sauntered down the deck.

"Bravo!" Lady Atline said, coming up beside M'greet. "But aren't you worried he might make trouble for you when we land in Spain? I hear he works for the British government."

"If he so desires, I will have to slap his other cheek," M'greet replied.

Indeed, when the ship disembarked at Vigo, Hoedemaker was right behind her. She could hear his cloddish boots stomping down the gangway. He sat behind her on the train to Madrid and tailed her all the way to the Palace Hotel. He never spoke a word to her, but M'greet felt threatened by his presence anyway.

As soon as the bellhop raised the blinds in her room, M'greet spotted Hoedemaker across the street, staring in her direction.

After a few days in Spain, M'greet tried to cross the border into France, but was refused. She immediately returned to Madrid and headed straight to the Dutch Consul to complain about her treatment. An assistant there revealed that she had been listed by Britain as being "suspect."

"Suspect? First I am undesirable and now I am suspect? If that is the case, why did they let me leave the Netherlands at all? What am I to do now? Stay in Spain until the end of the war?"

"I'm sorry, madame." The clerk did indeed sound sympathetic. "Not even the intervention of the Ministry could help you now."

"I shall reiterate that my sympathies are pro-Allies," M'greet replied loudly. "Surely that will make a difference."

"Good luck, madame," the clerk called after her as she left the consulate.

She did as intended the next day, but was once again refused entry into France.

"Do you know who pays your salary?" she asked a rather stupid-looking border guard.

"The French government."

"Yes, but a man named Jules Cambon signs your paycheck. Do you know him?"

The guard shook his head.

"He is a personal friend of mine, and has recently been promoted to secretary-general." Cambon was another of M'greet's former lovers. The name-drop had the desired effect, and, after casting a confused look at his companion, the guard moved aside to let M'greet pass into France.

It had taken her a weary six weeks to return to Paris, but, as M'greet checked into the Grand Hotel on the Boulevard des Capucines, she figured it was all worth it. There had been no sign of Hoedemaker since she'd left Spain. The Parisian weather was beautiful, and there were handsome men in uniform swarming the streets. The hotel clerk had mentioned something about a big battle looming somewhere nearby, but M'greet, as usual, did not pay much attention.

She decided to take advantage of the weather and ordered a taxi to drive her down to the Seine. As they passed the Arc de Triomphe, M'greet felt that she had arrived home.

She took a walk along the banks of the river, reflecting on how she had been an alien her whole life, first, as a child, abandoned by her father in the austere Netherlands, then in exotic Java, frequently deserted by her brute of a husband. Paris was the only place in the world that had ever seemed truly home to her. There, she had been able to make her own fate, and never needed to put her faith in anyone else.

And for that reason, she realized, she would never betray the beautiful city, no matter what the Germans would pay her. *Consider the 20,000 francs repayment for the goods you took from me,* she told an invisible Kaiser. *I will never provide you information with which you could destroy gay Paris.* With that, she pulled the despised vials of invisible ink out of her purse and dumped them into the river.

As she strolled back along the Champs-Élysées, intent on visiting all of her favorite shopping haunts, she caught sight of two plain-clothes men following her a bit too closely. These same men were waiting on a bench when she finished her manicure, and tailed her all the way back to her hotel. Although she was used to men following her, there was something about the way they tried to remain elusive that puzzled M'greet. *Why didn't they ever venture to introduce themselves?*

CHAPTER 39

ALOUETTE

OCTOBER 1915

When Alouette returned to Madrid, the Baron greeted her with an uncharacteristic coolness, stating, "I've purchased you an apartment."

"Pardon?" Alouette's hands felt clammy. Had von Krohn found her out, or was this his subtle way of disposing of her as a spy?

He patted his almost non-existent hair. "Arnold Kalle is still suspicious of our relationship. I needed an excuse to keep up the guise of our meetings, so I thought an apartment would be a good cover."

Alouette's heartbeat returned to normal.

"Come," he started toward the door. "Let me show you your new living space."

Alouette narrowed her eyes at his turned back, but followed him to a nondescript building steps away from the Calle del Alcalá, the most fashionable street in Madrid.

The apartment consisted of a suite of five rooms on the second floor above a beauty parlor. The décor was sparse, the scant furniture done in a modest style.

Von Krohn led her into a small room beside the back staircase. "This will be my office."

"Your office? I thought this was my apartment."

"It is, but Kalle has taken to having my house watched. Here I can meet with my contacts without worrying about him knowing my business."

"But—"

"Don't worry, Alouette. I won't be sleeping here. I'm not sure my marriage could survive that."

As he retreated down the stairs, a slow smile developed across her face. She could now see the opportunity this apartment presented for widening her schemes.

The next afternoon, Alouette lay stretched across the settee in the living room, wearing a simple dress of pale yellow, tied at the waist by a sea-green silk sash.

The Baron entered the room, and, upon catching sight of her, declared, "Your contrasting belt and gown remind me of the waves on the Atlantic shore."

Her stomach churned at the compliment. She gave no reply. The Baron was smoking one of his heavy, cloying cigars, and she lit a cigarette, purely for the purpose of neutralizing his cigar smoke. The surrounding air grew thick as storm clouds formed in Alouette's mind. "My dear Baron, I do declare how bored I get when you make such a nuisance of yourself."

He moved closer to her on the couch. "I wasn't completely honest with you earlier. It is not only Kalle who is suspicious of your new role in my life. It's also my wife."

Alouette blew out a ring of smoke. "Why do you suppose that is?"

"You don't think it's obvious to everyone that I'm secretly in love with you?" He said it so casually that she wasn't sure if he was serious.

She faced him, choking down the repulsion she felt. Her instincts told her to fling the lit cigarette into his face. She squashed it into an ashtray instead, racking her brain for a way to shut him down without completely alienating him. "Hans, perhaps if things had been different, we could have had a relationship." Luckily the lie exited her mouth with ease. "But you are my handler, and we must keep our contact chaste. For your wife's sake. Not to mention Zozo's."

To her immense relief, his face softened. "You're right, of course. Had you been German, and fifteen years older, or better yet, if I'd been younger, we would have made a great couple." He heaved a sigh as he got up from the couch. "Now, if you'll excuse me, I am expecting a visitor shortly." He glanced at her. "If it's not too much trouble, I ask that we be left alone for the next few hours."

"Oh, don't worry about me, Hans, I have plenty of unpacking to do."

Alouette installed herself in the kitchen, at the window that looked out into the back courtyard, keeping watch for von Krohn's mysterious visitor. As she waited, she reflected on their earlier conversation. Ladoux would probably have been thrilled if she told him she took advantage of von Krohn's affection to get more information. But she knew all too well the murky line between manipulation and seduction. She'd been down that road before, years ago, after Karl Mather, the lover she'd followed to Paris, spurned her. Too proud to return to Nancy, she had to find some way to support herself. She'd then met a madam who had trained her in the art of being a *courtesan*—a companion to rich and powerful men, who delighted in having beautiful, intelligent women on their arm. Especially one that wasn't their wife. While Alouette had never actually slept with any of the men she entertained, she'd come close enough to decide never to do it again. Thankfully Henri had come along and proposed marriage before she became really desperate.

The sound of the Baron's heavy footsteps pacing in his office brought her back to reality. She looked up to see a stocky brunette in her mid-forties entering the back door.

Alouette crept into the dining room, which was next to the Baron's office. She did her best to eavesdrop on the conversation between von Krohn and the woman, but, as they were both speaking Spanish, could only understand snippets. She noted that von Krohn called the woman 'Maria' and instructed her to visit his office for a handbag and a train ticket to Cerbére.

When she overheard the woman's voice say, "*Muy bien, señor,*" Alouette hurried to the living room. She heard a series of doors close and then heavy footsteps in the hall.

Alouette sat in an armchair with her head between her hands. Presently she could sense von Krohn standing in front of her. "Is something wrong?" he asked.

"I've got an awful headache," she replied in a low tone. "Maybe all of this unpacking finally got to me."

"Is there anything I can do for you?"

She looked up. "Do you mind buying me some antipyrine?" She felt a guilty pleasure in making him purchase the supplies she needed to communicate his secret plans to her boss.

He returned in half an hour to drop off the medicine and then left again, saying he had to attend a dinner at the Embassy. Alouette took advantage of his absence to write a detailed letter in secret ink to Ladoux, informing him of the spy named Maria and her instructions to go to Cerbére.

She was still involved in her task when she heard von Krohn return. Although her heart was hammering away in her chest, she set her pen down and swallowed the rest of the antipyrine as casually as she could when he entered the room. Luckily the secret ink had already dried on the paper.

"How do you feel about traveling to Morocco?" von Krohn asked in a pseudo-casual voice.

Alouette matched his tone. "What for?"

"I need you to send a coded message to the tribal insurgents."

"But Morocco is a French protectorate. Won't I have trouble getting there?"

Von Krohn dismissed her concerns with a wave of his hand. "Like everything else French, the French Secret Service is so negligent they will never know. I will accompany you as far as Algeciras on the coast of Gibraltar. I can make arrangements for our accommodations immediately."

"Separate rooms, of course," she replied.

"Of course."

As soon as von Krohn left, Alouette began another letter to Ladoux, asking permission to go to Morocco. She paused midway through the first sentence. Sending a coded letter through the post would take a minimum of four days to arrive, and then she'd have to wait another four days, at least, for his reply to reach her. By then she could have gone and returned. The pen fell from her hand as she realized von Krohn might have been on to something: the French Secret Service did seem somewhat haphazard, especially in contrast to the efficiency of the Germans. But if Ladoux did not have prior knowledge of her plans, and an uprising in Morocco took place while she was there, she might get blamed for it. She ripped the paper into shreds, recalling Ladoux's warning that if she got into trouble, she'd have to find a way out of it, alone.

They were put up in the Hotel Cristina, an ornate building overlooking the sea. The Baron honored her request with separate rooms, but ones that adjoined through an inner door. Alouette didn't complain as this way she could still be aware of what von Krohn was up to.

He left early the first morning to retrieve his messages from the German Consulate. When he returned, he stood in the doorway of the two rooms, a red leather-bound book in one hand and a wooden ruler in the other. "I have a difficult job to tackle just now," he stated loftily. "I would be very thankful if you wouldn't disturb me for the next hour or so." He put his hand on the doorknob.

"Oh, there's no need to shut the door, Hans. I plan on reading a bit." Alouette was desperate to know what he was going to do with the ruler. "I'd like to know you are nearby," she added.

He frowned, but left the door open. She chose a chair that gave her a vantage point into the other room, watching over the top of her book as he took a paper out of his coat pocket. He stood stooped over a table, moving the ruler across the paper and mumbling as he wrote in the notebook.

When he'd finished, he put the ruler away in a desk drawer before tearing up the paper. *It must have been a telegram he decoded*, Alouette mused, remembering what Ladoux said about the Eiffel Tower intercepting German messages. She watched as he threw the remnants of the telegram in the wastebasket before stalking into her room.

He stood at her window and Alouette joined him. They could see the Strait of Gibraltar and beyond, the coast of Morocco.

"Here is where Spanish and British waters meet," von Krohn stated, half to himself. He pointed to a distant white speck. "That's Tangier. One of these days the war will be there, too."

"How do you know?" Alouette asked.

"Are you in the pay of the French?" he demanded.

She willed her mouth not to drop open. "Why do you ask such a question?"

"Major Kalle seems to think that you are, and that one day you will betray me."

She took von Krohn's clammy hand into hers. "I would never do such a thing." *Curse that Kalle, whoever he is!* She rubbed his arm, prepared to go further if necessary, but he seemed reassured by the touch of her hand.

He shot her an apologetic smile. "I know, but a man in a position such as mine has the right to be suspicious."

She squeezed his arm before letting go. "I've heard the French have no money to pay me, so I could never be a double agent."

His smile widened, his good eye crinkling at the corners while the glass one stared straight ahead. "I have to return to the Consulate for a few minutes and then we can have lunch."

After he left, Alouette crept to his room, her eyes focused on the waste basket containing information of vital importance to her country. She started toward it, but then paused, realizing that the simple task of retrieving the shredded paper could result in her standing before the execution post at Vincennes. She went back to the window and fixed her gaze on Morocco instead.

Less than a minute later, the door to her room burst open. The Baron's first glance was not at her, but at the basket in his own room. Alouette covered her grin with a gloved hand. "Did you forget something?"

He looked relieved. "No."

"I may be a spy, Hans, but I loathe being spied upon."

"I'm not sure what you are talking about." He dug again in his coat pocket and handed her a packet of papers. "Here are your visas to travel to Morocco."

Alouette congratulated herself on resisting the lure of the waste basket; it was clear now that she had destroyed the last shreds of doubt in von Krohn's mind.

"The British have only given you a qualified visa, which means you are not immune to arrest in English waters."

"But I have to pass Gibraltar, and the English are very active there." She did not have to fake the look of worry on her face. "I don't want to be detained."

"You have nothing to fear. Neither the English nor the French have a shred of evidence against you. And this mission will prove to Kalle once and for all that you are a trustworthy agent."

She wasn't sure that was true: it must have been obvious to everyone in Algeciras that she was the Baron's companion. The British Intelligence Service was surely aware of von Krohn's role in German espionage and, since the French and English Secret Services did not readily communicate with each other, they would most likely be unaware that Alouette was under the Deuxiéme Bureau's employ. The prospect of being arrested was a very real threat. But then again, if she could get word to the Allies, they might be able to curtail any possibility of a Moroccan rebellion. "When will I leave?"

"In the morning." Von Krohn retrieved a box from his desk. "You will take this box of notepaper with you. It appears as if it has never been opened, but half of its bulk has been written on with invisible ink. It is obviously a parcel of great importance."

"To whom will I deliver it?"

"When you disembark, a black man with a pencil mustache will present himself to you. And now I really do have to return to the Consulate," von Krohn stated.

As soon as he left, Alouette put on her widest hat, complete with a lace veil, and hurried to the British Embassy. She told the secretary that she needed to speak to the Consul as soon as possible.

"And why is that?"

"Because I have news that could save the Allies."

He didn't seem impressed and maintained his suspicious expression. *Of course he was suspicious, just as Kalle was, as von Krohn was, as Ladoux was.* Distrust was deeply rooted in every line of work during the war, but especially in the business of espionage, where one false move could endanger your life.

Finally, the secretary relented and she was shown into the office of the British Consul. She refused a seat, not wanting to waste any more time on pleasantries. "Tomorrow I will be meeting a Moroccan rebel to whom I shall pass on instructions from the German Secret Service, written in invisible ink." She gave a few more specifics before stating, "If you wish to have me shadowed by one of your agents, and I prove to be a traitor, you can have me arrested upon my return."

The Consul listened without interrupting. When she'd finished, he rose and held out his hand. "I am prepared to accept your word. We will find a way to intercept this information." He paused to readjust his glasses. "In twenty-four hours, I shall have details about you from Paris, and, as you say, if we suspect anything, we will arrest you."

Alouette's resulting grin was so large that it must have been contagious, as the Consul also smiled. He shook her hand warmly and wished her luck.

She headed back to her hotel, thinking about how the English were a strange hybrid of naivety and shrewdness.

Alouette's crossing over the Strait of Gibraltar proved uneventful, though she kept her eyes out for anyone tailing her. If the British Consul had given orders to have her shadowed, they chose someone nearly invisible.

When the boat reached Tangier, she waited until all of her fellow passengers had disembarked before heading down the gangway herself. She gripped the railing with whitened knuckles as she wondered whom this trip would end up helping: France and her allies, or the beastly Boches.

As she reached the dock, a dark-skinned porter approached her. He grabbed her bag, stating, "I know a hotel where you will be comfortable."

Alouette noted his thin mustache before she wordlessly followed him.

. . .

After Alouette had checked in, the porter offered to show her to her room.

"Welcome to Morocco, S-22," he stated as he dumped her bag on the bed.

Fighting back a wave of misgiving, she handed him the box of paper.

"When are you leaving again?" he asked. Now that he no longer had to pretend to be a humble porter, Alouette could see he carried himself with a great deal of dignity. Perhaps he was a chief of one of the insurgent tribes.

"I'm going back by the first available boat tomorrow morning," she replied.

"Very good. I will meet you at the door of the harbour restaurant at seven-thirty a.m. I have something to give to you."

Alouette spent a very restless night in Tangier, wondering if the British had secretly come to her aid or if she had truly paved the way for a Moroccan uprising.

She arrived at the appointed place and time the next morning, but could see no sign of the supposed porter. She waited with bated breath, not daring to think that he might have been held up. At a quarter to ten, she allowed a sigh of relief. The English must have detained him, which meant that her mission had been accomplished. Impressed with the methodical efforts of the British Secret Service, Alouette boarded a boat for Spain.

A few days later, Alouette read in the French papers that U-boats laden with munitions intended for Moroccan insurgents had been inter- cepted. While the submarines themselves managed to get away, the potential for rebellion had been annihilated. As Alouette folded the paper, she once again marveled at the efficiency of the English. It all had gone down in such a discreet manner that von Krohn had never suspected he'd been double-crossed.

CHAPTER 40

MARTHE

*A*fter the death of Agent 63, Marthe's new instructions were to deliver any communication to a chemist's shop off the Grand Place. She had to admit that passing notes over the ordinary counter, although much less dangerous, was not nearly as intriguing as maneuvering past German soldiers in dark alleyways well past curfew. There was not much information to pass on anyway, as ever since the Kaiser's failed visit, things in Roulers had been quiet.

She was serving in the café one evening when she heard raised voices. She pretended to be rooting through her bag as she listened to two men arguing. One of them was Hauptmann Fashugel, who was currently billeting in Otto's old room. Fashugel was a stocky fellow with a friendly face, a machine gun company commander, whose men all adored him.

"What time did you say this blasted parade starts tomorrow?" Red Carl demanded.

"Nine o'clock," Fashugel replied. "But we'll have to be up a fair sight before then in order to march to Westrozebeke." He held up his nearly empty glass of wine. "This must be our last drink—we need to be in bed before long."

Red Carl blew out a ring of smoke. "I wish they would be content to send the padre to visit us instead of the other way around."

"Say, Marthe," Fashugel said upon catching sight of her. "If you please, we will be needing breakfast at the crack of dawn tomorrow morning. As if we don't already have enough work to do without spending our Sunday morning traipsing about the countryside."

"Oh my," Marthe remarked. "A parade? Doesn't a big gathering like that seem dangerous?"

"Indeed," Fashugel replied. "The Supreme Command wants all of us licentious soldiers to hear a bishop explain how to look after our souls. But it would serve Division right if the Seven Sisters bloody well blasted the bishop and the commanders to kingdom come."

"I hope they don't do that," Red Carl remarked. "Although I agree that our bloated chiefs would learn a lesson if that happened, the Seven Sisters might blow us up too."

Marthe pulled an embroidery hoop from her bag, as if that was what she had been looking for all along, and sat in an empty chair. She ruminated over the meaning of the conversation as she pulled the needle in and out. *A whole division on parade in Westrozebeke tomorrow morning!* They would indeed make a fine target for the Seven Sisters. There would be little place to take cover in her already shell-shattered former village.

Marthe waited for the two men to leave the room before she hurried upstairs and penned a message. The sun was setting as she rushed to the chemist's shop and it cast an ominous red light over the glass bottles as she handed the gray-haired man a tiny slip of paper. "Urgent," she whispered.

The chemist gave an almost imperceptible nod. Marthe, suddenly overcome with a terrible sense of foreboding, wanted to ask that they not harm the cheerful Hauptmann Fashugel. But she remained silent as she ducked out of the shop, knowing that would have been an impossible request.

She wandered home in a state of apprehension, trying to convince herself once again that this was wartime and anything that harmed the Germans was good for Belgium. She supposed she would never get over the agitation of causing harm to people's lives, no matter what side they were on.

All Sunday during her rounds, Marthe waited with trepidation for the news of the Seven Sisters' presence at Westrozebeke. As the military band started up just outside the hospital courtyard, she could hear the clomping feet of hundreds of men and dozens of horses as they began their journey to her hometown. And then silence descended on half-deserted Roulers.

She was therefore startled when an orderly approached her, stating the Oberarzt wanted to see her.

She found him in the hospital lounge. "Fräulein Cnockaert." He nodded a greeting. "The bishop has asked that any injured soldiers who are capable of making the journey to Westrozebeke be allowed to do so. Headquarters is sending a lorry around, and, as some of them are still at risk of having a wound burst open, I think it would be best if you went with them. The ward is quiet this morning, so you shouldn't miss out on too much here." He took a sip of tea. "You have no objection, I suppose?"

Marthe opened her mouth, but nothing came out. The Oberarzt gave her a strange look, and she recovered her voice. "Of course not, Herr Oberarzt."

As she gathered medical supplies, she could only think about her own safety, now hoping that the Allies had not gotten the warning in time to assemble the Seven Sisters. But as she left the hospital and walked into the sunshine of a fine fall day, she realized that was ridiculous. Such an assemblage of Germans would be a boon to the Allies, and her presence would not change that.

She stared up into the blue sky, wondering if it would be the last time she would see such a sight. She reminded herself of all of those soldiers who would willingly give their lives to keep the Huns from ruling over Belgium: Jimmy, Arthur, Nicholas Hoot... even her own brother. If they could make such a sacrifice, surely she could as well.

She shut her eyes as the lorry began lurching its way toward her hometown, wondering if it were better or worse to be aware of your imminent death. That morning she had been relieved to hear Alphonse had not been commissioned to drive the ambulance. At that moment, however, she would have given anything to have him there by her side. *But that would mean he could be killed too.*

Marthe had not been back to Westrozebeke since the morning she'd left with Mother and the other women. The town had been nearly razed to the ground, though here and there a few stone walls stood in defiance of the shells and resulting fires. Her heart hardened as they passed the charred remains of her childhood home, where her father had almost been burned to death. The Germans deserved anything the Seven Sisters could bring.

The lorry halted just outside the crumbling Grand Place, where thousands of soldiers had gathered in close ranks. The bishop stood in the middle of the square, his arms raised. So focused were Marthe's ears on listening for the faintest sound of an airplane that she heard nothing of what he said. But, save for the droning bishop, no other sound broke through the warm stillness of the day. As the soldiers broke out in a final hymn, Marthe heaved a deep sigh, disappointment outweighing relief.

The brass band finished the hymn with a flourish, and the soldiers clapped dutifully. *Stop clapping you hateful Boches,* Marthe thought. *It's gone on long enough.* But then the men began to shout and she realized the thunderous sound was not coming from the soldiers on the ground: it was coming from the sky.

Smoke burned her eyes as she saw a plane swoop down, scattering men in all directions. She closed her eyes for a second, reminding herself that above all, she was a nurse and there to help people. She put her arms around the chest of an amputee and pulled him underneath the wheels of the lorry. An unscathed soldier who looked to be barely out of his teens was already installed there, his eyes wide with fright.

Marthe got into the young man's face. "You have the use of your legs and can run. This man cannot." She could see the soldier's Adam's apple move as he swallowed. The next moment he was out from under the lorry, running for dear life as one of the Allied airplanes swept low, nearly decapitating him.

Hordes of gray uniforms swirled everywhere, the rat-a-tat of machine guns breathing new life into men ready to collapse from exhaustion. A bomb hit nearby, showering the bare earth of Westrozebeke onto the heads of the soldiers running for their lives as Marthe continued hauling wounded Germans under the truck.

The Seven Sisters eventually stopped swooping, and slowed their machine guns. They got into formation and then headed off somewhere else, probably content with the damage they'd caused. The gray masses returned, moving much slower this time, hampered by both exhaustion and the bomb craters, broken instruments, and dead soldiers that obstructed their path.

Marthe was assisting her charges in emerging from underneath the lorry when a senior officer from the hospital approached her. "Fräulein, you must return to Roulers immediately. Inform the Oberarzt they must send as many ambulances and doctors as they can spare and that the hospital should prepare to receive a great many wounded men."

She nodded, hoping he'd never know she was the one who'd caused the destruction in the first place.

Thankfully she did not have much time to think for the rest of the day, and well into the night, as she did her best to make the wounded men comfortable.

When she arrived home early the next morning, she was relieved to see that the door to Fashugel's room was ajar and she could see movement inside. She was too exhausted to greet him.

After she'd gotten a few hours of sleep, she woke up, her stomach rumbling.

Red Carl was already seated at a table.

"Shall I fix you and Hauptmann Fashugel breakfast?" Marthe asked.

Red Carl's eyes widened. "It will be just me from now on, Fräulein Cnockaert. The hauptmann was killed yesterday by one of the Seven Sisters' machine guns."

"I'm sorry," Marthe said, and meant it.

"Yes. He was a bloody fine officer, our Fashugel. We'll not get another commander like him, not even if this war lasts another eternity."

CHAPTER 41

ALOUETTE

DECEMBER 1915

Christmas in Madrid was a magical time. Although the war dragged on, the Spanish citizens remained, for the most part, oblivious to it.

On Christmas Eve, von Krohn requested Alouette to meet him in the Santa Cruz Square market. As she wandered through the merry crowd, the smell of roasted turkey filling the air, she felt unexpectedly light-hearted. That came crashing down as she caught sight of the Baron, who was accompanied by his wife.

"Alouette, I believe you've met Ilse," von Krohn stated, rubbing at his collar.

"*Joyeux Noël,*" Alouette told her, recalling the Baroness's affinity for everything French.

"Thank you," the Baroness replied coolly, accepting a bag of spiced almonds from her husband.

"What are you doing later, Alouette?" von Krohn inquired, ignoring his wife's suspicious glance.

"Oh, I thought I would head to the Palace Hotel. I hear they give a marvelous party."

"That party doesn't start till 11," he replied. "You are welcome to come to our house. We are giving a dinner party for a few dignitaries." He pulled at his collar again. "The military attaché Arnold Kalle will be there."

"Really?" Alouette couldn't keep the surprise out of her voice.

"Oh yes, it would not be acceptable for Kalle to dine alone as a bachelor on Christmas Eve." The Baroness's tone implied that the same could be said of Alouette.

Alouette, reminded of the last time she attended the von Krohns' dinner party, demurred. "I'm afraid I must decline in favor of a much-needed nap."

Von Krohn murmured in her ear, "I will be at the Plaza by 1 in the morning."

Alouette pretended she hadn't heard him and took her leave.

That evening, Alouette was seated at a small table near the dance floor. She had just ordered a drink when she heard a thumping sound.

"*Excusez-moi,*" a young man said. The tables were very closely placed together and he seated himself at the table beside Alouette's with difficulty. As he picked up his upper thigh, readjusting his leg, she saw that the portion underneath his knee was wooden. He reached out his hand. "Lieutenant Jack McKenna of the British Army."

Alouette noted how blue his eyes were before she put her hand in his. "Alouette Richer."

"Pleased to meet you."

"Did the Germans do that?" she asked, nodding at his wooden leg.

"Yes," McKenna answered with a laugh. "Your good friends, the Germans."

"*My* good friends?" she repeated.

He put both arms on the table. Though his words seemed unfriendly, the tone in his voice remained amiable. "I've seen you around with von Krohn."

She gave him an apologetic smile. "I knew the Baron in Switzerland before the war. He has taken it upon himself to introduce me to Madrid society."

"Do you believe he is a desirable dinner companion?"

"Maybe not as desirable as yourself." Even if he had an alternative reason for bringing up her German affiliation, it felt good to be flirting with a handsome soldier.

"Oh, I don't know about that," McKenna asserted. "It would be difficult for an officer in His Majesty's service to—" he frowned. "How can I say this without offending you?"

"Say what?" Alouette prompted.

He took a drink of his wine. "Let's put it this way—a British officer should take care not to get caught in a Lark's trap."

She paused, contemplating whether he knew of her codename, or if he was simply alluding to the English translation of her first name. She raised her chin. "Are you engaged with British Intelligence?"

McKenna neither confirmed nor denied anything. "Why do you ask? Because you are a spy for the Germans?"

Alouette sighed. "It seems to all you men—whether British, German, French, or what have you—women are like birds of prey, sent out to blind an unfortunate hare and make it easier for the hounds to hunt it. Have you no other thought than to accuse every woman of espionage?"

McKenna frowned. "Well, for me, I cannot think of a better way to win this war. Women make the best war laborers, even if the nurses couldn't save my leg." As if to soften the blow of his remark, he continued, "How could I not have a grudge against the enemy, when it is their fault I can't ask you to dance with me tonight?"

She let out a tinkling laugh and was rewarded when McKenna's face relaxed. But his tone was bitter as he said, "Here is one of them coming to invite you in my place."

She turned her head, expecting to see the Baron. She was therefore surprised to see a slim man with a full head of dark hair standing beside her.

He bowed. "Madame Richer, I am Arnold Kalle."

Her heart sped up at finally getting to meet the archnemesis of the Deuxiéme Bureau, and, for that matter, von Krohn.

Kalle held out his arm. "Will you give me this fox-trot?"

Alouette was torn: part of her wanted to stay and chat more with McKenna, conscious that they might be of use to each other. But then again, as a formidable foe, Kalle also played an important part in her mission, and here he was, presenting her with an opportunity to get to know him better.

She placed a gloved hand in Kalle's open palm. She didn't dare glance back at McKenna as Kalle led her to the dance floor.

Kalle appeared to be slightly younger than von Krohn; Alouette figured him to be somewhere in his forties. Unlike his counterpart, Kalle had a handsome face and carried himself with a manly grace.

"Pardon me if I seemed rude earlier," he said as he led her in the dance. "But our mutual friend the Baron sent me to warn you that the man with whom you were flirting is an agent of the British Intelligence Service."

Alouette studied Kalle's clean-shaven face. It was unlikely that von Krohn would have done such a thing, but if Kalle was lying, his expression betrayed nothing. "Please thank the Baron for his thoughtful forewarning," she replied. "But please also tell him that I knew the man with whom I was dealing."

"Is that so?" Kalle narrowed his eyes, but did not miss a beat in his dancing. "You are playing a dangerous game. McKenna is considered a very astute youth."

"Dangerous for whom?" Alouette demanded. "For von Krohn, who gets jealous easily? Or for you, who, I fancy, does not?"

"Dangerous for us all."

In lieu of answering, she rested her head against Kalle's chest.

Encouraged, Kalle steered her to the sidelines and slowed his feet. "I see that little salon over there is now unoccupied. Should we rest for a minute?"

Alouette's radar flashed *danger*, but she nodded anyway.

Kalle hesitated. "Perhaps I should mention to von Krohn that I have indeed gotten you away from your English neighbor. Otherwise he might fail to understand—"

"Don't bother," she said coolly. "He doesn't own me." With that, she marched into the little salon and set down in a blue velvet armchair. She crossed her legs, noting Kalle's eyes following her movements. "And now, Herr Kalle, I wish to know why you have been following me since I arrived in Madrid."

"Did von Krohn tell you that?"

"No," she lied. "Is it not the duty of a spy to know everything?"

Kalle looked anxiously around the little room, but they were alone. "Once again, madame, permit me to warn you that you have involved yourself in a treacherous situation."

"You are not the first to tell me." Alouette folded her hands over her lap, wishing she had the foresight to bring her wine with her. It might have given her more courage to deal with this sinister man. "Tell me, Kalle, why were you given the Iron Cross? I was under the impression that, like the French *Croix de Guerre*, the German Iron Cross was given only to those who had been in the firing line. Is it because your profession is really so risky?"

Kalle's already narrowed eyes grew positively beady. "If I were decorated, madame," he spit out with vehemence, "it was for defending my native country."

She lowered her fan and pasted a toothy smile on her face. "Do you mean to accuse me of betraying my native country?"

"I do not yet know whether you are defending or betraying it." His face relaxed and a muscle played in his cheek, as if he were trying not to smile. "What I do know, madame, is that you are as keen as a knife."

She lowered her head. "And you are as well, Kalle. And in order that we do not risk putting out each other's eyes while playing with such sharp weapons, I propose a truce."

Alouette studied the effect her words had on him, as if she were gauging the range of an airplane's guns from the cockpit. Every bullet must have hit its mark as he appeared taken aback. Nevertheless, he replied, "I'll accept your offering."

She shook his outstretched hand. "I wonder what young McKenna has been doing while we've been conversing." She rose. "I had already succeeded in making him tell me that the British Admiralty soon hopes to eliminate the disastrous consequences of your submarine warfare…"

Kalle managed to recover his voice. "He told you that?"

"Yes, but seeing as it was naval, it's more von Krohn's domain than yours. I didn't think it concerned you."

He shook his head in amazement. "You are indeed the devil and must get the better of everyone you encounter."

"I am not the devil, Kalle. I'm just doing my best to navigate this, as you put it, treacherous situation."

He stood up. "Shall we meet again?"

. . .

As Alouette headed back to the table, she noticed McKenna had gone.

"Madame," a waiter called. "Señor McKenna asked me to give you this." He handed her a small envelope.

She sat at the table as she opened it. Inside was a hundred peseta note and his calling card. On the back of the card he had scribbled, "I did not dare to pay for your drink in your absence, but I beg you to consent to pay for it yourself."

She looked up to signal the waiter, noting that the Baron had taken a seat in the opposite corner of the room. She caught the waiter's attention. "Here," she said, putting the peseta note in his hand. "*Joyeux Noël.*"

The waiter's eyes widened. "*Feliz Navidad!*" he called as Alouette grabbed her drink and headed to the Baron's table, where he sat simmering.

"Did you have a good evening with your Englishman and with Kalle?" The bitterness oozed from his voice.

Alouette scrunched her eyes, picturing von Krohn as a helpless hare which she had just succeeded in blinding with jealousy. "I did, thank you."

"Well, I've acquired some of my own news. It seems the German Navy is poised to win the war, and there is nothing your suitors can do about it."

"Oh? How so?"

The normally discreet von Krohn could not resist bragging to Alouette. "We have commissioned fifty brand new submarines—they are capable of remaining at sea for several months. They will be able to break through the blockade once and for all and Germany will triumph."

CHAPTER 42

MARTHE

MARCH 1916

*A*fter eighteen months of fighting, the war at the western front had turned into a stalemate, with both sides digging into trenches but making no major strides. Equally as unfortunate, Marthe's espionage antics since the death of Hauptmann Fashugel had also reached an impasse.

She was returning from the hospital late one night when she became aware of someone behind her. She quickened her pace only to hear the stranger doing the same. She glanced back, thinking she would see the ominous form of a gendarme, but the stranger was not in uniform.

"Would you kindly direct me to the Grand Place?" His voice was oddly familiar.

She paused in her walking, realizing that the stranger was Herr Jacobs, the safety-pin man who'd boarded at the grocer's house for a short while. He was dressed in threadbare clothes, his boots nearly worn through the toes.

"Follow me," she replied.

"I'm actually looking for the Café Carillon. Do you know of it?"

He stood in the middle of the road instead of on the sidewalk. "Even the houses have ears," he said in a low voice, nodding at the brick walls surrounding them.

"My father owns the Café Carillon."

Herr Jacobs nodded, clearly gathering that she and her father had finally been united. He pursed his lips and Marthe turned to see a group of soldiers standing on the corner of the Grand Place.

"Meet me at the Sturms' farmhouse tonight," he said quietly. "There's someone there I want you to meet."

She nodded her assent. Mevrouw Sturms was a Flemish farm-woman who was staunchly proud that two of her twelve children were Allied soldiers. Marthe had previously helped her pass letters to and from her sons.

Herr Jacobs grabbed her hand and said loudly, "Thank you, nurse. I will pass on your sound advice to my poor mother." He touched his hat and then strolled off. He carried his left shoulder as straight and strong as Marthe remembered, but his right one was hunched now, as if he'd suffered a grave wound.

Marthe had no trouble making her way out to the farmhouse that night. Mevrouw Sturms did not say anything as she ushered Marthe inside and led her to a small, sparsely furnished room before shutting the door and walking away.

The room was poorly ventilated and smelled like stale cigarettes and rotting wounds. A man lay on the bed, and, as he struck a match, Marthe caught sight of his face. "Max!"

Her brother paused to look at her, the match nearly burning his fingers. "Marthe?"

She rushed to the bed.

"Oof," he said as she embraced him tightly.

She pulled back. "Are you hurt?"

"Only a little."

She didn't believe him and undid the few intact buttons of his shirt with her deft nurse's fingers. His shoulder was covered with rough bandages, which she removed, revealing a deep cut, the hastily-finished stitches doing nothing to seal the wound.

As if on cue, Mevrouw Sturms reentered the room and handed Marthe a tray of first aid supplies before retreating again.

"It's lucky the bullet just grazed me," Max stated. "Otherwise I might have had to answer some awkward questions from a Hun doctor."

Marthe dipped a washcloth into a bowl of warm water and dabbed at the wound. "What sort of questions, Max? What are you doing here?"

"What am *I* doing here? A better question is what are *you* doing here? They told me some woman named Laura was coming."

"I am Laura."

Max moved her hand aside. "What do you mean, you're Laura?"

She resumed her cleaning. "That's my code name."

He laughed, a hollow laugh, not his normal deep chuckle. "Code name? What all have you been up to?"

She gave him the short version of what had happened to her since the war started while she threaded a needle sterilized with iodine. "And you, Max? We've been worried sick about you."

"I've been fine."

"Clearly not," she scolded. "Not with this gash. Tell me."

Max's voice was uncharacteristically somber. "Have you heard of the Langenboom gun?"

She shook her head.

"It was a huge gun they used to bombard Dunkirk. It could shoot miles behind the line." He took a breath as Marthe continued sewing up his wound. "My commanding officer got word that there was one posted outside of Moere and needed someone familiar with the area to dig up information on what the Huns were planning." He shot her his familiar grin and her heart swelled. "So I volunteered."

"Max."

His grin grew impossibly wide. "My code name is No. 8. It seems spying runs in the family."

"What happened?"

"An airplane dropped me outside of Pitthem. I tried to get hired on at a nearby farm but the Boches wouldn't employ any new laborers near the gun. But then I noticed that they used prisoners to repair the road."

"And what did you do?" Marthe asked, fearing she knew the answer.

"I got myself arrested. I picked a fight with a Hun."

"Did you hit him?"

"Nearly. Settled for cursing him out, but it was enough to get me three weeks of road labor in the shadow of the Langenboom. Oh Marthe," he repositioned his body to face her. "You should see it. They've got underground ammunition compartments as big as Westrozebeke's Grand Place, buried under cement walls two meters thick. And even though it's patrolled night and day by Hun guards, they've surrounded it with barbed wire."

"Wow," Marthe breathed. "That's some gun." He shifted in the bed and she saw his face twist in pain. "What happened to your shoulder?"

"We slept in a hut not far from the bastion. Our guards, believe it or not, were lazy devils and three nights ago I managed to climb out of the hut and go exploring. I had just finished mapping the gun's position when a patrolman approached me. I ran off and nearly got back through the window but a bullet scraped my shoulder. I hid the wound from my guards until my term was up and they let me go."

"And now you're here."

Max nodded. "Herr Jacobs has just delivered my newest orders: I'm to destroy the Langenboom as soon as possible."

"No, Max. You're injured. You have to give yourself a few days to get your strength up."

"In a few days they could turn that gun loose on Moere and kill everyone in the town."

"Max," she admonished him. Although he was older by three years, Marthe had always been the more responsible sibling. Some things never changed.

"Marthe, please don't tell Mother and Father that I'm here. If something goes wrong..."

"What are you talking about? You know that I cannot keep this a secret from them. And if something does indeed go wrong—not that it will because you are going to stay in bed—they would want to see you one last time."

"I don't want them to have to lie if they are questioned by the

Boches." He waved his non-injured arm. "Come now, 'Laura,' you of all people should understand that."

"If Mother and Father found out that I knew of your whereabouts…"

"It's only until I can manage to blow up the Langenboom. Then we can all celebrate, together as a family."

Marthe sighed before glancing out the window at the rising sun. "I'd better go before they start asking questions. I'll just tell them I had to stay at the hospital all night." She rose and put her hand on his arm. "Will you be all right?"

"Of course I will. I've survived this long."

"I can use some of my contacts to see what they know."

"Don't you go blowing up that gun on your own, little sister. This is my job."

"It can wait a few days. Until then, you stay here and rest. I'll let Mevrouw Sturms know how to change your bandages and I'll be back the night after tomorrow to check on you."

"Good night, Marthe."

As she walked to work two mornings later, a small boy ran past her and slipped a note in her hand. She recognized the boy as one of Mevrouw Sturms', and Marthe's heart thudded in her chest as she read the note. "No. 8 is desperately hurt and wishes you to come as soon as you can."

She called to an orderly just entering the hospital gates. "Mein herr, please give the Oberarzt my regards. Something terrible has happened and I must return home."

He nodded. "Be here all the earlier tomorrow."

Marthe arrived at the farmhouse red-faced and sweating. Mevrouw Sturms greeted her wordlessly and led her back to the little room. Herr Jacobs knelt beside her brother, who lay in the same bed as before, a clean bandage on his shoulder, but now a red, raw wound stretched in a jagged line across his chest. Another bandage, this one stained with blood, covered his lower abdomen.

"Well, little sister," Max gasped. "It seems luck is not on my side, but I'll polish off the Langenboom yet. Just wait till I'm well again."

She took his clammy, pale hand in hers. "What happened?"

Herr Jacobs answered for him. "Last night No. 8, your brother, decided to blow up the ammunition compartments under the Langenboom."

Max gave a wry smile. "I was hoping that a little spark would blast the whole place to bits."

"And it probably would have," Herr Jacobs added, "if two German secret service men hadn't spotted him and tried to question him. He had on his person the complete layout of the bastion and several sticks of dynamite."

Max's voice had become a whisper. "I thought I had safely escaped, but a stray bullet got me, once again." He shut his eyes.

"Max?" Marthe squeezed his hand. To her immense relief, his eyes slowly opened.

"I'll give you some time," Herr Jacobs said, rising. "And Max," he paused at the door. "You did a brave thing."

"I only wish I could have finished the job." He still had that characteristic half grin/ half sneer on his face, but Marthe could tell that her older brother was dying. He focused his eyes on her. "Now, little sister, don't you go blowing up the Langenboom while I'm ill. This is my job."

"Max?"

"I'm going to get some rest now, Marthe. I'm very tired. So tired," he repeated as his eyes closed again.

Half an hour later, her older brother, her tormentor, partner in crime, and personal hero, was dead. Marthe sat by his side, losing track of time as she reminisced on their childhood: Max laughing, Max putting pinecones on her chair, Max pulling her braids.

When she finally rose and dried her tears, she took the plans for the Langenboom from his jacket and handed them to Herr Jacobs. She kept the two sticks of dynamite for no other reason that they seemed like useful articles for a spy to possess. And because they had once been Max's.

CHAPTER 43

M'GREET

MAY 1916

The Paris of 1916 wasn't terribly different from the one M'greet had grown to know and love. The Germans had been concentrating their attack on the historic city of Verdun, miles away from the capital, but close enough that soldiers at the front would come to Paris for rest, and to forget the horrors of war. And it was not just men from the main French and English troops, but those of their colonies, such as Algeria and Morocco, which, with their Zouave uniforms, gave the city an even more international flair than normal.

M'greet's patterns while she stayed in the city of lights did not change a great deal—she rose around 10 each day and went down to the lobby for coffee and yesterday's stale bread, and then returned to her room to get ready to visit furriers, shoe-makers, perfumiers, florists, jewelers, or whatever her whim was for that day. She then would return to her room to change her outfit for dinner. Having abandoned her mission, she never gave Fräulein Doktor or the rest of the Germans much thought whatsoever, besides missing her beautiful, confiscated furs on a particularly cold evening.

Though M'greet's overall routine didn't vary much, her dinner companions often did. First, she resumed her relationship with Freddy, but when he left again for the front, she took up with Jean Hallaure, and then Nicholas Casfield. She was quite used to being surrounded by admiring men, so when two men followed her on a shopping trip, she didn't give much notice, especially because neither was particularly handsome. But the same men trailed her the next day to a furrier, and then after that to a jewelry shop.

She complained to the front desk numerous times, but the clerk could do nothing. She began making it a game to lose them, spending van der Capellan's money on automobile taxis, gleefully watching the men's surprised faces as the taxi pulled away, splashing mud on their trousers.

Nicholas Casfield offered to accompany her to dinner one night at the end of May. She was, of course, late in meeting him and as she descended the steps of the hotel lobby, saw that he was engaged in conversation with another soldier.

"Nicky," she called, wanting his full attention on her. Both he and the other soldier looked up. She walked slowly down the stairs, knowing that her diaphanous dress would trail prettily behind her.

"Aren't you going to introduce me?" she asked in a slightly breathless voice once she reached them.

The companion stuck out a hand. "Vladimir Masloff," he said smoothly.

M'greet put a hand on her chest. "That's quite a mouthful. Are you Russian?"

"Indeed," he replied.

"I shall call you Vadim." This put a smile on the man's handsome visage. M'greet batted her eyelashes as she studied him. He was very young, perhaps around half her own age. Thick eyebrows framed his dark eyes and his cheekbones cut a line across his face, which was clean-shaven, the better to reveal his sensuous, rouge-colored lips.

There was something about those lips that made M'greet forget all about Nicholas Casfield. "Would you care to escort me to dinner?" she asked, tucking her arm in Vadim's.

Nicholas took the hint. He twirled his nearly empty glass. "I'm going to get another drink," he said before walking across the lobby.

"So, you are the famous Mata Hari." Vadim's French was slightly broken, his accent poor.

M'greet waved her hand. "Not anymore. I haven't danced for ages."

"What is your current name?"

"Margaretha Zelle-Macleod."

"That is even more of a mouthful than mine." He thought for a minute. "I shall call *you* Marina."

He told her over dinner of his background: he belonged to the 1st Special Imperial Regiment, a unit that was dispatched by the Czar himself to the French front.

"And you are an officer," M'greet stated admiringly. "You must be extremely talented to have your star rise so fast."

"Yes," he agreed. "I'm stationed at Mailly, in the province of Champagne. I'm only on leave for a few days before I must return."

M'greet touched his hand. "I shall keep you company until then."

After dinner he invited her for a stroll along the promenade in the Bois de Boulogne. When they returned to the hotel, M'greet encouraged Vadim to exchange his room on the second floor for the one that adjoined hers. After they'd said public goodbyes in the hallway outside, Vadim knocked on the inside door and M'greet invited him into her room.

They were inseparable for the next few days. M'greet wanted to soak up as much of Vadim as she could before he had to return to the front. She'd been a courtesan for nearly ten years, and had met many, many men, but Vadim was different. Perhaps it was because he still held a touch of innocence in this world of hardship.

He asked her to accompany him to the train station when it came time for him to return to his station in the province of Champagne.

M'greet wept openly. "I cannot wait for you to get leave again. I have to see you sooner than that."

Vadim pulled a handkerchief out of his pocket. "What will you do? You can't exactly follow me to war."

"No," she agreed. "But I will think of something."

The train whistle blew. "I'm sorry, Marina," Vadim said softly. "I have to go." He put both of his large hands on her face and tilted her head upward before kissing her mouth.

"I love you, Vadim," she called at his retreating back. "I love you and I will see you soon!"

He waved as he mounted the train. She took a deep breath as it began to pull away.

"Marina!" Vadim appeared in the corner of a crowded window. "I love you too!"

She waved the handkerchief, shouting "I love you," until the train was a tiny dot in the distance and the smoke had dissipated.

Jean Halluare was sitting on a velvet chair, pretending to read a book in the lobby of the hotel when she returned. Hallaure was a second lieu-tenant who had been wounded and then installed in the Ministry of War. M'greet had spent a few nights with him in the middle of March —he came from an exceedingly well-off family, but he was awfully boring.

Hallaure stood. He was tall and cut a handsome figure in his cavalry uniform but the sight of his brass buttons reminded M'greet of Vadim. Her legs felt weak. "Champagne," she croaked out.

Hallaure pulled out his pocket watch. "It's a bit early, but I suppose…"

M'greet sank into the couch. "No. Where is the Champagne prov-ince? I must get there."

He resumed his seat and put a tanned hand on M'greet's white one. "It's in the war zone."

"Name some nearby cities."

He sat back and rubbed his chin. "Reims. Calais. Vittel."

M'greet sat up straight. "Vittel. Yes, Vittel. I've been there before. The waters are said to cure any ailment."

"You would need to get a special pass to go there now. It's too close to the action." He patted her hand. "Forgive me for saying this, but, although you look stressed, you do not look that ill. Besides, there are plenty of other spa towns that are further from the front."

"I must go to Vittel," she told him firmly.

"Then you will need to procure a doctor's note and ask at the Military Bureau for Foreigners for a permit to travel to a war zone."

She put a hand to her throat and coughed before rising. "I will visit my doctor soon. For now, I must rest."

CHAPTER 44

MARTHE

JUNE 1916

*D*uring the first week in June, Canteen Ma failed to call for the first time since Marthe had met her. Another week passed with still no sign of the old woman.

One evening Marthe was returning from work when she saw that the man who brought the liquor supplies to the café was standing outside the back door.

"Good evening, mademoiselle," he said, tipping his hat and indicating the bottles at his feet. "Will you please check the voucher?"

"My parents normally take care of the café business," Marthe started uncertainly, but the man thrust the voucher into her hands anyway. She unfolded it and just caught a small paper cylinder as it fell. She gave the man a puzzled look, but he lifted his lapel to reveal two safety pins running diagonally underneath.

"Where is Canteen Ma?" Marthe asked as she handed back the voucher.

He shrugged. "I'm not sure. I was told that I will be your main contact from now on." His frown deepened. "I doubt you will ever buy fruit from Canteen Ma again." He gave her one last nod before walking away.

Marthe hefted the box of liquor, her heart weighing on her as much as the bottles of schnapps. She supposed that Canteen Ma's luck had run out, a fate that they all faced every day. Perhaps she had already gone before a firing squad, leaving nothing in her wake but a creaky cart, no one to recognize or honor all of the work she did for the Cause.

At any rate, Marthe would miss seeing the eccentric old lady.

A few weeks later, Alphonse approached Marthe in the courtyard and informed her in a low voice that the Germans were accumulating large amounts of rifle ammunition and using the grounds of a house near the Grand Place as their dumping ground.

"Should we let the Allies know this would make a good bombing target?" Marthe replied, her voice barely above a whisper.

Alphonse pulled at his lip. "No. They've also been constructing anti-aircraft guns, and I doubt the Seven Sisters could get close enough without suffering a great deal of damage of their own."

"We can't just let them stockpile all of this stuff to use against the Allies." Marthe thought for a second. What would Max have done if he was in the same situation? "Alphonse, I've got it." She gestured for him to follow her into a corner, away from any prying ears. "I've got sticks of dynamite. If we light them and toss them into the ammunition stores, that should be enough to turn it all into one big inferno."

"No. Marthe, that's madness. There's a ring of soldiers constantly patrolling the outside walls. We could never get the dynamite past them."

"We've got to do something. Even if it's just informing the Allies so they can come up with a plan."

Alphonse nodded. "You let your contacts know, and I'll try to think of an idea in the meantime."

A few days later, Alphonse pulled Marthe aside as she was leaving the hospital. "Have you ever heard anyone mention a secret passage underneath the hospital grounds?"

"No." She sat down on a bench underneath a yew tree. "Is there such a thing?"

Alphonse nodded, clearly too excited to sit. "In 1914, Roulers was bombed by shells. I had just finished an ambulance shift and joined a couple of orderlies who were investigating the craters left by them. One of them revealed a big black hole surrounded by stonework. We went down with torches—it seemed to lead for miles under the town, but we didn't have the leisure time, nor the strength, to follow it to its conclusion so we covered it over with some dirt and forgot about it."

"Do you think that the others have forgotten about it as well?"

"I believe so." Alphonse finally took a seat next to her. "Most of the men who went down with me have long been transferred, and the wooden staff hut was erected right over the crater. But look at this," he held up a history book. "Roulers, like many medieval towns, once had an open sewer running through the middle of the main street. Don't you see, Marthe?" He dropped the book. "This sewer leads right past where the ammunition store is located."

She began to see Alphonse's point. "If we could get into the sewer, we could work our way through until we were underneath the dump, set off the dynamite, and vanish, leaving the stores to incinerate."

"Exactly!"

"But," Marthe pulled at her bottom lip. "What if we misjudge the distance we've gone and stick our heads out of the ground in the middle of the Grand Place after curfew, or, worse yet, at the feet of one of the sentries?"

Alphonse pulled a cigarette out of his pocket and lit it. "Yes. It will be risky—we could even come right through the floor of the Town-Kommandant's office."

She slumped, crossing her arms across her chest.

He blew out a ring of smoke. "But if we are careful and use common sense, I don't think we will. It's possible to use careful calculations, at least up to a point."

At this, Marthe sat up again.

Alphonse picked up the book and flipped through it. "The sewer runs mostly straight—it had to. Look," he displayed a page. "We can use this old map to estimate how far it is to the center of the dump."

"Surely it's not that easy to know how far you've traveled underground."

He flicked his finished cigarette. "I've thought about that—we'll make a length of string 100 meters long. If the dump is 3 kilometers away, that's thirty times the length of my string. But I would need a partner to help me measure and hold the string taut. What do you say, Marthe?" He put a hand on her arm. "Are you willing to take on such a risk?"

The warmth of his touch seemed to seep inside her, filling her blood with an unexpected fire. Alphonse must have seen something peculiar in her face because he removed his hand to dig in his pocket for another cigarette.

"Of course," she replied once her insides had returned to a normal temperature. "Especially if the reward is seeing all those potential weapons being blown to bits. When do we start?"

"Tomorrow night seems as good a time as any, provided they don't send me to the front with the ambulance. Find a reason to work late at the hospital, and meet me at nine in front of the staff hut." He glanced over at her. "But be sure to get some rest tonight, Marthe. We are going to have quite a series of hard evenings ahead of us."

As soon as the town clock struck the nine o'clock hour, Marthe set out for the staff hut. Most of the other employees had long gone home, and only the orderlies on duty were in the wards. A lone figure, shadowy in the closing dark of the evening, stood outside the long wooden hut.

"Hello?" Marthe spoke with a disguised tone in case the person was not who she thought it was.

To her relief, a familiar voice answered, "Hello, Marthe, you are right on time. Sit down for a moment."

She sat as the dim figure of Alphonse paced in front of her. "I've done some more reconnoitering, and I think our plan is sound. This hut," he reached out and set his palm on a wooden slat, "is slightly raised to keep out the dampness of the ground... and the rats. It leaves us enough room to crawl beneath and slip right into the hole, without having to raise up floor-boards, only to replace them again when we leave."

The ever-practical Alphonse had worked out even more logistics than she'd anticipated. "What's in the sack?" she asked, nodding at it.

"Cement, a hammer, a saw, a strong chisel, and, of course, plenty of nails." Even in the extensive darkness, she could see his white teeth flash as he grinned. "I'll not be able to visit the canteen for at least a month, now that my pay is pledged for all of this gear."

He beckoned Marthe to follow him inside the little hut. "The first thing we need to do is," he gently placed his sack full of supplies on the floor of the cabin, "hide our light." He grabbed a bunch of newspapers, and the two of them covered the windows. Alphonse then lit a lantern and gestured to several loose wooden planks in the corner of the cabin. "These were left by lazy workmen. They'll form the floor of the sewer beneath us."

"How deep is it?" she asked as she helped him move one of the planks toward the gap.

"It's about a 2.5-meter drop." He paused to gaze at her. "This is going to be a messy job, Marthe. I hope that cloak of yours is an old one."

Once again, she felt her face heat up, but ignored the feelings that her proximity to Alphonse ignited. "How will we get out again once we are down there?"

"That's where these will prove incredibly useful." He dropped a plank and then the sack into the black hole they'd uncovered. He then gave her a mock salute before sliding into the darkness.

It seemed like an eternity before Marthe heard a faint thump. She peered into the dark hole, only just able to discern the gleam of a torch.

"Well, Marthe, I'm safe in the sewer." Alphonse's voice was garbled and she heard him spit. "Just remember to keep your mouth shut tight."

She drew her cloak around her and then scooted to the edge of the hole, feet first, the way Alphonse had done. She dropped down, and he caught her waist.

"Thanks," Marthe murmured as she stood unsteadily on the loose rubble of the sewer. He moved away and raised his torch. She could see they were standing in a passageway, the walls and ceiling paved with flat stones, surrounded by a cold, damp stillness.

"We should get moving." He rummaged around in the sack and produced a length of cord. On either end were wooden pegs. He handed one end to her and took the other, setting off down the passageway.

Marthe stood still, watching the light from his torch growing fainter as the cord tightened. She reached up to rub at her eyes and brushed a mesh of cobwebs. The dust it uncovered caused her to sneeze as she felt the peg in her hand jerk. As she started forward, she heard rustling in the opening above. She froze, certain that they'd been caught even before they'd made headway into the sewer. She raised her torch to reveal two beady black eyes. She maneuvered through the sewer as quickly as possible.

"What's gotten into you?" Alphonse asked when she reached him.

"I saw a rat," she breathed.

"Yes," she could hear the laughter in his voice. "You'll run into quite a few of them."

They spent an hour in the subterranean sewer, taking turns walking with the string until it pulled taut, signifying another 100 meters. The only sound besides their own footfalls was the ever-present scurrying of the rats who managed to stay just beyond the reach of their torchlight.

At last they'd made 30 passes. Marthe joined Alphonse underneath where he suspected the store lay. He scraped up a little mound of dirt with his hands and drew a cross with white chalk to mark the spot.

She lifted her lantern to contemplate the seemingly impenetrable stone above their heads. "The roof above might collapse if we try to pull away that rock," she stated.

"My father was a miner," Alphonse replied. "Do you know what a miner would do if he had to remove rock but wanted to preserve his head?"

She shook her head.

"He'd put props against the roof before he picked at the mortar."

"The loose planks?"

"Exactly." He held out his hands, measuring distances. "We're going to need a ladder to help us get to the ammunition dump, and at the other end." He pulled out a pocket-watch and held the torch near it. "I've got to be in my barracks by midnight, or else I might have to answer some awkward questions."

Marthe moved closer to him. "Do you really think this will work?"

He lit a cigarette, the match casting light on a horde of rats scurrying away. "What do we have to lose if it doesn't?"

She pictured the piles of ammunition that, hopefully, lay just above their heads. The actual act of blowing up the dump loomed much more dangerous than walking through a sewer, but Alphonse's presence alleviated some of her nervousness. "Tomorrow night, then? Same time?"

"Same time."

They began their journey back to the hut. Now that the work was finished for the night, Marthe could hear her heart hammering, keeping pace with the rats' scampering. "I don't know that much about you, Alphonse. Who were you before the war?"

He lit another cigarette. "Who was anyone before the war? Does it matter at this point?"

She thought for a moment, picturing herself, little Marthe Cnockaert as a nursing student at University, ready to do anything she could to please her family. And now here she was, planning to blow up a German ammunition store. "Did you always know you wanted to be a priest?"

"No." His tone grew softer. "I wasn't sure I was ready to give up a family for God."

"But you changed your mind."

"Yes. There are some things worth sacrificing for, no matter what the cost."

She agreed with him on the statement in principle, but not necessarily with forfeiting the chance at love.

"What about you, Marthe? What will become of you once the war is over?"

"I suppose I'll stay a nurse. At least until I get married and have babies. That's what women do, isn't it?"

"Is it?" Even though he was right next to her, Alphonse's voice sounded far away. "Somehow I can't picture you in that role."

"*I* want a family," she stated, her voice firm. "I know that more than ever... now that Max is gone."

"I didn't know that you knew for sure about Max. Did you get word from the front?"

Glad for the change of subject, Marthe spent the rest of their journey back filling him in on what happened to her brother. "That's where I got the dynamite sticks," she told him as they reached the hole below the staff cabin.

"I wondered." They paused and looked up, feeling the air of the cabin on their faces. "I'm going to lift you up as high as I can, and you will have to pull yourself out."

Marthe nodded, feeling an unexpected ache when Alphonse put his hands around her waist. As he hoisted her up, she realized she wasn't as sure about her future as she'd sounded before in the pit. She didn't know if she wanted that family after all if it couldn't be with Alphonse.

CHAPTER 45

M'GREET

JUNE 1916

M'greet wanted nothing more than to be with Vadim in Vittel. She had not heard a word from him since he left for the front, despite asking anxiously at the Grand Hotel's front desk every day. Following Hallaure's instructions, she managed to convince her doctor, another former lover, that a mysterious illness had come over her and required her to go to the spa at Vittel as soon as possible.

When she obtained the doctor's consent, she set about trying to get a pass. The official at the Military Bureau for Foreigners appeared somewhat friendly and told her she wanted the Deuxiéme Bureau next door. 282 boulevard, Saint-Germain was an expensive-looking apartment building with tiled floors and high ceilings. She adjusted her straw hat with its fashionable gray plume before she went up to the front desk.

An officer greeted her and asked for her papers. He gave them a cursory glance before nodding at her. "Come with me."

He led her to an office where a large man with greasy hair and a too-small mustache that did nothing to hide his pock-marked face sat behind a desk. "Ah, Miss Mata Hari, come in, come in."

M'greet was only a bit startled that he used her stage name—her papers only gave her real name—but figured that her dancing fame had once again preceded her.

He nodded at her but didn't rise. "I am Georges Ladoux."

Taking the papers from the officer, Ladoux flipped through them with his fat hands. "Ah. I see you wish to go to Vittel. Are you not aware that it is in a military zone?"

"I am well aware." Although he was slow to invite her to sit down, M'greet arranged herself in a hard-backed chair anyway. "But it is also a resort that I have gone to before. You will see there is a note in there from my doctor so that I may be permitted to take the waters." She coughed delicately.

"It is difficult for foreigners to get a permit to go there. You are Dutch, are you not?"

M'greet searched her mind for one of her usual answers, but Ladoux's beady eyes made her think twice. "That is correct."

He picked up a paper from the pile and used the edge of the desk to straighten it. "It seems you have come under the suspicion of England."

She opened her eyes wide. "I'm not quite sure how. Was it that business in Folkestone so long ago?"

He put the paper down. "Folkestone. Yes. And this man, this Hoedemaker, he seemed to believe you were not being completely honest."

"Nor was he. He implied to the entire ship that he was in my room after hours."

Ladoux sat back and crossed his arms, focusing his gaze on her face. "The British are convinced you are a German spy. I, however, am not so sure."

She leaned forward. "You have to believe me when I say that I am pro-Allies. Completely."

"Your friend Jean Hallaure informed me that you would request to go near the war zone." He opened a desk drawer and pulled out a cigarette. "But, if you love France so much, you could render us a great service. Have you ever thought of that?"

Great service. She sighed to herself—here was yet another man asking her to spy. "I do love France, but this is not the sort of thing for which one offers themself."

Ladoux lit his cigarette in lieu of replying.

"Besides," M'greet added as a thought occurred to her. "My services would be very expensive."

Ladoux blew out the match. "What would they be worth to you?"

"I suppose, if I could deliver what you are expecting, a great deal. Although, if I were to fail, it would cost you nothing."

He exhaled a circle of smoke. "If I give you a pass, you must promise me you will not seduce any French officers at the airfields near Vittel. As far as aviators go, you never know what could fall upon you from the sky."

She folded her hands in her lap. "I wouldn't dream of it. There is a Russian officer I wish to see, and with whom I am very much in love."

"Ah." Ladoux flicked ash into a tray. "I have seen you having lunch with him."

She narrowed her eyes. This fat little man was the one having her followed all over Paris. "You have seen me, or your lackeys that tail me everywhere have reported such?"

Ladoux coughed and then waved smoke out of his face. "Their reports are mostly regarding you visiting the finest Parisian perfumeries and shops, but nothing else."

"Then this stupid game needs to stop." M'greet tapped a gloved hand on the desk. "Either I am dangerous, and you will expel me, or I am nothing but a pretty little woman who danced all winter and now that summer has come, wants nothing more than to be left in peace."

He stabbed his cigarette out. "I will grant you this pass with the understanding that you will meet with me again on your return from Vittel."

She rose to leave.

"And, madame, in case you are looking, you will find your friend Masloff in a hospital at the front."

She refrained from gasping aloud. Ladoux was clearly trying to get a rise out of her, but she refused to give in. "G'day, Captain."

"Good-day, Madame Zelle-MacLeod."

. . .

The following afternoon, M'greet went to the Quai d'Orsay to visit Harry de Marguérie. She was so used to looking upon Vadim's young face that Harry looked like an old man.

She told him everything. To his credit, he did not seem to be jealous about Vadim. After she'd finished her story, he ran a hand through his thinning hair. "Did it ever occur to you that little Normie, had he lived, would be the same age as Vadim?"

She opened her mouth, but couldn't think of anything to say. "It's not like that," she managed to croak out after a beat. "We're in love. I just want to be near him. And now this Ladoux man wants me to become a spy."

He laughed. "Another disguise, Marguérite?"

"This time it would be in the service of France, not to better my own life."

He shook his head. "You know, some people view the work of espionage as opportunistic and mercenary."

"Some would say the same thing about myself."

That old grin again. "True." His face grew serious as he asked, "How old would you say Ladoux is?"

"I don't know. Forty-something, though the fat might have hidden some of his wrinkles."

"Did you ever ask yourself why this, as you say, forty-something man is still a captain?"

"Does it matter?"

He put his steepled hands under his chin. "French men at the front have a survival chance of less than half."

M'greet frowned as she recalled what Ladoux said about Vadim.

Harry didn't seem to notice her reaction. "Officer promotions are handed out swiftly in order to fill these dead men's posts, so you'd think by now Ladoux would have a higher rank."

She supposed the points Harry brought up should have bothered her, but at that moment, she could think of nothing else but Vadim. "Maybe that's the highest rank he can achieve in his line of work."

Harry tucked his hand underneath his face and thought for a minute. "This line of work is, indeed, extremely dangerous, but if anyone can serve my country with such work, it is you, Marguérite. Ladoux probably knows that too."

She gestured toward the window. "If that's so, why do you suppose he is still having me followed?"

"Is he?" He went over to the blinds and peered out. "Two youngish-looking men, one in a brown suit, one in a green?"

"That's them. They've been tailing me for months."

"I wonder why Ladoux would offer you a position in the French Intelligence Service if he suspects you enough to have you tailed." Harry picked up his suitcoat from the chair. "C'mon."

"Where are we going?"

"We're going to have some fun. Watch what happens when Ladoux's flunkeys try to follow the Secretary of Foreign Affairs as he takes Mata Hari out to dinner."

The next day M'greet returned to Ladoux's office. She stalked in this time, displaying a confidence she did not quite feel. "Captain, in principle, I submit."

Ladoux's stern expression showed no surprise. "Does that mean you agree to work for me?"

"Yes, provided you will still allow me to go to Vittel."

He scribbled something on a piece of paper before sighing, "So be it. You will report back here when you return for further instructions."

His tone indicated that he had finished with the conversation, but M'greet was not satisfied. Yesterday he had seemed so interested in her affairs and now it was as though he couldn't care less. "Captain, is it possible for me to send a telegram to Vadim Masloff from this office? I have not heard from him since he left."

"Is this official espionage business?"

"Well, no, not exactly."

"Then I suspect you know the answer to your inquiry."

M'greet rose, but Ladoux did not look up as she left.

She headed straight to the post office, trying to shove off a nagging thought about Ladoux's indifference. *What did it matter?* She was going to Vittel to see Vadim! She sent him a quick note for him to expect to see her within the week.

CHAPTER 46

MARTHE

JUNE 1916

*M*arthe once again met Alphonse in front of the staff cabin a few days later.

"I made a ladder to get in and out of the pit," he told her. "So you don't have to worry about getting a mouthful of dirt this time."

She was about to ask when he'd found the time to concoct a ladder when he suddenly seized her in an embrace. She peered up at him. The seconds turned into hours as his lips grew closer and closer until they were upon hers. They were still locked in a passionate kiss, her eyes closed, her head whirling with questions, as the sound of marching soldiers broke her revelry. She opened her eyes to see three soldiers nearby, taking a shortcut across the hospital grounds.

"Fräulein Cnockaert does indeed have a lover," one of them chuckled as they passed.

When they finally broke apart, both of them panting, Alphonse apologized. "That just shows you how careful we have to be, Marthe. This is very dangerous work we're doing."

"Are you sure you want to become a priest?" She wiped her mouth with her cape as discreetly as she could.

"Yes," he replied, a tinge of sadness in his voice. "It is my calling. Just as much as this work we do."

Marthe forced her lips into something that could pass as a smile.

They lowered themselves into the sewer in silence. Their going should have been much easier this time, due to the hastily-made rope ladder, but Alphonse fumbled as he descended and dropped his torch. Luckily it was not harmed, and, as he lit it, Marthe saw that another ladder lay at the bottom of the sewer, accompanied by a flat wooden circular piece.

"It's a lid," Alphonse said, upon catching sight of her puzzlement. "To camouflage the hole we'll make at the other end of the tunnel." He handed her a pickaxe. "Ready?"

Silence descended once again as they made their way through the sewer. Anytime she felt something at her ankles, Marthe lowered her torch to scare away the rats, watching them flee into the corridor with a feeling of satisfaction, as if she were frightening off her own worries at the same time.

Once they'd arrived under the stone marked by the white chalk, they set to work. Alphonse had already propped the loose planks to form a tetrad against the stone ceiling so it wouldn't crash on their heads as they worked. Half-blinded by the descending dirt and dust, perspiration dripping down her burning neck and shoulders, Marthe attacked the stone ceiling with her pickaxe. After half an hour, he stopped working and peered up at the stone. All of the mortar was gone from around it.

"Stand back," he told her before removing the prop. The slab refused to give way. He reached into his sack and grasped a crowbar. As he inserted the crowbar to wiggle the slab loose, she closed her eyes, hoping nothing would fall on his head. Suddenly he leapt backward as a piece of the slab crashed down. The echo reverberated through the tunnel and Marthe said a silent prayer that the Germans hadn't heard it above ground.

After a little more work with the crowbar, Alphonse had opened a wide gap, through which they could discern moonlight. They moved the other ladder into position and he ascended it. "Marthe, we did it," he called down. "Hand up the lid."

The stone lid was heavy but she was able to lift it high enough for Alphonse to grab onto it.

"And now the dynamite," he said when he'd reappeared. She carefully transferred the dynamite into Alphonse's strong hands.

"You can come up now. We are protected from view of the sentries by piles of ammunition."

As Marthe climbed the ladder, she could see giant tarpaulin-covered mounds extending in every direction. "We did it," she giggled once she was on solid ground.

"Stay here," he commanded when he'd finished maneuvering the camouflaged lid into place. "I'm going to look for a good spot to place the dynamite," he stated before vanishing among the piles of ammunition.

Soon she could hear the measured click of a sentry's boots and cowered into a nearby mound as best she could. She saw the glimmer of a bayonet as the sentry passed by, but thankfully he took no notice of her.

She started visibly as she heard another sound behind her, but it was Alphonse returning from his reconnaissance mission. He pointed off to her right. "Over there is a pile of petrol. Place one of the dynamite sticks in there and then lead the fuse to our hole." He took hold of the other stick. "I'm going to put this one in that stack of rifle bullets."

Marthe lifted up the tarpaulin and was about to place the stick as directed when her foot slipped, striking a stray can of petrol. The faint metallic sound of the petrol can hitting another sounded like a gunshot in the otherwise still night.

"Is someone there?" called a gruff voice.

She maneuvered herself against a pile of ammunition, this time careful not to strike any more cans.

"Hello?" called the voice again.

After a few more beats, the voice was silent and she was able to put the dynamite in place.

She found Alphonse waiting by the hole.

"Did you hear anything?" she whispered, too embarrassed to reveal her blunder.

"Nothing," was his terse reply.

She helped him prop up the camouflaged lid before he drew the two fuses together. "What a shame we won't be able to see the sentries' reaction when the whole thing blows." He struck a match and shielded it with his hand. "Okay, Marthe, get back into the sewer. As soon as my head drops below the parapet, knock away the prop, but mind you not before—I don't want a bump on my head."

After she'd climbed back down, she watched Alphonse bend to touch the match to the fuses and then she heard a fizzling sound. After he was satisfied they were burning, he descended the ladder. She reached out with the crowbar and hit the prop, causing the lid to drop into place.

"Now run!" Alphonse commanded, and she sprinted as if the whole German army were after them.

They had only gone a few meters when a loud rumble shook the tunnel. Their hands went instinctively to their heads, but nothing fell. Another boom sounded, and then silence.

"Well," he said, a grin stretching from ear to ear. "Well, I think we did it."

Marthe began to laugh uncontrollably. As if her giggles were contagious, Alphonse did the same. It was as if the explosion had also cracked the thick veneer of austerity that surrounded his heart. Whooping madly, he spun her around. She nearly collided with the walls of the tunnel before she realized that, in their mirth, they'd accidentally extinguished the torchlight.

A hand found hers in the darkness, and then something soft touched her lips. The moment she'd been dreaming about was finally happening again—Alphonse was kissing her! And this time there were no soldiers around to fool.

She reached up and entangled her hand in his hair.

When they finally broke their embrace, both of them were panting.

"I—" Alphonse began, but Marthe touched his lips with her finger before placing her lips upon them once again.

She had no idea how long they kissed in the darkness of the sewer.

He finally stopped to light a cigarette before he bothered to light the torch.

They walked back toward the staff cabin in an exhilarated silence, Alphonse's strong hand still wrapped around Marthe's.

When they emerged into the night, they could see an orange glow coming from the direction of the ammunition stores. She expected Alphonse to pull away again, but he squeezed her hand. "I have to go back to my barracks before I'm discovered, but you might be able to see some of the commotion on your way home."

His face was close to hers, so she kissed him again, a quick, gentle kiss this time, not the long, needy ones of the tunnel. "Good night, Alphonse."

"Good night, Marthe."

CHAPTER 47

ALOUETTE

JUNE 1916

$\mathcal{T}$he tension between the military attaché, Kalle, and von Krohn continued to grow throughout the first half of 1916. The Baron often accused Kalle of appropriating naval matters which were supposed to be under his own jurisdiction.

Von Krohn returned to the apartment one night in June in a foul mood. Alouette found him stuffing papers from his desk into a hand-bag. "I have to leave for Cadiz as soon as possible," he stated in a weary voice.

"Am I to accompany you?"

"No."

"Oh Hans." She threw herself dramatically into a chair. "Every time you are in a conference with Kalle, you come back in the most devilish temper. And then you try to wall me up even more in this gilded cage."

He stopped. "I'm sorry, Alouette. But great events are happening with the German navy that will allow us to end this war, which has come to an impasse in the trenches."

She'd found that sarcasm usually worked to draw out information when he was in such a state. "You are going to win a victory from an armchair in a Cadiz office?"

"Do not question me further, Alouette." His voice contained more than a hint of warning. "I would pay anything to see Kalle's face in a few weeks when he hears the news, but for now we must have patience."

She put a hand on his arm. "But Hans, I was really hoping for a vacation on the coast. It's so hot in Madrid." She moved her hand to his face. "And maybe this time we could share a room."

His face relaxed. "Well," he cleared his throat. "I suppose…"

"I'll start packing," she said quickly, before he could change his mind.

It turned out that a German submarine was to be interned in the Cadiz port. Alouette realized the significance of this right away: the ability of U-boats to come and go as they pleased in Spanish waters could be considered a violation of Spain's neutrality. It might eventually anger the Allies enough to declare war on Spain.

Von Krohn was obviously taken aback when Alouette requested to see the submarine soon after entering their hotel room. "That's an impossible task, and you well know it."

She placed her bag on one of the two beds, willing herself not to wonder if von Krohn expected to share it with her. Instead of resorting to anger and demands, she forced her voice to take on a soothing tone. "Can you tell me, Hans, who is in charge of a submarine when it enters into neutral waters?"

"A commander is the master of his own vessel," von Krohn stated, opening his suitcase. To her relief, he dumped his clothes on the other bed. "But in a case like this, he does not dare move without receiving permission from the Minister of Marine Affairs of the neutral country." His voice boomed. "As I am the German naval attaché in this country, the commander of the submarine is subject to my orders."

"Well, if that is the case, why do you hesitate to take me aboard the submarine? What difference can it possibly make now that the submarine is interned?" Von Krohn's face remained stony, so she tried a different tactic. "I'd love to see the vessel that is currently at your beck and call."

At last his expression changed, to that of a dreamy one, and Alouette wondered how it came to be that this man whom she detested had become so infatuated with her. He nodded his assent. "I'll step out of the room so you can dress properly."

They took a boat from the other side of the harbor, as von Krohn said the fewer people that saw them board, the better. As they crossed in a fisherman's dinghy, the Baron told her, "Alouette, one of my greatest thrills is to give you any pleasure that lies in my power."

Her grip on her purse tightened, but he obviously had other pleasures in mind than the one she most feared.

"Now you will have an idea of the scientific superiority Germany has over the Allies and you will see firsthand how resourceful my country is. But," he glanced down at her, "remember to never tell a living soul that I allowed you to board a U-boat. And, Alouette, please don't speak French to anyone on board. If you need to say anything, say it in Spanish."

The submarine—according to the block lettering on the side, was named U-52— was anchored to the left of the port, hidden by a large brick wall. Alouette could see how easily it could sneak in and out of the harbor without being noticed.

The commander, an athletic-looking man in his mid-thirties, received them on the bridge. "I like your dress," he told Alouette in Spanish.

She looked down, brushing imaginary dust off her black and yellow skirt. She'd paired it with a red blouse, purposefully dressing in the colors of the German flag. "Thank you. I wanted to show tribute to your sailors." She nodded toward the crew, who stood at attention in full naval attire.

"*Sie sind mutige deutsch,*" the commander said with pride. They are brave Germans.

Alouette was taken off guard for a moment and nearly answered back.

Noting her bewildered expression, the Baron explained that she did not speak the language.

She took the commander's arm and resorted to Spanish. "As an airwoman, I am especially intrigued by the submarine's motors. Can you explain how they work?"

He grinned before leading her down the deck. "Of course. Let me give you a full tour."

Von Krohn was forced to tag behind, though he intermittently cut the commander off in his explanations. It was obvious to Alouette that he was trying to reestablish the commander as his underling.

As they went back on deck, von Krohn said in German, "I won't be back again." He moved to examine a fitting. "I give you *carte blanche* to decide when to launch. If, however, there turns out to be any hitch, ring me up at once."

Alouette sighed inwardly. Von Krohn must have been referring to the submarine leaving for a mission, probably to torpedo Allied boats, but, even though he spoke in a language he didn't think Alouette understood, he was being deliberately vague.

The commander nodded before saying, "Alouette, before you go, I'd like to show you our megaphone." He shot an apologetic smile to von Krohn. "If you don't mind, of course."

Von Krohn's mouth turned downward as he nodded.

The commander led her down a narrow hallway to show her a brass funnel. "It dramatically increases the volume of the human voice."

She ran her hand along the words crudely printed along the side. *Gott strafe England.* "What does this mean?"

He gave her a wry smile. "May God punish England."

She reached for his hand and squeezed it. He responded back with another squeeze. "I'd like to see you again," he told her in a low tone.

She turned to him with wide eyes. "I'll be in Madrid in July. Perhaps you could visit me? I'll be alone," she emphasized.

"July is impossible. But perhaps we could meet in the fall."

She pursed her lips into a pout. "Why not July?"

A look of sadness passed across his face before he smiled. A forced, mechanical smile, Alouette noted. "God keep you until we meet again, fräulein."

He led her back to von Krohn, who helped her into the dinghy. The commander waved at them until they were out of sight of the submarine.

"What was that about?" von Krohn asked gruffly.

She shrugged. "I may be engaged, but I can still be flattered by the attentions of a handsome young man, can't I?" She pointedly accentuated the words "handsome" and "young," hoping von Krohn would take the hint that he was neither.

It worked. Von Krohn sulked the rest of the night, and, mercifully, did not venture over to her bed. Alouette fell asleep to the sound of the Baron's snoring.

As soon as she got back to Madrid, she sent Ladoux a letter regarding what she'd learned about the submarine. She never received a reply.

CHAPTER 48

MARTHE

JULY 1916

A few days after the ammunition store explosion, Alphonse called on Marthe at her house to offer to walk her to work. "They opened an inquiry as to the blast, but cannot find out any information," he told her, the glee obvious in his normally stoic voice. "As all of the sentries remained at their post, they had nothing to report. None of them were injured, either." His grin widened. "I'm not sure if that is a good thing or a bad thing."

"What was their conclusion?"

"That somehow an explosive device had been packed among the stores and ignited by accident."

"So we're in the clear."

"Indeed." They had paused outside of the Grand Place. Alphonse leaned in for a kiss and Marthe returned it willingly.

"What time do you need to be at work?" he asked as they broke for air.

Marthe lifted her arm to check the time, but froze as she looked upon her bare wrist. She realized she hadn't seen her watch for at least several days.

"Is something wrong?" Alphonse's sturdy voice broke through her panic.

"No," she smiled up at him. "I just forgot my watch."

When she got home from work that evening, she searched her room thoroughly but found no trace of the watch. The clasp had been loose for a while, and she'd meant to get it fixed, but obviously the plan for the ammunition dump had taken priority. It could be anywhere: under the hut, in the tunnel, at the dump itself.

Or maybe she'd just lost it during rounds at the hospital. For that reason, she decided not to tell Alphonse about her missing watch.

CHAPTER 49

M'GREET

AUGUST 1916

M'greet traveled to Vittel by train. She waited impatiently at the train station for the hotel motor-car and was disappointed to see a plain old horse and carriage pull up.

"Where are the automobiles?" she demanded as the driver pulled his horses to a halt.

"Requisitioned for the front, madame," he replied.

"And where do you suppose we put these?" she gestured to her trunks. She was traveling lightly this time and had only brought four.

He made a face as he took stock of them. "I suppose I'll have to come back."

"You there," M'greet called to the two men standing near the ticket office, pretending to be preoccupied with a bulletin board. The taller man looked up and, as suspected, she recognized him as one of the same men who had been following her around Paris.

"Yes?" he asked.

She gestured to her luggage. "Do you mind helping me with those? I imagine we are going to the same hotel."

He shot a bewildered glance at his partner. His partner shrugged in return and the two of them hauled three of the trunks to the side of the road.

The driver held out a hand to assist M'greet into the carriage before dumping the other trunk unceremoniously next to her.

They drove to the Grand Hotel of the Baths, where M'greet was installed in Room 363. She took the waters the next morning and, upon returning, requested that room 362 be reserved.

Vadim arrived that evening. He had a silk patch over his left eye, tied by two ribbons.

"Oh, my poor darling!" M'greet covered the right side of his face with kisses, deliberately avoiding the patch. "What happened?" she asked when she was satisfied she'd kissed every square centimeter of skin.

"German gas. My mask had a leak in it." He carefully sat on the bed. "The doctors say I might completely lose my eyesight."

"Oh, my Vadim, I'm so sorry."

"This war is horrifying, Marina, in a way you will never understand." His face was as white as the bandage wrapped around his eye. "I was a boy when I first signed up. Then, at my first battle, I became a man. And now, now I don't know what I am... a walking wounded, a cripple, a should-have-been left for dead."

She grasped his hand. "You are none of those things. You are a brave soldier who will quickly recover from his injuries."

"Marina," he turned to her and she was once again shocked by his appearance. "Surely if this terrible thing comes to pass, you will not stay with a blind man."

"Vadim, how can you say such a thing? I would never leave you. Never."

A small smile appeared on Vadim's lips. "I thought you might declare as much. In that case, will you marry me?"

She clapped her hands. "Of course! I'd be delighted!"

That night M'greet made a vow to herself that she would never deceive Vadim with other men; she would let go of the Marquis, of van der

Capellan, even Harry. Of course, that meant she would have to ask Captain Ladoux for enough money to get by, to rent an apartment in Paris for her and Vadim to live. She had no concern of Vadim losing his eyesight. But if he did, she reflected, it meant he would always remember her as being beautiful, even as she inevitably became older, with deepening wrinkles and graying hair. As she drifted off to sleep, she dreamed of being the happiest woman on Earth.

CHAPTER 50

MARTHE

AUGUST 1916

*A*lphonse no longer spoke about being a priest. Instead, he'd make plans for the both of them for when the war finally ended. "I will probably stay on as an ambulance driver in Roulers and walk you to work until we can get a place of our own," he stated one morning when he met her at the café for breakfast. "Maybe I'll even take classes to become a doctor."

"A doctor?" Marthe asked.

"How else will we make money when you start having babies?"

"I don't know," she said with a laugh.

"Think it over." He glanced at his own watch. "I can't walk you to work this morning—I've been called in early."

He kissed her before striding off.

As Marthe passed by the Grand Place on her way to work, she happened to glance at the town bulletin board and a "Found" notice caught her eye:

A soldier of the Army of Württemberg has been arrested for theft. A number of articles found on his person appear to belong to the citizens of this town. Any person who thinks he recognizes the following articles should report to the Town-Kommandment's office during normal business hours.

Fourth on the list was "a gold watch with the initials M.C. engraved on the back."

Marthe gave a sigh of relief, pleased that her watch had been located. The thief had either discovered it on the street or stolen it from someone who had.

Without thinking, she strolled across the street to the Town-Kommandant's office. The secretary gave her a funny look but told her to go through the inner office door.

Marthe had met the Town-Kommandant a few times—he was there when she'd been awarded the Iron Cross. He nodded at her and bid her good morning. After she told him her business, he opened a desk drawer to pull out an envelope, which he then tipped onto his desk. Everyone else must have already claimed their stolen articles as only her watch fell out of the envelope. "Is this yours?"

She picked it up and fingered the engraved initials. "Yes, Herr Kommandant. It was a gift from my father and I'm very glad to have it back."

"Well." His smile did not reach his eyes. "Then I am pleased to at last find the owner of the watch."

As the clasp was still broken, she put it in her purse and forgot about the whole affair until she got home that afternoon. It was a slow day at the hospital and the Oberarzt had let her leave early.

Mother was at the door, a worried look on her face. "Where's Alphonse?" she asked by way of greeting.

"He was called to the front. I haven't seen him all day. Why?" Marthe asked.

"The gendarmes were here this morning."

"Looking for hoarded food again?"

"That's what they told me, but the way they went about their task this time, I don't think it was food they were looking for."

"What do you mean?" Marthe's voice rose. "Did they mention my name?"

"Not directly."

"Then there's nothing to be concerned about."

. . .

An hour later, Marthe was eating dinner when one of the waitresses told her that a roughly-dressed man was at the back door of the café, asking if the letter for Fräulein van Eurne was ready.

"What do you mean?" Marthe demanded. "I don't know anyone of that name."

She went to the back door. The man's clothes were indeed shabby, but his look was too shrewd to be that of a laborer.

"Meneer, I believe you have made a mistake. I do not know anyone with the last name of van Eurne," Marthe told him.

"Are you sure?" He leaned in, his breath smelling of bratwurst. "You can trust me."

She tried to control the shaking in her voice. "I have no idea what you are talking about."

His face seemed to drop with disappointment as he bowed. She watched him walk away, feeling vaguely frightened.

She quickly walked back in the direction of the hospital, toward Alphonse's barracks. The door to his cabin stood open, and it appeared to have been ransacked, but there was no sign of Alphonse.

When Marthe returned to the café, she found an officer of the Brigade Staff, along with two soldiers and a gefreiter waiting for her.

"I have orders to search these premises," the Brigade officer told her. "Gefreiter, place your men at the doors so that no one can come and go while we conduct our search." His steely eyes landed on Marthe. "Fräulein, please hand me all of your keys."

Mother made a small cry as her daughter surrendered her key ring.

"Your search will be fruitless," Marthe told the officer with more assurance than she felt.

He ordered her and Mother to wait downstairs. They sat in silence, listening to the sound of drawers falling to the floor and the clanging of a metal trash can being tipped over.

Marthe could feel Mother's eyes boring into her, but she focused on the pictures of the former owner and his family that still decorated the café walls. The same pictures Alphonse had once commented on so long ago. Marthe dug little crescents into her palm with her fingernails. *Alphonse.* She could never forgive herself if anything happened to him. She wasn't worried whether or not she would be arrested—from the noise upstairs, it was clear the Vampires were intent on finding something incriminating. Just that morning she had written two coded messages to deliver to the chemist later that night. She'd hidden them under a loose strip of wallpaper in her bedroom.

Heavy footsteps descended the stairs and the Brigade officer got into Marthe's face. "You see what I have found, fräulein?" He opened his enormous palm to reveal her messages. "You will come with me to the Kommandant's office to be formally charged."

Mother let out a cry, but the officer ignored her. "We have enough evidence to put you in front of a firing squad at our leisure. Gefreiter, grab her."

"Please, no," Mother begged.

Marthe did not say anything as the gefreiter took hold of her arms and marched her out of the café. She recalled what Aunt Lucelle had told her when she recruited her: *If you are caught, in all probability it will be your own fault.* She could feel a tear work its way down her cheek, but the gefreiter still had hold of her arms and she had no choice but to let it fall.

CHAPTER 51

M'GREET

SEPTEMBER 1916

M'greet and Vadim's time together had been ideal: they'd taken the waters, posed for a formal photograph, and spent the rest of their time in her room, away from the prying eyes of the detectives, who resumed their pattern of following her every place she went.

She returned to Paris to find a mountain of bills waiting for her. She shuffled through them: outstanding balances from many of the fancy hotels she'd stayed in over the past few years and invoices from a myriad of dressmakers and perfumiers. Of course, she had nothing to pay them off with—she hadn't worked for a long time, and had spent a good deal more money in Vittel.

She decided to call on her lawyer, Edouard Clunet, to see if he could be of help.

He examined the bills in silence, his characteristic austere expression deepening into a frown. "Some of these are nearly half a decade old."

"I know. You'd think at some point they'd just give up."

"We're talking about money here, M'greet. People will pursue debts long after you are lying in your grave." He looked up. "Do you have any savings?"

"No."

He took off his pince-nez glasses to rub at his face. "We are going to have to start a repayment plan to get some of these bills under control."

"But I have just become engaged and plan on moving in with my fiancé as soon as he is back from the front. There is no money for repayment."

"You are getting married again?" Clunet threw his head back and laughed. "I never thought I'd see the day."

M'greet grabbed the bills from his desk and shoved them into her purse. Clunet had been her lover many years ago and was clearly just jealous. "It's true. I will become Mrs. de Masloff as soon as I can manage."

"Good luck, M'greet," Clunet said ominously as she left.

She headed straight to Ladoux's office. "I need money," she said by way of greeting.

Ladoux gestured for her to sit down. "How much are you talking about here?"

"A million francs."

As usual, Ladoux's expression showed no surprise. "To earn such a sum would require you to produce extremely sensitive information from the German High Command. The kind of information that would end the war. For you," he gazed at her dismissively, "that kind of accomplishment would be nearly impossible."

"Oh, not so impossible, Captain." M'greet thought quickly, hoping to persuade Ladoux not to send her to Germany, where they might ask questions as to what happened to the 20,000 francs they had paid her. "I know just the man who could provide such information."

Ladoux leaned in. "Who?"

"One of my ex-lovers was friends with the German army's biggest supplier and can come and go as he pleases at the Grand Headquarters in Antwerp."

"What is his name?" Ladoux demanded.

"General Von Bissing." She'd once been introduced to the governor-general of occupied Belgium by van der Capellan. They'd only exchanged pleasantries at the time, but M'greet was sure that he, like most men, would easily fall prey to her considerable charms.

"And if you are caught?"

She waved her hand. "I've been in scrapes before. I can take care of myself."

"Of that I don't doubt. But this job is quite dangerous and you are taking the greatest gamble of them all—you will be playing with your life."

"I am an adept gambler." This was not true, but Ladoux did not know that.

He gave a loud harrumph. "I always bet on red in honor of France. Red is the color of the blood that flows for freedom at the front. Black represents your German friends. I warn you: red will win while black loses. Reflect on that before placing your bet. You have tonight to think it over."

"I have already thought it over. I will play red."

Ladoux pulled a cigarette case out of his desk drawer. "Do you care for one?" he held the case out toward her.

M'greet took a cigarette and put it in her mouth. "Thank you."

He held a lit match up to the end of her cigarette. He took a puff of his own before asking, "Do you know how to use invisible inks?"

She refrained from rolling her eyes. "No. That sort of trickery goes against my nature. And anyway, I will not need them. I don't intend to laze around for months, picking up tiny bits of information to send to you. I will make a grand coup, tell you all what I have learned in person, and then be finished."

"You didn't learn of secret inks when you were in Antwerp?"

M'greet froze, the cigarette halfway to her lips. "I'm not sure what you mean by that."

Ladoux sat back and crossed his left arm under the one holding the cigarette. "I'm sure that you do."

She recalled what Harry had said in his office that day after she'd first met Ladoux. "If you are so convinced I am a German spy, why do you propose to recruit me?"

"Well, for one, I am hoping you will betray some of your associates to me."

She stabbed her cigarette out. "Even if what you are accusing me of is true—which despite all your little agents and your dirty tricks, we both know it is not—I would never denounce anyone."

Ladoux lit another cigarette. "You act as though spying is a dirty practice when you yourself are to become one, most likely a double agent. You, who makes a living off of other women's husbands, refuse to reveal the names of fellow spies?"

M'greet held a gloved hand to her lips and coughed. "Even I have standards that I will not forsake."

When she returned to the hotel that evening, she found that some of her debtors had gotten a court order for her trunks.

The desk clerk handed her a bill for five hundred francs. "They are saying they will surrender your belongings if you can pay half."

"I can't pay any of it," M'greet responded, the desperation obvious in her voice. How was she supposed to seduce men in the name of France if her magnificent wardrobe was not complete?

She sent Ladoux a *pneumatique* asking the same question that evening. When she didn't hear from him for two days, she paid yet another visit to 282 boulevard, Saint-Germain.

Ladoux did not seem pleased to see her. "I had heard that you were quite the revolving door, but didn't think I'd have the pleasure of witnessing this behavior myself."

"Nonsense," M'greet snapped, well aware of his double entendre. "Did you get my request?"

"If you mean the uncoded *pneumatique* you sent—the one that anyone could have confiscated and read for themselves—then yes."

"And?"

"And my superior refuses to give you an advance. Had you taken a bit more precaution, I could have maybe argued for a little money." He reached into his desk and pulled out a packet of antipyrine. "I can teach you how to make a simple invisible ink with this stuff."

M'greet snatched the packet.

"You are willing to learn about secret inks?" The hopefulness was too obvious in his voice.

"No," she snapped. "You are giving me a headache."

The frown returned to Ladoux's face.

She sat down. "You cannot expect me to pay for all of my expenses on my own."

"What about your Belgian lover?"

"If van der Capellan knew what the money was for, he would refuse to pay, and I would no longer have a protector in Holland."

"Well then," Ladoux gave a dismissive wave. "I guess you'll just have to find someone else to pay your way."

In a huff, M'greet left his office and then went to the post office, where she sent a letter to Anna, begging her to ask van der Capellan for six thousand francs. She couldn't write to the Baron directly, for fear his wife would intercept the letter. She then sent an express letter to Vadim, paying for it with credit, reaffirming her love and promising to secure an apartment for them in Paris.

CHAPTER 52

MARTHE

OCTOBER 1916

arthe awoke to a sliver of sunlight shining on her face. At first she wasn't sure where she was, but then reality came crashing home: she was confined to Roulers' military prison, formally charged as a spy.

A guard opened the heavy door of her cell, and set down a tray containing a mug of tea and a dirty plate of black bread before leaving, locking the door behind him.

Marthe ate automatically, washing down the hard bread with the tasteless tea. This scenario had been playing out for weeks: in the afternoon, the tray contained thin soup and at night the same soup accompanied by moldy potatoes. No one had spoken to her, and she occupied her time lying on her bed, staring up at the tiny window slit, not wanting to think of what had happened to Alphonse, least of all daring to dwell on what would become of her.

Finally, a detective entered her cell. He was a large man with a deformed lump in the middle of his nose, as though it had been broken and never healed correctly.

"You are going to die in a day or two," he told her. "You might as well tell me the truth. We have your friends and they have confessed to your involvement in their crimes."

Alphonse. Just thinking of him was like a blow to her heart. But something about what the detective said didn't sit right with Marthe. Alphonse would never have revealed her name, not even under the pain of death.

The detective shook his fist in her face, and she had the mind to strike him across that hideous nose. "Speak," he demanded. "Who were the other people helping you? Your mother? Your father? Out with it!"

She sat on the bed. The detective was lying when he said he had her friends. He knew nothing.

He grabbed her arm and pulled her to her feet. "Are you going to tell me, or should we resort to other measures?" His face was next to Marthe's, his spit showering her face. "We have ways of making sure people talk, especially women." When he let go, her form went limp and she fell to the bed like a rag doll.

The detective tried one last time. "Who were those notes for? What did the codes mean?"

When he realized that Marthe was not going to speak, he left, stomping his feet as he walked out of her cell.

He came back a few hours later, bursting into the room while Marthe was sleeping, cursing and spitting at her until she woke up. This continued at all hours for the next two days; if it wasn't the broken-nosed detective, it was another man, a cadaverous bald man, who hissed and whispered his curses instead of screaming them.

Marthe thought she would go insane with hatred for the horrible men, but she consoled herself with one thought: they didn't have Alphonse, for if they did, they would never go through such lengths to get her to confess. She desperately hoped he was safe, wherever he was.

. . .

The detectives at last ceased their visits, and Marthe was once again left alone. A few days later, a young lieutenant entered her cell. He unfolded a piece of paper, and, after clearing his throat, read, "By order of the General Officer of Occupied areas, you are to be tried by a court-martial. You will be arraigned under Article 90 of the Military Penal Code, Section 2, which concerns the destruction of munitions and Section 4, regarding your service as an enemy spy."

He folded the paper and clicked his heels together before peering at Marthe.

"I've been asked to act as your defending officer."

Marthe's voice was hoarse. "I do not wish for a defending officer."

He sat in the rickety chair, the only other furniture she had besides the hard bed.

"You do not trust me. But, rest assured, I will not tell the authorities anything that you disclose."

"I have no reason to mistrust you, Herr Lieutenant." She was pleased to hear her own voice grow stronger. "It is just that I do not believe you can help my case."

He nodded. "From what I can see of the evidence held against you, you are probably right."

"Is it possible you could explain what information the prosecution has?"

He sat back in the chair and crossed his legs. "I have been informed of the events leading up to your arrest. One day a passing soldier spotted a group of children playing around a hole in the ground near the supply dump which had gone up in flames under mysterious circumstances. Below the hole, the soldier discovered a stone shaft, which led straight to Roulers Hospital, upon which was found a concealed exit."

Marthe nodded.

"A gold wristwatch was found in the tunnel, about half-way through."

At this, she froze, remembering Alphonse spinning her around, right before he kissed her.

The lieutenant continued, "Suspicion fell upon you, since the watch bore your initials and you were an employee of the hospital. You know what happened after that."

"And they have no knowledge of anyone else involved?" Marthe asked.

"Not at this time. But if you are willing to give up the names of your accomplices, I could probably argue for a lighter sentence. Life imprisonment, perhaps, instead of the death penalty usually reserved for spies."

"I will never reveal any names."

"I thought as much." He stood. "Should you change your mind, I am at your service."

"Thank you, Herr Lieutenant."

He knocked for someone outside to unlock the cell. "Whatever you did, fräulein, I believe you did it for the good of your country, same as the rest of us. May luck be with you." He bowed as the door opened and Marthe was left alone once again.

CHAPTER 53

M'GREET

NOVEMBER 1916

*T*he Baron's money finally came through in early November and M'greet was at last able to retrieve her confiscated trunks. She rented an apartment on avenue Henri-Martin and left the belongings she wasn't taking to Holland there. She then sent Vadim a letter, telling him all about the apartment and included a money order in his name for five hundred francs. As she signed it over, she realized that was the first time she'd ever given a man money.

She left Paris on a night train to Spain on November 5th. In Vigo, M'greet boarded the S.S. *Hollandia*. Even though the ship was from a neutral country, it was forced to dock in Falmouth for a routine inquiry by British authorities.

Two women were employed to search M'greet's cabin. They were surprisingly thorough in searching through her trunks—they even removed the mirror from the wall and peered under her bed with the aid of an electric lamp.

M'greet watched them with derision, figuring the women, who were both dressed very plainly and had short hair, were the suffragette type. She wasn't worried about their meticulousness: after all, she was employed by France, an ally of England.

The suffragettes finally left and M'greet lay on the bed to take a short nap.

Not more than ten minutes later, her rest was interrupted by a loud knocking. She opened the door to find a man in a khaki uniform and short mustache holding her passport.

"Yes?" she prompted.

"Madame, is this your passport? Are you Margaretha Zelle-MacLeod?"

"I am."

"Have you ever traveled under any other name?"

"My stage name is Mata Hari, but I don't use that name on official documents."

He stared at her fixedly for a minute. Once again, M'greet was not overly concerned and met his gaze. He pulled a wrinkled picture out of his pocket. "Is this you?"

She took the photo from him. It was an amateur photograph of a woman in a white mantilla, one hand placed on a hip and the other holding a fan. The woman was shorter and more muscular than M'greet. She recognized the woman as Clara Benedix, the spy she'd trained with under Fräulein Doktor.

"That sort of costume is not my style, sir. That picture is definitely not me."

"I think you'd better come with me," he replied.

The officer and one of the suffragettes, who turned out to be his wife, escorted M'greet by train to London. Luckily, they decided to unload her trunks from the ship before bringing her to Scotland-Yard, where she was put in a room by herself.

The questioning began the next day. They provided her with a translator, but, in M'greet's opinion, he spoke Dutch like a dirty Flamand. When he told her interrogators that M'greet had a German accent, she decided she'd had enough and demanded to carry out the rest of the examination in French.

The main investigator was an elegant gray-haired man with bright blue eyes. He introduced himself as Sir Basil Thomson, head of the Special Branch of Scotland Yard. His companions both worked for the Criminal Investigation Department.

Worried by the mention of Scotland Yard, M'greet asked Thomson if he thought she was a criminal.

"Tampering with a passport can be judged as a crime." He produced her papers. "Someone here has changed your age, as you can see. A very clumsy forgery, indeed." He tapped on the age, which M'greet had changed from 38 to 30 when she had first received it.

Under the circumstances, she figured a few white lies wouldn't hurt anyone. "It is not a forgery." She folded her shaking hands under the table. "Is it possible the Dutch ambassador can be present during this questioning?"

"Why do you need the Dutch embassy? Clara Benedix is a German."

She sighed. "I am not Clara Benedix."

"Did you ever have an inflammation of the left eye?"

Taken aback, M'greet replied that she'd never had anything wrong with her eyes.

"But one of your eyes is more closed than the other."

She touched the left side of her face. "It has always been so, but nobody is usually so rude as to comment on it."

Thomson ignored that last retort. He pushed the photograph of Clara forward. "The woman in this photograph also has this peculiarity."

"Perhaps, but that is not me."

He decided to change tactics. "Just before you left for Paris, did you receive the sum of 10,000 francs from anyone?"

M'greet's heartbeat sped up as she recalled the money from Karl Kroemer and Fräulein Doktor. She crossed her still hidden fingers. "No."

"We have information that Mata Hari received thousands of francs from the German Embassy."

Her throat went dry. "Is it possible to have a glass of water?" she asked one of the other men who stood behind Thomson. He nodded and left.

When the man returned with the water, M'greet took a long sip before setting the glass on the table. "I was not going to say anything, but you might as well know that I am employed by Captain Ladoux of the French Secret Service."

From the skeptical look on Thomson's face, he didn't appear to believe her. "Is that so? Why didn't you tell us this before?"

"I didn't think it proper to inform you of Ladoux's business."

Thomson seemed at a loss for words and glanced at each of his companions in turn, who shrugged. "I will inquire further into this," he replied finally.

Three days later, Thomson called her back into the examination room.

"You should know that Ladoux is claiming that he never hired you."

M'greet couldn't keep her mouth from dropping open. "Why would he say that?"

Thomson raised his eyebrows in an uncharacteristically inelegant fashion. "I don't know. But," he continued, relaxing his face, "our thorough search of your possessions has failed to turn up anything incriminating. In addition, we've received telegrams from several prominent men all insisting upon your identity as that of Margaretha Zelle-MacLeod."

Flattered at the mention of these prominent men, M'greet demanded to know their identities.

One of Thomson's lackeys handed him her file and he flipped through it. "Let's see. The Baron van der Capellan, Robert Henry de Marguérie: Secretary of French Foreign affairs, and the Marquis Frederic de Beaufort—he signed his telegram as Freddy." He shut the folder. "Therefore, we have no choice but to release you."

She heaved a great sigh of relief. "I am to go to Holland, then?"

"No. You will return to Spain."

"But—" she insisted.

Thomson held up his hand. "Spain."

CHAPTER 54

ALOUETTE

NOVEMBER 1916

*K*alle's agents had become a constant presence outside the Calle del Alcalá apartment. Consequently, Alouette had only been there infrequently in the past few months, and the Baron had given up going there altogether. He had invited Alouette to stay with him at his house, as the Baroness was away on a visit to relatives, but she had, of course, refused and instead returned to the Palace Hotel.

However, Alouette could not alienate von Krohn completely, so when he extended a lunch invitation one day in mid-November, she had to accept. She found him seated in his office, intently studying the map before him. An electric desk lamp was lit, but the rest of the room was dark. Without raising his eyes from his work, he waved her toward the seat in front of him.

Alouette knew better than to disturb him, so she waited in silence, refraining from drumming her fingers on the desk.

Finally he looked up. "Ah, Alouette, I'm glad you came." He picked up a pencil and tapped it a few times.

"What is it?" she asked, as nervous as she always was when the Baron had that gloomy expression in his eyes.

"This fiancé of yours…"

"Zozo."

"You mentioned once that he was an anarchist."

Alouette shook her head, not recalling that particular conversation, but it was true that the man Zozo was a Bolshevik.

"Can you send for him to come to Madrid?"

"Zozo?" she repeated dumbly. "What would you want with him?"

"I've been tasked by the German Secret Service to start a propaganda campaign to, as they put it, 'beat down the morale of the Frenchmen.' They gave me several hundred pesetas, so obviously they mean business."

"I could write to him…"

"Do it. And as quickly as possible. I want to beat Kalle in the race."

Accordingly, Alouette wrote to Zozo, imploring him to visit her in Spain. She also wrote to Captain Ladoux to ask that he send Zozo as soon as he could. She mentioned the money von Krohn was willing to pay, thinking that, at the very least, would elicit a swift reply from Ladoux, but she was wrong.

With each day that passed without a reply from either Ladoux or Zozo, Alouette grew first perplexed, and then worried. What was happening at the Deuxiéme Bureau that was causing them to ignore her request?

The Baron, too, grew impatient. "Why is there such a delay in getting your fiancé here?" he asked her one day.

Alouette could only murmur a half-hearted reply about him encountering "unforeseen difficulties."

"If he doesn't come soon, I will have to look for someone else to unload all of these pesetas on."

To her chagrin, Alouette read of the sinking of the *HMS Nottingham* in August. The German submarine responsible was said to be U-52, the same boat she had been aboard a few months earlier.

Still, Alouette heard nothing from France. Her fellow countrymen in Spain continuously snubbed her, thinking she was a German spy. She longed for an end to all of the lying, all of the scheming. And most of all, she longed for an end to her contact with Von Krohn. If only Ladoux would respond! She didn't need praise or encouragement, necessarily, although either would have been welcomed. What she really wanted at this point was acknowledgment. But Ladoux continued his silence.

Alouette walked home from yet another tedious lunch with the irritable Baron, asking herself what the sense was in carrying on such a dangerous task now that she had lost communication with the Deuxiéme Bureau. She kicked every stone in her path and heaved a heavy sigh as she entered the Palace Hotel.

She was so wrapped up in her discontent she barely noticed the tall man in the aviator jacket standing in the foyer. He turned, the familiar grin finally registering.

"Zozo!" she shouted.

He met her eyes and then bowed his head, his eyes dropping to the ground.

Alouette understood: he was cautious about the hotel staff overhearing them. *Trust no one.* She flagged down a porter and said in the loudest voice possible, "I am expecting some letters in the next post. Please send them up to Room 11 as soon as you can."

She had just shut the door to her room when someone banged on it. As expected, Zozo was standing outside.

She waved him in before she started questioning him. "What is happening in Paris? Why has the Captain not answered any of my letters? What took you so long to get here? Is Paris in danger? Are we?"

Zozo opened his mouth, but Alouette wasn't done yet. "Every week I write to the Deuxiéme Bureau, but I never get a reply. I'm beginning to wonder what my purpose is here, and whether I should continue on. Captain Ladoux has deigned to reply to none of my last twenty letters, and von Krohn seems to become more suspicious each day that passes. I am nothing but a lion in a cage here, and I'm fed up!"

Zozo collapsed into a nearby chair, holding a hand to his forehead.

After a beat, he put his arm down and peered at Alouette. "Captain Ladoux has been quite absent, I'll agree. The last I knew he had been working with new recruits, including a supposed double agent, whom he was setting up to expose. After your last letter, I was at 282 boulevard, Saint-Germain, for three days straight, my finger on the bell, but no one answered. Finally, I called on Captain Ignatieff, the head of Russian Intelligence in France. He was the one to pay for my fare to Madrid."

"But what of Captain Ladoux?" Alouette's voice was growing shrill, but she couldn't help herself. "Why was the submarine able to escape from Cadiz despite all of my best efforts? I've been completely let down and I don't think I can hold out much longer."

A puzzling smile appeared on Zozo's handsome countenance. She was indignant at his obvious amusement, which grew more intense as he said, "What do you want me to do about it? Captain Ladoux is confident in your relationship with von Krohn." He cocked an eyebrow. "When do I get to meet the esteemed Baron... and take his money?"

"I could telephone him now and he'd come straightaway." For some reason, Alouette felt the need to prove to Zozo the extent of the Baron's attachment.

He nodded toward the door. "Be my guest."

An hour later, Alouette and Zozo were indulging in aperitif drinks, a sherry for her and a bourbon for him, when von Krohn knocked on her door.

As she rose from her seat to answer, she apprised Zozo, "You are the most dangerous of anarchists."

He gave her a mock salute and Alouette opened the door.

Von Krohn did not utter a word of greeting to either of them, but nodded at Zozo as he took the chair across from him. "You are a Bolshevik?"

"Yes," Zozo answered. "I was a co-signer with Vladimir Lenin of the Socialist Revolutionary Pact."

"What you have done in the past doesn't fully inform me on how you can help in the future. France has proven to be far from open to revolutionary ideas, as was your Georgia."

At this Zozo sat up straighter. "I am well familiar with Russian order. I cannot see much difference between that of Russia and France." He gave a hollow laugh. "Nor can I discern the difference between that of the German order, which resulted in multiple revolutions, and is, as we speak, drowning out strikes with streams of blood."

Von Krohn had his hand over his chin, obviously absorbing every word Zozo spoke. Finally he replied, "Bourgeois order is the same everywhere."

Zozo rose and stood ramrod straight. "The people are starving— that's the order. There is no justice for working men—that's the order. Education is not for every man, only the rich—that's the order."

As if to slow the tirade, the Baron held up his hand, but Zozo was not finished. "It is like a grave in which the slaves, chained to their shovels, have been digging without respite for centuries, under the promise of the whip, and for the profit of a few slave traders. Don't be surprised if, when the millions of disillusioned soldiers come home, they annihilate this so-called social order and replace it with decrees that are more humane."

Now von Krohn stood, both hands in the air. "And yet Alouette tells me you have fought side-by-side with the French bourgeois against the Germans—"

"You don't get it." Zozo's voice rose in anguish.

Whether it was false or real, Alouette wasn't sure. Regardless, she was enjoying the showdown between von Krohn and her fake fiancé.

She grabbed a biscuit off the table and took a bite as Zozo continued, "The French watched as I fought single-handedly against five German airplanes. They believed that I was serving France against the Germans. Hence this medal." He touched the *Croix de Guerre* pinned to his chest. "But they were wrong." He shot a glance in Alouette's direction before focusing once more on von Krohn. "Each decoration they awarded me was like a stroke of the master's whip, trying to get the slave to germinate the seed. But all it was germinating was the harvest of revolutions to come."

Alouette crunched on her biscuit. *This is really good.*

Von Krohn sat before holding up a wary hand. "If you would be so kind as to tell me what you plan to do with the money I will entrust to you."

Zozo folded his arms across his chest. "I have no desire to serve you or your country, only my Russian brothers in their task for revolution." He paused to gaze again at Alouette, who raised her eyebrows. *Agree with his plan.* "But," he added, "if that includes galvanizing Frenchmen to rebel against their own government, I suppose it's all for the Cause."

The Baron nodded slowly, but Alouette could discern his barely-contained delight. She shot a grin at her compatriot. His ruse had worked!

Von Krohn stood once again. "I shall give you five hundred pesetas for your propaganda campaign." His eyes traveled from Zozo to Alouette, forming a look of wounded pride as he left.

"Well," Zozo took a biscuit before refilling his drink. "That was interesting."

"It certainly was," Alouette replied. "How much of it was true?"

He shot her a grin. "I am a Bolshevik."

She felt a pang of jealousy. "You are lucky you can maintain your cover without having to pretend to be someone you're not."

He sat next to her on the couch. "Do you mean pretending you care about that callous Boche?"

"Yes. I'm just tired of all the games in general. I wish I could go back to France for good. I wish this terrible war had never started, that my husband had never died…" her voice trailed off.

"Somehow I can't picture you married."

She shifted to face him, bringing her knee next to his. "You knew him, back in our flight days."

"That old man you were always with was your husband? I thought he was your dad or something." He shook his head. "I feel as though, had he lived, you might have died yourself, of boredom."

"Well, that's because you are the type to date a new woman at every aerodrome."

Zozo put a hand on her arm, and she didn't pull away. "Right now we're both grounded. And I'm the only one who knows your secret."

"Don't forget Ladoux."

He dropped his hand. "And Ladoux."

Ladoux. She felt nothing at the mention of his name. For the first time in months, the feelings of indignation and abandonment had vanished. All that was left was the feeling she was no longer alone, an outcast spy, alienated by the Spanish and the French alike. Zozo had come to her aid; he was now a comrade in her lonely battle. Alouette scooted closer to him and retrieved his hand. This time she put it on her leg.

"Are you sure you want to do this?" he asked.

"Like you, I'm a spy." She knew exactly what kind of man Zozo was: there were no secrets with him. But he was also a warm body and she had been so lonely. "Why can't I also be a woman who sleeps with someone she doesn't love?"

He pulled down the collar of her shirt and kissed her neck. "Well then, be sure not to fall in love with me."

"Don't worry, I won't."

CHAPTER 55

M'GREET

DECEMBER 1916

M'greet had no idea why Ladoux had denied hiring her to Thomson, but she knew she needed to do something to impress him if he was ever going to deliver the money he'd promised. She was stuck in Spain, and, as she had failed in meeting von Bissing in Belgium, she decided to seduce a German envoy in Madrid. Of course, in order to do so, she would need an introduction.

After she checked into the Palace Hotel, she asked the clerk for a diplomatic list. She ran her finger down the sheet, looking for a military attaché. She paused at the first one that did not list a wife. "Captain Arnold Kalle," she said aloud.

"*Perdóneme?*" the clerk asked.

"Can you get me an envelope and a pen?" she barked in return.

He did as bid and M'greet hastily wrote out a request to meet with Captain Kalle.

A messenger from the embassy delivered a note the next day, inviting

M'greet to Kalle's apartment for tea. She took great care in choosing her outfit, dressing in a raccoon-trimmed gray suit and matching hat.

A servant answered the door and led M'greet to the study. Kalle was tall and well-built, with an ample dark mane and no facial hair. He gestured for her to sit down and spoke in halting French, "I am not in the habit of receiving ladies who may have been sent to me by our enemies, but I am sure this is not the case with you."

She laughed. "Why are you so sure about that, Captain?"

"Well, for one thing, I was promoted to major quite a few months ago. I am certain that Allied intelligence would be better informed as to my rank."

"Oh, is that so?" M'greet asked, tucking a piece of hair behind her ear. "I am sorry then, Major Kalle."

"I noticed from your calling card that you are Dutch. *Sprichst du Deutsch?*"

"*Natürlich*," M'greet replied smoothly in his native language. She decided to tell him that her heart was with the German cause, and explained to him of her arrest. "But I am clearly not Clara Benedix."

He held up his hands. "I have promised the King of Spain that I would not get involved with intelligence." He picked up his drink and took a sip. "You are to be commended on your German accent."

"I lived in Berlin for quite some time."

"Is that so? Did you ever meet any officers?"

She turned her shoulder. "A few. I knew Alfred de Kiepert quite well."

"Ah." Kalle sat back. "Now I remember you. I saw you once at dinner with him at the Hotel Adlon."

M'greet batted her eyelashes. "I'm not sure I remember you."

"But you are most unforgettable." He nodded to himself. "I believe your arrest had been ordered in Barcelona." He offered her a cigarette, which she accepted.

"Why Barcelona?" she asked, puffing prettily on the cigarette.

"I am not sure, but I can inquire of Baron von Krohn, the head of German intelligence in Spain."

M'greet filed the name away in her head. She could see that Kalle was beginning to fall under her spell. She lounged back on the chaise. "What is life like in Madrid?"

"Tiring," was his snappish response.

"Oh?" She straightened.

His expression softened. "Please forgive me for my rudeness. I've been arranging for the disembarkation of German officers and munitions from a U-boat off the coast of Morocco. It's been taking all of my concentration lately, which accounts for my exhaustion."

"Of course." She got to her feet, offering Kalle a full view of her décolletage as she did so. "I wouldn't want to disturb you any more than necessary tonight. I will take my leave."

"I would like to meet you again, though."

She gave him her room number at the Palace Hotel. He kissed her hand before she left.

M'greet wrote to Ladoux as soon as she returned to her room, giving him the name Baron von Krohn and revealing the information about the submarine landing in Morocco. She called for a porter and told him to send the letter through the post straightaway.

"Yes, señorita," the porter said, bowing.

CHAPTER 56

ALOUETTE

DECEMBER 1916

*A*louette and Zozo continued their casual relationship until he returned to Paris in early December. As the Baron had left on holiday with his wife, Alouette was once again alone in a foreign city.

One evening she found Major Kalle in the dining room of the Palace Hotel. He was accompanied by an exotic-looking woman with an olive complexion. They sat at a middle table, directly under the electric chandelier, which revealed a few stray gray hairs in the woman's otherwise luxurious black locks.

"Arnold?" Alouette called as she approached them. "What are you doing here?"

"Ah, Alouette, I'd like you to meet the famous Mata Hari."

Alouette held out her hand. The woman looked as though the last thing in the world she wanted to do was to shake it, but she did anyway.

"Sit down," Kalle told her before turning to the woman. "You must forgive her. Alouette may be French, but she has the most interesting background."

The woman leaned forward. "You are French?"

"Yes, but I've adopted Spain as my new homeland," Alouette said, casting a sly glance in Kalle's direction.

"Is that so? I do love Paris," the woman commented. "Although it is necessary for me to return to the Netherlands as soon as possible. I was just going to ask Arnold here for his assistance."

"You would have to pass through several borders," Alouette replied. They both looked at Kalle for his reaction.

"Impossible." He waved his hand. "I'm sorry, Mata, but I cannot."

"I see." The woman took a sip of her drink. "It must be very difficult to disembark troops from a submarine off Morocco's coast. How will you pull off such a coup?"

Alouette nearly spit out a mouthful of wine. To her delight, she could see Kalle's face turn dark with anger.

"Beautiful women must not ask too much," he replied before getting up from the table, nearly spilling everyone's drink as he did so.

The woman seemed to have no remorse for Kalle's sudden departure. Alouette waited until he was out of earshot before leaning in and saying in a low voice, "I was like you once."

"What do you mean, like me?" the woman snapped. "You don't know me."

"Oh, but I do. I too had to depend on men for my livelihood. But I was fortunate to meet a man who loved me for who I was, and never tried to keep me in that gilded cage we both fear."

"What happened to him?"

Alouette played with the stem of her wine glass. "He died in the war."

"I'm sorry." The woman sounded genuine this time.

Alouette decided to lend the poor thing a hand. It was obvious the woman was in way too deep with Kalle. "I know someone who might be willing to help you."

"Oh?" The woman relaxed her face into an expression that appeared almost friendly. "Who?"

Alouette straightened her finger, as if about to tap on her wine glass, but instead discreetly pointed to a man across the room. "That is Colonel Joseph-Cyrill Denvignes, a senior attaché to the French Embassy."

If the woman was suspicious as to why Alouette was indicating one of Kalle's mortal enemies, she didn't show it. "Thank you."

"No problem," Alouette replied, her voice once again low. "We Francophiles have to stick together."

CHAPTER 57

M'GREET

DECEMBER 1916

M'greet left the tall blonde woman to make her away across the room.

"Colonel Denvignes?" she asked, approaching the stocky man with salt-and-pepper hair. She held out both hands for him to grasp. "It's such a pleasure to make your acquaintance."

A warm smile appeared under his substantial mustache as he took her hands. "Aren't you the woman who came in with Arnold Kalle?"

"Yes. I'm surprised you noticed."

"I couldn't help it. I have never seen anyone more breathtaking. What shall I call you?"

"Mata Hari," she said, withdrawing from his grip.

"And what is your purpose in visiting Madrid, Miss Mata Hari?" His voice held the tinge of a challenge. Noticing an empty sitting room, she motioned for him to follow her.

"Don't worry, Colonel," she hissed once they were out of earshot of the dining room. "I am one of yours."

"Pardon?"

"If only I had met you a day earlier, I would not have had to go

336

through the trouble of sending a letter to Paris. I could have given you the letter and you could have taken care of it."

"What information?"

She relayed to him all she had learned from Kalle, figuring that, even though she had just met the man, his position in the French Embassy meant he was trustworthy.

"Is it possible for you to get more specifics?" he asked when she'd finished.

M'greet frowned. "I tried to at dinner, but Kalle seemed reluctant to provide any more."

"Try again." He must have sensed her hesitation as he patted her hand. "For France."

She nodded.

Denvignes rose. "You are a very beautiful woman, Mata Hari, a true Parisian flower. Is it possible for you to join me for lunch tomorrow? That is, if Kalle does not call."

She gave him a seductive smile. "Of course."

For the next week, Denvignes took on the role of both substitute spymaster and ardent suitor. He seemed enamored with M'greet, and plied her with lavish gifts. At lunch one day, he rather reluctantly informed her he was to start out for Paris in the morning.

His hand reached toward M'greet's bosom, and to her surprise, plucked a posy from her corsage. "I will carry this to France to remind me of my Parisian flower. Can we continue this relationship when I return?"

"I would love for that, Colonel, but unfortunately I must be leaving Madrid soon."

"I see. Well, then perhaps we shall meet again in Paris. I'll be staying at the Hotel d'Orsay." He wound a ribbon around the posy before adding, "Is there anything I can do for you while I'm gone?"

"Yes." She leaned forward. "Will you please pay a call on Captain Ladoux and tell him how well I've done?" She pursed her lips. "Since I've been here, I haven't heard a word from him. Going forward, I'd like for him to treat me with more respect."

"Of course." He set the beribboned posy down. "In the meantime, should you retrieve any new information from Kalle, pass it on to my replacement at the embassy instead of sending it back to Paris."

"I will," she promised.

Perhaps as not merely a coincidence, only hours after Denvignes departed, Kalle sent an invitation for M'greet to pay a call to his apartment.

As soon as she was shown into his study, he stated, "I've heard your French friend was ordered to return to Paris."

M'greet's heart sped up. "Have you?"

He poured himself a drink. "You must have repeated what I'd told you, for the French have sent their radio messages everywhere, asking when the officers will alight in Morocco."

"It wasn't me," she insisted. She brightened as a thought occurred to her. "Maybe it was that blonde woman at dinner?"

"Alouette? Most certainly not."

M'greet decided to change the subject. "How do you know what the French are telegraphing?"

Kalle took a long gulp of his drink. "We've had the key to their cipher for months now."

"Oh." She walked over to him and put her hand on his arm. "How very clever."

She could feel his arm muscles relax. He set his drink down on the bar. "I can forgive such a beautiful woman as yourself, but if Berlin knew it was me who told you this information, it could cost me my life."

"They will never know," she assured him, unbuttoning her blouse. He took her hand and led her into the bedroom, where she let him do what he wanted with her.

Afterward, he lit a cigarette. "This war will perhaps lead elsewhere. There are among us Germans some officers who are nothing but brutes."

M'greet took a puff on his cigarette. Was he wishing to confess something? "The German army has some of the bravest men in the world." She turned toward him, offering a full view of her naked body.

"The French do as well," he conceded. "Especially the aviators. They have one right now who flies over our lines to deposit a passenger, a spy behind enemy lines, that we must search for. But we also have our own agents in France who are very well informed."

"How do these agents get word to you?"

"There are many means. We use couriers instead of sending letters."

"Well, I find that astonishing. I have traveled a great deal during this war and, judging by the inspections to which I have been subjected, I wonder how anyone could pass the security checks with secrets. In England, they even examined my hatpins."

He reached out to caress her bare thigh. "But it is not with women like you that one transports such things. Our couriers are a little dirty, people whom one doesn't usually notice. They carry the reagents to our ink formed into little white balls in their ears and under their fingernails."

M'greet gave a fake moan of pleasure. "My God, such inventions!" She shifted abruptly, as if a thought had just occurred to her. "I only wish that I could return to my home country for a trice. I have a daughter there I haven't seen in ages."

Kalle blew out a ring of smoke. "I told you I cannot assist you with the border guards. But," he sat up and reached into a desk drawer. "Maybe this will help." He dumped several bills in the space between them.

M'greet counted them as soon as she left his apartment. Kalle had given her $3500 francs.

CHAPTER 58

MARTHE

JANUARY 1917

$\mathcal{T}$he months before Marthe's trial dragged by. She wished to get the whole business over quickly; knowing that the trial would be a sham and her condemnation was certain.

Finally, the stomping of a great many feet could be heard outside her cell and the door flew open, revealing a German unteroffizier and two privates, their callous eyes staring straight ahead. To them, Marthe was already a convicted spy, and, in a short while, they would aim their rifles at her heart with the same lack of interest they displayed now.

The unteroffizier gave her a curt nod and Marthe followed him, the privates walking behind her. They left the confines of the prison and marched across the grounds to the courthouse. She had not been outside in months and she took a deep breath of the winter air, noticing everything: the smoke wafting from the prison kitchen, the bird poised on a leafless tree branch, the German flag waving in the breeze in front of the courthouse.

In too short a time, Marthe was inside the courtroom, facing eight officers in impeccably neat uniforms seated at a long table.

She was led to a shorter table with two empty chairs. She sat in one and pulled it forward. It squeaked along the floor, causing the jury members' frowns to deepen. She offered no apology. Instead, she placed her folded hands in front of her and stared straight ahead.

Another officer stood. He was short, with glasses that emphasized his stony eyes. *The prosecution.*

He began pacing the narrow space between the accused and the judge. "Marthe Cnockaert, a Belgian subject under the jurisdiction of the Imperial German Government, is accused of grave offenses against the Military Code. These offences are treasonous to our great country and are punishable by death." He paused to see the full effect of his words, but the only sound to be heard was a rustling of papers.

Marthe remained frozen, refusing to follow the little man with her eyes and thus only caught sight of him when he stopped directly in front of her.

"I will prove the guilt of the accused fully and conclusively. After leaving her home village of Westroosebeke, she took on the role of nurse in order to carry out her destructive deeds. There is no doubt she was dangerous even from those early days, working under the façade of being a ministering angel, while all the while passing on secrets regarding our army's positions." He pointed at Marthe. "This woman has caused the death of hundreds of our comrades-in-arms!"

The jury refused to show any verbal response to his accusations, but this time the sound of paper rustling was accompanied by the furious scribbling of many pens.

The prosecutor continued, "I will call witnesses who will testify to her guilt. We must remember, gentlemen, that these are times of danger; our Fatherland and the safety of our soldiers fighting in the trenches must be ensured. No sentiment toward womanhood must cloud our judgement. The only fate for the operative responsible for the destruction of the stores of our armies is death!"

This time there was absolutely no other sound as the prosecutor took his seat.

The judge straightened. "These are very serious charges, Fräulein Cnockaert. What say you?"

Marthe refused to speak the language of their so-called Fatherland and replied in Flemish. "*Ik zeg niks.*" I say nothing.

The judge peered at her over the top of his pince-nez glasses.

"Who were your other associates in the burning of the ammunition dump? It is well known you worked with the spy Lucelle Deldonck." Marthe was a stone wall.

"Fräulein, I have to warn you, you are hurting your own case." The judge took off his glasses to plead with her. "Be frank with the court. These messages were signed by 'Laura.' Are you Laura?"

After another moment of silence, he nodded at the prosecutor. "Proceed with the evidence."

Over the next few hours, the prosecutor called several Germans to testify against Marthe, including the brigade officer who had arrested her, the gefreiter who had discovered her watch, and the secretary to the Town-Kommandant who had heard her claim the watch. It was well into the afternoon when the detective from the prison came to the stand.

Marthe stiffened when she saw his face, with that hateful distorted nose. She tried to focus on the wooden desk in front of her instead of listening to his testimony, but when the detective stated, "The prisoner admitted her collusion with the enemy more than once to me," she could no longer restrain herself.

"That is a lie," Marthe stated quietly. "This man invaded my privacy night and day—when I was weak from hunger and lack of sleep, he threw me against the wall and shook me, threatening to kill me. And I never admitted such a thing. This is the kind of man you will listen to under oath?"

The judge held up his hand. "We concern ourselves only with facts in this court. If your charges are disproved, you will be released."

"I do not recognize this court or its verdict," Marthe replied, her voice so low that every man in the room leaned in to hear her. "I am well aware that my fate had already been determined before I even walked into this room. But if you think that your country can keep down the Belgian spirit of freedom, you are mistaken." She stood up, her voice growing stronger. "I see myself as a soldier in the field, with the same rights to defend my country against an invader who has ravaged our land, raped our women, and who has rewritten our laws for their own convenience."

This finally elicited feedback from the jury, who buzzed with anger as she sat down.

"Do you intend to call any more witnesses?" the judge asked the prosecutor when the court had quieted. The prosecutor shook his head.

Just then the unteroffizier came in and handed a note to the judge before saluting and exiting as quickly as he had entered.

The judge read the note, his eyebrows knitting together and his frown deepening. He then called the prosecutor to the bench and the two spoke in furious whispers.

The prosecutor threw up his hands and retreated back to his table as the judge cleared his throat. "Although this is against the usual procedure, the court has decided to hear the evidence presented by Herr Doctor Herbert Stolz."

All heads in the room, Marthe's included, swiveled to the back as the Oberarzt entered.

After he was sworn in, the Oberarzt began his testimony. "The accused has worked untiringly under my command for more than two years and has always taken great pride and generosity in her work as a nurse. I have come here on my own will to testify to her excellent character and her endless willingness to alleviate the sufferings of our wounded countrymen."

Marthe could feel her facial muscles relax as she looked upon her former boss.

The prosecutor rose and walked toward him. "Would it surprise you to know that the accused has confessed to her guilt?

"That does not concern me."

The prosecutor spat out his retort. "What should concern you is that the accused obtained the job of nurse at a German hospital in order to conduct espionage against said countrymen."

"She may have conducted espionage in the interests of her country, just as you and I act in the interest of our country. But it is my opinion that Fräulein Cnockaert carried out her duties as a nurse purely in the interest of helping humankind." The Oberarzt turned to the judge. "This woman was awarded the highest honor that our Fatherland bestows—the Iron Cross."

At this, several men in the jury gasped.

The judge banged his gavel. "The sentence for the accused will be announced in four days' time. Remove the prisoner and clear the court."

CHAPTER 59

M'GREET

M'greet's stay in Madrid proved to be more than fruitful. Armed with all of the information Kalle had provided, she intended to return to Paris and demand payment from Ladoux. The only question was how to get back.

She'd befriended two Spanish envoys: the senator Emilio Junoy and his assistant, Diego de Leon. Their relationship was strictly platonic, as her only concern was getting them to sign her travel papers. To emphasize her intentions, M'greet told them all about Vadim, who, to her knowledge, was still at Verdun.

"But señorita, the Battle of Verdun ended weeks ago," Junoy replied.

"Oh." M'greet's face wrinkled unintentionally. "I wonder where in the world he is now?"

She was surprised when Junoy told her over lunch the next day that he had been approached by a "handsome Slav, clearly in the employ of French intelligence" who had demanded to know why they had been seen in the presence of someone clearly hostile to the Anglo-French alliance.

"He couldn't have possibly meant me," M'greet insisted.

"I couldn't agree more," Junoy replied. "I told him we knew you as a charming, intelligent, spiritual woman, and that no word of politics had ever crossed your lips."

"In fact," de Leon added, "when we asked you about the where-abouts of your soldier fiancé, you had no idea. If you were indeed an enemy spy, you'd be much more informed of military operations."

There was no way M'greet could argue with that statement.

"But I do have good news." Junoy produced a French visa. "You'll now be able to return to Paris as soon as possible."

"Oh thank you!" she blew him a kiss with her gloved hand.

One of the first things she did after checking into the relatively inex-pensive Hotel Plaza Athénée was visit her customary hair salon, to touch up her hair color and cover her emerging grays.

Afterward, she called on 282 boulevard, Saint-Germain.

"Captain Ladoux is not in," a suave, dark-haired stranger told her.

"Do you know when he will return?" she asked.

"I'm not sure." The dark-haired man shot her a wide grin, as if he already knew the answer to his question. "Do you care to wait for him?"

"No." M'greet frowned. How was she supposed to get paid if Ladoux was nowhere to be found? "Do you know anything as to the whereabouts of Colonel Denvignes?"

"Ah, yes." He scratched at his unruly beard. "I believe he returns to Madrid this evening."

Denvignes had implied he would be in Paris for several months. M'greet forgot all of her carefully cultivated demeanor as she demanded, "What?"

"If you can get to the Austerlitz station in time, you might be able to catch him before the train leaves." He stepped into the street to wave down a passing taxi.

. . .

The passengers had already boarded by the time the taxi arrived in Austerlitz. M'greet hailed a conductor and begged him to inform the French military attaché that she was in need of his presence.

She was relieved to see Denvignes appear at the door of his carriage a few minutes later.

"Yes?" he asked coolly, as though he didn't recognize her.

"So this is the way you leave town, Colonel, without a word. Have you seen Captain Ladoux?"

He stuck his head out of the doorway to look up and down the platform before replying in a small voice, "No, but I did pay a call on his chief, Colonel Goubé. He told me that your information was very interesting and that you must be an intelligent woman."

"Is that all?" she demanded. "Did you explain our relationship?"

His grip on the railing tightened. "I told him I had met you briefly in Madrid."

Briefly? M'greet narrowed her eyes at the person standing before her, clearly of a different mind than the one who had once been so affectionate toward her. "Why did you lie? Did you forget about your Parisian flower?"

The train began to pull away. Denvignes called after her, "*Je suis désolé mon petit.*" I am sorry my little one.

Early the next morning, M'greet arrived again at the offices of the Deuxiéme Bureau and requested to see Ladoux. After being kept waiting for over an hour, she was told to call the next day after 5 pm.

When she was finally allowed entry into Ladoux's office, she refused a seat. "Who questioned Senator Junoy about my allegiance to the Cause?"

"I don't know what you mean," Ladoux insisted. He took out his customary cigarette case, but didn't offer one to M'greet. "In any case, you must not forget that you do not know me and I don't know you." He struck a match. "It is certainly not this office who sent someone to interrogate the senator."

"Why have you not responded to my calls? Where are the thanks for the services I have rendered you?"

Ladoux's face was blank. "What services? That stuff about Baron von Krohn and the submarine? We knew that already."

She threw her arms up. "Did you know of the information about the code-breaking, or the aviators dropping spies behind enemy lines?" When Ladoux's expression did not change, she cried, "The secret ink hidden under their fingernails?"

"This is the first I've heard about any of this."

M'greet collapsed into a chair. "Didn't Colonel Denvignes tell you anything about my exploits in Madrid?"

"No." He stabbed out his cigarette. "And there is no way the Germans have our codes. Kalle was feeding you what we call *intoxication* —fake news."

"But…" She was not going to leave his office without the promise of payment, no matter how small. "Isn't there any chance that Kalle's information is correct and the Germans have been intercepting our messages this whole time?"

Ladoux put his hand under his chin. "I would be very surprised if that were the case." He appeared to soften under M'greet's desperate gaze. "Let me see if I can uncover any further information regarding this mess." He gave her a meaningful look. "Do not leave Paris until I've had the chance to get to the bottom of this."

CHAPTER 60

MARTHE

JANUARY 1917

*T*he days between Marthe's trial and her sentencing felt like
years. As her German wardress delivered her dinner on the
third night of waiting, she finally spoke to her. "You are a fool not to
admit your guilt and throw yourself upon the court's mercy." She
dumped the tray of bread at Marthe's feet. "You must not think that
the Oberarzt's intervention can possibly help you. There is but one fate
for a spy, and that is death!"

Mercy of the court? Marthe pictured her jury's faces: cold, grim, as if
carved from stone. She could not imagine those granite faces granting
her any mercy.

In the morning, she once again awoke to the sun's rays through the
slats of her window, imagining that soon the time would come when
there would be no more sunshine.

As if on cue, the unteroffizier arrived. "Have courage, fräulein. The
time of your sentencing has come."

The nightmarish walk was repeated and Marthe followed the

unteroffizier up the stone steps to the court house. The judge and jury were in the same positions as last time.

The judge began reading in a formal tone, "It is a terrible thing to condemn a fellow human being, especially when that creature is a woman." He fixed his grim gaze on Marthe before continuing, "You have been the cause of the deaths of many Germans. It has been decided that you will suffer death by firing squad."

To her credit, Marthe did not cry. She thought about what the wardress had advised her. Clearly begging for mercy would not help, not that she could ever bring herself to stoop so low. The tragic farce had indeed been played out. Now all she had to do was wait for death.

CHAPTER 61

ALOUETTE

JANUARY 1917

ozo returned to Madrid in mid-January, taking the room next to Alouette's in the Palace Hotel. Von Krohn requested a meeting with him to find out how the campaign was going thus far and to introduce a new part of the plot.

"It is now time to completely shatter the morale of the French troops at the front," von Krohn stated. "I am going to give you a copy of a French newspaper. You are going to follow its format as closely as possible, for I want the French soldiers to believe they are reading actual news reporting the giant losses of Allied troops and the likelihood that Germany is going to win the war."

Zozo shot a warning look in Alouette's direction, as if he expected her to gasp aloud or otherwise give herself away. But she remained as cool as ever. "I am confident in Zozo's ability."

Instead of looking reassured, von Krohn's face flashed with something else. Jealousy perhaps.

Alouette decided to provoke him further and captured Zozo's hand in hers. Their affair wasn't the sort where they demonstrated affection in public, but Zozo squeezed her hand back.

"You may set your mind at rest, Baron von Krohn," she told him. "I will carry out your wishes to your satisfaction."

"Very well then." The Baron's face was steely. "I have changed pesetas into 300,000 francs. You are to return to France as soon as possible. As you cannot cross the frontier with such a large amount of money, we will bring you to the border in a car tomorrow evening. I will hand over the money at that point, and men in my charge will take you to France."

Zozo bowed gracefully as Alouette's heart unexpectedly filled with indignation. He was going back to France while she was stuck here!

Zozo claimed he had something to do the next day, so Alouette spent the afternoon alone. When she exited the hotel to meet von Krohn, Zozo was standing on the corner, his hands in his pockets.

She joined him on the sidewalk, wishing she could join him on his journey. Not necessarily because she wanted to be with him, but because he was the last link to her real identity. Of course she couldn't tell him any of that. "What will you do with the newspapers?" she asked instead.

He cast his eyes up and down the boulevard, but no one was in sight. "Burn them, of course."

"And the money?"

"Most of it will go to the Deuxiéme Bureau. Not all of it, of course," he said with a wink. "I have to spend a little of it myself."

"Of course."

He took one hand out of his pocket to offer her a cigarette. "I'll miss you."

Alouette accepted the cigarette as she thought of a reply, but just then the Baron's car pulled up to the curb.

"Do you have the money?" Zozo asked the Baron as he got out.

Von Krohn gestured toward a leather bag on the floor of the front passenger side. "300,000 francs."

"That's a lot of money," Alouette commented.

"It's not so much when you think about how this plan could save Germany months of fighting," von Krohn replied as his chauffeur loaded Zozo's bag. "That is, if your friend can see it through."

"Fiancé," Alouette corrected him, noting with satisfaction the glower that appeared on the Baron's face.

"But, Herr Davrichachvili, I must warn you." Von Krohn grabbed her from behind. "If you dare betray us, I shall hold Alouette hostage."

To her dismay, Zozo grinned. "The Russian General Martinoff told me the exact same thing at Tiflis. I had to leave my then-fiancé, a different woman," he added, "as hostage, pledging my word to the general that I would not incite the peasants to rise up."

Von Krohn relaxed his grasp on her arms. "What happened?"

"I incited the peasants to uprise, and we held the Russian army at bay."

"And your then-fiancé?" the Baron asked. Alouette was going to ask the same thing, but flicked her cigarette with feigned indifference instead.

"She told me to do what I must do for the cause. Exactly as Alouette would do, isn't that right Alouette?"

She shrugged.

"The Cossacks killed her," Zozo continued. Alouette glanced up, giving him a helpless look, but he ignored her. "Two days afterward, General Martinoff was blown up in his carriage. So you see..." he blew out a ring of smoke, "her death was not in vain."

"Luckily we are traveling by motor-car today," the Baron put in.

"Horse-carriage or automobile, what does it matter?" the supposed Russian nihilist stated. "Every man—or woman—is responsible for their own destiny."

Von Krohn stood stiffly by the door of the car as Zozo crawled into the backseat and Alouette followed.

"Heinrich," von Krohn called to his chauffeur. "I'll drive tonight. I know these roads well."

As von Krohn started the car, Zozo tried to make more anarchist conversation. Alouette sat with her hands folded across her chest, stewing. She hadn't expected Zozo to part with declarations of undying affection, but she also didn't expect him to admit to the Baron he'd sacrifice her life if it meant seeing his mission through. *At least he admitted that he'd miss me.* She glanced in the rearview mirrors to see that the Baron's narrowed eyes had left the road and were focused on her.

All of a sudden, bright lights blinded Alouette. Then there was the sound of metal striking metal, and the feeling of being shoved against the door. She passed out for what seemed like hours, but was probably only mere seconds. She awoke, coughing from the smoke in her lungs, and realized the car had stopped moving. They had struck a utility pole.

CHAPTER 62

M'GREET

JANUARY 1917

$\mathcal{A}$ s she waited for Ladoux to get back to her, M'greet resumed her usual rounds of shopping and visits to the manicurist and hair dresser. She knew she was once again being tailed, but paid no attention to her followers. Soon, Ladoux would see for himself that she had done a great service and would call off his lackeys for good.

Vadim was due back in Paris on January 8th. When he did not arrive, M'greet grew worried, writing to him twice a day to affirm her undying love and demanding a response from him. After a week went by with no reply from Vadim, she decided to write to Anna, begging her to contact van de Capellen to send more money.

When Anna sent a letter confirming that she would do her mistress's bidding, M'greet noticed the envelope's seal had been broken. Someone had been steaming open her letters.

Daring to hope that her lover's replies to her had been confiscated, she called the Grand Hotel, where she and Vadim had spent many pleasurable hours together, to see if they had any information on when he would arrive.

"Vladimir Masloff?" the clerk repeated.

"Yes," M'greet stated impatiently, expecting him to demand her to spell it out, something she wasn't entirely sure she could do correctly.

"It appears that he checked in yesterday."

She almost dropped the phone. "Please let him know that a visitor will be arriving to see him shortly.

"Can I also supply him a name?"

"No," she replied before hanging up the phone.

Vadim greeted her with a sheepish smile on the good side of his face. He was still wearing the eyepatch and stood stiffly in the lobby.

M'greet mirrored his stance. "Why haven't you answered any of my letters?"

The grin turned to a look of bewilderment. "I did. Did you not get my explanation?"

"Explanation of what?"

He glanced toward an empty couch. "Let's sit." He attempted to put his hand on her back, but she shrugged him off, wanting to make him suffer for the long months of silence, even if they weren't completely his fault.

He sat down across from her and took a deep breath. "I was under the impression that you already knew, and you were coming here to reprimand me."

"Knew what?" she snapped.

"Why I can't marry you."

Her mouth closed involuntarily. She bit her tongue and widened her eyes, willing herself not to cry. "And why is that?"

"My colonel received a letter from some French officer, who claimed you were a 'dangerous adventuress' and that you are only after money."

"We both know that's not true."

The good side of his face softened. "I do know that. But my colonel is forbidding me to see you again. I can't marry you," he repeated.

"Quit the army."

He reached out to pat her knee, but she moved her leg away just in time. "I can't desert. In case you are unaware, Russia is in the middle of a revolution. I would be killed if I went home."

"We can go to the Netherlands. It's neutral—they don't care about accepting deserted soldiers into their borders." She had no idea if that were true or not, but it sounded good.

Apparently it wasn't good enough for Vadim. He stood. "I'm sorry, Marina."

"Don't call me that. You no longer get to refer to me with a nickname. If you must mention me, which I hope you never have to do again, use 'Mata Hari.' That's apparently the woman you think I am, anyway."

With that, she walked out of the hotel and out of Vadim's life forever.

When M'greet caught sight of the same familiar men waiting for her outside, she decided she'd had enough. She hailed a taxi and gave the driver strict orders on where to turn so that they zig-zagged erratically through the Parisian streets.

When they'd finally lost the detectives, M'greet directed the driver to the office of her lawyer, Edouard Clunet.

She strolled in, not caring if he had a client at that time, which he did not. "I want you to send an official letter to Captain Georges Ladoux at 282 boulevard, Saint-Germain," she declared.

Clunet glanced up from his paperwork. "Is that so? That is the headquarters of the Deuxiéme Bureau. What business do you have there?"

"Nothing more, apparently." She nodded at the inkwell in the middle of his desk. Clunet sighed as he picked up the pen.

She began dictating: "Captain Ladoux, I do not ask your secrets and I do not wish to know your agents. Do not discuss my methods, do not ruin my work with secret agents who can't possibly begin to understand me. I desire to be paid as soon as possible for I wish to leave Paris."

Clunet set his pen down. "Don't you think demanding payment sounds a bit mercenary?"

"If I am not ashamed to accept money, then I must not be ashamed to say so." She snatched the letter from him. "If you want, I will mail it myself."

He handed her a stamped envelope. "M'greet," he started, but, envelope in hand, she was already out the door.

M'greet had just settled down to eat breakfast a few days later when she was disturbed by someone banging on the door. As soon as she unlocked the latch, the door burst open and a well-dressed, middle-aged man with an upturned mustache barged in. The man paused in front of her while five gendarmes filed in and began ransacking her room.

"What is this?" she demanded.

"Margaretha Zelle-MacLeod?" the man inquired.

"Yes?"

"You are under arrest for the crimes of attempting espionage against France and passing on intelligence to enemy countries."

She was taken to the Palace of Justice and shown to a tiny office. The room was so small that it could only accommodate a table and three chairs. Both of the seated men got up as she entered. The shorter one introduced himself as Pierre Bouchardon, investigative magistrate of the Third Council of War.

The other man nodded without saying anything before sitting down again. As he picked up a pen, M'greet realized he was just a clerk.

Bouchardon struck a match and soon the room was filled with the stench of his cigar. "Have you been informed of the charges against you?"

"I have."

"You have the right to call a lawyer."

M'greet waved smoke out of her face. "I do not think that is necessary at this point. These charges are clearly a result of a miscommunication between myself and Captain Ladoux of the Deuxiéme Bureau. I am innocent of all charges." She assumed that there had been another mistake, such as that tiresome Clara Benedix incident. She rose. "If you would just contact Ladoux, he can explain everything."

"I'm afraid it's not that easy, Madame Zelle-MacLeod. Captain Ladoux was the one who started this investigation."

"But—" She racked her brain, but could not come up with a suitable way to finish her argument. *That lying imbecile has betrayed me.*

Bouchardon's next words were addressed to the clerk. "Please make arrangements to deliver Madame Zelle-MacLeod to Saint Lazare."

She gave a horrified cry before grabbing Bouchardon's arm. "Please, monsieur, please don't send me to prison. I am of a delicate constitution—"

He shrugged her off. "Oh, we know all about your lodging preferences." He opened the door. "We will continue our conversation in a few days."

That first night, M'greet was placed in a padded cell, in case the shock of the day had caused her to develop thoughts of suicide.

The prison doctor paid her a visit, and, after examining her, asked if she was in need of anything.

"Yes," M'greet replied sullenly. "A bath and a telephone."

"Neither are available for prisoners at Saint-Lazare." He gestured toward a stained bucket in the corner. "That is for you to relieve yourself, and you can wash up with this bowl of cold water."

M'greet went over to the bucket and lifted her dove-gray skirts. She hadn't gone to the bathroom all day and told herself that doctors were used to seeing all types of bodily fluids.

"You know, this prison was used to house 18th century prostitutes with venereal diseases." He gave her a withering glance. "Fitting, wouldn't you say?"

Her eyes became slits as she rearranged her skirts. "How dare you."

He moved toward the door and she realized he was about to leave her alone in this horrid place. She changed her tone to a high-pitched plea. "Please sir, can you arrange a different room for me? Take pity."

But the heartless doctor left without further comment.

CHAPTER 63

ALOUETTE

FEBRUARY 1917

𝒯he Baron, who had been driving the doomed car, suffered only cuts and scratches from broken glass. Alouette's face was also cut, but her left ankle, which had been broken previously in an airplane accident, was fractured and her left knee was pulled out of its joint.

After a night or two in a Madrid hospital, von Krohn had Alouette transferred to his house. He claimed he wanted to protect her from the prying eyes of journalists, but she knew his real reason was to maintain his semblance of control over her, especially since her supposed fiancé, whose arm had been broken, remained at the hospital.

For weeks she lay helpless on a bed in the Baron's office. After she was able to put weight on her leg, she'd trek back and forth between the guest room and a pull-out bed in the office, spending her days lamenting over the money Zozo would never receive. Von Krohn must have already hired someone else, who was most likely not a double agent and might actually earn it by writing German propaganda to further lower the morale of French troops.

. . .

One day she was standing at the patio door of his office, propped up by a crutch, enjoying a little sunshine, when the Baron came in.

"How are you feeling?" he asked, the tenderness obvious in his voice.

"Fine," she snapped. All the tenderness in the world could never change the deep resentment she held toward him.

A maid popped her head in. "Señorita Maria is here."

"Tell her to wait in the parlor and I'll be there in a minute." Von Krohn reached for Alouette's hand. "We will continue this conversation later this afternoon."

She recalled that Maria was one of von Krohn's other female agents, one she'd warned Ladoux about months ago, but had yet to be arrested.

Alouette made her way toward the closed double doors that led to the parlor, balancing on her crutch with her ear to the door. Von Krohn's tone was low, but she could still discern most of what he said. "Very good. I'll send Antonio to look for two fountain pens. Call again tomorrow at the same hour and I'll pass them on to you, along with full instructions."

Alouette hobbled over to the nearest chair and sat, deep in thought. She had to find a way to warn Paris and have an agent shadow Maria immediately. She frowned at her bandaged foot, thinking the normally straightforward task seemed nearly impossible.

As soon as von Krohn returned, she remarked, in as casual a voice as she could manage, "I say, Hans, I can't go on wearing your wife's undies indefinitely. I should like to purchase some new ones."

He smiled an oily grin, probably picturing her in sexy lingerie. "I'll take you out after my afternoon siesta."

"No. I'd like to go on my own."

The grin disappeared. "You cannot manage an outing such as that by yourself. Not yet."

"But the doctor has given me permission to walk a little bit at a time. And I've managed so far on this crutch just fine. Besides," she racked her mind for a reason for him not to accompany her. "I must pay a visit to Zozo and see how he is getting on."

This produced the reaction she desired. "Fine. If you want to risk your healing leg just to see him, go ahead. I do not wish to be disturbed."

He left the room, the door banging behind him.

The servants helped her into the motor-car, and Alouette instructed the chauffeur to first drive her to the Palace Hotel so that she could pick up her mail.

The desk clerk deposited a pile of letters in front of her and gave her a satisfied smile before walking away.

Alouette wondered what was behind his reaction as she flipped through her mail. One of the envelopes contained a newspaper clipping sent by one of the Deuxiéme Bureau's clerks. She picked it up and read the headline: "The Spy in the Car," before she tossed it aside with shaking hands. She could only imagine what the newspaper article had speculated about the reason why the prized airwoman of Nancy was in a car with the German naval attaché and a known anarchist.

Someday, Alouette promised herself, shoving the rest of the letters into her purse. *Someday they will all know what I've sacrificed for France.*

She summoned the clerk, now surmising that his smirk had been because he too thought she was a German agent, to help her back to the car. She asked the chauffeur to head to her apartment on the Calle del Alcalá. The driver helped her upstairs before Alouette dismissed him, stating that she was going to change and then lie down for a few minutes.

She went to her desk and pulled out a piece of paper and a packet of antipyrine. After a moment, she threw them both onto the floor, cursing loudly at the lack of organization in the French Secret Service. Even if she did write to Ladoux, there was no way he would receive the information in time to prevent whatever it was Maria and von Krohn were up to. Not to mention she had no guarantee the Deuxiéme Bureau was even receiving her letters at this point. She racked her brain before calling the Palace Hotel.

"May I speak to General Denvignes?"

The hotel clerk put down the phone for a moment before informing her that the general had left for Paris several days ago.

Alouette hung up, barely able to refrain from banging the telephone receiver against the wall. She had no one left to contact. There was no way she could visit the French Embassy and demand to speak to Denvignes' replacement: not only would her crutch attract attention, but Madrid was so teeming with German spies that von Krohn would hear of it within the hour.

She returned to the Baron's house in utter defeat, claiming that her foot was too sore to attend dinner.

A few days later she was seated in the parlor when von Krohn entered. He tossed a French newspaper on the table in front of her, and Alouette's heart hammered as she picked it up. The headline read, "German Incendiaries Blow Up Munitions Factory Near Bayonne. Total Dead and Wounded: 90."

Her confusion slipped into horror as she realized what von Krohn had sent Maria to do. With no one to stop her, she probably accomplished her mission with ease. Alouette shoved the paper aside.

"Is something wrong?" von Krohn asked.

She glanced at the Baron, taking in the grin of triumph lighting up his ugly face and realized she was supposed to be delighted at the murder of her fellow countrymen. "A tremendous accomplishment," she managed to croak out. He nodded with satisfaction before reaching in his desk and taking out a fresh piece of paper, probably to brag to his superiors about the outcome of his bloodthirsty scheme.

CHAPTER 64

M'GREET

MARCH 1917

*B*ouchardon continued his interrogations of M'greet on a near daily basis. For one particular session, her lawyer, Edouard Clunet, was allowed to join them.

After Bouchardon re-established her life narrative: where she grew up, what her father did, etc., he tried to get into the specifics of her marriage and little Normie's death.

"I do not wish to answer any more questions about that period of time," M'greet stated with a wave of her hand. "It has no bearing on anything you have accused me of."

Bouchard glanced at Clunet, who shrugged. "Very well then," Bouchard replied. "Tell about this Vladimir Masloff."

"Oh." She blinked quickly. "It was a grand love on both sides."

"Is that so?" Bouchard asked, the doubt obvious in his voice. He flipped through some papers. "Would you claim the same about the Baron van der Capellen?"

"No," M'greet replied. "He was married."

Bouchard frowned. "What about the Marquis de Beaufort?"

She flicked her hand again. "A tryst. But fun while it lasted."

"And the German, Lieutenant Alfred Kiepert? Or the Berlin police inspector, Walter Griebel?" He looked up. "I need a separate file just to keep all of your men straight."

M'greet leaned forward. "What exactly am I on trial for? My morals?"

"Well," Bouchardon said, shuffling some papers. "I wouldn't exactly consider you a respectable woman."

She glared at her lawyer, who was chewing his fingernails. He took his hand out of his mouth. "Now, Monsieur Bouchardon, as you have no hard evidence of espionage activity, I would request that you allow Madame Zelle-MacLeod provisional liberties."

"You know that I cannot grant her any liberties," Bouchardon's tone was patronizing. "She is a suspected German spy. You should also be aware that cases of this kind rarely rely on physical evidence. It is more about witness testimony and character analysis of the accused. Now," he turned back to M'greet. "Let's talk about your meetings with Arnold Kalle. Did Captain Ladoux tell you specifically to contact this man?"

"No. Ladoux never gave me explicit instructions," she replied testily.

"So you were not obeying orders." He nodded at the clerk to make sure he wrote that down.

"There were no orders!" M'greet insisted. She relayed how she decided to contact Kalle after being sent back to Spain by Scotland Yard. While she was explaining what had happened, Bouchardon got up to pace up and down the tiny room.

"Let me get this straight," he said after she'd finished. "You sent the information you picked up from Kalle using your own handwriting, writing in the open for anyone's eyes. When you got no reply, you repeated said information to a stranger—Denvignes—just because he was with the French Embassy."

"But—" she was going to argue just that: Denvignes' position made him an ally since Ladoux wasn't responding.

Bouchardon held up his hand. "If you are to be believed, that would make you the worst spy I have ever encountered. And," he resumed his steps. "That would mean that Captain Ladoux, the esteemed head of the Deuxiéme Bureau, had engaged an amateur and completely unqualified agent, with no clear instructions on how to disguise intelligence nor deliver it in a secure method."

Clunet examined his hands and then selected one of the longer fingernails to continue gnawing on. M'greet shook her head at her lawyer's uselessness. She could at least refute one of Bouchardon's points. "Ladoux tried to get me to use his secret ink, but I refused."

Bouchardon looked at his watch. "I think we are done for the day."

M'greet got unsteadily to her feet. "Please do not send me back to prison. I cannot bear it for another night. The conditions there are so foul. I am not the same as those other women prisoners, but they treat me as though I am. I won't make any trouble for you, I promise!"

Bouchardon fixed her with his condescending stare. "From what you have told me, you are very much like 'those other women.' You are a courtesan, they are streetwalkers. The difference is only in sobriquets: under the law you are all prostitutes."

Clunet put his hands, with their bloodied cuticles, on the table. "Now see here."

But Bouchardon wasn't done yet. His gaze still fixed on M'greet, he continued, "You've lived your whole life having delusions of grandeur. If you choose to imagine yourself better than your fellow prisoners, so be it. But there is not much of a leap from being an, as you call yourself, 'international woman,' to a traitor. Both are evidence of a lack of morals, as you yourself have demonstrated time and again."

Once again M'greet blinked back tears. The last thing she wanted to do was go back to that hateful place, but she would not reduce herself to begging. "If that's what you think, then my grave has already been dug."

Bouchardon left the room without a reply.

The clerk began collecting his things as M'greet turned to Clunet. "What was that all about?"

"M'greet." He coughed into a wrinkled hand. "I am an expert in business law, not criminal proceedings. I'm afraid I'm in over my head."

"*You're* in over your head?" M'greet flung her arms into the air. "What about what they are doing to me?"

He buried his face in his hands.

"Edouard?"

He finally looked up. "I wish I could help you more, M'greet, but, as you said, it sounds as if your case has already been decided. They are going to keep questioning you until, out of desperation, you tell them what they want to hear. I cannot attend any more: under the French system, you are only given legal representation during your first and last interrogation sessions. We are lucky they allowed me to be here today."

"What am I going to do?"

"I would be as honest as possible with them. You have nothing left to lose at this point."

This time she let the tears flow freely. "That place is so horrible, Edouard. There's filth, so much filth. I just want to be in a clean hotel, with all of my nice things..."

He reached out to pat her hand. "I know, M'greet. I know."

Not only was Saint-Lazare filthy, it was cold and damp. M'greet was transferred from her padded room to a smaller, even dirtier cell.

As she lay in bed that night, she could hear the rustling of small creatures: rats, maybe, or cockroaches. She had thought her tears had dried, but she cried all through the night, with no one to hear her, thinking she might go mad with worry. What had she done to deserve such treatment? *Only what she had been told to do.*

In the morning, her unwashed body was covered with tiny, itchy red bumps. For once she was grateful not to have a mirror around; she was sure her face was swollen and her eyes rimmed with red. If only she had her make-up, she could have easily fixed that, but her cosmetic kits had been sent to a chemist for analysis, to see if secret ink could have been made from them. As if she would have wasted her precious ointments to make ink!

As predicted, Clunet was absent from the next interrogation. Bouchardon began with the question: "Whom have you served? Whom have you betrayed? France or Germany?"

M'greet replied in a quiet voice, "My goals were to aid France and damage Germany, and I believe I succeeded in both."

367

"Were you ever recruited to work for German intelligence?"

A denial formed on M'greet's lips, but then she remembered how Clunet had told her to tell the truth. "Yes. Karl Kroemer recruited me. But I only agreed because Germany owed me money! I considered it payback for the furs they stole from me at the beginning of the war."

"Why didn't you tell Captain Ladoux about this beforehand?"

"I never intended to do their bidding, so I didn't think it was relevant." She also didn't consider it important to tell them about Fräulein Doktor.

Luckily Bouchard didn't ask. "You entertained many officers in Paris. Did you pass on military information you solicited from them to Germany?"

"No. I love officers and have loved them all my life. I would rather be the mistress of a poor officer than a rich banker."

He grimaced. "I don't think that statement rings particularly true. What about your affair with Harry de Marguérie?"

M'greet gripped the arms of her chair. "What's he got to do with any of this?"

Someone knocked on the door to the little room. "Ah, right on time," Bouchardon stated before answering the door.

She looked up in surprise as Ladoux stalked in.

"Please sit down, Captain," Bouchardon gestured toward the empty chair across from M'greet.

Her hands were tingling and she looked down to see that she was clutching the chair rail so tightly her knuckles had turned white. She removed her hands to flex them.

"Would you care to make a statement, Captain?" Bouchardon uncharacteristically remained seated this time.

"I would," Ladoux replied smoothly. "The accused was never under my employment."

"That's a lie!" M'greet countered.

Bouchardon's directions were sharply put. "If the accused would remain quiet during the captain's testimony."

Ladoux continued, "The accused had never been given money, nor an agent number, nor was any communication protocol put forth."

"But you promised me one million francs as payment if I succeeded."

Ladoux glanced at the clerk before stating slowly, with perfect enunciation, "Let the record show I made no such promise."

"And with good reason." Bouchardon repeated what M'greet had told him earlier about Karl Kroemer.

Ladoux sat back and clasped his hands. "I knew all along she was a German agent, though she never cared to admit that to me."

M'greet folded her arms across her chest. "I didn't feel obliged to reveal that to you, because," she shot a look at Bouchardon, "once again, I never intended to carry out tasks for them."

Ladoux dug a sheaf of papers out of his briefcase. "That's not what these telegrams say." He pushed the papers toward Bouchardon.

"What telegrams?" M'greet asked.

"They are from Kalle to Berlin," Ladoux stated to Bouchardon. "We intercepted them via the Eiffel Tower."

Bouchardon picked one up and read it to himself before summarizing, "Kalle is recommending that German Intelligence pay H-21 ten thousand francs." He shifted through them and selected another. "Here Kalle says he paid H-21 3,500 pesetas." He glared at M'greet. "Did you ever receive money from Kalle?"

M'greet could feel her face growing red. "Yes, but only because…"

Ladoux's fat head was nodding furiously. "You see, the Germans gave her a code name, and paid her great sums of money, something France never did."

She banged her fist on the table. "I've already told you I never provided any information to them. Kalle only gave me that money to help me return to France, since no one at the Deuxiéme Bureau was responding to me."

Bouchardon leaned forward. "We must make clear that, from our point of view, maintaining contact with the enemy is legally considered a crime equivalent to actually furnishing intelligence to said enemy."

"Is that all?" M'greet started to get up. She'd rather sit in her dingy, disgusting cell than continue this conversation.

"Not quite," Bouchardon waved at her chair. "There is the matter of Lieutenant Masloff's deposition."

M'greet heaved a sigh before resuming her seat.

Bouchardon passed a paper across the table. "As you can see, the lieutenant denies ever having been in love with you." He tapped at a sentence. "He called your affair 'merely casual.'"

She shoved the paper back at him. "I have no reply to that statement."

Ladoux stood, his short, fat body towering over the still-seated M'greet. "If you do not reveal the names of your German accomplices, you will be shot as a spy."

She had finally reached her breaking point. "You know nothing of my character, nothing! Because of my travels, my foreign acquaintances, my manner of living, you think poorly of me. But…" she stuck her finger in Ladoux's fat face. "You are a petty, small man. It is not my fault you did not know how to employ me properly. This is all your doing, not mine." The tears coursed their way down her face, but M'greet did not bother to wipe them away. "Everything I thought I once knew is collapsing all around me. Never would I have believed that such cowardice could come from him," she nodded toward the awful paper with Vadim's statements, "a man for whom I would have gone through fire." She rose. "I will defend myself, and if I fail, it will be with a smile of profound contempt."

CHAPTER 65

ALOUETTE

*A*louette was still seething over the explosion of the French munitions factory. What was happening at the Deuxiéme Bureau? The answer came, once again, in the form of a newspaper. The headline read: "Arrest of Famed Dancer and German Spy." Perusing the article, her eye caught the following sentence: "Lady MacLeod was the mistress of the German naval attaché in Madrid."

Struck with inspiration, Alouette hobbled into von Krohn's office, intent on getting more information out of him. She threw the newspaper onto his desk. "One of your women spies has been arrested in Paris."

His face turned white as the blood drained from it. "One of my women spies? What is her name?"

"Mata Hari, the dancer."

The color returned to his face, but it still held a look of bewilderment. "It is possible that this woman is in the pay of Arnold Kalle, but I know nothing about her."

Alouette tucked her crutch under her armpit in order to fold her arms in front of her. "Prove it."

He sighed before going to his locked cabinet. He took a set of keys out of his pocket and opened the drawer to retrieve a file. He carefully locked it again before setting the file down on his desk.

Von Krohn opened the file to reveal a pile of photographs of women, some with a typed paper stapled to it. Alouette assumed the typing contained vital information about each woman's position and location, but von Krohn flipped through them too fast for her to make anything of it.

She decided to force him to slow down. "There!" she shouted, pointing to a picture of a dark-haired woman. "That's Mata Hari!"

Von Krohn frowned as he read the information before shaking his head.

Alouette already knew it was not the woman in question, but at least it got him to go through the file at a slower pace. When he reached the last picture, he shut the file firmly. "I told you, she's not one of mine."

"Is it possible she was employed by the Embassy?" Alouette was dying to know what else was in that locked cabinet.

"I suppose it is possible." By this time, von Krohn seemed almost as eager as she to find out if Mata Hari were employed by Germany. He extracted a few more files, but they could find no evidence whatsoever that Mata Hari had been sent to Spain by Germany.

CHAPTER 66

M'GREET

JUNE 1917

M'greet's trial was the farce she had predicted it would be. The prosecution called six witnesses, the first being one of the two men who had followed her all throughout Paris. His name turned out to be Police Inspector Monier, who spoke about M'greet meeting her lovers in fancy hotels and expensive restaurants and of her extravagant shopping trips, but gave no evidence of espionage. The second witness was the man who had arrested her, Commissioner Priolet, who, once again, could provide no proof of her spying for Germany.

Next up was Ladoux, who said pretty much the same as he did before: that he had never employed her as a French agent, but pretended to do so in order to prove her employment for Germany. He was followed by Ladoux's boss, Colonel Goubé, who claimed that M'greet was "the most dangerous spy he'd ever encountered," but offered no reasoning as to why he thought that.

The last two witnesses to give so-called evidence of her guilt did not physically make it to the stand. The prosecution read aloud a statement from Lieutenant Hallaure, the man who'd suggested that M'greet go to

373

the Deuxiéme Bureau in the first place. He claimed he wasn't aware of the supposed sickness that required her to take the waters in Vittel.

To M'greet's chagrin, the last testimony was that of Vladimir Masloff. Bouchardon read the same proclamation, the one where Vadim claimed he'd never loved M'greet, aloud to the jury.

Clunet had elicited several people to come forward in M'greet's defense, but the only one who dared show his face in court was Harry de Marguérie. Of all the men who had claimed to love her, had showered her with adulation and money through the years she'd been Mata Hari, only Harry stood by her side. He began his testimony by insisting she'd never discussed military matters at any point.

Bouchardon paced in front of Harry in his typical manner. "Are you saying that you spent multiple days in the presence of the accused and never once mentioned the subject that has all of Europe obsessed —namely, the war?"

"We spoke of art and music. You are right, the war is a constant topic of conversation in my line of work, and it was a relief to not have to chat about it endlessly." He looked directly at M'greet as he continued, "Nothing will ever spoil my good opinion of this lady."

As Harry left the stand, instead of showing obeisance to the jury, he bowed to M'greet.

Despite the lack of evidence, the jury needed less than half an hour to declare her guilty. Not only was she condemned to death, but the tribunal also stated that all of her precious possessions were to be sold in order to reimburse the French Government for the cost of her trial.

"It is impossible!" she screamed after the verdict was read.

Clunet put a restraining hand on her arm. "I will appeal," he stated. But M'greet knew that all had been lost: they had condemned her not because she had given the enemy any information, but because she had refused to play by society's rules.

CHAPTER 67

MARTHE

JUNE 1917

*T*hose days waiting for her execution were the longest of Marthe's life. Each morning she awoke, she wondered if she were twenty-four hours closer to the firing squad.

One day, the same unteroffizier who had escorted her to her trial and then sentencing, appeared at her cell door. "Please come with me, fräulein. The judge has summoned you back to court."

The judge was in his customary position, as were the jury but Marthe noted the absence of her prosecutor this time.

The judge picked up an order. "It has previously been decided that, as a convicted spy, you will be put to death by firing squad."

She nodded bravely, realizing they must have finally scheduled the date of her execution. *At last these months of torturous waiting can come to an end.*

"But..." as he cleared his throat, Marthe looked up, not allowing herself to dare hope. "There has been new information to come to light." He addressed the jury. "One of our own men, Alphonse Martin, has come forward."

Her face colored at the mention of Alphonse's name. Why had the judge said that he was one of theirs?

He continued, "The accused knew him as an ambulance driver for the hospital. But he was also a double agent, one who exposed many Belgians spying for the Allies. He had been working on finding out who this 'Laura' was. According to him, it was not the accused, but rather an old woman who sold fruit out of a farm cart, and who'd previously been discovered and taken care of. Herr Martin insists that the accused is innocent of nearly all charges."

Marthe willed her racing mind to focus. It was obvious they thought Canteen Ma had been operating under the code name Laura, which was not true. But what was that about Alphonse being a double agent?

The judge set down the paper. "Based on this information, plus the fact the accused has been awarded the Iron Cross, and the special testimony provided by our own countrymen, Herr Martin and the Oberarzt at Roulers Hospital, the Commander-in-Chief of Areas under Occupation has graciously decided to commute her death sentence to one of imprisonment for life." He turned his stern eyes to Marthe. "Do you have anything you wish to say?"

She shook her head numbly. She couldn't have said anything if she tried.

The unteroffizier led her back to her cell. Marthe supposed she should have felt elation at escaping the death penalty, but she felt nothing. The judge had to have been mistaken. There was no way Alphonse was a double agent. If their relationship had been based on the simple matter of him trying to trap Marthe, he would have never lied to the judge about Canteen Ma being Laura. And if the judge were correct, then she didn't know the first thing about Alphonse. Why would he have helped her blow up the ammunition dump if he was working for Germany?

. . .

Marthe was moved to a new cell, where, as a prisoner for life, she began a soul-numbing routine. She was awakened at dawn to a tray of tea and black sour bread and then taken to another room, where she, along with twenty-five other women, were expected to repair German uniforms, before being returned to her cell for a dinner of bean soup. The endless sewing was difficult on her eyes and fingers, but she welcomed the few hours away from her thoughts.

The lack of food and fresh air depleted her health. The prison warden sent for a doctor from the hospital, and, to Marthe's delight, it was one with whom she had been friendly. He was deeply shocked at her appearance and slipped her some extra bread.

"Do you know of the ambulance driver named Alphonse?" Marthe asked once she had swallowed the bread; it was dry but much more palatable than the prison rations.

The doctor frowned. "I believe so. Tall, brown-haired?"

She nodded. She wasn't sure how to broach the subject of Alphonse being a double agent.

"He no longer works for the hospital."

"What happened to him?"

The doctor shrugged. "I think someone once said he intended to become a priest. Perhaps he's gone on to seminary school."

For once, Marthe wanted to be alone with her thoughts. "Thank you, Herr Doctor."

He patted her leg. "Don't worry. The war must be over soon: humanity cannot stand much more of it."

As she watched him leave, Marthe thought to herself there wasn't much left of humanity. But she forced that thought away. Just because she had been imprisoned, and the man she loved turned out to be an enemy spy, didn't mean that there was not still good in the world. Or even in Alphonse. Maybe he'd only pretended to work for the Germans. After all, it was partly on his word that she hadn't been sentenced to death. Or maybe all the things he'd done to convince her of his loyalty were based on lies.

Knowing that she would never again lay eyes on her lost love, Marthe hoped that he would find peace, either as an agent of Belgium, or Germany, or God. As for herself, she now had no idea what her future would be. Whether for good or evil purposes, Alphonse had stolen that from her. For the first time in many days, she started to cry.

CHAPTER 68

ALOUETTE

OCTOBER 1917

*I*n mid-October, von Krohn handed Alouette yet another newspaper. She read the headline aloud: "Mata Hari put to death by French firing squad." She paused, her mouth still open. After a moment of reflection, she stated "I never thought it would come to this." Although she herself had lived in fear of standing in front of a German fusillade for the past three years, it never occurred to her that the French government would send one of their own to the execution post at Vincennes. And that it would be Ladoux to hammer the last nail into the proverbial coffin.

Von Krohn took the paper and refolded it. "She was either a terrible spy or else an incredibly accomplished one."

Alouette recalled how the dancer had revealed Kalle's involvement with the Moroccan submarines at dinner. "I think it might be the former."

"Well, both possibilities make her boss, the head of this so-called Deuxiéme Bureau, look like an incompetent buffoon." His lips turned up into a sinister smile. "Or else maybe he's a double-crossing fraud and we should be recruiting him for our side."

"Hans, didn't you say that you believe the French cracked your government's code a few months ago? That they could decipher whatever telegrams they intercepted at the Eiffel Tower?"

"Yes. That's why we had to switch to a new cipher last fall."

"Did Kalle know that?"

"Of course."

She shook her head. Ladoux must have known that too. He must have figured out that Kalle was setting Mata Hari up, feeding her *intoxication* of no use to the Deuxiéme Bureau and then using a code he knew the French could interpret to lie about her involvement. Kalle probably sacrificed Mata Hari to keep his other agents from suspicion. She had simply been a helpless pawn in Germany's game, yet Ladoux let her go to her death anyway. *Why?* There was only one person she could ask, and he was in Paris, a place Alouette couldn't suddenly go jaunting off to without good reason.

Luckily von Krohn presented her with an escape route. "I'm going to Malaga for a few days."

Alouette pretended to be elated. "When do we leave?"

His face fell. "I can't take you, Alouette. I'm sorry."

She pursed her lips in a fake pout. "Why not, Hans?"

He patted the hand holding the cane that had replaced her crutches. "You're not strong enough yet. Besides, I'm going to be paying a visit to my wife."

Alouette nodded, making up her mind that she'd take the Paris express as soon as he left.

After she'd boarded the train, Alouette opened that evening's paper. All of Europe, it seemed, had caught Spy Fever, seeing agents of espionage in even the most innocent of people. The paper listed some of the more famous cases. The Germans had even arrested a Belgian nurse to whom they had previously awarded the Iron Cross.

For once in her life, Alouette had to admit she was in over her head. She longed to return to Paris for good, but knew she wouldn't be able to until she'd put an end to the German Intelligence's Spanish branch. And that meant the end of von Krohn.

An overwhelming feeling of depression swept over her. She felt that she was no closer to stopping von Krohn than when she first started. She thought of that stupid filing cabinet in his office, hiding all of his secrets. If only she could get access to his keys, she could reveal every bit of information contained in those files.

As she stared at the passing landscape, a plan formed in her mind.

Of course, the first thing Alouette did when she reached Paris was to pay a visit to 282 boulevard, Saint Germain. Against all odds, Ladoux was actually present.

"How dare you not answer any of my letters. You are keeping me a virtual prisoner in Spain!" She used her cane to point at him.

He looked understandably shocked at her condition: she'd lost a fair bit of weight, and she was still not able to walk without support. "Is that all from the accident? Monsieur Davrichachvili told me about it."

So Zozo had made it back to Paris. She hobbled to a chair. "Yes, it was from the accident. Something you would know if you deigned to read any of my letters."

"I assure you, I've read them all. I just haven't been able to respond. There are circumstances underfoot about which you don't need to know…"

"Oh I know. I know you are the one who sent Mata Hari to her death. I just don't know your motivation."

Ladoux held up his hand. "Alouette—"

"We all know these are the consequences you risk when you agree to play your little game, Ladoux."

He seemed about to explain his side of the Mata Hari plot, but Alouette wasn't in the mood to hear any more lies. "I want you to help me with one last coup, and then I'm out." She told him about von Krohn's filing cabinet. "There are names and photographs of all of the Baron's contacts, not to mention there must be oodles of other information of worth. If I could slip some sort of drug into his drink, I could steal his keys and then empty the safe."

"That's too much of a risk."

"No." She glanced at her cane, which lay just out of reach, longing to bang it on Ladoux's desk. "I'm on the verge of a nervous breakdown and need to leave Spain for good."

He threw up his hands. "Leave then. No one is stopping you."

"My conscious is. Something you probably know nothing about. I have to do one last mission for France." She fixed a pleading gaze on her boss. "Help me."

"I can see that you are extremely tired and overwrought." He lit a cigarette. "But…" she could tell he was about to deny her again so she changed her expression to one of menace. "Very well." He dug into his desk drawer. "I'll permit you to try out your plan, if only to prevent your resignation." He passed her a visa, along with two little packets. "Drop one of these packets of powder into the baron's beer. It will not take long to act, but be careful not to overdose him, as the results could be fatal."

Alouette's lips curled into a smile as she tucked the packets into her purse, thinking it wouldn't be so terrible if von Krohn died of an overdose after all.

Ladoux mimicked her smile, though his twitched with something else. Irony? "Good luck, Alouette."

She decided to pay a visit to Zozo and see what he thought of her plan. He had healed remarkably fast, though his arm would carry permanent scars.

He invited her into his predictably messy apartment. She sat down on a cigarette-burn scarred couch, the only furniture he possessed, and told him about her encounter with Ladoux.

"Let me see these powders," he said, holding his arm out.

After she'd handed a packet over, he ripped it open and then sniffed at its contents. "Give me another one."

She obeyed and he poured both into a beer before drinking it.

Alouette was momentarily stunned. "But Ladoux said you could die from an overdose."

Zozo grinned. "Did he now? Just you wait to see the results of this so-called devastating drug."

She scrutinized him, searching for any possible effects, but she couldn't detect any change whatsoever.

He returned her gaze. "You look too skinny. Let's get you something to eat."

. . .

They went to a café down the street. Zozo's gait was steadier than Alouette's as he held her arm. If anything, he was even more alert than normal.

"Why would Ladoux lie to me?" Alouette asked after polishing off a sandwich. "It's obvious he had little appreciation for my plan."

"I'm sure he had good reason for not backing your scheme." He changed tactics when he saw this statement did not cheer her in any way. "Don't lose heart. Ladoux has a lot of things going on right now."

"Right now? Mata Hari's already dead. What else could be happening?"

Zozo set his beer down. "Just things."

"Did you know Mata Hari?

"I met her once or twice, and Ladoux asked me to interview her contacts in Spain. I don't think she was the sinister spy they made her out to be."

"Did you know the Germans were lying about her through a code they knew the French had broken?"

"No." He wiped his hands on a napkin. "Her lawyer asked me to deliver her final letters to her daughter, as well as to the Secretary of French Foreign Affairs: Harry de Marguérie and someone named Vadim, but Ladoux ordered them to be destroyed."

"Why did Ladoux hate her so much?"

Zozo put his hand over hers. "France is not in a good place right now. The soldiers are threatening to mutiny, and I think Ladoux needed a scapegoat. He hired her thinking she was a German spy, and I guess she never managed to change his mind. She was a hapless victim of Ladoux's propaganda."

"He should have saved her, not let her die." Alouette's rage was boiling over. What if Ladoux had done the same thing to her? "*You* should have saved her."

A look of confusion passed over Zozo's fine features. "Me? I couldn't have—"

Alouette grabbed her cane and got to her feet. "If you knew she was such a 'hapless victim' then you should have said something. Now it's too late."

"Ladoux is just trying to do what we all are: stay alive."

She hobbled toward the door. "Well, I'm not going to play his game anymore."

"Alouette, wait—" Zozo called, but she didn't stop.

As soon as Alouette saw the Baron, she could tell something was wrong. She had been a careful student of his facial expressions for so long that she knew the particular one he demonstrated now was a barometer of consternation.

"What is it?" she demanded with more than a touch of impatience.

"I've just returned from a conference with Prince Ratibov, the German Ambassador. One of our submarines has torpedoed a Spanish steamer, endangering relations between my country and this one. Spain might even decide to side with the Allies. I expect to receive my marching orders at any moment."

"And what of me?" Alouette asked, the desperation in her voice real.

Von Krohn turned to face her. "You will stay here and take my place. I'll arrange for you to receive money and instructions through Portugal."

She frowned as it occurred to her that if the Germans cleared out of Spain, the information contained within von Krohn's safe would be utterly useless.

"I have full trust in you, Alouette. You will head the information bureau here, and when the war is over, Germany will hail you as a queen."

There was no way Alouette would allow any of that to happen. She was employed as a double agent in order to supply France with information regarding its enemies, but she had no desire to rise any higher up the ranks of German intelligence.

Before she could reply to von Krohn, he gathered up a pile of papers from his desk. "I've got to return to the Embassy and see if we can clear up this matter."

Alouette remained seated in his office after he'd left, staring at the filing cabinet. It was, of course, still locked. She pulled out a blank piece of paper to write the Deuxiéme Bureau regarding this new information. She asked for a visa to return to France, having given up the notion she'd ever infiltrate the Baron's safe.

Ladoux never replied.

The Spanish eventually relented and rekindled their diplomatic relations with Germany. Von Krohn would be staying in Spain after all. But that didn't change Alouette's mind any further.

She was on her way to meet the Baron for lunch in the Palace Hotel's restaurant when a desk clerk called her over.

"Madame, I am afraid you are going to have to change hotels."

"What do you mean?"

He had the audacity to not be embarrassed. "Your room is being reserved for a Frenchman. My manager has decided to no longer cater to German spies."

She glared at him. "Fine."

She walked away slowly, not wanting to reveal the burning lump that had formed in her throat from the injustice of it all. As she strolled outside, a hot wave of hatred swept over her. Hatred for the war, for Germany, but most of all, hatred for von Krohn, who'd gotten her into this mess. Someday that stupid desk clerk would learn how he'd misjudged her while she was fighting heart and soul for her country.

Her sour mood hadn't lightened when she sat down for lunch.

"What's wrong, Alouette?" von Krohn asked. "Another headache?"

"No. I'm fed up with Spain, with living in exile." It was rare for her to be completely honest with the Baron, but this was one of those moments. "I want to go back to France."

His eyes widened. "You are exhausted and clearly in need of a vacation. Have patience and we can visit Morocco in a few days' time."

"I want to go back to France, now!" She banged a gloved fist on the table for emphasis, causing the glassware to rattle.

"You can't do that, Alouette. It would mean your death, and you know it."

"And whose fault is that?" she asked, bitterness dripping from her voice.

"Wait until the end of the war. It can't be too far off now. The minute it is over, I will make arrangements for you to go to Germany."

She clenched her fists. "I am a Frenchwoman! A Frenchwoman! Do you know what that means?"

He shook his head dully.

Ladoux's betrayal, coupled with the embarrassing situation with the desk clerk this morning, had finally pushed her over her limit. "It means that, from the first day I met you, I've been working for my own country. I have kept records of all of your movements and reported them to Paris. That's what it means to be a Frenchwoman." She jumped to her feet, her eyes on von Krohn.

A confused smile formed on his thin lips. She could tell he was wrestling over whether to believe her or not, probably finding it very difficult to accept he'd been duped by a woman.

She leaned in toward him, resisting the urge to spit in his face as she shouted, "*Ich bin eine Französin!*"

His face puckered in horror to hear her speaking a language she claimed she didn't know.

For the *coup de grâce*, she dug a ticket out of her purse and waved it under his nose. "As you can see from the date on this, I've been to Paris quite recently."

He stood, turning purple with rage. "You—"

"Yes, me!" She pumped a fist in the air, wanting the entire restaurant, if not the whole of Spain, to hear her next words. "Get this into your thick head, Baron von Krohn, naval attaché to Wilhelm II, Emperor of Germany. I came to Spain to serve my country and spy on you for France's benefit."

He struck her across the mouth with such fury he broke one of her teeth.

Alouette put a hand to her bleeding mouth, knowing that, had they not been in a public place, he wouldn't have hesitated in killing her with his bare hands.

She turned and fled as fast as her legs could go, leaving her cane on the ground beside the Baron.

CHAPTER 69

ALOUETTE

*T*he person who answered the door at 282 boulevard, Saint Germain, was not familiar to Alouette. "Where is Ladoux?" she demanded.

"He is not here."

"I am the Skylark and I demand an audience with him."

"As I said, he is not here, but Colonel Goubé will see you."

Colonel Goubé was a bald man with a thin graying mustache. He rose when Alouette entered his office. "You should not have left Madrid without our permission."

She paused, dulled by his reception. "I came here to speak with Captain Ladoux," she finally replied in an acid tone.

"Captain Ladoux no longer works here."

"Very well then, I will meet with his successor."

"I am his successor, Madame Richer," he replied, his face turning amber. "And, I demand you to return to Spain."

"I can't," she spit back at him. "I've compromised my position, after managing to ruin von Krohn's career."

"Another will be sent in his place."

She bowed her head, deeply hurt. She didn't want any monetary reward, but thought Goubé could at least show some appreciation for all that she had accomplished. Even Ladoux could, possibly, have been capable of that. "By the time they've set someone else up in von Krohn's position, the war will be over. Where's Zozo?"

"Monsieur Davrichachvili has gone back to Russia to help Lenin and the Bolsheviks in their revolution."

She could feel her disappointment mounting. Now that she'd finally been able to retire to her home country, all of her supposed allies were gone. "Would you please tell me how to contact the captain?" she asked Goubé in a pleading tone. "It was he who had originally engaged my services, and seeing that they have come to a conclusion, it is only fitting that I should tender my resignation to him."

His face appeared to soften. "I'm afraid that is not possible."

"Why not?"

He leaned his elbows on the desk. "Captain Ladoux has been arrested on suspicion of betraying France to our enemies."

"I see." Alouette's heart sank even lower. *Another tragic end to spy mania.* Whether or not Ladoux was truly a double agent was no matter at the moment, but it was another sign that it was time for her to be done.

She held up her hand and gave a resigned wave before exiting 282 boulevard, Saint-Germain for the last time.

CHAPTER 70

MARTHE

OCTOBER 1918

*A*fter almost two years of being imprisoned, Marthe was awoken one morning by the urgent clanging of church bells. The shouting in the courtyard came closer, and soon she could hear the stomping of many boots along the corridor of her prison.

She braced herself as someone threw open the door to her cell. A disheveled man with a ragged beard stood in the threshold. "The war is over!" he shouted. "You are free to go!"

Marthe found Roulers in near ruin. The British had almost bombed it out of existence; there was hardly a building with an intact roof in the entire town. She knew that most of the inhabitants had been evacuated months ago. Mother had sent word that both she and Father had found shelter at the Sturms' farmhouse outside of town, the same place Max had died. An ironic twist to be sure. *Those kinds of ironies had occurred since the beginning of the war*, she mused as she came upon a deep trench carved into the ground and found herself gazing into the sewer where she and Alphonse had their first kiss. *Good luck to you, Alphonse. Wherever, whoever you are.*

The sound of a hurdy-gurdy brought her out her revelry, and she watched as a group of civilians began dancing on the street corner, reminding Marthe this was a time for celebration. There would be plenty of time later to mourn those who were lost.

She grinned as she realized the men patrolling the streets wore the light blue uniforms of the French and the khaki uniforms of American doughboys. There was no need to check for safety-pins now as the Vampires and the rest of the Germans had been forced out of Roulers.

She arrived at what remained of the Café Carillon where a party of British officers sat on the ruined patio, eating their lunch.

"You look hungry," one of them said, passing her a sandwich. He laughed as Marthe devoured it. "You *were* hungry," he stated as he dug in a nearby box for more food.

"I belong to the British Secret Service." Marthe sat down, arranging her tattered skirt. "But I've been a prisoner, and have no money. My parents—"

"Just eat now," the officer said, handing her another sandwich.

She could feel him staring at her as she chewed. She couldn't help noticing that his eyes were as blue as the sky over Roulers, and that one of his legs was wooden. Though he was unshaven, his facial features were well-defined. He wasn't exactly handsome, but he had a dependable air about him that Marthe immediately found attractive.

"This will help to wash down those sandwiches," he said, producing his canteen. "I'm Lieutenant Jack McKenna."

"Marthe Cnockaert."

Not long after the end of the war, she married that handsome young officer and became Marthe McKenna. They built a new house among the burned ruins of the old one in Westrozebeke, the house where Father had nearly burned to death. They also restored the garden, planting flowers as fragrant as those of the 1914 Kermis, when her adventures had begun.

EPILOGUE

Marthe **Cnockaert** was eventually awarded British, French and Belgian honors for her work in World War 1. In 1932, she and her husband, John McKenna, published "I was a Spy," about Marthe's espionage adventures. Winston Churchill penned the foreword for the book, stating, "Her tale is a thrilling one. Having begun it, I could not put out my light till four o'clock in the morning." More spy thrillers followed, making her a minor celebrity. The couple never had any children and McKenna left Marthe in the 1950s. She died in 1966 in Westrozebeke, at the age of 74.

Alouette (Marthe) Richer married Thomas Crompton, a financial director of the Rockefeller Foundation, in 1926. His death two years later left her a wealthy widow. She received a French Legion of Honor in 1933 for her espionage work during the first war. Her minor fame was extended when Georges Ladoux published the book, "The Skylark," in which he called her "Marthe Richard," a name she eventually took on. She published her own memoirs, entitled "I Spied for France," in 1935 before resuming her spy game in World War 2 by befriending several members of the Gestapo in German-occupied Paris. She ran for political office after the second great war and championed the closing of Parisian brothels. She died in 1982, at the age of 93.

Margaretha Zelle MacLeod's body was not claimed by any of her survivors after she was executed at Vincennes and it was sent to the Museum of Anatomy in Paris. Some claim the body was then dissected by medical students and disposed of. Her head was embalmed and at one point became part of a display of infamous criminals. It was discovered to be missing in 2001.

When John "Rudy" MacLeod was informed of his ex-wife's death, he stated, "Whatever she did, she didn't deserve that." Their daughter, Non, died less than two years after her mother, at the age of 21.

In October 2017, 100 years after her death, Mata Hari's files were declassified. The evidence for her actually being employed as a German spy is scant, though she herself admitted to taking money from them in compensation for her stolen furs. Whether or not the intercepted telegrams were a set-up by Kalle, Ladoux, or both, remains a mystery.

Georges Ladoux was arrested under suspicion of espionage four days after the execution of Mata Hari. He was eventually committed to house arrest and spent the rest of the war undergoing interrogations, similar to what he'd put his supposed double agent through. Although the case was dropped after the cease-fire, he was arrested once again for concealing evidence for a colleague at the Deuxiéme Bureau. The case was acquitted on May 8, 1919. In 1923, he was finally promoted to the rank of major. He wrote several books, including a somewhat fictionalized biography of Marthe Richer and another of Mata Hari, in which he maintains his belief that she was a German agent. He died in 1933 at the age of 58.

A NOTE TO THE READER

Thanks so much for reading this book! if you have time to spare, please consider leaving a short review on Amazon. Reviews are very important to indie authors such as myself and I would greatly appreciate it!

Read on for a preview of *The Spark of Resistance: Women Spies in WWII!*

Also, please feel free to send any comments or suggestions to kitsergeant@gmail.com

Stay tuned for the next installment of the World War Spy Series! Sign up to my mailing list at kitsergeant.com to be informed of my next release featuring women spies!

For more information on the real-life women featured in this book, be sure to visit my website: www.kitsergeant.com!

SELECTED BIBLIOGRAPHY

Craig, Mary W. *A Tangled Web: Mata Hari: Dancer, Courtesan, Spy*. Stroud: History Press, 2018.

Ladoux, Georges, and Warrington Dawson. *Marthe Richard, the Skylark: The Foremost Woman Spy of France*. London: Cassell and, 1932.

McKenna, Marthe. *I Was a Spy!* London: Jarrolds, 1933.

Proctor, Tammy M. *Female Intelligence: Women and Espionage in the First World War*. New York: New York University Press, 2003.

Russell Warren Howe. *Mata Hari The True Story*. Little Brown, 1995.

Richard, Marthe, and Gerald Griffin. *I Spied for France*. London: John Long, Limited, 1935.

Shipman, Pat. *Femme Fatale: A New Biography of Mata Hari*. Harper-Collins, 2009

THE SPARK OF RESISTANCE
PREVIEW

Read on in the Women Spies Series- *The Spark of Resistance: Spies and Traitors in World War 2!*

PROLOGUE

MAY 1945

*V*era Atkins barely recognized the woman standing alone on a platform at Euston railway station. She was clad in a bedraggled coat, unusually thick for this time of year, that hung too loosely on her frail figure. "Yvonne?"

The woman turned. At only eighteen, she had been one of the youngest hired, and still bore the look of a child, though now a starved one with dark circles around her eyes and matted blonde hair.

Miss Atkins had the mind to hug her, but was afraid she'd either break the girl's bones or Yvonne would collapse under the weight of her former boss's arms.

"I'm sorry to keep you waiting," Miss Atkins said instead. "Was your journey all right?"

Yvonne attempted a smile. "As good as could be expected."

Pleased as Miss Atkins was to see Yvonne, her thoughts were eclipsed by one, niggling inquiry. She voiced it after they had settled into the car, Miss Atkins sitting as straight as always, Yvonne's head leaning against the seat. "What do you know of the other girls?"

Yvonne's eyes flew open. "The other girls?"

"Yes. Who else was with you?"

Yvonne closed her eyes again, scrunching her face in recollection. "I saw Rose at Ravensbrück, and they said there was another British woman there, Lise, but she was in solitary confinement and I never got a good look at her face. And I encountered Corrine, Nadine, and Ambroise at Saarbrücken when I was taken there, temporarily. I remember going into a prison hut and seeing them, and thinking, 'The whole women's branch of F Section is here.'"

Miss Atkins mentally matched the code names with the real identities of her girls: *Didi Nearne, Odette Sansom, Violette Szabo, Lilian Rolfe,* and *Denise Bloch.* Nearly forty women had gone into the line of fire, and most of them, except Yvonne, were still missing in action. "I've been looking into it, but I was notified that there had been no British females held at any concentration camp."

Yvonne turned to her. "I never told them I was a British agent. I thought I would have a lighter punishment if they believed I was French. But I knew that Corrine, Nadine, and Ambroise felt differently." She shook her head sadly. "They were moved out of Saarbrücken the night before I was."

"And what do you think became of them?"

"I don't know," was Yvonne's terse reply. "I'd heard they were brought to Ravensbrück, same as me, but I never saw them again."

They arrived at Yvonne's father's house. Miss Atkins reached out, as though to touch her former employee's tangled curls, but thought better of it. She folded her hands across her lap. "Don't worry," she told Yvonne as the driver helped her out of the car. "I will find them."

THE SPARK OF RESISTANCE
CHAPTER 1

MATHILDE

*H*e moved through the crowded restaurant with the lithe limbs of a Gypsy. Indeed, his eyes were as black as a Roma, though his hair was styled like a Frenchman's.

Those dark eyes now focused on Mathilde. "Do you mind if I sit here?" He did a good imitation of a Parisian accent, but she could detect a hint of something else.

"Not at all." Jeanne leaned forward, the décolletage of her velvet top dipping low. She patted her impeccably coiffed hair. "And you are?"

"Armand Borni." He glanced over at Mathilde, as if to weigh whether or not his perfectly French name fooled her.

Mathilde stretched her lips into a thin smile. It was one of those dull evenings at La Frégate, the kind when she questioned just what she was doing there. Jeanne had requested their usual seat near the entrance, the better to watch the comings and goings of wealthy Parisians attempting to escape the gloom of their lives under the Occupation.

The undoubtedly fictitious Armand arranged his napkin on his lap. He met Mathilde's eyes for a split second before hers dropped, focusing on his teeth, which, like his accent, were obviously fake. She tucked a piece of her own unruly dark hair back behind her ear as she caught sight of a pair of German officers entering the restaurant.

The crowd immediately fell into a palpable hush, the way Mathilde's classmates used to at boarding school whenever the subject of their gossip came into earshot.

"Feldwebel Müller," Monsieur Durand, the owner, rushed over to the newcomers. "How good of you to come." He reached out to pump the German officer's hand a few times before turning to his companion and repeating the gesture.

Armand's face showed the tiniest frown before it returned to its carefully staged neutral expression.

Jeanne looked up. "It's Feldwebel Müller and Leutnant Fischer again. They come here every Friday night."

Mathilde, still unversed in the Wehrmacht ranking system, glowered as Monsieur Durand led the men to his best table, where an older couple was already seated. The restaurant owner gestured for a passing waiter to assist in moving the couple. "Those Nazis must be pretty important for Durand to oust the Bergers from their table."

"Of course they're important," Jeanne responded pointedly. "Even though they are low-ranking officers, if La Frégate becomes part of the *Gaststätten für Reichsdeutsche*, Monsieur Durand will probably get a pay raise."

"What is the *Gaststätten für Reichsdeutsche?*" Mathilde's tongue stumbled over the unfamiliar German words.

"It means 'restaurants for the German Reich.' My husband's printing house was told to make pamphlets for the visiting German soldiers. They have lists of all the vendors promising accommodations for them, even..." Jeanne leaned forward to whisper, "brothels." She sat back and took a sip of wine. "Any business in the pamphlet gets special treatment and won't be subject to rationing." Her voice dropped once more. "Not to mention Durand's mother-in-law is half-Jewish. He probably hopes to work his connections so she doesn't get deported."

Mathilde, never the type to conceal her emotions, shuddered. It wasn't enough to see the grayish-green suited soldiers marching around her beloved city. The notion of watching them ravage a meal in her favorite restaurant made her sick to her stomach. "I don't understand how we let them into Paris so easily in the first place, and now here we are, catering to their every whim."

"What do you mean?" Jeanne asked. "You are not wishing that we are still fighting them, are you?"

Mathilde sighed. "No. What was to be done was done. But I still hate that they are here. I cannot stand to see the swastika flying over the Eiffel Tower."

Throughout the woman's conversation, their new guest had remained silent, but chose that moment to speak up. "You cannot just hate the Germans."

"What do you mean?" Mathilde asked, turning toward him.

He laughed. "I've only known you for a few minutes, but even I can see that you deal in absolutes. You cannot simply hate them, you must despise them with every thread of your veins."

She put a manicured finger to her lips as she glanced at the oblivious Germans across the room, indulging in a steak meal even though today had been declared a meatless day. "Why leave anything half-finished? If one is to hate, one must do it fully."

Armand's expression deepened for a brief moment before he dug into his salad, stabbing at a piece of lettuce with more force than necessary.

"There are ways, you know," Armand's statement as they left the restaurant was carefully casual.

"Ways to what?" Mathilde asked, her eyes on Jeanne, who was several steps away, trying to wave down a cab.

"Defeat the Nazis."

"I'm not sure if you know this, but our soldiers refused to fight them here." Mathilde spoke deliberately slowly, as though Armand were half-deaf, not concealing the fact she recognized he was a foreigner. "We signed a peace treaty that resulted in our soldiers being captured as prisoners of war. And now they've taken over our city and shame us every way they can." She nodded toward a nearby placard that had been printed in German above the old street sign. Because of the blackout, the streetlights remained unlit and the French sign was barely visible, but the black-lettered words on the German one were quite legible, though unpronounceable. *As bulky and awkward as a swastika*, Mathilde thought. *As unwelcome as the Germans themselves.*

"I am well aware of Paris's plight," Armand replied. He leaned in closer, his voice low. "What would you think if I told you we could establish communication with London to pass on our own propaganda? To encourage our compatriots to challenge the Germans any way they can?"

Mathilde's mouth dropped open.

Armand glanced at Jeanne's back. "I cannot say anything else here. There are spies everywhere. But not the right kind."

Jeanne finally succeeded in her task and turned to Mathilde as the cab stopped.

"Aren't you coming?" Jeanne demanded. "Curfew is in half an hour." They all looked at their watches. Mathilde had once thought time was beyond being owned, but the Germans had even taken control of the city's clocks and turned them all to Berlin time, two hours ahead of Paris. As a result it seemed even the sun was reluctant to confront Hitler; with winter looming, it set earlier and earlier in the evening, shrouding the already-dispirited city in even more darkness.

Armand shut his pocket watch with an audible click as Mathilde waved her friend along.

"Come to my apartment," Mathilde said once Jeanne's cab had pulled away. She wrapped her thin fingers around Armand's and led him down the street.

"I know nothing of espionage," she told him when he was comfortably seated on her couch.

"But you know France... much more than an exiled Pole."

Mathilde nodded to herself as she fixed them chicory coffee. "You're Polish. What happened to make you hate the Germans so much?"

He laughed. "Besides being from Poland?" His tone dropped as Mathilde sat beside him. "I was a fighter pilot before I was taken prisoner by the Nazis. They sent me to a POW camp."

Mathilde's eyes widened. "Did they torture you?"

"I managed to escape before they could do their worst. A widow hid me in her house and then gave me her husband's papers." His voice grew hoarse. "But my brother is somewhere in one of those camps. And my parents are still in Poland." He put his hand over hers. "You have to help me. I will not accept that Poland is defeated."

She squeezed his hand. "I think the same of France. And now that the occupiers refuse to hire me as a nurse, I have more time on my hands."

His face hardened. "I should warn you that this work will be extremely dangerous—"

"I don't mind the risk," Mathilde interrupted. "As you said, I do know people in most parts of the country, especially in the Free Zone." This included her husband, but she of course made no mention of him.

He took on a dreamy look. "Can you imagine you and I plotting against the Germans? You'd become the Mata Hari of the Second World War."

"Mata Hari? Didn't she betray her own country?"

He laughed and Mathilde couldn't help but smile. She paused to mull over what Armand was proposing. In what he would probably claim was her characteristic, all-in way, she decided to be the best spy the Allies had. "If we are to be working together, I suppose I should know your real name." She said it both out of curiosity and as a test, to see if he trusted her fully.

He did not hesitate. "Roman Czerniawski."

It was her turn to laugh. "That's quite a mouthful. I shall call you 'Toto.'"

"Toto? As in the dog in the *Wizard of Oz?*"

"Yes." She touched his arm. "As in my dependable sidekick."

"Oh, so now I'm your sidekick? It was my idea in the first place."

She shrugged. "You're cute, with big brown eyes just like Toto."

"What's your full name?"

"Mathilde Lily Carré."

He put his hand on her knee. "I think Lily suits you better than Mathilde. I'm going to call you Lily from now on."

She bestowed her most seductive smile on him, thinking in her head that he wouldn't be the first man to refer to her by that particular name.

Enjoyed the preview? Purchase *The Spark of Resistance: Women Spies in WWII* now! Thank you for your support!

. . .

Books in the Women Spies Series:

355: The Women of Washington's Spy Ring

Underground: Traitors and Spies in Lincoln's War

L'Agent Double: Spies and Martyrs in the Great War

The Spark of Resistance: Women Spies in WWII

ACKNOWLEDGMENTS

Thank-you to my critique partners: Ute Carbone, Theresa Munroe, and Karen Cino for their comments and suggestions. I am eternally grateful to the gracious Kathy Lance for her superb editing skills.

And as always, thanks to my loving family, especially Tommy, Belle, and Thompson, for their unconditional love and support.

Printed in Great Britain
by Amazon

59873034R00248